ISBN 978-0-483-68372-3
PIBN 10489856

FB &c Ltd, Dalton House, 60 Windsor Avenue, London, SW19 2RR.
Company number 08720141. Registered in England and Wales.

For support please visit www.forgottenbooks.com

THE

STAR AND THE CLOUD;

OR,

A DAUGHTER'S LOVE

BY A. S. ROE,

AUTHOR OF "A LONG LOOK AHEAD," "I'VE BEEN THINKING," "TO LOVE AND BE LOVED."

NEW YORK:

Carleton, Publisher, 413 Broadway,

(LATE RUDD & CARLETON.)

MDCCCLXIV.

THE STAR AND THE CLOUD;

OR,

A DAUGHTER'S LOVE.

CHAPTER I.

It was in the month of April, 18—. On one of the last days of that beautiful, yet fickle month, a lad—he could scarcely be called a young man—was riding a very pretty roan pony along one of the by-roads that diverged from the main path of travel, near to, and parallel with, the banks of the Delaware river; and in that portion of New Jersey distinguished as the county of Hunterdon. In the month of April, especially if it be such weather as we have reason to expect, and for which we are all looking, nature has put forth some of its most pleasant aspects. The earth is quite green with the fresh springing grass and grain—the trees, many of them in full leaf, and others just opening to the sun, yet none with that dark rich color which the month of June brings out. Beautiful, though, they are, to the eye so long accustomed to the bare tendrils, and the white or brown coverings of winter. The air is fragrant too, and fresh, and the heart of man sympathizes with bursting buds and springing grass, and his pulse beats more lively, and his mind exults in the fact that the icy chain has been broken, and life again in motion.

But this is not our story, although it has something to do with it, for that lad on the roan pony was filling his heart with the delights about him, and seemed so much to enjoy the beauties that met his eye from the thick hedge that lined the road on either side, that he suffered his pony to walk, and occasionally stretch his neck to nibble off, from a projecting branch, the opening buds.

The face of the country was pretty, but not distinguished for boldness, or grandeur. There were mountains, but they could only be seen in the distance, lifting their blue summits against the eastern sky. They gave, however, a fine finish to the panorama of green fields, heavy forests, pretty vales, and gentle acclivities, that met the eye in that quarter; while in the west, beautiful wide-spreading meadows, with occasional glimpses of the waters of the Delaware, formed a scene of most pleasing character.

Young persons, however, are not fastidious about such matters. In general, the free, open sky, the pure air, the trees, and the fields, have an influence sufficiently powerful, without any special beauty in their combination, to animate their feelings, and satisfy their desires. They are very apt likewise to exert a dreamy imaginative power over the youthful mind, and many an airy castle is erected, and many a fair vision of the long future, beguiles the still hours, as the young wanderer plods along country roads, or across open fields, or through the dense woods. The country is evidently the place where youth finds its most satisfying enjoyments.

That the youth in question had been for some time indulging in entrancing day-dreams, there can be no doubt, for he had not noticed that huge masses of dark vapor were rolling up from the west in token of a severe storm. He may not have noticed the fact, however, from the circumstance, that for a long stretch of the road he was traveling, a thick wood obscured almost entirely his view of the west, and only at intervals was there any opening through which an observation could be taken. His attention was at length arrested, and his dream dissipated, by a heavy roll of thunder, and casting a look toward that quarter of the heavens, he perceived there something darker than the foliage of the woods, and remembering that it was April, and how short a period it took in that fickle month to gather up quite a tempest, he reined up his pony, rode a few paces at a brisk gait to an opening, and then stopped and began to consider.

A shower was at hand without doubt, and no common affair either, if the rugged black heaps that were mounting up, and with great rapidity too, could be taken as a sign. For a moment he seemed in doubt as to his proceedings, and then, turning the head of Roan, began to retrace his steps; starting him off at a very lively canter, evidently designing to gain a shelter with as little delay as possible. The road was one of those winding paths so common in the country, where reference was had rather to the convenience of those who first traced it, than to the directness of the route, which, by the way, is the very sort of road to be in unison with nature. Turnpikes and railroads have their origin and end in cities, and are mere continuations of their long straight streets, and are ever reminding one of stiff straight houses, and all the other unnatural straightnesses that mark their conventional arrangements.

There were, however, no railroads at that day, and but few turnpikes: the only short cuts were across fields, or through woods, and our young friend not being able to take advantage of either while on the back of Roan, could only shorten his distance from his place of destination, by causing the latter to use his legs with all possible agility.

As we have said, the road was winding, and did not allow objects to be seen far ahead, and on this account he had not noticed another traveler upon it; not until he was so near, that a young lady started to one side of the road, and Roan to the other, and he started too, for he felt that he was open to the charge of rudeness in riding at such speed so near a foot passenger, and that a lady too; and so quickly did he pass that he had no time to make an apology, or even a slight obesiance; which good manners in the country demanded of those who met upon the road. His glance at the countenance of the lady assured him that she was not one he had ever seen before; and although it was but a glance he could give, he was struck with the perfection of beauty that shone upon him. He wished heartily that Roan had not used his legs quite so nimbly, for he would have been glad to have had another look. Suddenly a heavy clap of thunder not only banished all idle wishes, but brought him to a sense of the proprieties; he reflected a moment upon the state of things, reined in his pony, and made a halt. The storm was coming on with fearful haste—broken masses of clouds were coursing immediately above, and he could see in the distance where the tempest had already burst; and the wind was lifting up the huge black line of vapor, that would in a few moments bring its forces directly upon him and his fellow-traveler.

Thoughts fly faster than the pen, and even faster than the clouds when a hurricane is driving them; and very soon, it was but an instant after he had brought his horse to a stand, when his conclusion was arrived at, and he was riding rapidly back in the direction of the young lady.

"You will excuse me, miss," he said, as he sprang from his horse, and stood beside her, "for addressing you, as we are strangers to each other; but the storm is rapidly approaching, and I can not bear the thought of leaving you exposed to it alone, as there is no house that you can possibly reach in time."

"You are very kind, sir. I am on my way to the Barrens to see Mrs. Barton; perhaps I can reach the house before the storm breaks here."

If he had been at a glance affected by the beautiful expression of her countenance, he was much more so as it beamed full upon him; and heightened by the most musical tones of voice he had ever heard.

"Oh, you can not! certainly, you can not! I was on my way to Mrs. Barton's, too; but fearing the storm might last all the afternoon, concluded to return home. Can you ride my pony?"

"Not with that saddle."

"Can you, if I remove it?"

"I could, but what would you do?

"Oh, I don't care for myself if you can only get to a shelter." And he at once caught hold of the girth to remove the saddle.

"Oh, pray do not; I can not think of allowing such a self ish arrangement. Will your pony carry double?" And in spite of the terrific aspect of things, the young lady smiled as she asked the question.

"Oh, that he will—but we must lose no time." A light shawl which she carried on her arm was at once used as a pillion; the pony reined to the side of the low stone fence; and the sprightly girl soon adjusted herself behind her gallant attendant.

"Now you may ride as fast as you please."

"May I gallop him?"

"Yes, you may put him to a run."

"Hold fast, then, for it will be a tight race."

And the fair young girl, with as much confidence as if he had been a brother, grasped closely with her little hands to his sides; while he, sitting very erect, and keeping himself with much care in a steady posture, urged his horse to his utmost speed.

"Does he go too fast for you?"

"I am firm, if you are. Do not check his speed on my account."

The little house of Mrs. Barton, or Aunt Luckie, as she was generally styled, was situated on the very edge of an immense track of woodland, consisting for the most part of white and yellow pine. The forest was of primeval growth: none of the present living race remembered when its trees were small; they had increased in size greatly, no doubt, since their memory, but so gradually that none had noticed that the large trees which for miles and miles covered this portion of the country were ever any smaller. As the youth looked ahead, he could see the cottage about a quarter of a mile distant; but the tops of the taller trees were already moving, and the roar of the tempest, which was raging on the western side of the forest, could be distinctly heard even above the clatter which the feet of Roan was making on the hard gravel-road. And now a cloud of dust was seen above the tops of the trees, and the trees, but a hundred rods from them, to bend beneath the blast. A new stimulus was given to the pony, the cottage was near at hand; but so was the tempest, and furiously the little beast tore along the road.

"Oh, you dear child, how have you got here?"

"Do, dear Aunt Luckie, try to make him come in—it is such a dreadful storm."

"Who! who is it?" said Aunt Luckie, as she ran to the door.

"I do not know; but he has been so kind! Oh, dear!" This last exclamation was uttered in terror, as a blinding flash of lightning, accompanied on the very instant by a peal of thunder that seemed to have torn open the very beams and crushed every thing around them to the dust, burst upon the two dismayed females. The young girl sank upon a chair by which she was standing, and the widow fell prostrate upon the floor. They were not, however, seriously injured; and the younger one soon arose and made efforts to relieve the elder, who, although able to sit upon the floor, was apparently in a confused state of mind.

"Are you badly hurt, Aunt Luckie?"

"I hope not, child—it seems to be going off; my head turns, though, like a top, and my limbs is all in a tremble."

"I fear something has happened to the young man—why does he not come in, Aunt Luckie?"

"Oh, dear!—what *do* you say?—who is it—where is he?"

"The young man that so kindly turned back because he feared I should be caught in the shower. He brought me on his pony; and if he had not done so, I should have been exposed to this terrible storm."

The old lady rubbed her eyes and her head, and by degrees seemed to comprehend something of the case. And at last, looking with an air of great concern at her attendant,

"I'm afeer'd he's been struck. Oh, dear! what shall we do?"

Resolved not to forsake one who had been thus gallant to her, if possibly her aid could be of any service, the girl at once threw an outer garment over her head and rushed from the house. The violence of the wind had abated, but the rain still continued, and the lightning blazed fearfully amid the pines, and the roll of the thunder, as it tumbled from cloud to cloud, and down to the earth amid the dense forest, would have appalled her under usual circumstances. But now she had forgotten herself, and thought not of danger.

She could see nothing of the horse or the young man in any direction that she looked; and had begun to think that he had remounted and rode off. But to be certain, she turned an angle of the house to take a more complete view; and to her horror, just beneath a small rough shed, constructed against the side of the house, lay, apparently dead, the noble youth who had so kindly waited upon her.

At once she was by him. He lay nearly on his back; his hat had fallen from his head; and his dark hair, matted by the rain, covered his face. The rest of his person had been almost completely shielded by the shed.

She knelt beside him, smoothed the hair from his face and forehead, and began rubbing his temples. His countenance was pale, but his flesh was not cold; he evidently breathed. She increased her efforts, rubbing his hands and wrists, as she had his temples. Soon a slight sigh escaped him.

"Are you in pain?"

"My head."

And again her delicate hands were rubbing his fair temples and pressing them by turns.

"O, how kind you are!" he spoke in a very low voice, and his bright eye was fixed upon her. At that moment Aunt Luckie appeared; she was, herself, still weak and trembling. The moment her eye fell upon him, she clasped her hands and exclaimed,

"O dear! if it ain't Mr. Clarence!" and she, too, forgetting her own weakness, began rubbing him, and saying all manner of kind things to him.

"If we could only once git him in the house, and on the bed; do, Miss Carrie, you try and help him that side." And Miss Carrie, as she was called, did so with as ready a hand as if he had been her own brother. With their united aid he was able to assume an erect posture, and soon gained the cottage; and, although much against his will, at the command of Mrs. Barton, laid down upon her bed.

"And now," said Mrs. Barton, "I want you to tell me how it was you came here so together; and how it is that you have both known one another, and I all the time a knowing nothing about it."

"We do not know one another, Aunt Luckie, according to the common rules of becoming acquainted; and I doubt whether either of us can call the other by name."

Carrie was standing near the bed; for Aunt Luckie's bedroom, sitting-room, and kitchen, were all in one apartment. And as she spoke she looked at the youth and smiled, who immediately replied,

"I must ask the favor of you, Mrs. Barton, to give me an introduction to this young lady—that is as to her name—her character I believe I already understand."

"Well, dear me, if it don't beat every thing! Do tell, now, don't you know one another's names? Well, I can soon tell you. This is Miss Carrie; Carrie Leslie; and she is just like an own child to me; seeing I was brought up in her grandfather's family, and tended her when she was a baby; and many happy days have I had there; and many weary ones since; but the Lord does all things right." And Aunt Luckie said this because she truly felt it; her heart had learned to trust in a Heavenly Father; and there, even as on a rock, she firmly rested.

"And now, Mrs. Barton, if you will tell this young lady who I am, I shall feel at liberty to offer to shake hands with her, and thank her for so generously venturing out in the storm to look for me, and for the efficient aid she rendered when she had found me."

And as he held out his hand, the young lady, without hesitation, offered hers to him.

"Oh la, yes; why this is Mr. Clarence Ralston; I've known him from a little boy, and a good boy he has always been to me, and, I guess, to every one else."

"That will do, Mrs. Barton; I expect Miss Leslie will not care to hear a very long account of my past history."

"O, I like to hear about *good* boys; I have some little brothers at home, who are always wishing me to tell them stories, and about boys in particular."

"Well, I could tell you a long story about him—"

"Not now, I entreat of you, Mrs. Barton; please not now."

"Well, I am so glad that you know one another, any how; for you are so much alike. I wonder I never thought of it before."

"Our introduction could not have happened better. We have become more intimate than we might otherwise have been in many months; and if we are to be good friends, as you say we are so much alike, it is well that it has turned out so; as I have only a week longer to stay here, Mrs. Barton."

"Oh, dear! only a week!"

"That is all; I am as sorry as you are; I should much rather stay here than go home."

"Then I fear," said Carrie, smiling, "you are not such a very, *very good* boy after all. Good boys love home."

The look which young Ralston gave her was one that sank deep in her heart, and in connection with his reply, caused her most sincerely to regret what she had said.

"Perhaps you know *home* only as a place where you meet with kindness and love. Do you think you would prize it so highly if you expected no loving looks; no kind words; not one heart to which you could go with any joy or grief—all stern, cold, selfish, and grasping."

Carrie stepped up and took his hand.

"Forgive me; I know too well the value of a loving home to trifle with the feelings of one who may not be so fortunate. But I hope yours is not what you have represented it."

"I may, perhaps, some day tell you more about it."

Their conversation was interrupted by an exclamation from Aunt Luckie,

"Oh children, children, *do* come here; come and see here, Carrie."

Carrie hastened to the door.

"Did you ever see such a sight? See what the lightning has done!"

One of the largest trees of the forest had been literally torn to pieces by the furious bolt. The tree was broken off some thirty feet from the ground; and the trunk, which was standing, presented a mass of huge splinters, one of which, as large as the body of a common-sized forest tree, had been torn completely off, and was sticking upright about ten feet from the parent trunk where it had been carried, and forced into the ground.

It was a striking evidence of the terrible power which had been about them, and of that mercy which had given direction to the stream of electricity. What might have been the fate of the cottage, and those within the little tenement! and as Carrie made mention of the probable consequences, Aunt Luckie replied,

"Yes child, it is a terrible power, and we all felt it a little; and that poor boy had like to have felt it to his cost. But the rain helped him. The lightnin', though, has got a Master, and He sends it just where he pleases, and it can't go nowhere else; ain't you glad of that, dear?"

"But if it had come, Aunt Luckie, we should all have been destroyed."

"That is if it had been His will; then, you know, it would have been all for the best."

Carrie did not reply. She knew that God was good and great; and she had a hope that her heart had been renewed by divine grace. But life was very pleasant to her. All the influences about her were such as bound her with strong ties to the scenes of earth; she did not like to say what she did not feel, and therefore made no reply.

But where all the time is pony? the faithful little beast, that had carried the two young travelers so rapidly to a shelter. Young Ralston could give no account of him. He remembered nothing, after seeing the young lady enter the cottage.

"The crittur has gone home, you may depend on it. The thunder frightens 'em dreadfully. He has gone home, and your father and mother will be frightened to death; they'll think may-be you 've been thrown off and killed, or something or another."

"That is true, Mrs. Barton;" and young Ralston left the bed as he spoke.

"That is true, and I must hasten home; for I know they will be very uneasy, and I would not cause them needless anxiety; I must go home immediately."

Mrs. Barton had begun her preparations for tea, and was anticipating a pleasant end to their visit. But she entered at once into the feelings of the youth, and forbore to urge his stay.

"But where are *you* going, Carrie?" She saw that the young lady was putting on her hat.

"You would not let me be so ungenerous, Aunt Luckie, as to allow this young gentleman, just off from a sick bed, to walk through the lane alone. I must accompany him a little way at any rate."

Whether the young gentleman felt a little dubious of his own strength, or was unwilling to lose the pleasure of such company; it is not of consequence enough to inquire. He only remarked,

"I fear I shall be the means of shortening your visit."

"Oh, well; I can make that up the next time. I shall be here next week, Aunt Luckie."

And giving the good woman a hearty kiss, and renewing her promise to come the next Saturday, she stepped off from the house, a little in advance; as she thought young Ralston wished to speak with Mrs. Barton in private.

Carrie did not try to catch the meaning of any part of the conversation; she could not, however, help hearing the last words which Aunt Luckie said, as she raised her voice to quite an animated strain,

"Never, never, never, Clarence, dc you do such a thing as that!"

And now perhaps, the reader may say, "Is it not time to give a little insight to matters as to these young people? Who they are; what they look like; whether they are boy and girl, or young lady and young gentleman; as sometimes they have been called by either appellation.

In regard to the last question, we find ourselves at a loss. The boy was not a big boy, nor the girl a large girl; she was a little, plump, rosy thing of about fourteen years of age, her hair of the golden order, falling in ringlets about her ears, and upon her neck behind; but all kept from her forehead and face by a long comb, that clasped her foretop, and restrained the rich locks from interfering with things in front.

Beauty of countenance is such an arbitrary matter, and is so independent at times of the particular form of the features, that a description of them will scarcely ever convey to the mind of the reader, or hearer, the full force of their power. We can say thus much, however: her complexion was of that delicate hue generally attached to sunny hair—snow-white, with a slight blending of the rose tint, on the cheeks, and a deeper hue of the rose upon the lips; her eyes were not a pure blue, either light or dark, but appeared to be a mixture of that distinguished color, with the hazel, and her eyelashes partook more of the shading of the eye than of her hair. These were long and heavy, and would have given almost too sober a cast to her countenance for one so young, had it not been for the counteracting influence of a dimple or two, not far from her finely arched rosy lips. Those dimples and those lips in connection with the eyes and their heavy fringes, and the other finishing of the face and neck, formed a combination of charms few could resist. She was not one that could be looked at with indifference. Her form was not yet complete, but the outlines of the mold could readily be perceived, and none could doubt the perfection of its beauty when matured.

The young gentleman was still dressed in boy's clothes: loose trousers; a roundabout; a vest; flowing collar; ribbon round his neck; and a neatly plaited ruffle protruding from his bosom. The color of his roundabout and trousers was blue, with brass buttons, very plentifully bestowed upon them, neat shoes incased his feet, and white cotton stockings were seen occasionally peeping from beneath his long trousers. His dress intimated that those who provided for him, had means to procure the best articles of their kind; and his manners showed that care had been taken to train him according to the best rules of that polite period. Independent of all these, however, there was that about him which young ladies, or those a little more advanced in life, are very apt to be affected by. He had a very pleasing countenance, of rather a serious cast, and the complexion pale and delicate. It was relieved from effeminacy by his dark hair and bright dark eyes. He had evidently never been much exposed to the weather, nor to rough work; for his hand (the young lady could not help noticing that), was almost as soft as her own. These matters, we know, are of minor importance, and in general, a boy or young man ought rather to be respected for having about him, at the age of our young gentleman, the marks of toil and exposure. But circumstances alter cases, and we are not willing that our readers should be prejudiced against him whom we are introducing to them, because he has them not. He was wealthy and had been, for the most of his life hitherto, a boarder. Those with whom he lived were well paid and had no right to make any demands upon his exertions for the sake of their interest, had they needed them, or been disposed to exact them. But they were far removed from any such thought, and had always been only too anxious, lest it should not appear evident to all, that the care over him had been of the tenderest kind. His hands had therefore been used chiefly in turning over the leaves of his lexicon, or in handling the bat and ball. No one who looked into his clear bright eye, or noticed the expression of firm and steady purpose that beamed in his countenance, could doubt of the manliness of his character, or fear that in an hour of need, or danger, he would shrink from duty. His age was just seventeen, and his height gave promise of something more than full medium stature when at maturity.

Now ladies—for to you is this story more particularly dedicated—if you may possibly have reached the period when wisdom takes the liberty of dropping an occasional lecture to those beneath you, or rather behind you in the journey of life, try to go back a few years: be girls again in thought and imagination. We wish you to do this, that you may enter into the feelings of our Carrie, for we shall drop all other titles which we have hitherto given that young lady. She is to be Carrie after this, and nothing else. Remember she is only a fourteen, a child of nature; free from affectation or prudery; a very honest-hearted, candid girl, and with warm and affectionate feelings. True, she has been but a very short time in the company of this young gentleman, by whose side she is now walking, and holding free and apparently agreeable conversation. But were not the circumstances of her introduction peculiar? She has already received very timely attention from him, and she has had her sympathies deeply excited for him, in a moment of peril. Was it not quite natural that she should overcome those minor obstructions, which are apt to interpose between the intimacies of young persons of her age, and that of her companion; and allow an advance in acquaintanceship of weeks, or even months of casual interviews. We hope you think it all very natural, because we wish to engage your good-will for one we love so much ourselves. But whether you can enter into her feelings or not, we must give the facts, and tell the story just as the events happened.

The sun came forth in splendor, and the grass, and shrubs, and trees, were glistening in his rays; and the air was perfumed with the scent of fresh opened leaves; and the birds were singing joyously; and all nature appeared so calm and beautiful, that one might have judged no storms could ever again shroud her in darkness and terror.

And those youths were as happy as the birds; that is if we judge them, by the lively prattle they maintained, and the smiles that came so readily upon their lips.

They made but slow progress however on the way down the lane; for there were many pretty things in the hedges, that demanded attention, wild roses almost ready to open; wild violets in the grass; maple keys, hanging close beside the path; squirrels running on the fences, and springing up into the trees. Birds too, were there in great variety; and the last mentioned objects gave occasion to the young gentleman to remark, perhaps for a special purpose,

"You must have lived in the county, I think, to be so well acquainted with the variety of birds."

"Oh, yes, I have always lived where there are plenty of birds. My father will not allow a bird to be shot near our house."

"Has he a farm?"

"Well I suppose they call it so. There is a great deal of land, I know. I believe he has a great many farms, all over. He has one up here: I don't know that you would call it a farm, for it seems to be all woods. He owns all that great woods around Mrs. Barton's house, as far as you can see. I believe, though, that belongs to mother; but I suppose it is the same thing. Pa always calls it the Hazleton property; and ma calls it our Hazleton property. Where we live—but do you know where we live?"

"I heard Mrs. Barton speak of Clermont: do you live there?"

"Oh, no; I am only there at school. My home is at Princesport—have you never been there?"

"Never."

"Oh, then you can have no idea what a beautiful place it is. Are you not fond of water scenery?"

"I think I should be; but I have had no opportunity to try my taste in that respect. I have only seen our Delaware here; and when away from here, at school, there was no water near. I have always thought I should admire an extended view of the water."

"Oh, then, you should come to Princesport. I wish you could see it. Why, from our house, we can look over a beautiful bay; and, at night, we can see the light-house, or rather the light of its lantern. Oh, it is so lovely to sit in our hall of an afternoon and watch the sloops sailing across the bay, and sometimes a large ship; but we always take a spy-glass when we see a ship—ships are at such a distance. Oh, I do wish you could see them. Are you not fond of sailing?"

"I think I should be; but I have never tried that either. If you will allow me, I should like to explain to you my reasons for speaking as I did about *my* home, and for which you reproved me."

"Oh, but I asked your forgiveness, and you said you had granted it. Please do not speak of that again. You know I spoke playfully, too."

"You were perfectly right in speaking as you did. I thank you very much for what you said, it has made me think more seriously on that subject; but I have wanted ever since to explain to you why I spoke so. I should be very sorry to have you leave me with a worse opinion than I deserve. I must tell you that I have two homes."

"Two homes!"

"Yes; the home of my parents, and the home where I have hitherto lived. When I was an infant, my mother had a violent illness, and it was necessary to seek some one to take care of me. Mrs. Rice—you know Mr. and Mrs. Rice, do you not?"

"What, Mr. Rice who sometimes preaches in our church at Clermont?"

"The same. He is a clergyman, and a very good man; but he has no regular place for preaching. Well, Mrs. Rice had lost her babe, and she offered to take me—and then she could not bear to part with me—and so I have lived there ever since, except for the last four years that I have been at a boarding-school.

"My own mother was a long time ill; and when she recovered, seemed to have lost all affection for me, and, indeed, would scarcely allow me to come to the house. I have only been there occasionally, for a few days at a time. My father is very much taken up with his estates. He speaks kindly when he sees me; but that is all. My brothers only seem to look upon me as a stranger, in whom they have no interest; and, in fact, I should think from their conduct that they dislike me.

"Well, now, my mother, for some reason, she does not say what, has sent me orders to come home to live, that is, when not at school. And can you wonder that I feel reluctant to go, or that I expressed myself as I did?"

Carrie could not reply. While he had been speaking, and with the frankness of youth, telling the sad story of his life, she had been calling to mind her own dear home, her fond and loving parents, her confiding little brothers, younger than herself, but wound about her heart by cords of most tender affection. And how could she but feel, deeply feel, for one who had no such experience, and whose heart seemed panting for a resting-place. She could not help it; right or wrong, her young warm feelings were all worked up, and they must have vent.

They were just then passing a large flat rock which lay by the side of the road, and the young gentleman, perhaps a little wearied himself, or more likely anxious to prolong the interview, as the road which led to his home would very soon cross the path they were then on, pointed to it as a convenient place for resting.

"That rock offers a good seat; are you not tired?"

Carrie really was not tired, and had not thought of needing rest; but her benevolent heart at once suggested to her that possibly *he* might be, and without making any opposition, prepared to try the good seat which had been designated.

"Do you think," said he, as he spread the shawl upon the rock for her benefit, "I am so much to blame if I can not love such a home as I have described?"

"Oh, I don't know—I feel very sorry. I am sure it must be a dreadful thing not to be loved at home."

"And do you not think I should be justified if I should run away, and go off and try to make friends among strangers?"

"Oh, dear! that would be dreadful, too! But I thought you said that your parents had ordered you to come home?"

"Yes, they have; but if they treat me as they always have done, ought I to make myself miserable just to gratify their whim?"

Poor Carrie felt almost sorry that she had taken the seat. She did not relish the subject of conversation, and the last sentence her companion uttered grated very harshly upon her sensitive feelings. She must answer, however, and clear her own conscience.

"It is not right for us, is it, to speak of our parents' wish as a whim?"

"I know—you must forgive me again. But what else can I call it? and why should I obey their command, or wish, when I know that all they care about me, is to regulate my property? It is not to make me good, or happy, that they want me home."

"But do you think you could be happy away from home if you were acting contrary to their wishes?"

"I do not know that I should be happy—I do not expect to be happy anywhere;—but I am certain of being very miserable at home. It is nothing but one continual jar about money. It is nothing but money, money, money I hate the very name."

"Yes, but you are no doubt very glad to have money when you are in want of any thing. Your pretty pony, and your handsome saddle and bridle, must have cost money, and a good deal, too; and if your parents had no love for you, why would they give you such pretty things? And do you not remember what the fifth commandment says? It does not say, 'Honor your father and mothe if they are good, and kind, and love you very much, but it is simply 'honor thy father and mother.'"

"How can I honor them when they do not act so as to command my love and respect?"

"I do not think it makes any difference. The Bible does not say so, as I remember. Do you not think you would feel very bad to see a child treating his father rudely, because perhaps he was overcome with liquor, or had been guilty of any other crime? Would you not think better of him if you saw him trying to hide his father's faults? You told me a little while since that you had been confirmed. Do you not when you are confirmed bind yourself to keep all the commandments? And then only think! Do you not remember about Ham, how he was cursed, and all his children cursed, just because he mocked his father when under the power of too much wine? We had better do right, had we not? just right, or as right as we know how to do, even if our parents should do wrong?"

The youth was sensibly affected by the simple, artless manner in which the holy precept he was in danger of violating, was held up to his remembrance. There was also no little power in the kind, yet earnest look that beamed upon him, accompanied by tones so soft and musical, as if the speaker wished to make the truth she was dealing out, as pleasant to him as possible.

As he made no reply, she continued,

"Shall I tell you how I think I should do, if I was so situated?"

"Oh *do* tell me. I will do any thing that you would do."

"Oh, dear me, how you do go from one extreme to another; you do not know, but I might tell you to do something that was very difficult to do, and it migh' not be right after all, for I do not pretend to be very wise, and besides, I only said, or was going to say, what I thought *I* should do, if I was placed in your circumstances. But are you not rested? had we not better be getting on?"

"Am I rested? oh, yes; why, I only stopped, you know, to let *you* rest. I have not been tired yet. But *do* tell me what you was going to tell; what would you have me do?"

"There again! now, mind, I did not say any thing about your doing, but only what I thought *I* should do if I had parents, whom I thought did not love me, or brothers and sisters, that did not love me."

"Well, please tell me then what you would do."

"Why, in the first place you see I should love them, if they did not love me; and I should do any thing to show them my love, by taking a great deal of pains to please them in every way; and to make them happy. If they should speak hard to me, I should speak kindly to them; if they were in pain or trouble, I would do all I could to help them, night or day: I should take a *great deal* of pains, you see, more than I do now. Now, I do not have to take any special care to please them, to show them how much I love them; for they know that I love them, and I know that they love me."

"But what if you did not love them, nor they love you?"

"Oh dear, it is too dreadful to think of; I do not know what I should do. But I suppose I know what I ought to do."

"Do tell me."

"I think I ought to do every thing just as I would if I loved them very much; I ought to mind every thing my parents commanded; and do—and do—all my duty toward them. But is not that your pony I see on the road?"

"Yes, there he is. He concluded that he might as well stop and take a bite, as the shower has gone over; and now, that he is safe, may I not accompany you home? I am not the least tired."

Carrie hesitated a moment, and no doubt blushed very much; for she felt all at once as though the weather had become very warm; she hardly knew what reply to make; perhaps her own feelings would have dictated an affirmative answer. She had become strangely interested in her companion. He manifested so much deference for her opinion, and was so very attentive, without the least approach to forwardness, and seemed, in fact, to exercise such a fraternal dependence, that without being able to account for it, or even trying to do so, she felt in his company as she had never felt before toward one so lately a stranger to her.

But there were some considerations aside of her own feelings, which must be attended to. The lady under whose care she then was, might view things very differently; and she might be called upon to explain all the circumstances of her interview with him. She therefore followed the dictate of prudence, and answered,

"Oh, I thank you; I have not far to go now, and your pony ought to be attended to; his saddle, you know, is yet at Mrs. Barton's, and you will be obliged to go back for that, will you not?"

Clarence would have met that difficulty, if no other objection had been in the way. But believing, that for some good reason, she would prefer to go the remainder of the distance alone, he at once ceased to press his wish.

"And then, I must part with you here, and perhaps never see you again!"

Carrie's eye was fixed full upon him, as he said this. She did not smile, nor make any attempt to pass off his remark in a playful manner. She saw that he felt really sad.

"I hope our interview will bear thinking about, even if we never do see each other again. But perhaps you may yet visit Princesport. I know my father and mother would give you a hearty welcome, for I shall tell them, when I go home, all about my adventure this afternoon; and they will be very happy of an opportunity to return your kindness, and attention to me."

Clarence offered his hand, which she hesitated not to take. The tones of his voice evidently had a tremor to them as he spoke in reply,

"*I* shall never forget our meeting, at any rate. It has changed all my purposes, and I hope has affected my character for the future. But whether I shall ever see you at your own home, or elsewhere, will depend upon the will of others. I shall go at once home, as my mother has requested; I shall follow strictly the suggestions you have given me; I shall obey them to the letter, and do every thing in my power to win the love of my friends. But, what would I not give for such a sister, as I believe you to be, to counsel and comfort me!"

"Have you no sister?"

He merely shook his head in reply.

"Well, you know if you do your duty, or try to do it, you will have a friend." She was intending to say—*Almighty and ever-present*—but her feelings were just then too keenly excited; she could restrain them no longer. He saw her beautiful lip trembling, and the tear lying on her fair cheek. A gentle pressure he ventured to give the little hand he had been holding, and then turned and walked away.

CHAPTER II.

MRS. BARTON, or Aunt Luckie—as she was called by those most intimate with her—had been brought up in the family of Mrs. Leslie: when married, had left them to reside near a tract of woodland owned by that family. The husband was employed in cutting wood and timber, and taking a general oversight of things, and preventing too large a liberty by those who might otherwise have done more than glean the refuse. The necessity for this care was increased from the fact, that the property lay contiguous to the Delaware river; and much valuable timber might with ease have been purloined and floated off to market without the knowledge of its owners. Mr. Barton was a very honest man; but much better calculated to look after the interests of others than his own.

It happened, very unfortunately for him, that soon after his marriage and removal to their present location, he had been successful in the purchase of a pair of horses. They proved to be superior animals, and were distinguished for beauty of form, as well as bottom and speed. He purchased them while they were suffering severely under an attack of horse distemper. And as the person who owned them feared they would, one or both, die on his hands, concluded to tempt some purchaser by an offer of them at a very low price; on the principle "that half a loaf, or even less, was better than no bread." Mr. Barton became the purchaser—the horses recovered; seemed animated with new life, and to be much improved by their illness. The finale of it was, that Mr. Barton cleared five hundred dollars by the operation. It was, however, the only five hundred dollars he ever cleared by any of his speculations in after life. And the worst of the thing was, that this first success gave him a turn for transactions of that nature. He became quite a dealer in sick horses; and would at times have some half a dozen feeble, bony, uncouth-looking creatures grazing in the road near his premises, while much of his time was taken up in decocting doses for them, and using expedients to put life into their systems, and flesh upon their bones. But the business did not pay. Some of the beasts had internal ailings and some external injuries that baffled his skill. Some made flesh, but never could be got to make speed—and, like Pharaoh's lean kine, devoured voraciously whatever they could get, but kept lean still; and although Mr. Barton would point out the marks which indicated the superiority of the animals, yet, not being able to get the anatomies covered with flesh, other people could not be brought to realize them.

How long Mr. Barton might have continued his speculations, there is no telling, had he not unfortunately run himself thereby out of all means, either of buying horses, or stuff to feed them with. Sheer necessity compelled him, at last, to drop the trade. He was not a lazy man, nor a bad husband; but except in the matter of the first pair of horses, his transactions were not successful, and the living he made was what might in general be called a poor one.

Mrs. Barton had the very happy faculty of making the best of every thing. She made the best of her husband. That is, she never found fault with him; tried to help him along in doctoring his horses—she always called Mr. Barton's management of horses "doctoring"—encouraged him under some pretty hopeless cases, where the creatures were not only lame, but had remarkably bad coughs; and seemed never to be wearied in gathering allacampane and yellow dock roots, and in making such preparations as he had "heerd on" to be good.

And it was not till things had come with them to the very last scrapings, that she ventured to suggest, "that old horses, and sick horses was not profitable to venture much on."

Mrs. Barton also made the best of whatever she had to make with. She knew how to cook up nice little savory dishes out of very slender materials. Her bread was always light, and well baked, and her butter had a sweet rosy flavor; and all the plates and dishes had a wholesome polish; and her cupboard had a delightful fragance, whenever the doors happened to be open. You would feel certain that there was there lurking in some of its corners, pies, or cakes, or sweetmeats, or ripe fruits. Her floor, and her bed, and her tables, and her walls, were made the best of. They were all clean, and whole; and above all, she made the very best of herself—no one ever saw Mrs. Barton with a ragged cap, or tumbled hair, or greasy apron. And no one scarcely ever beheld her clean, wholesome-looking face, without thinking of sunshine. Clouds never hung about it; her smile kept them all away. And perhaps this was the reason why so many, both of rich and poor, would drop in at Mrs. Barton's.

Sorrow visits both classes indiscriminately. It is kept back by no wall of outward circumstances, and finds its way to the heart through the splendid gateway of the affluent, and the lowly portal of the destitute. And it must be assuaged often by means beyond those within the sufferer's command. And Mrs. Barton's sunny smile was just the kind of light that pleased a weary heart. All things to her appeared tinged with it. It shone a little, even in the deepest gloom; and she had a happy faculty of making others see it too. But doubtless the secret of the charm lay in the fact that Mrs. Barton was one of those meek, and quiet, and loving Christians, whom we meet occasionally, and only occasionally; in whose bosom the fire once kindled never goes out, nor even smolders. She knew not much from books, for her education, in that respect, had been very limited. She had learned to read, and nothing further; but that had enabled her to search into the rich storehouse of the written word; and in that search, had her humble mind been engaged for years, and every day she kept on searching, a little at a time; and she treasured up what she found, and she lived daily upon those stores. And when she wanted direction as to any steps in duty, or support under any trying circumstance, there she searched, and was sure to find what she wanted. That book had no mysteries to her that gave her any trouble, and she often wondered why some found stumbling-blocks and others were disturbed with doubts. She believed it to be the word of Him who had made her and the world she saw around her, and as there were so many things in her own existence, and the earth on which she breathed, that she could not see into, it was no wonder to her simple mind, that there should be dark sayings in this Book. But all that she ought not to do, and the feelings which she ought to cherish, and the hope that shed light upon the grave, were all plain, and satisfied her.

Although Mrs. Barton was very far from seeking the notice of others, others sought after her. The sick liked to have her about their bed. She knew how to do things in just the right way. And the dying, whether rich or poor, would often send for her. She seemed to know what to say at such an hour, and although much attention was paid to her by those in a superior station, it did not lift her mind above her own humble duties, and her own humble place in life. We need not wonder, then, that those who knew her so well as Mr. and Mrs. Leslie, should have felt great confidence in permitting her to keep a motherly watch over their little daughter, during her absence from home; and had given it as their wish to the lady Principal of the school, she attended and with whom she lived, that Carrie might be permitted to visit Mrs. Barton, as often as the interruptions of school would permit.

And almost every week, when the weather allowed, Carrie's favorite walk was toward the woods, or Barrens, as they were often called, to see Aunt Luckie. Nor was she the only young person who delighted to take that walk; for Mrs. Barton was fond of the young, and had great patience with them, and many a good word she gave them at parting that they would be apt to keep in their mind.

Clarence Ralston had found the way there, and had not only learned a great many good things as he sat by Mrs. Barton, while she kept her spinning-wheel going; but having plenty of spending-money to use as he thought best, often bought many nice little things in the way of tea, and sugars, and spices, and such extras as she would not be so apt or so able to get for herself; and being naturally a sedate lad, and as she thought, of a very affectionate and confiding disposition, she had taken a great fancy to him; and he having confidence in her, communicated freely all the peculiarities of his situation, and of his feelings. It was but two days after the scene recorded in our first chapter, that Clarence and his pony were again approaching the humble cottage at the Barrens. He was near the house when he met Mr. Barton, busily employed on one side of the road, trying to get up from a recumbent position what seemed to be a sick cow. He stopped at once, and asked if he could be of any assistance.

"Well, I don't know but it's a gone case; her eyes seem to be most sot."

Clarence looked at the poor beast, and thought within himself, "it did indeed look like an extreme case." The bones were frightfully visible, only covered by a rough coat of hair, each apparently standing alone and independent of its fellows. Her eyes stared wildly, and her breath was very short.

"She bleeds well, though; see that—" Clarence saw that quite a pool of blood lay where her tail had been. He exclaimed,

"Who has done that?"

"I cut it off, you see; first I bored her horns. Her horns is cold as death. It must be the horn distemper. I thought bleedin' might may-be start natur a bit. She would have been a mighty good cow, and I got her a great bargain. She'd bring forty dollars any day; but I'm afeard it's a gone case. Her eyes don't look good. But here comes wife; I wonder what she's got!" and sure enough there was Aunt Luckie herself, looking very fresh and fair. She had a bottle in one hand, and a cord in the other.

"Good morning, Mr. Clarence, we're doctorin' agin, you see."

"I'm afraid it will not do any good, Mrs. Barton; she is past help, I think."

"Do you? Well, I'm sorry; it would have been such a comfort to have a cow. I don't think much about horses; they're a deal of trouble, and risky critters. A cow, though, is worth havin'; don't you think, husband, you could git this down her? it's pepper tea, nice and hot. I've got this cord; I thought may-be you could tie her to the fence, or to a tree, or something, and put it down that way."

"There's no need of a rope, wife; she's still enough now. I'm afear'd it's all up with her, but I'll try to git it down.

So Mr. Barton raised the head of the poor animal, and succeeded in pouring down the liquid, but its only effect was to cause two or three weak spasmodic coughs. Her head fell again to the ground as soon as he withdrew his support, and in a very little while his fears proved true. She was a gone case.

"Well, I am sorry," said Mrs. Barton, "for the beast, and for ourselves, too. For if she had have lived, it would have been such a nice thing to have a cow. I guess, husband, you won't think it best to buy any more critters of any kind, that have any thing the matter on 'em."

"I sha'n't, I tell you. I'm done now buying sick critters; it 's an unsartain business. I'm done onst for all. Her skin, though, will bring most half what I gin for her; that 's somethin'."

And so Mr. Barton made preparation to save what he could from his purchase; and Mrs. Barton, with Clarence leading his pony, walked to the cottage.

"I feel sorry for Barton, though I tell'd him it warn't best to venture any more on *sick* critters, or *old* ones, either; but I guess he will be done now; only it would have been such a nice thing to have a cow. But so it is; and now come and tell me all about your walk home."

"Oh, Mrs. Barton! I never took such a walk before, and I am afraid I never shall again."

They had just entered the room as Clarence gave her this reply, and taking her seat and placing it close by the chair he had taken, she looked at him very earnestly.

"What do you mean?"

"I mean just what I say. I never expect to have such a walk again. She is an angel—but I want you to tell me about her."

Mrs. Barton had to think a little before she dared to speak.

"And so you got home well; and was Mr. and Mrs. Rice alarmed about you?"

"They knew nothing about it, Mrs. Barton; you see I found the pony feeding along the road, and not caring to ride back here myself, I hired little Bill, who, you know, came for the saddle, while I sat down upon a rock—you know the large flat rock about half way to the village?"

"Yes, yes; many and many a time have I sat down and rested me on it on a hot day."

"Well, that rock I shall never forget. I spent the happiest time there I ever had in my life. When Bill came back I just jumped on and rode home. I said nothing to the old folks, for they did not know *her*, and could understand nothing about it: but how can I see her again?"

"Oh, la me! Mr. Clarence, how you do go on! You will forget all about her, so soon as you get home, and see all the fine things there; and all the great folks. You are like all young boys, soon pleased and soon over it."

"But I shall never get over it. Why Mrs. Barton, I

scarcely slept at all that night. I could feel those dear little soft hands on my temples all night, and I could see that sweet, earnest look, that met my eye when I awoke from that shock; and the tear on that pretty cheek, and her rosy lips trembling when I parted from her: I shall never forget it, Mrs. Barton, to the end of my life. But she is so good! her heart is better than her face, though I never saw any face so beautiful before."

Mrs. Barton had too much feeling for the boy to laugh, and in fact she did not feel like laughing, but she knew somethings in reference to him, that might cause this warmth of feeling to be a trial to him; and her judgment warned her to be cautious what she said. She wondered not that he was so affected, for she herself could never look upon the beautiful, artless girl, without thinking that she must be loved by all who knew her. But she dared do nothing to cherish that, in one she thought so much of as she did of Clarence, which might give him sorrow in the end. So, with a very serious air, she replied, after a moment's thought,

"Well, child, we must be thankful that there are so many beautiful things yet in the world, and so many good and pretty beings, that we meet with. God made the world, and all the things that give us pleasure, and some of our fellow creatures He has made so kind, so true, so full of loveliness, that we can't help loving them. But children, you know, are pleased with many things which they don't care about as they grow up; and young people like you find that what they think, at your age, they don't think when they be grown up men and women."

"Yes, I know all that, Mrs. Barton; but when we love a person not only for their looks, but because they have been faithful to us, and tell us our faults, and try to make us do right, and keep the commandments of God. No, Mrs. Barton, I shall not forget—and I am going home now, and mean to follow her advice in every thing; and mean to try my best to do every thing my parents tell me; and see if I can make them love me."

"Dear child, I know you have many trials, with all the pleasant things that you have, and very strange trials. Money is sometimes very bad to make trouble and hard feelings; and I hope you won't love it so as to change your kind nature. I sometimes think, though, that it is a great pity that you have been left as you have. It ain't your fault; you couldn't help it, and all you can do, since your grandfather has willed it so, is just to try and do as much good as you can with it. But I'm afear'd sometimes it will give you trouble on account of your mother."

"I expect it, Mrs. Barton; I expect nothing else. I shall be watchful, and very careful—my mother will want, I know, to make just such a match for me as she has made for my brothers. She will want me to marry, I suppose, some one who has as much money as I shall have; and no matter how good a person might be, and how much I cared for her; if she were poor, I do not believe my mother would ever give her consent. And now I want to ask you what you think? If I go home, and am obedient in all things, bearing patiently their cold treatment, and doing all I can to please my mother, and father too, do you think when I come to be of age, and should want to marry one that they did not fancy, because she had not so much property as I have, or as they thought she ought to have, do you think it would be wrong in me to take my own way?"

"Well, child, it ain't best for us to look too far ahead, and say what we would do, and what we would not, some years to come. You, just like a good boy, go home, and do all your duty, and the Lord will make all things work right when the time comes. But I am so glad to hear that you have given up the dreadful thoughts that you spoke to me about, the other day. I hope you will never, never think of doing such a thing again. 'Submit yourself to them that have the rule over you,' and trust in the Lord to take your part, and you will see how it will turn out."

"But I want you, Mrs. Barton, to tell me all about her. She told me where she lived; and, from what she said of her home, I think she must have a very pleasant one."

"Hasn't she, though! why, she is the idol of her father. He clean doats on her. He will wait on her to her parties, and home again; and no matter what she wants, and he knows it, he will git it, cost what it may. Why, what do you think! he heard her mention, one day, what a pretty pony such a one had, and what does he do, but the first thing she knew, a day or two after, the prettiest little horse ever you see—just about the size of yours, only that it was black, and yours is speckled—and a pretty saddle and bridle, all came home together. And when he took her out and asked her how she liked it, she just ran up to him and put her arms about his neck and kissed him, and kissed him again, and again. 'Oh, my dear papa,' she says, 'how good you are!' And then, how pleased he was to see her ride. She soon learned; and he would ride out with her every day. I do believe if any thing should happen to her it would kill him outright."

"That 's the way, then, she learned to ride so well?"

"Ride! I wish you could see. She seems to go just like a bird flying through the air, and afraid of nothing."

"Is her father rich?"

"Well, I don't know as to that. They've got a good deal of property about in different places. Why, this great woods, all about here, belongs to them. You see, his father was one of the old proprietors, just as your grandfather was, and had worlds of farms, but they didn't always bring much profit. I guess a good many has been sold, and people living as they do, you know, keeping horses and carriages, and all such things, and a world of servants, eats up fast. But I guess he is well to do. But ain't they got a beautiful place! and such a view from it! The house is, for all the world, just like your father's, if you hadn't that great big wing to the end of it, and the back part running out so—"

"Has she any sisters?"

"Not a living one. She 's got three brothers, and that 's all; and she 's the oldest on 'em all; and that 's the thing that makes her father doat on her so. But then, that ain't all; she is so good; every body loves her, rich and poor; she treats 'em all alike. She ain't got no more pride than if she never had no notice taken of her."

Clarence did not find his feelings at all relieved by all Mrs. Barton was saying; in fact, the good woman had forgotten for the time, her thoughts about prudence, and was only adding fuel to the fire. She sat in silence a moment after she ceased speaking, which she did in consequence of the really serious countenance which she saw her remarks had caused.

"I can not go away, Mrs. Barton, without seeing her again. When will she be here?"

"Oh, well, she thought may-be she might come next

Saturday. It may rain, though, or she may not feel like walking through the heat; and many things might hinder. If it should be very warm; or may-be the madam may not give her leave; so you see it is all uncertain."

"And I must go home on Friday! I have a great mind to stay over until Monday."

"Did your parents wish you to come Friday?"

"Yes, they said, or my mother did, that they should expect me on that day."

"Well, then, child, as you was sayin' you was going to try to do your best to home, you'd better begin right. Your mother might ask you what you staid for, and you know she is keen to see into things; and you would want, you know, to tell her the whole truth. That might make words, and lead on from one thing to another, till there was hard feelin's—no, no—I think you'd better let things be as they be."

"Why can not I go then to the house where she is staying, and just bid her good-by; what harm in that?"

"Oh, la me! there would n't be no harm in it, that ever was. But you see she lives to the boarding-school; and you know the madam is so particular about sich things. She would want to know if you was a relative; a brother, or at furthest, a near cousin. And what could you say? Why, there ain't one on 'em that dares to stir out without she is with them, and sees just what they do, and who they speak to, and all that. Carrie has got leave from her father to come here whenever she has a holiday, if she wants to. But she dare n't for the life of her go out of the track straight from the boarding-school here. I suppose it is best to keep young girls so, they're flighty, you know, sometimes; and I 'spose there's danger in lettin' 'em have too much their own way. No, I would not have you go there for nothin'. You might git your feelin's hurt; for the madam is a high piece, they say, and makes all mind her."

"I almost wish I had never seen her. No, I don't either. Well, Mrs. Barton it is pretty hard; but I will try to do as you say, and I will try to keep in mind all the good things you have ever said to me. I shall not forget them; and I shall never forget what that dear girl has said to me.

"And now, Mrs. Barton, you have been very kind to me,

and I feel under great obligations to you; and I want to leave you some token that you may remember me by. Here is some money that will buy you a first-rate cow, that has not the horn distemper, nor any other ailing. Take it and use it at once for that purpose, and remember to pray for Clarence."

"Oh, you dear good child!"

And Mrs. Barton, without taking the money, put her apron to her face, and indulged in a hearty cry. It was some time before she could compose herself sufficiently to speak, and when she did, her voice was much broken.

"Oh, you are so good! But I dare not take it. I thank you, though, all the same. And may God bless you for your kind wishes."

"But, Mrs. Barton, you must take it. If you refuse, I shall go and buy a cow with it, and drive her here to your door. The money is mine. I can spend it as I please; and my parents never ask how. And I am certain they would be quite well pleased if they knew it had been thus used. So say no more about it. Buy the best cow you can, and call her Carrie. Will you, now?"

"Oh, well, dear, don't you want it now for yourself? May-be you want clothes, or something else?"

"I want nothing only one more look at that dear little creature. Clothes! why, I shall have more than I can carry home. I am going to give little Bill, who came here for my saddle, enough clothes to last him for a year. So here, dear good Mrs. Barton, take it and give me a kiss for good-by."

And then as he mounted his pony, and rode on his way, Aunt Luckie implored heartily a blessing for him, and sat down and wept at the thought that it might be a long, long time before she should see his face again.

CHAPTER III.

On the beautiful banks of the Delaware, within the county of Hunterdon, were settled some of the most wealthy proprietors of New Jersey. Their immense estates spread for miles along the borders of that river, extending from thence far back among the pleasant hills and valleys that diversify that region and give such a charm to the scenery. The mansions of the "lords of the manor" were in correspondence with their large property; and the style in which they lived differed but little from that of the aristocratic circles of England, from which some of them originated, and which all endeavored to copy, so far as they could in a comparatively new country.

Whether the habits thus continued from the old world were appropriate for the land in which they had found a home, is none of our business. So long as their means were equal to the expense of their establishments, no one has any right to complain. It was to outward appearance a very comfortable style for the owners thereof. The array of servants within doors, and the swarms of laborers in the woods and fields, required from the master and mistress merely the exercise of judgment in directing their labors. For themselves, there was no need to make the most trifling effort with their own hands.

Among the most wealthy of this class was Randolph Ralston. He had inherited from his father, previous to the war of the Revolution, a very large property—immense tracts of land, a noble mansion, and large amounts of money, loaned on property security, were all placed in his hands at the age of twenty-one.

Not in the least dazzled by the means with which he found himself possessed, he lanched out into no new extravagances. Steadily he stepped into his father's track, and gave as much attention to all the minutiæ of his affairs, as if his livelihood depended upon his making the most from every source of income.

Not satisfied with the wealth which had descended to him, he very carefully looked about for a companion who might bring with her other virtues a respectable amount of what he considered the "one thing needful," and made his choice at length of one whose expectations were all that his wishes craved. This lady was the daughter of Alexander Williamson, a merchant of the city of New York, who by close application to business, and judicious investments, had accumulated a large fortune. Mrs. Williamson had been a partner in more senses than one, in all his concerns—she assisted her husband in "tending his shop," consulted with him in all their investments, advised him in most of his successful speculations, and was as well acquainted with the routine of business as himself.

Whether the fact of her thus attending to the management of their affairs had created a love of money, or whether she had inherited that unfeminine passion, it is not worth while to inquire. But its manifestation was so notorious, that her name at the time was synonymous with whatever was close and grasping.

Mrs. Williamson was also noted for her pride of family. By no means humbled in her own opinion by servile drudgery behind the counter she held "a high head" from the fact that she could claim relationship with a titled family in the "fatherland;" and although fond of hoarding her pennies, lavished large sums in furnishing her house in the city in a style that few could vie with in those days. Her walls were tapestried with leather of the richest colors. On her floors were spread the most costly Turkey carpets, and from the ceiling to the floor immense pier-glasses reflected the full forms of her favored guests; while the mahogany sideboards, with their marble slabs, groaned under massive waiters, tankards, and goblets of solid silver.

One only child was to be the sole inheritor of all this wealth, and *she* gave rich promise to her parents of being all that they could ask as a successor. She was proud, close, and fond of show. If any thing, more tenacious of family dignity, than her mother; so much so that many supposed no aspirant to her hand would ever be successful who could not in his own right claim a titled rank.

Such chances, however, being rare, and Miss Williamson not remarkable for personal attractions, with the exception of a tall and commanding form, she thought best to accept the addresses of a plebeian in the person of young Randolph Ralston, of Clanmore Valley, as his homestead was named.

The fact that she was the richest heiress of her day, and must in time bring to his store of wealth a handsome addition, was sufficient to atone, in his estimation, for an apparent want of amiability, and for many of those qualities which a young man generally looks for in a companion.

He courted, won, and married her, and in his splendid family coach, bore her off as a valuable addition to his own estate.

We shall not attempt, dear reader, to portray the scene of connubial bliss that followed—you can anticipate without, our aid, the result of such a union. It was a cold business contract. A joint-stock association, in which the holy sympathies of nature were set aside as of no value. "They had their reward."

In the course of years, nine children had been given to them; of whom, at the period when our story begins, six were not.

Of the three then living, two had arrived at manhood, and had married, under the sagacious management of their mother, heiresses. They had both been trained to regard wealth as the one great good of life, in comparison with which the affections of the heart were of no account.

Wealth either in possession or expectancy, was the great motive power by which the will of the parents had been enforced. It was addressed to their fears whenever the sons manifested a disposition to rebel against parental authority. And the hope of a larger share of the inheritance by obsequious acquiescence, was the mainspring which regulated the conduct of each son alternately. "Which parent it was their best interest to court for the time being," was not unfrequently a subject for each singly to calculate. For which might have the largest amount to bestow was not easily decided.

An event, however, occurred soon after the marriage of the eldest of their sons then living, which tended to change materially their views and feelings, and create a new element of wrangling and discord.

A few years before the death of Mr. and Mrs. Williamson, the parents of Mrs. Ralston, the latter became the mother of another son. At his birth she was seized with a serious illness, attended with violent delirium. She could take no care of her babe, and the little stranger was sent from home into a family that had just then been bereaved, and where the mother was willing to receive him in the place of the dear one committed to the tomb.

Whether from the effect of the delirium, or from some other cause, Mrs. Ralston, after her recovery, refused to own her child, and he was left to be brought up in the family where he had been first nourished. Whether it was that the parents of Mrs. Ralston feared lest this younger son might be disinherited by his parents, or whether they acted from the wish to keep what they had earned as long as possible in the family, by bequeathing it to the youngest, we know not; for there was no reason assigned, but on the death of Mr. Williamson, it was ascertained that the whole of his property had been left to Clarence Ralston, the infant son of Randolph and Gertrude Ralston; one half of which was to be placed in his hands on his arriving at age, and the other half on the death of his mother; the mother to have the exclusive use of the whole income until he reached his majority, and of the one half during her natural life.

This fact of itself was sufficient, in the minds of a family thus trained, to cause feelings not of the most desirable kind. But aside from this, the perfect dissimilarity of character which this younger son manifested to that of his parents or brothers, so soon as it began to develop, caused him to be looked upon as a stranger to their sympathies. The reason of this difference may be easily accounted for.

The Rev. Malcom Rice and his lady, whose kindness had given this deserted child a home, were persons of no ordinary character. They were both possessed of more than a usual share of the better feelings of our nature, and, beyond this, were endowed with that kind of piety, which, while it obtrudes not its possessors into the notice of the world, creates immediately around them a charmed atmosphere, where love abides, where soft words utter the pure thoughts, and gentleness wins obedience; and all that is impure or selfish, meets the silent rebuke, and shrinks away.

They had loved in youth, and the love of youth had strengthened with advancing years, and kind attention to each other had increased as they progressed along the downward valley, and walked the closer, and seemed the more attached, as the world beyond them spread a wider circle, and receded from their sympathy.

In this atmosphere of peace and good will, this youngling had spent his earliest days. Days when the future man was forming, when the thoughts and feelings were taking the impress that was most likely to be abiding.

That great care had been taken with the moral training of their charge, was clearly manifest, as the child grew into the boy, and the boy into the youth.

Clarence was also far superior to his brothers in personal attractions; and perhaps on this account as well as others, of a purely selfish nature, the heart of the mother had begun to soften toward him. At first, he was sent for occasionally, to visit his parental home, and finally, as we have already seen, the mandate was given that recalled him to take his natural position in the family. He was now seventeen, had completed his course at school, and had just entered college. As usual, he had gone to the home of his foster-parents, for whom he had a sincere regard, to spend his vacation, when the summons from his mother broke up his plans, and much against his will, but with a firm resolve to do his duty, he was now on his way thither.

"Oh, how beautiful!" he exclaimed, as, on reaching the summit of a hill, his eye at once rested on Clanmore Valley. Far as he could see on either hand, lay, spread out before him, the beautiful panorama. The valley ran from east to west, lined on each side by immense forests, covering the hills to their tops, with occasionally a pleasant green opening, where acres of trees had been leveled, and were now covered with the rich young grain. The plain itself between the hills presented the variety of a highly cultivated country, for many miles in extent, intersected at intervals by sparkling streams running from the hills, and forming by their united volume a small winding river, that found its way through the opening of the valley in the west, into the Delaware. A stranger would have judged it to be a country settlement of well-conditioned farmers, for numerous dwellings were scattered at no great distances from each other, through the whole valley; all of them in good order, and speaking of substantial comfort. But Clarence, as he looked down upon the prospect, and admired its beauties, knew that the whole scene before him was the possession of his parents; it was Clanmore. It had been, he well knew, an object of intense interest to his father and mother, and his brothers too; the cause of many a hard thought, a monument of pride, and, he feared, the subject of unhallowed wishes. Had it not been Clanmore, he could have enjoyed the view with a greater zest.

It is a sad thing to look upon a home that has no fond associations in our hearts. Especially sad is it, for youth in its freshness, when its affections are putting forth their tendrils, and seeking for objects around which they may cling for life, to have them rudely thrust aside, the sport of every wind, drooping to the earth, or curling back from whence they started.

Clarence paused awhile, and then descended the hill. The road he had been traveling was the common highway that crossed the valley. On reaching the plain beneath, he soon turned into that which led directly to the mansion. It was a fine passage way—the traveled path smooth as a floor, and lined on either side by trees of native growth. The road was winding, too, and more beautiful on that account; winding as the little river by whose margin for the most of the way it ran.

Laborers were busy with their plows in the adjoining fields, and the lively voices of the drivers echoed from the nearer hills and woods; while birds in countless numbers chirped, and twittered, and sang, and flew, from bush to bush, and on the large oak, and on the stone-fence, from whence they would pick the old berries that yet clung to the branches of the cedar.

At length he is in full view of his father's dwelling, a substantial edifice of brick. The main building, a large double house, with portico, and heavy pillars, and a wing of proportionate dimension, attached to one side. Every thing that the eye rested upon was in keeping. All finished in the same manner. All in complete order, and looking as fresh as though the work of the past year, while, in truth, nearly a century old.

As Clarence alighted from his pony, and gave him into the hands of a servant, a lady, very stately in appearance, and moving with slow step, approached from the hall door across the porch, even to the steps up which he was ascending. Her look was severe at first, but as he took her hand, and smiling, said:

"Mother, I hope I see you well," there was evidently a relaxing of the rigid muscles of the face, and his smile was almost returned. It was the nearest to it he had ever noticed on that face before.

"Master Clarence, you are welcome home—walk in."

It seemed to him, however, as he followed his mother into the hall, and then through that to an adjoining room, that there was a strange chilliness to the air, and all looked cold and stiff; and as his mother took her usual seat, a high back arm-chair, of ample size, cushioned, and covered with leather, edged with gilt, and made a formal signal with her hand that he should be seated too, he could scarcely suppress a sigh; it was all so cold, so unlike home.

"You are welcome home, sir; sit down. I had almost expected that on your return from college you would have made your first call here. But since you have been so prompt to obey my request, and as you will no longer have such an opportunity for seeing those with whom you have so long resided, I shall find no fault with you. Did you leave Mrs. and Mr. Rice in their usual health?"

"They are in good health, and desired me to present their respectful remembrance to my mother and father."

"That is all well. Your father, and Mr. Ralph Ralston, your elder brother, have gone to Cornwall. Mr. Richard Ralston, you doubtless know, has been lately established on that estate, and there has been some little difficulty in regard to the true boundary line between that property and the Hazleton tract. Mr. Leslie, who owns it, or, more properly, has the management of it, as it in right belongs to his wife, is to meet them, and I expect, unless something should occur of an unpleasant nature, he will return with them on his way home."

Clarence must have been excited by something his mother had just said; for having her eye keenly fixed upon him, as was her habit when addressing any one, she perceived no doubt that the color had suddenly arisen and spread over his face. She paused in her address a moment, and then asked,

"What is it, Master Clarence, that has excited you all at once?"

"Oh, nothing, mother; surely, I am not excited." And he tried to smile away her suspicion.

"But, surely, you are excited. Is there any thing in what I have said to you about the business on which your father and brother are engaged, or in the name of the gentleman who is with them, that could have disturbed you?"

He was about to say, "Oh, no;" but it occurred to him at once that it would scarcely be an honest reply, and in accordance with the resolutions he had made, he therefore said:

"I confess to you, mother, that the name of the gentleman did, on its mention, make my heart palpitate more rapidly than usual. But I was not aware that my face so readily expressed my feelings."

"Have you known Mr. Leslie?"

"No, mother; I have never seen him. It was merely the name that startled me." And then with all the frankness of a son who has a mother by him, he gave the particulars of the scene with the young lady.

"And if you were to see her and knew her, mother, you would not be surprised that I have become so much interested in her."

The countenance of Mrs. Ralston changed not in the least during the whole revelation which her open-hearted son was making. She kept her eye fixed upon him in the same cold, stern manner; but not more so than before.

"I am not at all surprised that you have been fascinated by the arts of such a young person. She seems to have been possessed of a good share of forwardness. She, doubtless, like many others, would be very glad to attract the attention of one who is known to have such large expectations as you have, Master Clarence. But that, on your part, you must consider is all child's play. In due time, with a suitable connection, it will be my pride to see you well established; but be very careful to allow no liberty on your part, nor make any advances to any young lady, beyond the mere civilities of a gentleman. And here let me take the opportunity to say a few words to you about your expectations. Every young man situated as you are should be made to feel his position. It might prevent great confusion and mortification to a whole family. To say nothing of what your parents are able to endow you with when you shall come to be settled—that is of course conditional upon your strict compliance with our will—nor of the much larger amount you will have bequeathed to you at our death, provided you demean yourself as an obedient son; to say nothing of all this, which alone will be sufficient to place you in a high position, you know, as I suppose you do, that by the will of my father, your grandfather Williamson, you have been made his sole residuary heir; and, moreover, when you shall arrive at majority, one half thereof comes immediately into your possession. It is not generally known how large an estate your grandfather left, and, perhaps, some parents would be very solicitous to hide from their children the fact in such cases. But I think differently. If you were a native of my parent country, Great Britain (Mrs. Ralston had no sympathy with the separation), and been born to a noble rank, you would not be kept in ignorance of it. You would be trained for it, and receive consideration from other youth on account thereof, and of course would not think of forming a family alliance without due consultation on the part of each head of the families to be allied. And therefore it is that I think it best to inform you of the peculiar advantages you possess. The amount my father left will exceed three hundred thousand dollars. In time this must be all yours; and I tell you in order that you may feel your position as you ought, and realize how highly unbecoming it will be for you to allow yourself to be influenced to make any family arrangement by a freak of fancy. Your parents will not be unmindful of your interest in this respect, and will in due time introduce you to one who may be your equal." As Mrs. Ralston thus delivered her views, she maintained a very upright position in her high back chair, and uttered her words with great deliberation, emphasizing with much care such portions of her discourse as she wished him to lay up more especially in his mind.

As Clarence felt that no reply was expected from him, the dictatorial manner of his mother being evidently intended to prevent all argument on the point, he was happy to have the opportunity to change the subject, as she seemed to have finished what she had to say. He therefore ventured to ask after the health of his father and brothers.

"The health of your father is good for his years. He is, indeed, advancing far in life; in fact, he may be called an old man, already beyond the threescore years and ten. But he is still able to manage his large property, without any aid beside my own advice."

"And does brother Ralph live at home again? I have understood that his wife has returned to her parents."

"Your brother, Mr. Ralph Ralston, is at home as you have heard, and his lady has also returned to the home of her parents. Her temper was beyond endurance. And it is a very fortunate circumstance that your father was so decided in refusing to make a settlement upon her before marriage. The Crawford family held out a long time before they would consent to the marriage, insisting upon it that the Glenville Estate should be made over to her, in her own right, and to her heirs. It was very fortunate, indeed; for we should now have the mortification of seeing that handsome property at the control of strangers. As it is, no harm has come of the arrangement. Mr. Ralph Ralston is home again, and has brought with him what furniture, plate, etc., we gave him; and the lady has gone to her parents, and taken with her whatever she brought. The house stands empty, to be sure. But it had better remain empty, than have gone out of the family. The children are young, and very cross and troublesome, and they are out at board, where the parents can see them when they feel like it. Upon the whole, the matter is quite satisfactory. I wish that your brother, Mr. Richard Ralston, was as well situated.

"The arrangement for Richard's marriage was made without any difficulty; for she was an orphan and had no friends to interfere. Her property, indeed, is entailed upon her heirs. But she seems to be losing her mind. Nothing attracts any notice from her. It is said that her mother died an idiot. I can not say how she will go, but she appears to be tending that way. Richard gets a large income by her, and your father has built him a handsome mansion, and has put the Cornwall estate in fair condition, and they are settled upon it; and very handsomely settled, indeed, and with the exception I have named, Richard's prospects are very bright."

Clarence still continued silent. He only wondered what there could be, in the circumstances of his brothers, out of which his mother could draw any comfort. But she evidently was not at all distressed. He could not help thinking, however, that it was a sad recital he had been listening to. His brothers must, he knew, be miserable. Clanmore itself, with its three thousand acres, would not be worth having, with a wife whose temper was so bad that even Ralph could not control her; or with one like Richard's, whose mind was running down into the imbecility of childhood. Did his mother indeed estimate property so highly that all the love of the heart was of trifling value in comparison? The thoughts of Clarence troubled him exceedingly. And it was quite a relief when his mother intimated that she had nothing further to communicate at present, and that he might go and take a ramble, if he pleased.

"I will take some other opportunity," she remarked, as he made his obeisance, "to hold converse on some other matters touching yourself."

He was glad once more to be abroad in the open air, and at liberty to indulge his own musings.

There were delightful spots about the place just suited for retirement and rest. Clumps of trees, with short, velvety turf at their roots, standing on gentle declivities, and inviting to repose. Clear babbling brooks coming down from the hills, and winding about; sometimes coming through the open meadow, and then almost hidden from view by an intervening knoll, studded with trees, around whose base it glided; and then under a bank where willows grew and spread their long yellow branches over it. These were just such places as a youth would select to throw himself at ease upon, and enjoy his pleasant day-dreams—and Clarence was fond of day-dreams. He loved to indulge his fancy; and the more so, as he had so few realities, in his social condition, upon which he could dwell with satisfaction. He walked through the garden, and from thence into the orchard, and across a little bridge that spanned one of the brooks alluded to above, and then close by the bridge he found a rustic seat, resting upon the large roots of a giant oak, that had swelled above the green sward. He noticed what a quiet spot it was, and that the hedge and garden wall defended it from observation, and that the spreading branches of the oak made a large circuit, through which in the full summer heat no ray from the sun could pierce, and that even now when the leaves were just opening, it formed a pleasant shade. And he threw himself upon the seat, and listened to the murmuring brook, which found here more than usual obstructions, almost a dam having been formed by the stones and gravel washed down by its current. And in the deeper water above this dam, small fish could be seen darting across the sparkling surface.

The seclusion, the shade, the gentle babble of the brook, all invited to repose and silent musing. Clarence had never noticed the spot before; but he intended hereafter to be a frequent visitor, that he might enjoy its beauties. Again he is up and off, to explore the woods which were near at hand; First a pretty copse, where the underbrush had been cleared up, and every broken limb removed; and cattle were browsing on the thin young grass which had already attained quite a growth; and on the further edge he passed another brook and then on into the thick forest. He marked the large shagbark hickories, where nuts would no doubt be in plenty when the autumn came, and the bushes, where hazel-nuts might be found, and persimmon trees that stood alone near to the forest, in the open field, and he thought how he should like to visit them, when the first sharp frosts had come; and he marked where the clumps of cedars grew, and thought how fat the robins would be when the berries should have ripened, and that there would be the place to find them; and he noticed where he heard the partridge drum, and every hedge from which the quails started, and ran into their covert or buzzed off into the deep woods. That Clarence thought of nothing beside the chances for game, and winter fruit, must not be imagined, for he made a long excursion, and these objects which have been mentioned, merely obtruded themselves, as he was passing on, and gave a momentary turn to his ideas; he had much to occupy his mind about the past, but of deeper interest still to him was the present and the future, nor were persons excluded from the diorama which flitted before his view, and one above all others, held a conspicuous point, and around her clung the tenderest thoughts, thoughts that were garnished with the richest colors, and sent their quickening rays deep within, and changed the whole aspect of nature to him, and fringed his life with their rainbow hues.

Again he has reached the large oak, which shadowed the little bridge and the rustic seat, and has designed to rest a while in that secluded spot. But he has suddenly stopped, and in a moment stands looking at a female form, that has most unexpectedly been thrust into his path. He almost thinks his busy thoughts have led him into fairy land, and that all about him is a dream. But she has risen from her seat, and her hand is stretched out toward him, and her first words of greeting were:

"And so we have met again!"

"Can it be! is it reality? Oh, how glad I am! you are indeed welcome here."

"Thank you; but I little thought of meeting *you*, when papa called upon me this morning to take me with him on a ride."

"And I am so glad to welcome you to my home; and *that* Mr. Leslie, who has gone with my father and brother, then, is your father!"

"Oh, yes, he called to see me at Clermont, this morning, but as he was in such a hurry to get on to the place where he had appointed to meet some gentlemen, and we had so much to talk about, you know, that he proposed to take me with him; and then I could have time to ask all my questions, and hear all about home. He then only thought to be gone a few hours, but it seems they could not finish their business to-day, and it may be I shall have to stay all night."

"That is better yet, and then I can have time to show you about our place, and we will go on horseback; you shall try my pony alone this time, and I will take my father's hunter, old Hector; he is a noble horse. But how did you find this spot?"

"I found it without looking for it. The grounds about your house appeared to have so many pleasant spots; I thought I would just ramble abroad and visit them. Your mother gave me leave, and so I came through the garden, and over the stile, and there I saw a path, leading somewhere, and I followed it, and when I got here, this seat looked so inviting, that I just sat down, and have been watching the little fish darting about the pool, and the turtles sunning themselves on the stones, and listening to the woodpeckers; there is one up in this tree somewhere now; how merrily he works away! But what a beautiful home you have! I should think you would enjoy yourself greatly."

"I hope I shall feel differently about it, from what I did before our conversation on that rock. You smile—but I am in earnest—and I have been this very day amusing myself, in going about principally through the woods. It does already appear pleasanter than it used to; if I only had some one to ramble with me, somebody that admired the same things I did, that loved flowers as I do, and the birds!"

"And who would tell you your faults?"

"Yes; oh, I should be willing to hear my faults told to me, if any one should do it with the same kindness of manner, and who could feel for me when I told my causes of unhappiness. But come, sit down again, please do, and talk to me as you did on the rock."

And the artless girl accepted the invitation, and there they sat together and talked of all things, most congenial to their youth. They little thought how their hearts were entwining, nor what trials might spring from this hour of innocent enjoyment. She avoided, however, entering into such matters as related to his personal interests at home; and with the tact for which woman is so distinguished even in her early years, the lovely girl, whenever he would introduce the subject, by some happy turn to the discourse, would lead the conversation in some other direction; and Clarence could not help following where she led. There was such a fascination in the tones of the voice, in the motion of those rosy lips, and the honest glances from those softly shaded eyes.

No matter what she said, it was music to him; he loved to listen to it; he was in no haste to leave the spot; he feared to hear a word dropped that might intimate a breaking up of the delightful scene. He almost had superstitious thoughts about it; "as that it would be the last time;" and years might pass before they met again; "it was such a happy circumstance, evil must be following somewhere near."

It was thus he thought, and perhaps those thoughts were shadows flitting on before the realities soon to be experienced by him.

There is a charm in the first touch of woman's love when

the heart is yet in all its freshness, and the youth has not yet tasted the bitter in life's cup, and knows nothing of care, and has no troublesome doubts about expediency, nor is disturbed with calculations for the future, that can never be felt in a maturer age. The affection may not be so strong, and when its bond is sundered, the heart may be soon again at rest; yet while its power is felt, the sweet influence has no alloy—the purest draught of pleasure man can ever quaff—and Clarence was drinking it now. No wonder that time flew by unheeded, and that the present was so enchanting that he thought not whether the sun was high above him, or about to sink behind the western hills. His companion, however, pointed out to him the fact; and then her little bonnet was put on, and taking his proffered arm they crossed the bridge, and walked along leisurely through the orchard, and through the long, wide garden path, plucking flowers as they passed onward to the house.

"And there is my papa! and there is your father!"

"Is that your father walking with mine on the piazza? how young he looks!"

They were now sufficiently near for Clarence to observe what a fine personal appearance Mr. Leslie possessed. How erect his form!—a little above a medium stature—how fresh his countenance seemed! and how mild its expression! And he could not help contrasting it with the anxious, stern look which his own father's had ever worn.

Mr. Leslie was the first to notice the young couple, and hastened to meet them. A pleasant smile accompanied his greeting.

"Aha, my pet, you have found company, have you!" taking her hand, "and who is this young gentleman who has been so kind as to bring you back, Miss Run-away?"

"This is Mr. Clarence Ralston."

"Ah, indeed!" turning toward Mr. Ralston, who still remained upon the stoop with his hands behind him, looking with his usual stolid air upon his son, whom he had not seen for months, but making no advance to meet him.

"This is another of your sons, sir?"

Clarence, of course, must give his hand to Mr. Leslie, although in haste to greet his father; for he saw, or thought he saw, more than the usual scowl upon his brow. Immediately he stepped quickly forward.

"Father, I am very glad to see you."

The hands were released from their clasp behind, and one of them offered to the son. But the embrace was far from being a warm one, and the heart of Clarence drooped at this first token of his father's feelings.

"Got home, have you?" He said nothing further; and just then the elder brother, Ralph, made his appearance at the hall door, and Clarence accosting him as "brother Ralph," stepped quickly toward him with his offered hand. But Mr. Ralph Ralston had no idea of allowing any such freedom. He therefore kept his hands in his pockets, and with his naturally stern, cold face, put on an air of surprise at the presumption of the youth.

"You make quite free, sir!"

"It is your brother Clarence," said Mr. Ralston, turning to Ralph.

"Oh! ah! it is, hey? If *you* say so, I suppose you ought to know. He is grown to be quite a youngster. Come home to stay, I suppose?"

"Yes, sir, he has," replied the father, who, to do him justice, had noticed with displeasure the marked ill-will of Ralph. His own reception had indeed been cold enough; but that was more to be attributed to his usual manner than to any feeling of indifference. Mr. Ralston had never cherished the kindlier impulses of our nature. No warm, generons emotions had ever excited his heart. In his earlier life one absorbing interest had shut out all others. His vast possessions had engrossed his attention. He had lived for them. His partner shared with him in the love for gain, but unlike a wife and mother, encouraged no tender emotions; and rather seemed to feel that they were weaknesses, that should be crushed and rooted out. Mr. Ralston had been unused to any fond epithet, and even the tone of voice in which Clarence pronounced the name of father, was so new, so strange, that it almost caused a tinge of shame upon his cheek, as though there was something wrong even in its warmth.

Clarence entered the hall, and retired to his room, where he could hide his feelings, and obtain that composure which he needed, to be able to bear patiently, as he had resolved to do, whatever he might meet with at his home that should be offensive and unjust.

"Lady Ralston would like to see you, miss, when it will be your pleasure to wait upon her."

This message was delivered to Carrie by the maid whose particular office it was to attend upon the person of Mrs. Ralston.

"Oh, certainly, with pleasure. Shall I go to her now?"

"If it 's your pleasure, miss."

And Carrie followed the messenger through the hall, who opening the door of one of the large parlors, curtesied as Carrie entered, and then closing the door, left her in the presence of the lady.

Mrs. Ralston was seated in her large arm-chair, appareled in a rich dress of the costliest fabrics of those days. Her hair crimped and powdered, and with her large spangled fan gently moving from the cushioned arm of the chair upon which her hand rested.

Carrie made a respectful obeisance as she entered, and a pleasant smile played round her lips. But it met no kind response; and the cold, severe aspect of the lady chilled her young heart at once. And instead of drawing any nearer to the arm-chair, she retired to the window, and took a seat upon its deep cushioned embrasure.

"I will thank you, Miss Leslie, to draw a chair and be seated near to me; I wish to hold a conversation with you."

Carrie promptly obeyed the order, although she was obliged to draw the chair. Her utmost strength would not allow her to move it in any other way.

"You and Mr. Clarence Ralston appear to be very intimate; may I ask how long you have been on such terms?"

Mrs. Ralston, from her chair of state, had watched the two young persons as they approached the house, chatting pleasantly together, and mutually noticing and enjoying the flowers that bloomed luxuriantly on either side of the path. Flowers that, but for the pleasure they, in their innocence, were extracting from them, might as well have "wasted their sweetness on the desert air."

The tone of voice, the stern compression of the lips, as soon as the words were spoken, and the piercing gaze of the lady's eye—all united to put the unsuspecting girl into such a state of perturbation, that her first thought was to run out and throw herself into her father's arms for protection. But as her conscience accused her not, she soon began to feel assurance enough to make a reply, when the lady interposed,

"I wish no equivocation—I want a direct reply to my question. It is of some consequence that I know who have been his associates, and to what extent he has allowed himself in intimacies with those who are strangers to our family."

Poor Carrie was one of those unfortunate beings who, just at the time when they need the use of their senses most, find them scattering in all directions.

She had a full share of common sense, and at times a ready wit, but these only could be in full command in an atmosphere of confidence and love. Now she was in a sad condition. Her heart throbbed violently. She felt her face burning, and the tears would probably have been forthcoming, if it had not been that Carrie, meek and gentle as she seemed, still, in a corner of her heart, carried her full share of womanly pride. It could not be noticed under usual circumstances, but there it was, and now aroused by this rude attack, hushed the tenderer feelings. She could not speak, and perhaps it was as well she did not attempt to.

"It matters not that you make no reply. I shall unfold my mind to your father, and make known my wishes on this subject. But lest you should indulge the idea that my son Clarence Ralston is one that you can safely set your affections on, I can tell you that other arrangements are designed for him, and it would be highly improper for you to encourage any intimacy. I shall lay my commands upon him, in reference to this subject, and shall expect to be implicitly obeyed. And it is my wish, as you are to share the hospitalities of our house to-night, that you avoid any private interviews."

Carrie's thoughts had, by this time, begun to collect themselves, and, rising from her seat, she made a graceful obeisance to the lady, and left the room. Immediately she sought her father; he had just stepped into the garden, and was alone.

"Dear papa."

"Ah, Carrie, is it you? What a lovely spot this garden is!"

"Dear papa, will you oblige me by ordering your carriage, and going with me to some other place for the night—please do not ask me why; I will tell you some other time."

"I will, my darling, if you wish it, by all means."

Had it been a mere whim on the part of Carrie, her father would have complied with her request, for he had never yet refused any wish she had expressed. But he saw now that she was truly in earnest, and he believed it was for no childish freak. He therefore lost no time in asking Mr. Ralston that his carriage might be got in readiness.

In the mean while, with Carrie still clinging to his arm, he entered the parlor to pay his parting respects to the lady. Mrs. Ralston, proud and overbearing as she was, and rudely as she had just treated his little daughter, was evidently somewhat moved at his entrance. His commanding personal appearance, his gentlemanly deportment, instinctively affected her. She almost rose from her seat as she replied to his courteous salutation.

"Mrs. Ralston"—he did not give the title which all the members of the family, except her children and many of her visitors, accorded to her—"I have come to make my respects to you, as I was about to leave. I thank you for your hospitality, and would be happy to accept Mr. Ralston's invitation to spend the night, but my daughter, I expect, is a little home-sick to get back among her schoolmates."

Carrie looked up at her father with much meaning in her countenance, but said nothing.

"I should have been happy, sir," there was evidently a tremor in her voice, "to have had your company this evening, as there are some things of a private nature which I wish to communicate. But as I am not to have the opportunity, I would merely now say to you, that our son, Mr. Clarence Ralston, has been much from home, and, perhaps, has not been as careful as he might have been in forming intimacies as we could have wished. You are no doubt aware, sir, that he is heir to a large estate; and, of course, sir, you, as the head of a family, can well appreciate our anxiety on that account. We have already arrangements in view for him which will preclude the idea of our consent to any other alliance."

Mr. Leslie waited patiently till the lady had finished her remarks, and then bowing low to her, merely replied:

"I wish you good evening, madam."

Having made an appointment with Mr. Ralston to meet him the next morning at Cornwall, Mr. Leslie was handing Carrie into the carriage when Clarence approached in haste, and apparently much surprised at their departure.

"You are not going away!" This he said to the young lady. She made no reply, her eye merely glanced at his as she took her seat. It was not an angry glance; but he saw at once that some sad change had come over her, for there was no kind notice of recognition, and as the carriage rolled away not even a silent salutation at parting. The dream had vanished. His fond youthful hopes lay dead; and he entered the house with a consciousness that he was but just tasting the evils which he had so much dreaded.

CHAPTER IV.

Among the domestics at Clanmore was a young woman, whose valuable qualities had given her, even in that family, where pride of purse was so predominant, and where the most lordly airs were indulged toward all its dependants, a consideration which few of that class even in our day receive. Maggie Bruce was a Scotch lass, who, having migrated to this country with her parents, persons of decent standing in their native land, was by their death thrown upon her own resources, and chose for her business of life domestic service. She had found a place in this family when about sixteen years of age, and had lived with them sixteen years and more; so that, although we have called her a young woman, it was rather because she had a remarkably youthful appearance, and was also the youngest among all the members of the family, except Clarence, who had indeed just begun to be numbered with them.

Maggie never got tired, nor cross, nor sick, nor weary of her position. She had a ready mind to learn whatever was new to her in the department of her duties. She could cook, if the cook happened to be sick. She could sew, if the seamstress was obliged to leave; and she could make most comfortable-looking beds, if the chambermaid was away. But her principal employment was in carrying out the views of the "mistress," as she styled Mrs. Ralston. She was generally near her person, or within call; assisted as lady's maid in the dressing-room, and did all the crimping, powdering, and curling that was required; and made herself so useful, that when any thing was needed, or any body was unwell, or help of any kind was required, it was only to call for Maggie.

She had been trained in the rigid principles of the Scotch church, and adhered to them; studied her Bible, or rather read that, and studied the Catechism, with all the proof texts;

had little faith in Episcopacy, and had a *very faint* hope that any of that denomination were in the way to heaven, and often said, "Gin they gat to heaven at a' it would be a muckle chance." But Maggie's heart was much more orthodox than her creed; and somehow she always contrived to comfort herself when any of her friends or acquaintances departed this life in the faith of that sect, and to find some consolation from the fact, "That there were many things we could nae see into, and one of them was the heart of man; there might be gude there that anither mortal could na see."

Now Maggie, faithful as she was to every interest of her employers, never forgot that she was a free woman, and had rights as such, which could never be merged in the will of another; and, true to her character as a child of Caledonia, would not hesitate to let out her mind, as she thought occasion required, to her "mistress" in plain Scotch terms. Mrs. Ralston would be at the time highly indignant; and often had Maggie been threatened with a dismissal, but the order to leave was never given. There would have been a sad vacancy in the household, if Maggie's cheerful voice had been no longer heard, nor her busy hands ready to do her necessary service.

It happened that Maggie, without any design of her own, had overheard the language used by Mrs. Ralston to her young visitor, and she had also noticed the happy young couple in their promenade through the garden; and she could give a good guess how matters stood.

And when Clarence came in after the guests had gone, Maggie met him in the hall on his way to his room, and she saw there was something wrong with the "lad," for his countenance was woefully distraught, and she saw that his bright "e'en was drappin' a tear;" and so she made up her mind that it was no more than her duty to "drop a word of comfort in the bairn's lugs." It was Maggie's business to see that the rooms were in order, and she had that day been putting things in proper train for the new "young gentleman;" and Maggio found some very good excuse for just "poppin' in," and when once in, she was at no loss how to "start a question."

"And a bonnie room the 'mistress' has given you, and I believe now a' things are right to your mind. And may ye hae many a happy day here, Mr. Clarence."

"Thank you, Maggie."

"And I'm thinking ye'll be the light of the house, for when there's na young about, things are dark, and waesome betimes; but a young face, and the smile of youth, are like sunlight on a murky day."

"It is hard to smile, Maggie, when the heart is sad."

"Hut tut, Mr. Clarence; and what can ye know about a sad heart? Ain't yere parents livin', and are ye no the hope of the house; for Mr. Ralph is ower old to mend his way, and he is not the obedient son **that** wins the blessing; an' Mr. Richard is awa, but there's nae luck to him neither, for there has been ower many hard speeches from him to them that begot him, to win a blessing either, and when the blessing is wanting, it is no worldly wealth that can give the true joy to the heart; waes me! and how could I be livin' now, and my heart light as yon bird that's swinging on the bough of that aik-tree, 'gen I could no look back to the hour when my parents blessed me with their dying breath: 'Ye've been a dutiful daughter, Maggie,' they said, 'and the blessing of God will bide wi' ye a' your days.' Ah, Mr. Clarence? I wad nae part wi' these words for a' the braid lands of Clanmore."

"But your parents loved you, Maggie!"

"And don't a' parents loe? forby they may have different ways of showing it. There were no lands or moneys for my parents to have a care of anent me; and sae a' their care was to keep me in the strait way; and I found it aitimes over muckle strait for my young wishes; but thanks be paid, I have not been permitted to gang far from the gait they wae ha'e wish'd me to walk in. Ye'll be discreet, I am hopin', my bairnie, and no be takin' miffs at a' the things which may be put upon ye. The Lord leads us by a long road sometimes, and many roundabout ways, but it comes out to the right place at the end; I hope ye'll mind that."

Clarence listened with deep attention to the speech of Maggie: the pleasant plaintive tones of her voice soothed his spirit. Much of the same pure truth he had heard from his friend Mrs. Barton, and from lips whose young beauty added a tenfold power to them. But just at this crisis, the fresh instance of faithful regard to his best interests was like a friendly shield interposed just as the dart of the enemy was whizzing in deadly flight against him; it was the word "spoken in season."

"And now, Mr. Clarence, ye'll be brushing up, and fixing for tea, and ye'll put on a bright face; ye may hae at times a hard tussle wi' your will, to make it run smooth and fair, agen hard words, and stiff ways; but ye must look *up* for the help that will be aye ready at the askin', and, ye mind Maggie, ye will hae a bright sundown at the last."

"I will, Maggie; I will try to do my best; and I thank you truly for your kind advice."

"The Lord be wi' you, then; and when Maggie can do you a gude turn, ye'll aye find her ready."

A word spoken in season, how good it is! And Maggie's homely remark proved to Clarence, just at that moment, what he needed to keep him from breaking over his good resolutions, and throwing himself away from parental restraint. It was indeed an hour to try his heart; his cold reception by those from whom he had reason to expect some little show of natural feeling, was of itself hard to bear. But in addition to this, the sudden departure of the one being, on whom his young heart had fastened with intense desire, and under circumstances that left no doubt upon his mind of some rude treatment on the part of his parents, one, or both, and which would forever preclude the hope that any intimacy could in future be indulged, or that he could with the least shadow of propriety throw himself again in her way. He felt indeed that the vision was at an end; and the warm feelings of his heart, which had been kindled by it must be smothered, and dust and ashes alone remain of that flame which had exhilarated and awaked into joyousness a heart long yearning for the sympathy of friendship.

Clarence had learned to pray, and he remembered the words of Maggie, "that he maun look up for the help that would be aye ready for the asking," and before he left his room he did "look up," and was enabled to possess his soul in patience.

The next day Mr. Ralston and Ralph departed to keep their appointment with Mr. Leslie; and on their return at evening, Clarence was further grieved at learning from them, that hard words had passed between Mr. Leslie and them, in consequence of a disagreement as to the boundaries of their contiguous estates.

"It is but a difference of a few feet, but I shall have my

rights," said old Mr. Ralston, "if I spend half the value of the estate at law."

"I guess you'll have to go to law alone then," said Ralph, who, when he could, delighted in a covert way, to irritate his father; "for Leslie said he should never contend about such a trifle."

"It is no trifle, sir; it is my right, and right is no trifle; yes, he pretended to be conciliating, and all that, but the true reason is, that he is cramped; he is short of money; he is selling his farms, and no fool would do that, if he were not obliged to."

"I should think he would be a fool if he did n't sell them, if he were short of money."

"You are a fool to say so; what! sell his family estates, that have been their property for generations! is that your creed, sir?"

Ralph found that he was going a little too far; he had better wait until the estates, which he was coveting, were in his possession; and the "*old fellow*," as he was used to call his father, was beyond the power of making new wills, or changing old ones. He therefore took counsel of prudence, and thought best to turn the battery away from himself.

"No; *I* have n't been short of money yet; but I guess you are right about Leslie. He is a little too free with the ready. I rather think that bright sprig of his will not have quite so big a lump to give her husband as her mother had. Hazleton estate, I am thinking, is bound for the market."

"That confirms my own opinion," said Mrs. Ralston, who had not yet joined in the conversation; but sat very erect at the head of her tea-table, with Maggie standing beside her near the large silver urn, which was placed on a small waiter of the same material, on the right of her mistress, passing the cups when filled in front of the lady who supplied the cream and sugar with her own hands.

"That confirms my own opinion. I rather think a certain young lady would not have been brought here, if it had not been known that there was a prize worth seeking for. But I was prudent enough to take knowledge of the state of things, and made such a declaration of my mind as, I think, will prevent any such attempts in my family from the same source again."

"Then you sent the young one off with a 'flea in her ear, mother!" answered Ralph, looking rather sneeringly at Clarence as he spoke.

"You are in the habit, Mr. Ralph Ralston, of late, I find, of using very low, and very common expressions. They are not quite the thing for a gentleman. I suppose you intended to say, 'that I sent the young lady away rather disappointed.' I did so; and think she will never be likely to come near a Ralston again; nor her father either."

Maggie fixed her eye upon Clarence; she saw the color rise upon his cheek and then go away, and leave it paler than before. She knew that he was ready to let out his feelings; but happily she attracted his notice by mentioning to Mrs. Ralston that Mr. Clarence's cup was empty, "and should she get it for replenishing?" and as he looked toward her, she very expressively put her finger to her lips. He read her meaning; and the influence that her wise advice and her kind attention had gained over him, caused him to obey her caution. He kept down the thoughts that were just about to be let out in words, and was saved a storm of rebuke and ridicule.

And thus, day by day, was some new trial pressed upon him, but he was enabled to get through the weeks of his vacation without having once been goaded to return an improper answer, or do aught which might give him cause for regret when he should have left his parents. He had not, however, given up all hopes of seeing Carrie once more, and had made his plans to visit his friend, Mrs. Barton, on his way to college, as well as his foster-parents; and then, if no other way offered, to go boldly to the school, and ask for an interview. Maggie had become familiar with all the facts of the case in regard to the young lady; for Clarence could trust her, and it was a great relief for him to have some one before whom he could mention her name, and to whom he could tell his feelings; and he had not kept from her the design he had in view. Maggie said nothing at the time, but the day before his departure from home for college, she seized a private opportunity to bring up the matter.

"Ye'll pardon me, Mr. Clarence, for making free wi' my advice fornent your affairs. But ye're a good bairn, and have withstood a' the temptations that surrounded ye with a strong will, like a man; and now to the last I'm assured ye'll knock the hot fat into the fire, and kindle a lowe that will gi'e ye sair trouble. Ye see, Mr. Clarence, in the first place, ye 'll be watched on your gait to the school or college, or where it is that ye are goin'; for your mother, the mistress, I can tell ye, is mistrusting that ye have nae yet got the lass out of your head, and that ye ha'e been keeping sae still just to put her aff the scent; and she will ken a' the way ye go, mind what I say to ye, and gen ye suld go as ye ha'e talked about, and see the lassie, wae's me! it would be muckle waur for her and yoursel' than at the first. And then I'm thinking ye 'll not be able to win a sight of the lass at ony gate, for she is a high spirit as even yoursel' or ony of your family had; ye can see that by the cut of her lip; and her father, too, is nae man, if my guess is right, that wad allow an insult to his bairn; and it is maist sure he might construe it so. Nae doubt he has cautioned her agen having a word to say to ye—not for any thing that ye ha'e done, but forby that she has been sae treated by the 'mistress;' and ye wad be sairly confounded suld ye gang to the house, and ha'e word that ye are nae welcome there. Sae gen ye will be guided by my counsel, ye will jist gae off quietly on your ways, and drive off all thoughts about the bit lassie. There can nae gude come of dinging your mind wi' that which canna onyhow be compassed."

It was a sad damper to the ardent feelings of the youth; but Maggie's suggestions appeared so reasonable, the more he reflected upon them, he concluded to abide by her counsel. And without engaging to himself or any one else to put an object of such interest out of his mind, resolved to go right onward to his place of instruction, and leave the future to *Him* who alone could direct concerning its unknown events.

CHAPTER V.

PERHAPS in no portion of our country, are the distinctions in society more rigidly maintained, than in some of the old towns of New Jersey. This State has neither commerce, nor manufactories to boast of, and in many of its settlements, but little change has taken place, in the relative position of its inhabitants, or it *had not* at the period of which our story treats. In these towns a certain number of families could be found living in a style differing from the masses. Their houses were in general substantial edifices, of a form of architecture common, in the middle of the last century. By no means designed for show, but finished with care, and with those marks of substantial independence about them, that even at the present day is not surpassed by those palatial residences, springing up from all the most sightly locations, near our metropolitan cities.

These families maintained a standing that was not disputed by other portions of the community. A kind intercourse was kept up between the two classes, but it did not extend to social visits, nor to the formation of family ties.

This form of aristocracy was by no means oppressive in its influence, and led to no results that were perceptibly injurious.

Some, belonging to the higher class, were the active and useful men of the State: judges of its courts, executive officers, legislators, and lawyers of eminence. Many, however, contented with living on the income which their estates produced, not apparently anxious to add to their fortunes, by engaging in the usual avocations by which money is acquired; commerce, manufacturing, or trade.

With most of the latter, it was a matter of prime consideration to possess a handsome establishment of horses and carriages; in the former of which they took great pride, and perhaps in no part of their expenses, were they more liable to run into extravagance than in the purchase and support of the best bloods, both for the family coach, and the contests of the turf.

Although their property consisted for the most part of land, they were not, in the true sense, farmers. The greater part of their estates were hired out to actual laborers; for the rent of which they received either a stipulated sum in money, or a certain portion of the produce. They, themselves, taking no further oversight of matters than to see that the stipulations made as to the kind of crops were adhered to, and that the woodlands which were of special value, should not be encroached upon beyond a specified point.

That such a state of living, was best adapted to call out the energies, or even to afford its subjects the highest enjoyment, we will not attempt to argue. It had its pleasant things no doubt, and to mere lookers-on might at times appear almost an enviable condition. But there were evils lurking beneath of a very serious character, and some of these, our story will in due time develop.

Princesport was probably at first settled with a view to commerce. It was finely located for that purpose. Its waters were deep: the largest ships could approach its docks. An island projecting into its bay, afforded a shelter from the eastern gales, and a short run would carry the voyagers into the open sea, or bring them away from the stormy ocean into a secure roadstead. But other things were found to be wanting, which are essential to a commercial dépôt. There was nothing either raised, or manufactured at, or about Princesport to be exported, and there was no market there, for any amount of foreign produce brought for sale. The country around for many miles was thinly inhabited, and the soil not sufficiently fertile to induce settlers to expend either money or labor upon it.

Another more important reason why its commercial prospects were blasted, or could never have been very flattering, was, that within the same inclosure that sheltered it from the ocean, lay a large port with superior advantages of every kind. And as in this world, the tendency is to the absorption of the smaller by the larger, Princesport could not be an exception.

It had, however, some advantages of which it could not be

deprived. The beauty of its location was a natural gift; its fine open bay, around which extended a sweep of land variegated by cultivated farms, and extensive forests; a beautiful island stretching immediately before it, and shrinking off into a narrow point, over which water again could be seen spreading on and on, even to the open sea; and a finely sloping bluff rising from the clear sandy beach, and rounding off toward the west, formed a semicircle of elevated ground, on whose uneven surface were sites for buildings, where each could have a view peculiarly its own, and yet all of them, more or less, a fair prospect of the panorama of land and water, for many miles in extent. Men of substantial means must certainly have been its founders, for most of its edifices that made any pretensions at all, were of the best order of that day. And they can be seen even now, by the travelers upon the swift boats that fly along its shore, standing upon the edge of its bluff, high and lifted up, defying the waters below, and the winds above, and some of them looking like bulwarks erected for defense against an armed foe. And there can be seen too, its small house of worship, with its pointed windows, and tall spire looking boldly off upon the open bay, and around it the dead of many generations, whose sleeping dust heeds not the lullaby of the gentle waves, nor their fierce howl, when lashed by the wintery gales, they dash and break in foaming fury on the shore beneath.

Princesport is an old place. It has an old look. It was old at the period about which we are writing, and it must have been long, long ago, that one could point to an erection of any note, and say, "Lo! this is new." But none the less to be admired on this account. It has a history of its own; and long tales to tell of the days that tried men's souls. There, in those very houses, hearts have palpitated in hope or fear, as the booming cannon and rattling peals of musketry were heard in the distance; and some felt for their *country*, and some for their *king*. For, side by side, in this ancient town, the partizans of each were to be found.

It is refreshing sometimes to visit such a place, where the besom of change has not swept the past away; where there are landmarks of by-gone years; where grave-stones are not all new and fine, and one can know a little by his own observation what man was more than a hundred years ago.

Thus much have we written to point out, to the curious in such matters, the location where the principal events of our story occurred. To the writer it is sacred ground, hallowed by memories of childhood's days, and friends long vanished from the earth, and scenes now strangely melting into dreamy visions. They were real once, but now, like fading mists, far, far off, on that mountain range that bounds the verge of early life.

Horatio Leslie, who has already been partially introduced to the reader, was the only son and heir of a family long distinguished at Princesport for its respectability, and, perhaps a little, for its aristocratic bearing. The founder of it was one of the proprietors of New Jersey, and a large holder of those rights. Succeeding generations from him had so divided these estates, that the father of Horatio could only be called a man of fair property. He owned, indeed, considerable tracts of valuable land in different parts of the State; but the income which they yielded was barely sufficient to meet the demands of his home establishment; and at times, even large tracts of woodland were of necessity laid under contribution when an extra call was made for outlay.

Every thing about his home, however, was kept in good condition; and his style of living in accordance with that to which he had been brought up, and fully equal to that of those in the same class of society. In process of time he and his partner were laid in the dust, and Horatio his son succeeded to his possessions.

The son had never been trained to any regular calling. His principal employment, after obtaining his education, had been to ride into such districts of the State where his father's lands lay, and attend to the collection of the rents, or the sale of timber, or the produce which might have been taken as rent.

He had never engaged in farming, as a business, and knew little about it, except what his observation might have taught him while among those who cultivated his father's lands.

That he was altogether satisfied with this kind of life we will not say. But it is not a very easy matter to change from the course to which we have been trained; and especially is this the case if neither the body nor mind have been drilled to labor. An imbecility that is ofttimes painfully felt, disables such an one for any change that involves responsibility or vigorous action. A consciousness of inefficiency holds him back, and keeps him treading in the old path.

The name which had been given to the homestead of the Leslies, was Chelmsford, probably after some residence in the old country, formerly belonging to their ancestors, or from some fancied similarity in location, or otherwise, to the place of that name with which they had been familiar there. It was, however, with or without its name, just such a homestead as one would be very likely to be much attached to. The house itself was a double brick building of two stories in height, well proportioned; with heavy cornices, solid doors, deeply-carved wainscoting, broad low stairs, a wide hall, a curiously ornamented portico in front, with a spacious piazza in the rear, running the whole length of the house. But pleasant, and spacious, and home-like as the house was, there were other things, external to it, peculiarly agreeable. A noble court-yard surrounded it, in which large weeping-willows waved their graceful branches to the morning or evening breeze, or hung motionless when the noonday sun was shining in his strength, casting deep shady circles at their bases, under each of which a whole family might repose at once. And other trees, majestic and beautiful, were scattered round, like guardian spirits. Generations had sported in that yard, and watched those trees when the storms were swaying their mighty branches, or when in the silent evening the sweet moonbeams stole trembling through, and painted fairy pictures on the velvet turf. And then, beyond the court-yard spread the garden, whose beds, and borders, and walks, had borne the same fashion for a hundred years. Old familiar walks, around it and across it, here and there, lined with the deep green box, that years had enlarged to good-sized shrubs. There fathers, and grandfathers, and great-great-grandfathers had walked, and marked the growth of flowers and fruits, and "meditated at the even tide." Men of fourscore years had, when but sporting children, rolled the hoop or played with the household dog in those smooth and hard paths. This garden was linked with the memories of childhood. It was no fancy place, formed after the newest fashion; no level patchwork of curious shapes, with circles and semi-circles, and little artificial mounds, and stiff mechanical fountains, and urns, and statues. It had none of these. Its ample size gave room for nature's own beauties; noble trees spread their wide branches at intervals, and left space enough still for the sun to do his necessary work. Old apple-trees thrived there, and hung their long low branches even to the ground, weighed down with the clustering fruit. Children had gardens of their own within its bounds, with little groves of nursling trees, where they could sit and tell their stories, or indulge their young day-dreams. You could not see it all at once, for it lay upon a rolling plot, and you must walk up, and down upon the other side. And there you could be alone, shut out from view; and you could take in from thence a long, wide stretch of country, as you cast your eye beyond its hedge of fruits. The distant hills, a river glistening in the sunbeams, and winding through the far-off meadows, green fields, orchards, cedar-groves, and dense forests.

And there within the noble mansion, as you sat in the wide hall, on summer days, all unobstructed to the view, lay the whole breadth of waters. The bay, the river, the island, the circling sweep of distant country, and the open space where the sky and water met, and the old church with its tall spire, marking a line through to the furthest headland that your eye could reach. All these had ever been the same; and they had all made their marks upon the memory, and were all associated with this home.

Soon after the death of his parents, Horatio Leslie married a lady of fortune, or such she was thought to be. But as her property consisted of a landed estate, although of intrinsic value, being a large tract of woods, it added nothing to their immediate income. If properly managed, in time doubtless it might yield a large sum; but she brought to her husband a richer treasure than any amount of wealth could have been: a loving heart, an amiable temper, and a good understanding.

She had, however, never been trained to take a part in domestic matters; servants had been about her from her infancy to wait upon her will, and attend to every want. Nor was her husband's home less bountifully supplied with domestics; they swarmed in the kitchen and about all parts of the house. What they all found to do, might be difficult to say, but they had no difficulty in finding their way into the store-room, and to their table; nor were they troubled much with care as to the ways and means by which the exhausting supplies were to be replenished.

In process of time, four children had been given to them, a daughter and three sons; and the fond parents seemed only to vie with each other in their efforts to make the lives of these little ones as happy as life could be.

Mr. Leslie had made no change in the style of living, to which he and his partner had been accustomed; nor did he, as many young beginners are apt to do, launch out into some new extravagance, so soon as the means which their parents have left, come into their possession. The old family carriage with its span of noble bays, was considered quite good enough. A few additions had been made, as the boys grew old enough to ride. Henry had his gray; and Charlie his sorrel; and Carrie her little black pony, which, with his own favorite saddle-horse, Bob Lincoln, a gift from his father, constituted his whole stud. It made indeed quite a family of quadrupeds to feed; but not larger than many in the same condition in life maintained for purposes of pleasure. The old servants were also continued in their places; they had been thought necessary during the administration of his parents, and his tenderness for his wife would not allow him to think but they were still needed, to relieve her from every burden, and to make her new home as easy and agreeable as that from which he had taken her. Neither Mr. Leslie nor his companion were anxious for display. The old family furniture remained unmoved; no material additions were made to it, and had they been left to their own will, few splendid entertainments would have been given to gratify their pride or the taste of friends. But this, unhappily, was not the case; Mrs. Leslie had brought with her, by the full consent and wish of her husband, a relative, to be a permanent member of the family, who, on many matters, was quite the reverse of herself. Miss Eunice Gould was a foster-sister of Mrs. Leslie; she had been adopted by her parents, when Miss Gould was an infant, and had been brought up as a daughter, and when the parents of Mrs. Leslie died, would have been dependant, either upon her own efforts for a living, or the charity of friends, if provision had not been made for her by their kindness. A small legacy had been bequeathed to her, which was sufficient to enable her to provide herself with such things as she might need, to appear respectable, but not enough to enable her to live in the style she fancied in an establishment of her own.

She was very efficient in all matters relating to the ornamental part of life, knew the true fashion for the dress of the hair, and the array of the person; understood all the etiquette of polite life, and was remarkably tenacious of all its forms; had knowledge of all the nicer ways of preparing luxuries for the table, and of arranging things to the best advantage for display. Miss Eunice was also remarkably tenacious of family dignity; she knew what was proper for persons of a certain condition, in society to do, or not to do; what families were respectable, and what were, as she called them, low; and would have thought herself much more degraded by contact with the latter, however virtuous or otherwise worthy, than by intimacy with persons openly vicious, provided they belonged to the class in which she ranked herself.

Miss Eunice was fond of dress; she laid great stress upon it; spent much time in attending to it, and the whole of her income in providing it, and what more she could get. Her temper was not an even, pleasant temper; it had its changes, and these were very sudden at times; and she had formed an idea, or appeared to have done so, that *her* feelings were matters to be regarded by all the world; especially by her own family; they were sacred things, that no one must injure, and of which all must be sensitive and careful; and she was very tenacious of her own judgment and taste; any opposition to either, affected her feelings, and if persisted in, made terrible storms sometimes. Mrs. Leslie had been taught to yield to her wishes, because Miss Eunice was an orphan and dependent; and in time, what had been done as a principle, became a matter of habit. Miss Hazleton, and afterward Mrs. Horatio Leslie almost entirely yielded her own will and better judgment to the caprice of Miss Eunice, or "sister Eunice." In process of time the title given to this lady, was "Aunt Eunice," and the prime question at the Leslie's, when any matter was suggested, or attempted to be carried out, was, "What does Aunt Eunice say?"

As with "Aunt Eunice," considerations of expediency or "propriety under the circumstances," were not a moment to be thought of, when the standing of the family, as a family of high consideration, was to be maintained; that was the chief end of the thing in her estimation; and whenever Mrs. Leslie or her husband happened to drop a word against any unnecessary expense, it was frowned away at once: "the dignity of the family required it;" or "persons of their standing could by no means do less than that."

Mrs. Leslie did not appear to have a strong constitution, was often confined to her room, and Aunt Eunice, by degrees, assumed almost entirely the control of family affairs; and being very handy about many matters, it seemed, at times, that she was such a necessary appendage, that, lest she should take offense, and throw up her responsibility, especially while his daughter was yet so young and engaged at school, Mr. Leslie was induced to let her manage in her own way, hoping that time might bring about a change, and his own more prudent views be established.

It must not be supposed, however, that all this made any unpleasant jar in the family. Peace reigned there. It was a happy home. Parents and children rejoiced in each other, and in all the agreeable variety that their home afforded.

Years roll on fast when children are growing up, and expenses are very apt to roll on too. They seem to be unavoidable; and if the *hearts* of parents had to be consulted, the cost would be of no moment. But it sometimes happens that the pocket is not so full of money as the heart is of love; and although the latter has its way, it is only accomplished at the expense of much anxiety and management, and perhaps direful sacrifice.

Five years have now elapsed since the reader was first introduced to Miss Carrie Leslie. She has finished her education so far as it was to be obtained at school, and has taken her place at home, and was quite contented to be there. Her absence from it has not weakened her attachment to the dear old spot. Above all, it has not impaired her love to her family. In all their interests she took a deep concern, and was ever ready with her lively, pleasant way, to cheer each heart, and shed gladness and sunshine around them. At her mother's bedside she was all attention and love, and never would weary in doing something to alleviate and comfort.

But although she no doubt has for her parents an equally

strong affection, her heart has for some time been more particularly drawn toward her father, for reasons of a peculiar nature. She has noticed changes in him that trouble her. He has not changed in his treatment of her, or of her mother or brothers; he was the same fond, indulgent parent and husband, never crossing their will, nor denying their requests. But there was evidently a preying care upon his mind. He was much away from his family, called abroad by business; and when at home he seemed absorbed in thought, walked his room alone, and late at night, and even when surrounded by his laughing group of children, did not enter into their mirth with the freedom that he once had done. Sighs often involuntarily escaped him, and his smiles seemed forced. He had visitors, too, that he preferred to see alone, and had long sittings with them. Tradesmen, too, called often, and his cheek was seen to lose its color as their names were announced and he went to wait upon them to his private room.

None noticed all this but Carrie, for her heart was sensitively alive to any thing that could affect her dear, dear father; and she had reached an age beyond the careless thoughts of childhood, and her reason told her that all was not right.

There were many things about family matters, too, that Carrie would have altered if she could. She saw what she thought to be useless expenditure in many ways, and had ventured at times to give her advice to Aunt Eunice, and in her gentle way to remonstrate. But Aunt Eunice met her admonition with her old adage, "What is proper for some families, is not to be a guide for people in our condition."

Carrie would have liked to make her own labors of some avail, too, in the family, for she did not believe in being idle; and felt that her hands were given her for a more useful purpose than to tambour or to make pretty flowers upon strips of lawn. But Aunt Eunice said: "Such work is menial, and would disgrace the family, and lower her in the estimation of the servants; some are made to work, and some are good for nothing else." This reasoning did not satisfy her; but Aunt Eunice must have her way, or disturbance would be made in the family, and her mother's nerves were weak, and so she yielded and tried to hope for the best. But there were shadows about her. The atmosphere seemed to be gathering darkness: a storm must be near at hand.

CHAPTER VI.

IT was at the close of a long summer day that Carrie took her seat by a window where she could have a full view of the western sky. The stars were just coming to view, and her eye was fixed upon one that she always loved to watch. She loved to look at it, because it was so bright, and shone so steadily, and seemed such an emblem of purity and peace, far, far above all earthly disturbances. It always gave to Carrie an idea of permanent brightness, and her thoughts grew more peaceful as she gazed upon it—the Evening Star.

A cloud was rising from the west—a heavy mass of vapor—and as it rose and spread its rugged edge near to the lovely planet, Carrie thought the latter grew more bright, and that its rays tinged the dark mantle—to her eye it did—and then the huge cloud covered all. A moment she was sad, then rose, and placed a lamp upon the round table, and drew a little basket toward her, and sat down by it. And from the basket she took a small article of fine linen cambric, in appearance a collar for a lady's neck, and this she laid down upon the table within easy reach of her hand; while, from a larger work establishment at her feet, she drew out an article of coarse fabric, and commenced working briskly upon it. Besides the cricket which was chirping away in his hiding-place upon the hearth, and the click of her needle, there was no sound in the room, nor from any part of the house. Quickly her needle flew, and every little while she was obliged to make new drafts upon the large basket; at the same time gathering closely upon her lap, and into as small a compass as possible, so much of the article as had already passed through her hands.

The appearance of things in the room, with that of the apartment itself, was highly respectable. The furniture was not new, nor of a fashion then in use, but it looked as if it had been well cared for, and like many men with even gray locks dangling about their ears, very little the worse for wear. The mahogany chairs, the long mantel glass, the marble table in the corner of the room, with its fancifully-wrought rim of brass around its edge, and the high-back sofa with its pictured chintz cover—all had evidently been the best in their day, and had lost none of their respectability, and were never likely to. The walls of the room were wainscoted throughout, and there were heavy moldings around the doors and windows, and a deep cornice, highly ornamented, around the ceiling, with heavy molding board at the base of the walls.

The fire-place was large, and its jambs completely covered with blue and white tiles, whose colors were as bright as the day they were put on.

Upon the mantel-piece, however, had been lavished the bounty of the builder; and, with the exception of some trifling blemishes, might have passed for a little gallery of the arts. There were figures of all shapes and sizes, and from those in curious little garments to none at all.

The young lady herself was, however, much the finest picture of the whole. Some years have passed since we have described Carrie. She has not lost any thing, however, by the change from the lively laughing girl to the staid and thoughtful young woman. The full, plump cheek has gone, and the round, full face, is now a fine oval. The hair has lost its bright sunny hue, and rich auburn locks rest on her fair neck. Her eye is darker than it was, and the deep brown lashes give a more pensive cast to her features; and her finely arched lip would still warn those who might feel disposed to take advantage of her gentleness. Her form, too, has now the grace of womanhood, and has realized all that the girl promised.

We could, if necessary, be even more particular in our description of Miss Carrie at this age; we could give her exact height, even to the fractions of an inch, and the very number of the shoe that fitted her pretty foot, and every mark of beauty on her lovely face. But these would scarcely interest the reader, and could not make them know her as we wish them to. They would, no doubt, could they behold her, arrayed in elegant simplicity, as she was wont to be, and view her graceful form as it moved before them, and have a full, fair look at her mild sparkling features, be charmed, no doubt;

they could not help it. But they could not know our Carrie even then. We hope to make them acquainted with her in a better way before we separate.

She has been sewing diligently, and gathering quite a heap upon her lap—when all at once her work is thrown aside and placed within the basket at her feet, and the basket shoved out of sight beneath the table, and the lighter work which had lain neglected by her is taken up. She has heard a footstep, and knows that Aunt Eunice is approaching.

"It is a sin and a shame; I must say it, and I will say it."

Carrie looked up in surprise at her aunt, but said nothing, being well aware that if the lady had any thing upon her mind of an unpleasant nature, it would be forthcoming.

"Yes, I say it," and she commenced a stately promenade about the room; "it is a sin and a shame; and I never could have thought your father would have thus treated a poor helpless woman."

Carrie laid down her work and fixed her bright eye firmly on the walking figure.

"Remember, Aunt Eunice, *I* am here, and can not listen to words that cast a shadow of reproach upon my father. If you wish, I will retire."

"No, don't go; you *shall* hear it," and the lady stopped and stamped her foot; "all the world shall hear it, that Horatio Leslie—" Carrie hastily arose, and was about to leave, when her father entered. She paused.

"If you have any thing to say against my father, Aunt Eunice, you can say it in his presence." Aunt Eunice had again resumed her promenade, having suddenly cut short her speech as Mr. Leslie entered.

"What is *that* I hear?" Mr. Leslie spoke in a low voice; he appeared perfectly calm, although he looked more sad than usual.

"I was about to leave the room, father, because Aunt Eunice was using language in reference to you, not proper for a child to hear."

"Eunice, why is this?" and Mr. Leslie now spoke with decided emphasis.

"Yes, I did say it, and I will say it before all the world; it is a sin and a shame to treat any woman as my poor sister has been treated; she was brought up a lady, and she had property enough to make her a lady, and to keep her a lady all her life; and to think that she should be cheated out of it, and have it all squandered away; and it is all your doing, and you know it is; and all your talking won't alter it."

Mr. Leslie did not immediately answer. He was either astounded by the harshness of the charge, or unwilling to trust himself, under the excitement it produced, to make a reply. He looked steadily at the lady, and then glanced his eye toward his daughter, as intimating the impropriety of her language, under present circumstances. Encouraged by his silence, and taking no notice of his significant reference to the presence of Carrie, Miss Eunice began in a more angry strain,

"I shall not hold my tongue for any body, I don't care who it is. A great wrong has been done, and you know it. I have held my tongue long enough. To think that my poor sister should be so treated; it is enough to make any woman's blood boil—yes, it is true, and you know it. To think of a poor helpless wife being cheated out of her patrimony!—you forced her to sign the deed, you know you did."

"Eunice—I have long borne with you, even to my own injury, and that of my family; you have now made a false charge against me, and that too in the presence of my child, and I now tell you, that unless you make a suitable apology for what you have said, and promise to bridle your tongue for the future, you must not remain another day under my roof."

"Under your roof! If all tales are true, there is not much of it yours. I shall stay here so long as my sister stays, and no earthly power shall drive me away."

Mr. Leslie was about to reply, apparently in a very excited manner, when his eye glanced at the lovely countenance of his daughter. She gave him an imploring look, and, as though a mighty charm was in it he paused, and walking a few times hurriedly across the room, took a seat, and buried his face in his hands. The lady had not quite "said her say," but the fire had nearly consumed itself. The order, however, to leave that roof, was such a bitter sting, that she could not very well get along without venting out a word or two more. She spoke in a much more moderate tone:

"You have said it, remember, Mr. Leslie, remember you have said it—yes, I am to be turned off now. The time was, and you remember it well, when you promised me a home for life. But my poor sister has no property now, and—and—well, I can go."

The lady made a low obeisance, held up the train of her satin dress, and swept away through the door, like a stately ship with a full breeze behind her.

Mr. Leslie raised his head, and heaved a deep sigh.

"And now she will go and worry your mother, and work her up into a nervous headache. Oh, dear Carrie! I am ready to say with Cain, 'My punishment is greater than I can bear.'"

Carrie immediately arose and stood by her father, and commenced smoothing his soft dark hair with her hands, while the tears, unseen by him, were quietly falling from her fair cheeks. She did not want to add to his grief, by exposing her own feelings; some moments therefore elapsed before she could speak.

"The hour for trial you know, dear father, is the hour for trust."

Another deep sigh broke from the father's breast. But he spake not; while the lovely girl continued to smooth his glossy hair. At first using her hands, and then taking a small comb from her hair, drew it gently through his long dark locks. For a while he sat motionless, almost apparently ready to drop asleep, under the magnetic influence of that hand and comb. At length the feelings of the husband are aroused.

"Carrie, dear, thank you, your gentle hand has acted like a charm upon me. But I feel anxious for your mother. Your aunt I fear is torturing her, with her unruly tongue, and you know how unable she is to bear any disturbance. I wish you would go to her."

Without making any reply the daughter at once obeyed. First stepping to the table to adjust the work, and then as she left the room, closing the door in the gentlest manner, as though she feared the effect of any unnecessary jar upon the feelings of her father, now so well at rest. But that father's heart was suffering under the power of a storm that could not be quieted even by the gentle ministration of a loving child. It had its own bitterness to bear, and the moment the charm of her presence was withdrawn, he arose from his seat, and paced the room. His downcast head, his folded arms, his quick step, all denoting the power of that contest the inner man was then enduring.

"The blow has been struck at last, and I am a ruined man! and all the secrets of my situation must be exposed to the prying curiosity, or the heartless remarks, of the unfeeling world; and what I am to do? where am I to go? to what quarter can I look for help? where is the friend that will come to my rescue? I am lost, crushed, helpless." And as though the sentiment he last uttered, had taken possession of every nerve in his body, he threw himself into his chair again; his head drooping on his breast, his hands covering his face, and the big tears dropping as freely as if he was a child again upon his parent's knee. Chide not, gentle reader, the weakness of your brother; may you never know the anguish which was then wringing his bosom. He was in the midst of one of those terrible storms which sweep across the path of life. It has been gathering for years. His props have been torn away, and he laid prostrate in the low depths of a valley where all around is darkness, and not a ray of light glimmers.

For a time the deep floods were poured forth, until wearied nature sank into listlessness, and he sat silent and stupefied, looking with beamless eye upon the light of the lamp, and watching its waving motion, as it swayed to the gentle touch of every slight current of air.

The step of his daughter through the hall at length roused him. He endeavored to compose his features, and obliterate all traces of his deep sorrow. His eye turned toward her as she entered. There was no smile upon her countenance, nor was there any mark of sadness. But her beautiful features were lighted up with an expression of earnestness, as though matters of great moment were brooding in her heart. Her hair was thrown back more than usual, and lay in slight curls behind her ears exposing her fair round forehead, and adding much to the air of strong determination. While her soft eye beamed with a fullness of feeling upon her father's sad countenance.

He tried to appear calm, but it was a vain attempt. Nor would it have been of any avail. She had come with a firm resolve that if there was any power in a daughter's plea, she would know the whole truth. She would sound the depths of that trouble which she had now for a long time perceived was preying upon her father's heart.

She approached his chair, laid one hand affectionately upon

his shoulder, and with the other parted the hair from his forehead, and then pressed it against his throbbing brow.

"How is your mother, Carrie?—is your aunt with her?"

"Mother is quite calm now, and Aunt Eunice has retired at my request to her own room. But father—*dear* father—I want to ask you—and I want you to tell me—all the truth about your situation. You are in great trouble of some kind; and from what Aunt Eunice has said—unkind as her words have been—I must believe that your pecuniary circumstances are the cause. *Do*, dear father, let me know the whole. The worst you can tell me will not, can not, be so trying to me as the state of uncertainty I am in."

She felt his frame quiver as she still kept her hold upon him.

"Do you think, dear father, that I have not noticed the change that has been coming over you for months past? How much you sit alone and look sad? How often the deep sigh escapes you, and how seldom there is a smile upon your face? Your very gait is altered. Your step grows heavy. Your brow wears the constant marks of care; and your hair is turning, I know it is, prematurely gray. Do you know that you seem to shun even *my* presence; and have not, except from some necessity, spoken to me for a month past?"

"Oh, don't—don't—dear Carrie—do not talk thus—you are harassing my soul to madness!"

She threw her arms about his neck, and laid her soft cheek to his.

"*Dear*, *dear* father, I love you more than life! My heart is bound up in you! I would not, for all the pleasure life can ever give me, add one pang to your heart! I will bear any thing for you! I will do any thing for you! But only let Carrie share your confidence, do—do."

Her trembling tones died away, and he felt the warm tear drop upon his chek. He drew her to his bosom, and pressed her fondly. But no word escaped his lips. His frame trembled beneath the terrible struggle within his breast. It was a powerful conflict between feeling and duty. The latter urged him at once to yield to the entreaties of the dear one who hung weeping upon him; but the former pleaded against oppressing her young heart with a burden he ought to bear him self. And he was almost ready to put her off with a fictitious revelation; again she pleaded,

"You do not know, dear father, how much I can do to comfort you. Do let me bear the burden with you."

He could no longer resist; it was, however, like a struggle against the grasp of death, so long had he buried his troubles within his own heart, and so untiring had been his efforts to conceal his circumstances.

"Dear Carrie, sit down by me;" and he drew a chair for her close beside his own.

"I fear you will blame your father when you hear the whole, but I can not help it. Carrie—*I am a ruined man!*"

He attempted to rise as he said this, but the hand of his child was upon him.

"Be calm, dear father—let me know the whole. Has it all gone?—all your property? Tell me just how it is.

He wiped the big drops from his forehead, while his daughter raised his hand which she had held and pressed it to her lips.

"I have not much to tell you, my dear child, beyond this. Do not ask me to go back and recount the particulars; I can not do it. For these six years past my difficulties have been accumulating—my debts have been increasing. Every thing has been going wrong. The worst has come at last—I'm a ruined—helpless man!"

"Only ruined, dear father;" and the sweet girl looked full upon him, her face beaming with the warm love of her heart. "Only ruined, dear father, as to the loss of your property. You have got mother yet, and Harry, and Charlie, and Willie, and Carrie. You have *us—all of us*—dear father; and, oh! you do not know how sweet it will be for us to do something to aid you. We can each of us do something. What would we not do just to see again the old smile upon your face, and that peaceful look it once had!"

"Ah, my dear child, you know not what you say. You have no idea what it means *to be poor;* and do not, I beg of you, talk about *your* doing something, or your little brothers. No, let me die first, before I see you or them driven to such a strait."

Carrie felt that it was not the moment then to reason with her parent, nor to unfold the plans she had been thinking of

He was too highly excited, and his heart almost broken, and needed all her power to soothe. And how her heart yearned over him, and how intense her desire to unfold to him that peace which, in this trying hour, she was conscious of enjoying; to tell him of that truth which God invites his covenant ones to place in His power and love.

But to tell him of *that* now would be only a mocking of misery, for as yet "God had not been in all his thoughts" as a Father and Friend. She knew, however, that he believed in his general providence, and she could think of no better way at present than to try as well as she could to lift his thoughts to a higher source of help than earth presented.

"You know, father, you have often said, 'The hour of trial is the hour for trust.'"

"Yes, yes, I know, my child, it has been a common phrase with me; I learned it from my mother; but I have used it without much meaning."

"But you believe in God's providence, dear father?"

"Oh, yes, He reigns above. I—I know it. He is a great Being, and terrible in His doings to the children of men."

"And you believe, too, that He is our Father; He calls Himself such; He has made you, and given you children, and given you a warm and loving heart; He knows at this moment all you suffer, all the agony that pierces your bosom, as you think of your children. Does He not temper the wind to the shorn lamb? and will He not temper the judgments of his hand to a father's bleeding heart?"

"Oh, Carrie! Carrie! my *dear*, *dear* child!"

He drew her toward him, and her head lay resting on his bosom.

"Pray for me, dear Carrie."

"I have long done that, dear father; I have prayed for you in reference to this very hour for, I have seen it approaching for a long time. And now I want you to feel that this trial, though severe now, may be only the beginning of better things for you and for us. I feel confident, that thus it will prove. And then, only to think, dear father, you will no longer be carrying this burden about with you all alone. We all know your trouble now; mother knows it too; and we will be ready to hold you up; I know we shall love one another more than ever; and no matter if we are to be poor; is not love better than great riches?"

"And does your mother know all, Carrie?"

"She does."

"Who has informed her?"

"Aunt Eunice has told her what she knew about the villainy of Thorne, the man to whom you and mother deeded the Hazleton Estate, and I have told her what I feared about your personal difficulties."

Mr. Leslie heaved a deep sigh, and was much agitated.

"And mother is much more calm than I could have hoped she would be. She only seemed to be troubled on your account, and said that we must all try now to hold you up, and do what we could to comfort you. So you see, dear father, that much of the evil you have so much dreaded is already nullified; and now, father, you had better retire for the night; you need rest, that you may be better prepared for the duties of to-morrow."

"But the dear boys! Harry, you know how peculiar he is; he seems already to carry about with him a sad heart; poor fellow; I fear he will be crushed under it; and Charlie is so sensitive; and my dear little Willie! Oh, Carrie! you do not know, you do not know what I feel!"

And Mr. Leslie arose and paced the room; his mind, somewhat calmed by the soothing efforts of his daughter, was again tossed by the terrible tempest. Carrie seemed powerless to still this new outbreak; and she sat, awe-stricken at the tokens of anguish which her father exhibited; she realized, as she had never done before, how sacred, how strong was a father's love. She could only listen to his sighs, and in silence see him wipe away the falling tear; and with all the fervency of her heart pour out her strong desires to Him, who alone could give relief; and there, too, as she sat, she vowed to be more true and loving than she had ever been, for she felt indeed that a parent's love was beyond price, a depth her thoughts had not yet sounded.

Wearied at length in body and mind, Mr. Leslie came up to where his daughter was sitting, and laying his hand upon her head,

"I fear, my dear Carrie, this scene will be too much for you; I will try to be calm; I will try to do the best. I am sorely perplexed, but perhaps there will be a way. Let us retire for the night;" and he stooped and received her warm kiss. They separated; he to ponder on the way in which he should meet the trials of the morrow; and she to her closet, to commune with her God, and commend the dear objects of her affection to her Redeemer and Friend.

CHAPTER VII.

In a small town it requires but a short time to communicate intelligence. Mr. Leslie anticipated this, and had written to all the tradesmen and others in the place to whom he was indebted, so soon as he knew that his circumstances must be subject to public notoriety, and made known what he designed to do for them, and invited them to call upon him.

He expected, therefore, early the next morning to be favored with visitors. Having resolved to act openly, and to yield all he possessed to them, he awaited their arrival, not without feelings of mortification and sadness, yet with a degree of composure.

It was, however, late in the afternoon before he was called from his room by the announcement that "old Mr. Thompson" wished to see him.

Mr. Samuel Thompson, or Uncle Sam, as he was more generally styled, owned the largest store in the place, and was considered as a man "well to do," but by no means a rich man. He had been a shoemaker during the earlier years of his life, and had, by diligence and economy in his trade, accumulated some hundreds, when, thinking that his profession was injurious to his health, he invested his funds in a stock of goods, such as a country town demanded, and being known as very honest, and also having the reputation of being a well-disposed, kind-hearted man, soon had quite a run. By degrees his stock was enlarged so as to embrace all the variety which families might want—dry goods, groceries, crockery, hardware, together with boots and shoes. He was plain in his habits, and made no pretensions to any thing further than honesty. How much he was worth neither he nor any one else knew, for he never had taken an account of stock, and kept no books that could be balanced. All he knew of the matter was, that he owed no one any thing; and his stock of goods and outstanding debts seemed to be increasing. Ever since he laid down his awl he had been gaining in flesh, until from being quite slender, with a consumptive look, he had become a portly man.

Mr. Leslie had always been on good terms with Mr. Thompson, and although he was aware that there must be quite a large bill due to his store, there was not one of his creditors he felt more readiness to meet.

The old man arose as Mr. Leslie entered the room and walked to meet him, and grasped him warmly by the hand. He said nothing, and his friendly salutation so affected Mr. Leslie, sensitive as he then was, that speaking on his part was no easy matter; so they both sat down, and for some moments not a word was said.

At length, in rather a husky voice and a broken tone, Mr. Thompson relieved the silence by first asking after the health of Mr. Leslie's family, to which Mr. Leslie made reply, and then took occasion to ask "Whether Mr. Thompson had received his note?"

"All right, all right; yes, I got it. Sorry, very sorry, that things has turned up so; howsomever there must be changes; there's no keepin' things agoin always the same way; can't be done; some goes up, and some goes down. For my part, I've been always so afeer'd of fallin' that I keep down. My women folks sometimes cry out agin this and agin that; one wants me to pull down the old house and build a new un; another cries out agin the old mare, and wants me to kill her, or sell her, or give her away, and git a new un. 'Hush up, hush up,' I say; 'let well enough alone;' a new horse might break their necks, and a new house would make 'em want so many new things in it, that it might clean be the ruin on us. But all this ain't what I've come about: it's neither here nor there; and I hope you don't think I meant any offense to you, sir, by no *means*. You have lived jist as you was brought up, and as I tell'd the folks to-day, it wasn't your fault that you lived in a big house, and all that; it was gin to you; you was born in it and to it. Here you had, as I telled 'em, the house, and the barns, and the horses, and the lands; all left to you, and what could ye do but jist go on and make the best use on 'em that you knew how. Some might find fault and say, 'Why hasn't he gone to work and done some kind of business?' 'Hush up,' says I, 'hush up; what business would you have him to do? a man must be trained to it.'"

"That has been my difficulty, Mr. Thompson; I have not known what to do; my father, you know—"

"Hush up, hush up, know all about it; the world can't fool me at my time of life. *A man can't very easy get out of the track he was brought up in.* Once in a great while it may be done, but it ain't common; and it ain't safe in general, nither; nor it ain't very easy stoppin' when a man gits agoin down hill; it 's a darned sight easier that it is goin up, tho' it may be sorely agin his will. But that ain't here nor there. The thing is, what 's to be done now? and that 's what I've come about, if I only can git at it. You see, Mr. Leslie, as the folks round got the notes you sent 'em, what do they do but come right straight down to me, to see what was to be done. 'Hush up,' says I, 'hush up,' as soon as they began talking, 'hush up; jist go in the back room, and as soon as the customers is sarved, I'll be there, and we'll talk about the thing among ourselves; for there ain't no use in a man's blabbing out his troubles afore all the world; it ain't none of their business. The first chance I gits, in I goes. 'Sit down neighbors,' says I, 'sit down, for I ain't agoin to stand. It don't suit me, no how.' So at it we went, and after they had told their stories, they all looked at me, to see what I had to say.

"'Well neighbors,' says I, 'it 's a pretty plain case. Mr. Leslie owes us all; some more, some less; and he acknowledges it like a man. He can't pay us only with what he's got to pay with; and as I understand it, *that* he proposes to put up to vandue, horses, and carriages, and cows, and furniture, and all he's got left, and sell off for what they'll fetch, right off, and we to divide it among us. Now,' says I, 'neighbors, what kind of a way is that?'"

"I thought it would be the fairest way, Mr. Thompson—"

"No doubt, no doubt. But what kind of a way is it, when a man has got but little to pay with, just to take and throw it away? We ain't, you know yourself, Mr. Leslie, but a small place here; and to sell your things to vandue! why it would be just like throwin' them into the river, or into the fire, to onst. It ain't in no ways a right thing, and so I tells 'em. 'Now, neighbors, says I, 'this is my mind. If Mr. Leslie feels so disposed to do the right thing, let 's us do the right thing too. He gives us what he's got. Now then, let us take 'em at a fair valuation. Let *him* pick out a man, and let us pick out a man; and let them two together say what each thing is fairly worth; and then we will lump our bills all together. If there's enough in that way to pay us in full, well and good. The accounts is squared, and marked off the book and no more to say about it. If it don't pay us quite all, then we'll divide what there is, fair and square, and call it all even at that, and so make an end on it. But your *house-goods*, we ain't not one on us a goin' to touch 'em, *at no rate*."

Mr. Leslie was much affected by this new view he had of the man who was speaking to him, and of those in whose behalf he appeared. He had feared that even the proposal he made would meet with opposition, and that he would be obliged to suffer many reproaches from the most of them. But to find such a liberal spirit manifested by those whom he had never treated as equals, and who had always been considered by him as among the lower orders, was a new phase to him of the character of men, and a startling rebuke of those sentiments in which he had been educated. He arose and took the old man's hand.

"Mr. Thompson, what I have heard from you within these few moments past, is worth to me all the experience of my past life. Your feelings are noble and kind, accept my hearty thanks."

"Hush up—hush up—good sir; there's no use of thanks. It ain't only what's right; nothin' more. You see, Mr. Leslie, I ain't tell'd you all yet. Just please set down, and I'll tell you the whole on it, for I don't believe you 've even heard a word about it before. You know I lost a daughter about six months agone?"

"Yes, sir, and I felt truly sorry at your loss."

"It *was* a great loss, sir; a great loss to me and mine. But I fear it would have been greater still if it had not been for your—your blessed daughter—Miss Car'line—"

A pause of some moments ensued, for the old man had ventured upon a theme which came too near his heart.

"I had n't thought when I began that I should feel so. But the sight of that dear child o' yours, or the naming of her name, brings all fresh back to me. Maybe you've never heard how much she was at our house?"

"I have not, particularly, sir. I knew that she called there occasionally, to inquire how your daughter was."

"Ay, ay sir, she did *that*—but she did a great deal more. You see, Mr. Leslie, I'm a most ashamed to say it, but it is too true; I never did much with my family in the way of religion. I know it 's all wrong to work so hard for this world, and then to do so little for the next. But so it has been too much—too much. Well sir, my, daughter, you see, was taken down all of a sudden, and we was all in trouble about healin' her body. What was to become of her soul, if any thing should happen? Well—we did n't think about it. But *she* thought, poor thing. Yes—but who could she speak to? Her mother had gone before her; her sisters, she knew, could n't tell her nothin' about it; and I—. Well, Miss Car'line called one day to the door like many others did, to ask 'how Mattie did?' and then go away. But she did n't do so; no, she asked whether she might n't go in and see the sick one? And so she went in, and went right up to the bed-side; and you know what an angel face she has, when she looks pleasant at you. Well, my daughter seemed to take right to her, and so Miss Car'line sat down and took off her bonnet and shawl, and then, says she to the girls, 'you go now and rest yourselves, and I'll stay here and do all that's to be done.' Well, I can't tell you what she said, for there was no one there to hear. But—but sir—well, no matter—nothing would do but she must promise to come again, and she did come again, and most every day, and they would have long talks together; and then after a while the sick one began to talk to her sisters, and to all of us; about—what we ought to do, and to be. And sich a happy creature as she was! no fear of dying; and such a pleasant look as she had, to the very last! Well, sir, just as she was a going, she asked them to cut off a lock of her hair, and they did it. 'Now fold it up,' she says, 'in a piece of white paper. I want this to be given to Miss Leslie when I am gone, and tell her it is to remind her of a poor sinner whom she led to the blessed Saviour; and who—hopes—to—meet her in heaven.'"

There was a pause of some moments.

"And now, sir, do you think I am goin' to take things out of this house, for the sake of a debt, while these hands is able to work? No, sir, I sha'n't do it, and there ain't one on 'em will do it; for they know as well as me what an angel that daughter of yours is. Ain't she all the time among the poor a doin' something or another for 'em? I don't know as you are knowin' to it, but it is said, she has done a deal of coarse sewing just to help along some poor person. Why, sir, it is said that she and one or two others that she led on to do it, made up all the coarse garments that poor Aunt Betty Cross took by the job from the folks that ship to the South. Aunt Betty was sick, and her gals' were ailin', and Folger was a dunnin' for his rent, and what could they do? So Miss Car'line goes to work and makes others help her, and they've clean made up the whole, and set Aunt Betty on her legs agin. No sir, there ain't one in this town that you are owin' to, that would take any thing out of this house that Miss Caroline has handled or put her dear little foot on; we sha'n't touch it. And now, sir, I have said my say, in regard to this business, and we'll fix all these matters just whenever you say the word. But I have one word more to say which concerns only you and me."

He had risen and taken his hat, and was holding the hand of Mr. Leslie:

"I can't say how matters may be with you, and I don't want to know any more than you may see fit to tell me; but if it would be any convenience to you at any time, to have any thing out of my store, just send down as freely as ever; and we can settle all about it one of these days when you may be better able to do it."

Mr. Leslie could only reply by a warm pressure of the hand, but the old man understood its meaning, and in silence they separated.

CHAPTER VIII.

Carrie had, in her own estimation, gained a great point, when, at her earnest solicitation, her father had been induced to unfold the state of his affairs. The barrier which had shut out his family from his confidence was broken; and they could now, in a great measure, share with him the trials he had so long borne in secret. But Carrie's views extended further than this—a great work had been begun, a work she had spent many lonely hours in devising ways and means to accomplish, and upon which her heart was fully set. To carry it on required an energy of purpose few of her age possess, but there was no faltering with her when once she had set out. The way was dark before her, and how the great end should be accomplished was by no means clear. But step by step she was resolved to tread, believing firmly that in the path of duty the pillar of cloud and of fire would be manifest as its guidance and protection should be needed.

With her father's consent, she at once wrote to her brothers, and summoned them from school. No longer with honor could they be sustained away from home, and duty clearly demanded their recall.

Her next aim was to put a stop to the great drain upon her father's means caused by their retinue of servants. There were many obstacles in the way of any reform here—the indisposition of her mother, and the fear that she might feel compelled, if any steps were taken to reduce their expenses in that way, to make efforts for which she was not equal; the will of Aunt Eunice, which Carrie dreaded to encounter; and the feelings of her father, which were so tenderly alive on the subject of her being compelled to active service in the house, or that her mother should be deprived of any attention that she had always been accustomed to.

But each of these difficulties appeared to melt away, or to

present less insurmountable barriers as the subject was earnestly approached.

Mrs. Leslie, true woman as she was, had seemed to forget all her own infirmities from the hour that she learned that the husband of her youth was in trouble. Her sympathy with him had acted with electric power, and imparted vigor alike to her mind and body.

Aunt Eunice had retired, not only from all active rule in the family, but had entirely secluded herself within her own room from the evening when her unruly tongue brought upon her the severe rebuke of Mr. Leslie; and all the report from her by the maid whose duty it had been to attend upon her, was, that "Mistress Eunice had a most shocking bad headache, and could in no wise leave her room."

And a way was happily provided to save the feelings of her father, and to accomplish her design in this matter, which Carrie, herself had never anticipated.

Mrs. Barton, or Aunt Luckie, with whom the reader is already acquainted, had lost her husband, and been living a widow for the two past years. Mr. Barton, as we might have expected, left nothing behind him of any consequence, as a means of support for Aunt Luckie. And as she was obliged to make her own way in the world after he had done working for her, she concluded to leave the home she had occupied when we first brought her into notice, and to return to the town where she had been brought up. She felt a little happier to be near the friends of her youth, and especially where she could see, as often as she pleased, the children she had taken care of in their infancy. She had hired a small tenement not far from Mr. Leslie's. It was very small, indeed, but still kept with the neatness for which she had ever been remarkable, and by her industry was enabled to provide for her wants, and to keep always on hand some "nice little things" to please the younger folks. To the children of Mrs. Leslie, Aunt Luckie's was the next place to their own home. There they felt free to ask for what they wanted, and sometimes even more free, when the mother happened to be confined to her room, and Aunt Eunice had sole charge of the keys. And when sickness overtook the family, and she thought she could be useful, the key was turned in her own door, and her place would be by their bedside.

It was not at all surprising, then, as soon as she received tidings that a new trouble had overtaken Mr. Leslie's family, that Aunt Luckie made quick preparation to be among them, "to see what she could do to help."

It happened as Aunt Luckie entered the parlor, that Mrs. Leslie had taken her seat there—the first time she had left her room for many weeks. And the good woman lifted both hands in astonishment.

"Why, Mrs. Leslie! I had no idee of seeing you here, and looking so bright!"

Mrs. Leslie smiled, remarking at the same time, "that she had not felt so well for many months."

"Well, that is good news, any how. I always think if a body can only have their health, other things ain't of so much consequence. You ain't a going to take my things, Miss Carrie!" Carrie had begun to untie the strings of Aunt Luckie's red cloak.

"Yes, I am going to take your things, Aunt Luckie; so do you sit still. You know I always make every one do just as I say."

The cloak and bonnet were soon put out of sight, and Carrie taking a seat by her side, in a very short time commenced the subject which had been so much upon her mind.

"Do you not think, Aunt Luckie, that I am old enough, and big enough, and strong enough, to help myself, and to help father and mother too, without the aid of so many servants?"

Aunt Luckie looked at her with a very serious air, but made no reply.

"I suppose you have heard how we are situated now?"

"I have heer'd some things, my dear; but I thought I would come straight down here, and know for certainty about it. Is it true that old Folger has got every thing?"

"He has so much in his power that if he should foreclose, we fear there would be little left indeed."

"Well, I fear if your father is in his power, he has n't much to hope for."

"*That* we all believe; and I think the best course we can pursue is to prepare for the worst, by stopping every unnecessary expense, and myself and the boys doing what we can to assist in supporting the family."

Aunt Luckie kept her eye fixed on the beautiful countenance of the speaker. She had loved her from the cradle; she had watched her growth to womanhood; had looked with pride upon the beauty of her person, and the grace of her carriage; had listened with delight to the praises of others as they spoke of her lovely countenance and lovely character; and had thought of her as one destined to fill some high place in life— as one day to be the mistress of some noble mansion, where wealth would surround her with all the elegance which it could purchase. "She was good enough, and handsome enough," she said, "for a prince or a king, either, if there were any such things about here." And now to hear her talk about poverty, and work, and doing something for herself— for her own support, and that of others! No wonder Aunt Luckie could not at once make any reply to the question put to her.

At length a tear began to steal down from its hiding-place, and then another, until they came so fast that Aunt Luckie had no way to help the matter, but to give right up and let her full heart have vent.

Crying is very catching, and Mrs. Leslie could not restrain the emotions awakened in her heart, any better than Aunt Luckie. It was the first time Carrie had ventured to touch upon the topic before her mother.

The contagion, however, did not affect her who had caused the tears. Calm as the evening star, and as unaffected in her brilliancy, her countenance beaming with the high purpose which her mind resolved, she sat and listened to their tokens of distress. She felt, indeed, that a dark cloud was spreading over her—it might be charged with a severe tempest. But she felt a strong assurance that if she went steadily on in the path of duty, the hour would come when, the storm having spent its fury, would pass away, the clouds be scattered, and the atmosphere more pure and bright than ever.

Aunt Luckie, however, was not one of those who had tears ever ready in sympathy with trouble but had nothing else to give. She took her cry out, and then was prepared to say and to do what was in her power to soothe the troubled spirits, and strengthen the hearts and hands of those she truly loved.

"Nature must have its way; but after all it ain't tears that is going to give help. As to what Miss Carrie says about doing something with her own hands, by way of support to the family—I hope it may never come to that. But be that as it may, it seems to me, if so be it is that things have come to the pass Miss Carrie tells of, the first thing to be done is to *stop the outgoes*. And now I can tell you just what I think you had better do: Let all the servants go—all five on 'em; they ain't altogether worth two good pair of hands—and I will just come and take my old place."

"Oh, Luckie! what *do* you mean?" and Mrs. Leslie looked at her with intense interest.

"Aunt Luckie!"—Carrie laid her hand upon her arm, and her eye was moistened with a tear—"what *do* you say!"

"I mean just what I say. Send away all your servants, or help, or whatever you please to call them. And I will come here, bag and baggage; and if I can't keep things in better trim than all of them put together—then no matter."

"But, Aunt Luckie, *how* shall we pay you?"

"It will be time enough to talk about that when I ask for it, my darling. You see, this is a matter I've been thinkin' of a good while. But I ain't seen no time, before now, when I thought the time had come to mention it. You had help enough, and more than enough, and it was not for me to interfere and try to get myself in, or to get them out. But your speaking to me now makes me free to say my say.

"You see I often ask myself what am I living for? Barton is dead, and I have no children to do for. The year comes and goes, and finds me just where I was before; no better off, and no worse. Here, you know, is my old home. All I love on earth is here. I don't mean the house—for may be you may not stay long in it. But your family is all the world to *me*. I want to *live* with you, whether you be poor or rich, and to *die* among you. And now, if you are all willing, there is no more to be said about it."

Carrie's warm heart could keep in its strong emotions no longer. She threw her arms around the kind friend who had thus manifested such tokens of true love.

"My own dear Aunt Luckie! may God pour into your heart His rich consolations, and reward you for all your kind feelings."

"Love is better to me, dear, than any thing else. I'm never afeer'd for a living. I've always had it, and I am willing to trust for the days to come. I am only thinking [illegible] happy we shall all be! Poverty ain't any thing so bad as fol[illegible] think for, if a body has only peace of mind, and them about 'em they can love. But let us dry up the tears, I hear your pa's step in the hall. We must have a cheerful face for him, [illegible]how."

And each endeavored as fast as possible to do as Aunt Luckie had said. It was evident, however, from the sad expression which marked the countenance of Mr. Leslie that the first sight of things had not been favorable.

He smiled, though, and seemed most agreeably surprised at seeing Mrs. Leslie.

"My dear Lucy! are you really able to be here?"

"I am; but I can hardly tell you, my dear, what has happened to me that I feel so much better. I do feel more like myself than I have done in a long while; I expect Aunt Luckie must have some of the credit."

"Oh, la, Mrs. Leslie, how can you say so?"

"Only to think, dear father, what Aunt Luckie has been proposing."

Mr. Leslie had passed a word with her when she was entering the house, and therefore had not said any thing as he came into the room. His mind, too, was absorbed with the interest his wife's unexpected appearance had excited. He turned toward Luckie now as Carrie spoke, and perceived she had been weeping.

"It is a sad time with us, Luckie."

"Oh, but, father, it is going to be a happy time with us. Just sit down and hear what we have been talking about, and what Aunt Luckie proposes."

And Mr. Leslie did as Carrie requested, and listened with deep interest to the whole recital. A heavy load seemed gradually to be falling from his mind. His brow relaxed, his eye brightened, and a smile almost settled on his lips. The subject was one that had caused some of the severest pangs his heart had suffered. He knew not how to retain such a burden as their domestic help had been, and yet he knew not how to spare them. He was well aware that a great amount of his family expenses accrued from the wages, and the board, and, above all, the waste of servants. But how to remedy the evil, he could not tell. He knew not but each was necessary in his or her place. To throw the labor upon his lovely Carrie was a thought he could not indulge for a moment. It was one of the darkest spots in the cloud that had settled about him. No wonder, then, that his countenance lighted up as this mist was dissipated, and his anxieties were thus relieved.

"Well, Luckie," he said, as soon as his daughter had done speaking, "you can have but a faint conception of the relief your offer has given to my mind. But it is a very unlikely time for you to cast in your lot among us—a very dark time. You can no doubt be a great comfort to *us*, but what can we do for *you!* How shall we—"

Aunt Luckie heard his voice tremble as he was endeavoring to speak of her pay and reward.

"Don't say nothing more now—there is no need—I understand all about it. And Mrs. Leslie and Carrie too. We have settled all that. If you are satisfied, it is all I want. I'm home again, just where I want to live and die."

Aunt Luckie now whispered to Carrie, who at once left the room. And then she continued for a few moments, in her pleasant way, endeavoring to make those who had been thus brought down to the stern realities of a state of comparative poverty, think of the mercies that still encompassed their path.

"To have such a child, too, as that dear Carrie! so sweet in all her ways! only thinking about her parents—and not at all about herself—only just what she shall do for all the rest. Ain't that enough of itself? But it is more than nature, depend on it. Carrie has something more than *that* to keep her up so. Why she seems to me to have her mind away up above the earth."

"That is true, Luckie. She does indeed. Ah, Luckie! I do not know where she has got, I am sure *I* can not take any credit to myself. It does not seem to me that I have ever lived to any good purpose whatever." And as Mr. Leslie said this, he arose and walked the room, while Mrs. Leslie covered her face in silence. She, too, was conscious that the past had gone like a long sleep; that life had been but as a dream. Its scenes as changing as the visions of night, and with as little steadiness of purpose in her mind.

"I never think it very good to be looking at the past, any

more may-be, than to make us thankful, or to make us try to do different. Now, you know, I don't mean any disrespect; but I've been often thinking over in my own mind, and counting up the families I have known, all broken up, and scattered to pieces, and most all of 'em have lived without acknowledging God. I hope you will take it kind of me, and not think I mean to bring any blame on you—either of you. You have n't either of you done any thing that has been at all out of the way; and you have been good supporters of the Church, and you have been kind to the poor, and have always helped the minister, and all that. But what I mean is, you know the Scriptures says, 'I will be a swift witness against the families that call not on my name.' Now, I don't blame you—nor I can't—you was so brought up. Your father lived just so—I mean old Mr. Leslie; and *his* father, the one who built this house—he did so afore him. I don't believe since this house was built, there has ever been a family prayer in it, except may-be when a minister has happened here overnight, or when the minister was called when some one was dying. Now don't, I pray you, think hard of me, I—"

"Oh, Luckie! Luckie! you say what is too true. I have thought of it a great deal these months past. Yes, we have lived for generations a prayerless family. I know it. We deserve to be scattered—to be broken up—and that is what hangs heaviest on my mind. The frown of God rests upon me. It has been upon me a long, long time; it has blasted all my plans and hopes."

"Oh, don't, don't, please, Mr. Leslie, don't talk so. You ain't blasted—you won't be broken up, nor scattered. Ain't there a blessing among you! Do you think the prayers of that dear child ain't a blessing! Yes, it is the beginning. I see it. This is only a rod; it ain't a blast. No, no. I have hopes to live yet to hear you, as the head of this family, calling us all together night and morning to bow down and acknowledge God, and praise him for his mercies."

"And I hope to live to see it too, Luckie." Mrs. Leslie had been weeping, and her husband had gone up, and standing by her held her hand. As she thus spoke, she looked up at him with all the tenderness of her true wife's heart expressed in her countenance, "But it has not been his fault, Luckie, as much as it has been mine. He has never denied the least wish I have ever expressed; and I know if I had made this request, he would have yielded to it. Dear husband, let us begin anew—"

"Lucy, Lucy, how can I do it? What mockery would it be for me, with my unrenewed heart, to pretend to pray, or to lead my family!"

"Please, Mr. Leslie, don't say so; I don't feel as though *I* was any one to teach what a person ought to do; but I know this. If your heart is not right, to whom can you go to get it made right? Oh, if you feel at all like wishing to begin to do your duty, don't stop, I beg of you. How can it be mockery for you to call your family together, and thank the Lord for your spared lives, and for all your other mercies! Couldn't you do it in good earnest?"

"I think I could, Luckie."

"And couldn't you acknowledge that you had sinned against Him, all of you? and couldn't you ask His forgiveness? and couldn't you honestly and earnestly ask Him to take care of you and yours, and help you and all of us to do what we can't do ourselves? and no mockery either?"

"But Luckie, at my time of life, it is hard to make changes."

"It is hard, Mr. Leslie, at any time, to make changes for the better, if we try to do it in our own strength. Oh, it is very hard; but it can be done. If the Lord helps us, our gray hairs will be no hinderance. But you are not an old man yet, only just in the prime of life, and the few gray hairs on your head, and the wrinkles on your brow, I know, has come more of trouble than of age. Only just look up to *Him* for help, and all will be easy."

Luckie had said all that she thought was proper for her to say, and she sat silently waiting, until some further notice should be given that her advice was needed. At length Mrs. Leslie asked,

"You would not think it wrong, Luckie, that Mr. Leslie should use the prayer-book, if he should think it best to begin as you advise; and as I believe both he and I think should be done?"

"Oh, no ma'am, by no means, by no means. I am, as you know, a Presbyterian, and have never been used to that way; but I never find no trouble in joining in the prayers when I go to the church, which I do when there is no meeting in the meeting-house. Oh, no; their prayers are good; so it seems to me, and just what all poor sinners can join in, if they only have the heart to do it. Oh, how happy I should be just to see it; just once to bow down with you all, and say amen when he had done."

"I believe you would, Luckie," said Mr. Leslie, as he came, and took her hand; "I believe you would heartily rejoice to see me do my duty; and God helping me, I will try."

It was too much for the feeling heart of Luckie.

"Oh, praise, praise the Lord. Oh, I knew it. I felt sure of it; I knew a blessing was coming to this family. You see it is a rod that is upon you, a father's rod, and there is a blessing in it; and you will all live to see the day when you will thank Him for it."

"I thank Him now for it. Yes, Luckie; I know not what is before me, nor to what depths of poverty I may sink. But if my present circumstances have been the means of making only *this* change in my course of life, I thank the Lord for them. I know I shall be happier with a crust of bread, if I acknowledge the hand that gives it to me, than I have ever been, or could ever be with every luxury, and no God to go to."

"Oh, dear, that is good; but do let me go and tell Carrie."

"Yes, Luckie, you may. I know it will make her heart glad."

It was not long before the light step of the lovely girl was heard approaching; there was joy in its tread; there was joy unspeakable beaming from her swimming eye, and her flushed face, as she opened the door, and looked upon the calm face of her father. She went straight toward him, and his arms were extended to receive her.

Not a word was spoken as she received his fond embrace, and then hastened to her mother, and wept upon her neck such tears of joy as only they can shed who have wept in secret places for those over whom their hearts tenderly yearned, and find at length that their prayers are answered.

It happened very favorably for Mr. Leslie, under present circumstances, that his servants had been as reckless of their own interest as of his. They had taken up their wages quite as fast as they were due; so that but a trifle was owing to any of them. This was immediately paid; the separation was somewhat painful to all parties, but the stern demands of duty required it, and Carrie as well as her parents felt that a great burden had been taken from the household, when Aunt Luckie was installed as sole mistress of the kitchen.

Bob, the coachman, had, however, not been classed with the hired servants, and nothing had been said to him in reference to a change of place. He had been brought up in the family of Mr. Leslie's father; that is, he had been purchased, when a young man, immediately from the coast of Africa. He was not a slave, though, to the present Mr. Leslie; his freedom having been bequeathed to him at the death of his old master.

But slavery to him had never been a grievous bondage; his wants had been well attended to, his duties had not been severe, and his pockets had always been supplied with loose change; and so great was his affection to the family, that their interest seemed to be his whole study.

Mr. Leslie had informed Bob, on the death of his father, that he was now a free man, and could choose his own situation, and offered to give him a written character to any of the gentry who might wish to employ him. The mention of a character, however, had like to have given him great offense.

"What fur, Master Ratio, me want a character? jist like a white nigger! Ain't Bob known to all de quality 'bout here! How me look goin' 'bout wid a dirty piece ob paper, and handin' de gentleman to read, and see if he want take Bob! No, no; if dey no take me widout a character, dey no hab me at all. But what fur I go away, Massa Ratio? you no want me?"

"Oh, yes, Bob, I should feel sad to have you leave me; for I should never expect to get one to fill your place that I should like so well; but I thought, perhaps you had lived so long here, you might wish to change."

"What fur me change? ain't I lived always in dis house? and ain't I always set by old massa and mistress? and ain't I known you from a boy? No, no; if Massa Ratio want me, I no go away while de house stands."

"But I must pay you wages now, Bob, which I will very gladly do; only say what they shall be. I will give you as much as the best of them get."

Bob looked a moment at his young master, and then broke out into a loud laugh.

"Ha, ha, ha, Master Ratio! go 'long, now. You jokin', ha, ha, ha!"

"But I am in earnest, Bob! you are a free man now; as free as I am; and it is but right that I should pay you for your services."

But Bob only laughed the louder; and in this way always met Mr. Leslie's offer of money as wages. Whenever he wanted, however, he would ask freely; but only for small sums. He seemed to prefer, and doubtless did, a childlike dependence. The idea of a separation from the family, such as wages implied, was perfectly at variance with all his ideas of happiness and of the propriety of things.

And thus he had lived to the present hour. It was therefore a matter for serious thought with Mr. Leslie how to dispose of this old and faithful servant. We call him old, however, rather because he must have been many years in the world, than from any appearance of age about him. He had never suffered from hard usage, or hard work, and was yet hale and hearty; able to manage the most fractious horse, or do a day's labor with the best man that could be found. To keep him as he was now situated, without the prospect of being able to offer him a home, when he should become helpless, did not appear to Mr. Leslie to be just.

And yet to propose a separation was a severe trial. It was no common tie to break, and one which can be only fully comprehended by those who have been brought up where the relation of master and slave is known. The idea may be ridiculed by those who have taken a violent stand against the institution in all its forms, and are resolved to destroy it, root and branch.

But the fact remains that there is between the kind master and the faithful slave a tie of strong attachment, rising above all the littleness of the selfish principle, and taking hold of the best feelings of our nature. Its evils are the dark shadows of the picture.

Mr. Leslie was, however, spared this unpleasant duty by the intervention of Carrie, and that without any design on her part, the feelings of the daughter being as much opposed to a separation as those of the father.

Carrie had been engaged by the side of Aunt Luckie, in the kitchen, being determined, as she said, "to learn how to do every thing that had to be done," when the fire, needing a stick to replenish it, she stepped to the adjoining cellar and was in the act of bringing a piece of wood, when Bob came in from without. He had not time to take it from her, although he hastened to do so, for quick in all her movements, it was in its place on the andirons, ere he could get to her.

"What fur you do *dat*, Miss Carrie? It no your place to bring de wood."

"Oh, never mind, daddy; it is high time I begun to help myself; you may be gone one of these days."

Bob said nothing at the time, but watching his opportunity when Carrie was alone, he asked her,

"What a you mean, Miss Carrie, a leetle while ago, when you sa , 'May be you be gone.' What a you mean by dat ?" y

"Oh, I did not design to say any thing that might make you feel unpleasant, daddy; but you know our circumstances are very different from what they once were. We must all now learn to help ourselves; you know, papa can not afford now to hire much help."

"You no call me hired man, Miss Carrie !"

Carrie saw that he was much excited.

"Oh, no, daddy, no! I believe you have lived with us and served us faithfully, just because you have loved us, and because we love you. But what can we do now for you, daddy? Papa is in trouble; his property is gone. Our home may be taken from us any day; and how selfish it would be for us to be keeping you here to labor for us, when you are yet strong and hearty, and able to get good wages, and to make provision for yourself against the time when you may be helpless."

"Miss Carrie, now me want you to tell me de livin' trute. Is Massa Ratio tired of Bob, and want to git him out of de way ?"

"Oh, no, daddy! Why papa will feel, when you should go away, that he has parted with one of the best friends he has got in the world; and so would all of us."

The old man wiped away a tear, and for a few moments made no reply, except by a motion of the muscles of his throat as though there was some obstruction thereabouts, not favorable to speaking loud. At length the words came out, not very clear, indeed, but sufficiently distinct to be understood:

"Well, den, Miss Carrie, dere need n't be no more said about it. So long as Massa Ratio live, or mistress live, or Miss Carrie, Bob no leave you till dey carry me to the grave-yard."

Carrie saw the big tears roll down his honest face. She knew his heart meant every word his lips had spoken, and she was not ashamed to let him see that she had feelings which could appreciate his strong attachment.

"Well, daddy, I can assure you that there shall ever be a heart to love you, and a hand to help you at your need, while one of us shall live."

So at the request of Carrie, Mr. Leslie resolved never more to say a word to the faithful negro about a separation. He knew that he was strong to labor, and doubted not that at least he would be no burden to them.

The arrangement which the kind-hearted Mr. Thompson had proposed, was carried into effect without delay; and all the loose disposable property which Mr. Leslie owned was taken at a liberal valuation.

It was indeed a severe trial to the family to see the noble horses they had prized so much led off by strangers; to be looked upon hereafter only as the property of others. But perhaps no one of them felt it more keenly than the faithful Bob, who had taken care of them so long, and had looked upon them as an important part of the family to which he belonged. On the day of their delivery he walked beside his master to each of the stalls, followed by the men who were chosen to assess their value.

One after another of the fine animals, Bob led forth at his master's bidding; and as their judgment was pronounced upon each, the old negro fixed his eye keenly upon the men. He said nothing; but the rolling out of his under lip expressed very decidedly his contempt for their opinion, and his dislike of the whole arrangement.

Five horses had thus been passed upon, and led away, when Mr. Leslie motioned to Bob to bring out the last. But Bob made no signs that he meant to obey.

"Lead out the horse, Bob."

Bob looked at his master with such an air of astonishment as only a negro can put on.

"Bob-o'-Linkum, Massa Ratio! No, no, Massa Ratio neber sell Bob-o'-Linkum!"

"Why not sell *him*, Bob? He is old and not so valuable as the others."

"Ah, Massa Ratio! Massa Ratio! me sorry to hear you say so. How many times you ride dat hoss! night and day dis twenty year. He born on dis place; me break him for old massa; old massa lub dat hoss; dat hoss follow me like a kitten all round de farm; dat horse no trive you take him away; he tarve to det. No no, Massa Ratio; Bob-o'-Linkum de only ting left old massa lub; 'cept Massa Ratio and Bob."

Mr. Leslie did not need to be thus reminded of the bonds which connected him with old Bob Lincoln. He had been, when a colt, remarkable for beauty and spirit, and was yet a serviceable horse. Could he prevent it, this relic of former days would not be permitted to pass into the hands of strangers. Conscious of his own weakness in the matter, he had purposely delayed to the last, the trying task of ordering the faithful old beast to be brought out. The remonstrance of the servant added to the difficulty; but it was too late to falter now. He did not care to violate the feelings of the old man by a peremptory command, and therefore in a persuasive manner endeavored to show him that there was a necessity for it.

"But," said he, "perhaps they will think him too old to be of any value; you had better lead him out, Bob, and let them examine him."

Bob obeyed, but as he led the old horse forth for inspection, kept a tight hold of the halter.

"You say he is twenty years old?" asked one of the assessors, looking at Bob.

"Twenty year! he more an dat; him twenty-five at the leetlest."

"Twenty-five! well he can't be worth much."

"How much you tink dat hoss worth?"

"Well I don't know; he is a fair looking horse. I should say he might do for a hack a while yet; he might possibly be worth forty dollars."

"Forty dollars! just look at dat hoss; see him legs; straight and smooth like a colt; look at him eye; bright as a dimond; feel him wind, no heave dere; all sound as a whistle. Forty dollar! dat hoss worth as he stand now on his four leg—five hundred dollar. *You no hab dat hoss.*" And in a moment more, old Bob Lincoln was in his stall and pulling away at his feed.

Mr. Leslie, unhappy as he felt, could not repress a smile at the sudden manner in which Bob had ended the trade. And yet he was sorely perplexed, for he knew how doggedly determined the old man was when his temper was raised. One of the gentlemen, however, entering into his feelings, kindly proposed that they should leave the matter for the present, as it might be possible there would be no occasion to assess the horse, as there were other articles of value they had not yet examined.

It resulted that there was enough at a fair valuation to meet all demands; and the old horse was left in his stall.

Bob, however, never forgave the insult shown to his favorite.

"Let me ketch 'em on de road! me show 'em! Bob-o'-Linkum go pass e'm like a bird, and leave 'em out o' sight in no time."

CHAPTER IX.

It is the usual way of speaking, when a man has made a wreck of his affairs, to say, "that he has been unfortunate;" and perhaps it is best to encourage this construction; it is a leaning to the side of mercy that speaks well for the heart of man.

But it may not be uncharitable to affirm that nine tenths of such cases are more the result of mismanagement than misfortune.

And no doubt, to the sensitive mind, this fact is the bitterest ingredient in the cup.

Mr. Leslie had suffered much during all the time his property was melting from his grasp—had passed many wretched days and sleepless nights, in his efforts, not so much to stop the waste, as to put off to some indefinite period an exposure of his affairs. And so entirely had his mind been absorbed with that one purpose, there was no room for proper reflection as to the means by which his condition might be altered, and the tide of ruin arrested.

But when the climax had been reached, and the hour he had so much dreaded had been fairly met, he had time to look back and perceive how madly he had acted. Then arose in all its terrible power, that hideous monster, Remorse. Then, he could readily see how a little firmness of purpose, a wise prudence in checking all unnecessary expense, a judicious disposal of unproductive property merely retained from a morbid sensitiveness as to the opinion of others, might have saved a vast amount of real trouble, and preserved a home for his family.

He had time now, also, to look ahead, and ponder upon the ways and means by which he was to provide for their future necessities.

A man who has been trained to a regular business or profession; who has been accustomed to the constant employment of his hands or mind in a systematic round of duties; who has learned all the ways by which success is to be obtained in the calling he has been brought up to—should he, by some untoward event, be prostrated, and all his present means swept away, and even a load of debt hanging upon him, has still a resource left. The knowledge of his trade remains —*a capital which nothing can destroy* while strength and health continue, and which, with the accumulated wisdom gathered from the school of adversity, is ready to be used with surer effect hereafter.

But as Mr. Leslie looked out upon the busy world around him, amid all the variety of useful avocations, there was not one in particular that he could call his own, or which he felt any confidence to undertake. How often, as he sat musing in silence by the window of his dwelling, and beheld the active step of the mechanic hastening to his daily labor; or the farmer in the neighboring field, walking behind his cattle, and holding the steady plow, did he heave a sigh, and sadly mourn that he had not even their ability to provide for his own. The false estimate which he had hitherto put upon the condition of respectability to which he was an heir; the false light in which he had viewed the different classes of society, were too glaring to escape the observation of a mind naturally just, and brought to right reason by a stern necessity.

Now he saw that the man of true respectability was he whose energies were directed to some useful end; who had learned to do something in the great workshop of life; who could administer to the physical or mental necessities of the world at large. Pride of birth, or of station, he now beheld to be but the tinsel drapery that shines so gorgeously by the lamp of the festal hall, of no intrinsic value amid the realities of daylight.

But to reason justly is one thing; to rise in the stern majesty of those dictates which reason approves, and breaking over all the barriers which a false education may have built up around us, go forth with courage in the heart to the new and untried course, is quite another.

As the suffering man then felt, no honest work that his hands could do would have been in his eyes degrading. But how would it affect those dear ones in whom his heart was bound up! how would they feel, to see the husband and father, who had hitherto walked before them as an independent man, whose wants had been always attended to by the ready hands of domestics, and for whom those tender feelings had been cherished which appear to thrive more luxuriantly amid the politer circles of life—toiling in the sweat of his brow to earn their daily bread amid the rough labors of life! Ah, how such thoughts already start the big drops upon his forehead! Their tender sensibilities, their warm affection, take hold upon every fiber of his being, and his frame trembles under their quickening touch! How can he thus lacerate the hearts that beat so tenderly for him?

The name of Folger has been already mentioned incidentally, in connection with Mr. Leslie's ruined fortunes. But as he will have a prominent place in the recital of events connected with this family, we must introduce him more particularly to our readers.

Tobias Folger was born and brought up in the city of New York. His business in early life had been that of a shipping merchant, and had been unusually successful; for although a young man when he withdrew from that branch of trade, he was esteemed wealthy. There had been, however, strange stories afloat that affected his standing among the high-minded and honorable men which compose that class of merchants in the great city; and perhaps this was his reason for relinquishing a business that had been so lucrative. He had lost caste among them, and therefore chose to employ his means where few questions would be asked as to how he came by them, provided he could purchase largely, and was ready to listen to every chance for speculation. He became a hanger-on in Wall-street, was intimate with exchange-brokers, and was always on hand when times of scarcity came on and honest men were ready to make great sacrifices to keep up their sacred credit. It is supposed, however, that even here he felt at length the blast of *scandal talk;* for after the death of his wife he broke up his fine establishment in the city, was no more seen "upon 'change," and departed none knew where. Princesport being a retired spot, where he might hope to escape the slights and whispers of "detractors" as he was pleased to style them—he had chosen it as a hiding-place, and had there selected a fine location, erected a handsome house, and set up as fine an establishment of carriage and horses as the best could boast of.

The death of his wife, however, can not be passed over in silence.

Trusting woman seems ever doomed to have her holy confidence abused by the very being who most needs her sweet influence, and is most dependant upon her unselfish love. Alas! for the honor of manhood! How many petty tyrants meet us at every turn! Big with their own importance, alive to every evil that affects themselves, absorbed in every trifling care that happens to engage their own mind, ready to lavish their means to gratify their own appetites and tastes, or to administer to their own peculiar pleasures; while the lovely beings that were courted on bended knee, and were gained through vows of constancy and love, now sit at home lonely and disregarded. Their pallid cheek and sunken eye no longer tell of the beauty that once sparkled there. No husband courts them now, nor loves to feel their warm breath on his cheek, or tries to cheer them amid their weaknesses, or throws the light of his accomplishments around their silent chamber. Their hearts have never lost the true beat, nor indulged one faithless thought, and would yet beat warmly, and the eye kindle with brightness at the tender appellation and the fond caress.

But the stillness of death has settled upon all such topics in which affection might manifest its presence. An icy sea shuts in the loving spirit—all in—to feed upon itself, and pine away, till the friendly hand of death cuts the earthly tie, and the spirit wounded here, goes back to its eternal home.

When Tobias Folger married the beautiful Lucy Barstow, she was like a budding rose in June—a sweet flower; plucked too from the pure fresh air of the open country. She was a farmer's daughter. He bore her in all her blushing loveliness to his house in the city, and, for a season, alas! how short! she was a petted toy; and then by degrees the toy began to attract less notice; and other more important duties than a wife's pleasure, took up his time; and then cold words, cold looks, those tokens of an icy heart, became familiar; the only answers to her words and looks of love.

And then at length strange rumors came to her ears. They came like the sudden thunder-clap, when no cloud has obscured the sun. They were the saddest tidings that a wife can hear. They ate into the very soul; and like the fatal worm consumed the life within. She would not, could not tell her wrongs; of what avail to her to let the fatal secret out! and publish to the world her own misfortune, and her husband's shame! Would that bring back his love? would that atone for her sad loss? No, she would not, could not tell the anguish of her spirit, and kept it all within. So the rose departed from her cheek; her eye lost its brightness; hope expired in her heart, and thus she drooped away, and the funeral procession followed her lifeless body, beautiful even in death, to the place of graves.

She left behind a little daughter, which had been named after its mother. A pretty child—but still, and sad, and unlike others of its age. It seemed to have a heart to love, and its large clear eye was ever searching round as though it could not find the thing it wanted. Whether the father loved the little motherless being it would be difficult to say. But he was kind and seemed to try at times to awaken joyous feelings and bring the pretty smile; but seldom did he succeed. And perhaps because of this he placed the child with strangers. It may have been that her presence was a rebuke he did not care to meet too often.

Tobias Folger had remained a widower; he had been now some years at Princesport. As has been said, he lived in good style; but he was not accepted by the "quality" of the place as one with whom they wished to associate. Whether any thing was known of his former history is not at all certain. If any knew it, the secret was well kept; for in general no other stigma was attached to his name but that of "Old Folger." By which was merely meant that he was "rather a tight man," and one that loved money.

His personal appearance was prepossessing; his stature tall and rather slender; his carriage graceful and his manner, when he wished to put on the gentleman, very winning; his countenance fresh and ruddy, his eye bright, and generally stern, except occasionally, when a peculiarly soft and tender expression beamed from it; and his laugh was as joyous as that of a boy at play. At the period we are now considering, he was not quite forty years of age; not a wrinkle marred his face or brow, and his hair showed no signs of age or care.

He was a keen observer of human nature, and had the art of keeping his own feelings in abeyance while prying into those of others.

That quality which is in general denominated sensibility, he seemed to be devoid of. Either he had never possessed it, or in the course of his dealings with mankind, had lost it; and another quality generally esteemed as valuable to man as a dependant in some measure upon his fellows; sympathy with human joy or sorrow, he never manifested; at least in such a way as gave persons at all disposed to be cautious, any confidence in its sincerity. The opinion of shrewd observers was, that he cared for nothing beyond his own interest; and to accomplish an end he had in view, could look far ahead; and had patience to make a very large circuit, if the object was not to be obtained by a straightforward course.

Mr. Folger had followed the practice of loaning money to those who needed it; and found at Princesport, small as the place was, those who were compelled to resort to such help. He had made some friends in this way, and a few enemies. But apparently it was a matter of no moment to him to which of these classes those about him belonged.

Mr. Leslie's difficulties had begun before his introduction to Folger, and even before the latter gentleman had become a resident of the place; and no doubt the climax of his troubles would have been reached much sooner if he had not found in Mr. Folger a banker whose resources were so abundant, and who seemed to loan him with such good-will and confidence. Folger doubtless understood well the difference not only in the character of those he dealt with, and that one man's word was much better security than another man's bond, but he also made his calculations somewhat on a man's station in society. He well knew that a fall from position was by a few dreaded as an evil of the worst kind. Mr. Leslie was of that class. He stood highest among those ranked as the heads of distinguished families. Every effort would be made, and every demand within his power acceded to, rather than suffer exposure. He also knew Mr. Leslie to be possessed of a fine sense of honor. His word would be sacred and kept to the very letter. Under such circumstances, then, it is not at all surprising that shrewd and money-loving as Folger was esteemed to be, he should have met Mr. Leslie's applications with so much freedom; and in return, the pleasant manner in which his requests were acceded to, and the unlimited confidence which appeared to be reposed in him, caused the latter to feel that the character of Mr. Folger was either greatly misunderstood, or shamefully misrepresented by those who openly spoke of him as an unfeeling, grinding man.

Time rolls rapidly on, and so does interest. In the course of six years from the time Mr. Leslie procured his first loan, he had become largely indebted; many thousands of dollars, in notes payable on demand, lay in the private desk of Mr. Folger. Suddenly an evident change took place in the bearing of the latter gentleman. He began to talk very seriously about the scarcity of money; and his inability to make collections; and hinted very plainly that the amount due to him must either be forthcoming soon, or sufficient security placed in his hands. Mr. Leslie became alarmed, and at once made propositions to liquidate his obligations by disposing of the property he had received by his wife. This could only be done to advantage by disposing of small parcels at a time. It was woodland; a very large tract—too large to find readily a purchaser for the whole. It was in a distant part of the State; too far from his home to allow him to attend personally to its sale; and the indisposition of his wife forbade the idea that he could be so long and so far away as he must be, should he attempt to manage the business himself. This difficulty was met by a proposition from Mr. Folger: "that the property in question, the Hazleton estate, should be deeded to a person well known to Mr. Folger, and partially so to Mr. Leslie." This person resided near the property; was a great manager of such business; and Mr. Folger had great confidence in him as he had so adroitly and profitably managed for himself, in a similar case. The thought of giving a warrantee deed of such a valuable tract of land for no consideration, and as a mere matter of trust, was at first by no means agreeable, and Mr. Leslie hesitated to make the venture. "But," said Folger, "I am willing, Mr. Leslie, under such circumstances—so confident am I of the good faith of Mr. Thorne (the name of the agent proposed)—to let the large amount due to me remain just as it now is; and am content to receive my pay from you just so fast and no faster than Mr. Thorne can make the sales, and receive the money."

The proposition appeared plausible, at least it was one that would relieve him from the sad necessity of placing his homestead as security in the hands of Folger, and in an evil hour the thing was done.

Not many months had elapsed before Mr. Leslie began to fear, and *Mr. Folger too*, that Thorne was not the honest man he was supposed to be; no letters ever came from him in reply to the frequent and urgent appeals of Mr. Leslie, for a statement of what he was doing, or for moneys he must have received; and finally, upon a personal application, Mr. Leslie was told, to his utter astonishment, by the gentleman to whom he had deeded the land, "That the deed was a good one, the land had *changed owners*, and that he, Mr. Leslie, need give himself no further trouble about it."

A representation to Mr. Folger of this act of villainy, did apparently fill him with ungovernable wrath toward the perpetrator; he swore terrible oaths, denouncing not only the gentleman in question, his former friend, Mr. Thorne, but almost the whole race of mankind; uttering likewise the belief, "that he, a poor innocent man, would yet be cheated out of all his hard and honest earnings; that there was no safety anywhere; no confidence was to be placed in any human being; and that he would never, after this, loan a penny without double security already in possession. At this interview nothing was positively said to Mr. Leslie, in reference to security of a more tangible nature, than that which he had been contented with in the matter of the Hazleton property. But Mr. Leslie felt assured that things would not be allowed to remain thus much longer. His heart sank within him, but he was helpless, and could only wait the end.

He did not, however, have to wait long. Mr. Folger was very gentlemanly in the manner of making the proposition, but his victim saw clearly that his wish must be acceded to, or violent measures must be the consequence, which was, that a mortgage should be given upon Chelmsford, and the lands connected with it. One saving clause was added, that he should not at present put the deed upon record, and would wait a reasonable time to see if Mr. Leslie could in any other way satisfy him for the amount. The arrangement was entered into, and Horatio Leslie left the house of Tobias Folger with the consciousness that he was no longer the real owner of a foot of land.

A chain was about him; he felt its galling fetters in his very heart. He felt it as he walked about his fields, or rested in his dwelling. The beauty had fled from the landscape. The sparkling waters, the distant shore, the white sails spotting the river and the bay, all were now only objects which he could not help observing, but they no longer awaked pleasing emotions. He had no sense of ownership in any thing around him; even the old mansion in which his dear ones nestled, seemed only a lodging-place from which they might be driven at any hour.

It was not long after the scenes described in a previous chapter, as Mr. Leslie was sitting in his room alone, absorbed in sad reflections, and turning over in his mind the various projects which at times had occurred to him, whereby he could do something for the support of his family, he saw the carriage of Folger approaching the house, and prepared to receive him. He knew that there was some unsettled business between them, and was therefore not surprised at his calling. As strong prejudices were entertained by his family against the visitor, he was glad that he happened to notice his approach, and at once opened the door himself.

"Good-morning Mr. Leslie; how to you do this morning, sir?" and his countenance assumed a very bland expression, in marked contrast with its aspect when they had last met.

Mr. Leslie received him courteously, and introducing him to the room in which he had been sitting, offered him a seat.

"Thank you, sir;" and the gentleman bowed as he took the seat with as much diffidence as if he was a visitor to one who owed him nothing, and to whom he felt infinitely obliged for a polite reception. Mr. Leslie could not but notice likewise that his visitor was dressed with more than usual neatness. Had he been about to call upon a company of ladies, his appearance need not have been more carefully attended to.

"And how are the members of your family, Mr. Leslie? I am exceedingly happy to learn that Mrs. Leslie has much recovered from her indisposition."

"Thank you, sir; I am happy to be able to say that she appears to be better than she has been for many months."

"Glad to hear it, sir. When the mother of a family is prostrated by weakness or ill health, it is a sad blur to a man's happiness. The wife, is after all, the light of a man's dwelling; although I know you are surrounded by a fine family, at least I have reason to believe so from what I hear, never having had the pleasure of an intimacy with them Your daughter, Miss Leslie, I had the honor of a slight introduction to, some time since. I think if she is a fair sample, you have great reason to be happy."

"I have reason, sir, to be well contented in that respect, Mr. Folger; and were it not for other things, few men could be more happily situated. But as things now are—even that circumstance adds to my trial." Mr. Leslie heaved a deep sigh, and for a few moments neither gentleman spoke.

"The fact is, Mr. Folger, I found it very difficult to bring my mind down to the sad reality of my situation."

"I do not doubt it, sir; I do not doubt it in the least. This world is so full of sad changes. But you know what Burns says: 'A man must n't hang his head because he happens to —to be poor; a man 's a man for a' that.' I must say, however, Mr. Leslie, that I have had, myself, sad moments of late. Perhaps you may not give me credit for as much sympathy as I do really have for you. I sometimes even wish I had let every thing go, before I had asked you to do what has brought such a trial upon you. Indeed I had no idea at that time, that such consequences would follow my recording of the deed. I heartily wish it was still in my own private drawer; if you had only hinted to me your true situation, we might have managed the matter in some other way, and prevented all this trouble."

Mr. Leslie was much moved at the apparent kindness of the speaker. He did not know that Tobias Folger had taken pains to make himself acquainted with the fact that he, Mr. Leslie, was largely indebted to various persons in the town, and he did not know that pains had been taken to let out the fact that a mortgage deed to Tobias Folger had been put upon record, covering all the property of Horatio Leslie, although not in a way that could necessarily be charged against Mr. Folger personally.

Mr. Leslie had taken but few lessons in the school of life. His own mind, generous and just, could not harbor the idea

that such duplicity could exist. He had indeed felt, at times, that Mr. Folger could change his course of conduct very suddenly: he had certainly done so toward him. But he accounted for it on the supposition that perhaps his temperament was not always the same; he might have become alarmed, and felt a necessity to take the course he did, for his own security. He was therefore not prepared to judge harshly, and even felt grieved at times to hear the expressions of prejudice thrown out by those around him. At the present moment his mind was quite disarmed; there seemed so much sincerity in the words which he heard, and in the manner of his visitor, that he really blamed himself for even having allowed an unkind thought toward him.

As Mr. Leslie did not immediately reply, Mr. Folger continued, "I have heard, Mr. Leslie—and on some accounts I must say it has given me great pain, but it has been reported to me—that your daughter, Miss Leslie, has thoughts of opening a school. I hope you will pardon me for mentioning it, but I have particular reasons for wishing to know whether such is the case."

"I believe, sir, my daughter has suggested something of that kind; she has a great idea of doing what she can to aid under our present difficulties. But I do not know; I do not know how—" His visitor interrupted by speaking out the words which seemed to linger on the lips of the warm-hearted father.

"Submit to it! I am sure, my dear sir, it must be very trying to you—a very trying thing indeed! and yet you know, Mr. Leslie, good sometimes comes out of evil. I am very certain that great good must result to those who may be favored with instruction from such a teacher, a lady of such accomplishments, and such a lovely disposition as your daughter is represented to possess. I am very sure, sir, that *I* should esteem it a high privilege to have a child of mine under such guardianship; and that leads me more particularly to the subject about which I have taken the liberty to intrude myself upon you this morning; perhaps you are not aware, sir, that I have a little daughter?"

"I was not aware of it, sir; does she live at home with you?"

"For special reasons, she is away from me at present; yes, sir, I have a little daughter, the relic of a lovely mother, of whom I have long since been bereft. She is now about eight years of age; I have boarded her hitherto among strangers, for special reasons which I will not trouble you with explaining. She is a remarkably quiet and docile child, and I feel well persuaded will cause very little trouble in the way of government. How apt she may be to learn, I can not say; that, however, is of comparatively little consequence. The moment I heard that your daughter, Miss Leslie, contemplated opening a school, the thought occurred to me, What a rare chance it would be if I could get the poor little motherless thing under such an instructress; and further—I hope you will pardon me for the liberty I am taking, but I shall be obliged to procure board for the child somewhere in the vicinity of the school, as my own residence is too far removed from the centre of the town to make it possible that she could live with me—would it be asking too great a favor, Mr. Leslie, that you would be willing to receive her into your family?"

Mr. Leslie was so taken by surprise as to be unable for the moment to make a reply.

"The remuneration, Mr. Leslie, shall be most liberal; fix your own terms: money is no consideration with me when the good of my motherless child is in question."

Mr. Leslie now began to understand why it was, that he had been treated with so much deference by his visitor, and the character of Mr. Folger opened in a new light. Hitherto he had appeared only as the money-lender, the man of business, civil, but cautious, and with a keen eye to his own advantage. Now he was revealed as a tender father, really solicitous, above all other things, for the welfare of his little one. "The poor little motherless thing." "The relic of a lovely mother." Mr. Folger had a feeling heart, after all! How little people understood him, who called him "old Folger!" Of what small moment is the opinion of the world at large!

As it was a matter Mr. Leslie could not decide, without consulting with his wife and daughter, of course "Mr. Folger would not for the world urge it; he merely ventured to make the request. Mr. Leslie, as a father, could well comprehend the motives which actuated him."

"And now, my dear sir," said Mr. Folger, "I have troubled you with my private affairs, allow me to ask you, in relation to your own matters, a question or two. I suppose, Mr. Leslie, you think of me, as I know many do, that I am very sharp to look after my own interest, and care little how others get along. 'Well, let them think so,' I often say to myself, 'let them think so; what, after all, is the opinion of the world at large worth? It does not alter the facts in the case.' I have also *my* opinion of them, and that opinion, my dear sir, is very different as to individual cases; as I said, I know not but you, Mr. Leslie, have thought at times that I was a little too cautious, a little too tenacious of security, and all that."

"Pardon me, my dear sir, for interrupting you, but you judge me wrong: I have not, Mr. Folger, indulged hard feelings towards you; I have blamed myself, and no one else."

"I am rejoiced sir, that I can make such an exception as yourself in my favor, and I believe when you and I come to know each other better, you will find that the close man of business knows how to be generous, and does not always seek his own selfish ends. I have a serious question to put to you Mr. Leslie. Have you as yet formed any definite plan for business? I ask you thus boldly, because you have before this mentioned to me, that you were looking for business or employment of some kind."

"I can answer very readily, sir, that I have not. The way before me is very dark; I feel the necessity of doing something, but what at present to turn my hand to, can not tell."

"Would you, sir, if employment could be obtained abroad, away from your home, I mean, feel ready to embrace it? I mean, of course, honorable employment, although perhaps, not very lucrative. It might lead to something better in future."

"I should feel it indeed a great trial to be obliged to leave my family, and remain away from them. But, sir, if my duty calls me, as I think it does, I should not hesitate."

"No doubt, sir, with such a family as you are blessed with, it must be a great trial—a great sacrifice. Well, sir, that is all I wish to know at present. Perhaps in a few days I may be able to say something definite to you, and you can then judge as to the propriety of your accepting it. Good morning now, sir, I have detained you much longer than I designed. My very best respects to your family, sir, if you think proper to present them."

And Tobias Folger departed, maintaining the same deferential deportment when he bade adieu as when he first entered the room.

CHAPTER X.

HENRY and Charles, the elder brothers of Carrie, were twins by birth, but very unlike in appearance and disposition. They were now about seventeen years of age, and had returned from school immediately on receiving their sister's letter. Charles, or Charlie, as he was usually called, was a bright active boy, with a fine open countenance, full of life and feeling. His eye a deep hazel, his hair a pure auburn, and his complexion fair, where not exposed, but varying as the seasons changed, or as he might be more or less in the sun and wind. His temperament was peculiarly excitable, and yet he was more truly docile than either of his brothers. Quick of motion, and impetuous to accomplish whatever his mind was intent upon, he was frequently the subject, of admonitions, and would at times appear ready to break away from all restraint. But the outbreak would be only momentary; his heart was full of affection, and soon regained its balance. The hasty impulse passed quickly away, and with a cheerful aspect he submitted to the check, or went at once to the task he had been required to perform."

He was rather under size for his age; and perhaps on that account, as well as his activity, he was most generally called upon to do errands away from home. Mr. Leslie of course continued to make what small purchases the family needed from the store of the kind-hearted Mr. Thompson, although he did not avail himself of the offer to have the articles charged. Nothing but an extreme necessity would now compel him to do that.

As some few things were wanted from the store a few days after his return home, Charlie was summoned to do the errand.

As he entered the store, and stepped up in his prompt way, and accosted Mr. Thompson in a respectful manner, the old gentleman put his spectacles up on his forehead, and looked very steadily at him a moment, apparently admiring his fair open countenance and his pleasing address.

"Whose boy *be* you?"

"Why, have you forgotten me, Mr. Thompson?"

"I don't know as I have forgot! It don't seem to me I ever knew you. You ain't one of the Leslie boys?"

"Yes, sir. Charles or Charlie, just as you please, sir."

The old gentleman then took hold of him with one hand, and held him off at arm's length, while with the other hand he placed his spectacles again in their proper place before his eyes.

"Bless my soul! It is you—ain't it! but how you are grown! and how white you look! You're hearty, ain't you?"

"Yes sir, very."

"Well, well, well—the young ones are growing up, and I am growing down, or going down. Oh dear me! how stiff I am getting! And how is all at home? How is that dear angel of a sister you've got? I tell you what it is, boy, don't you never go contraary to that sister in nothin'. She is too good for this airth. Oh dear, oh dear this rheumatiz! it's got right hold of my left leg and it won't hardly let me stir."

And the old gentleman, putting a hand on each arm of his chair, was making motions to get up.

"Mr. Thompson, don't get up, sir; just tell me where to get the tea and the sugar, and I will put them up; please do let me."

The old gentleman saw that the boy was in earnest and ambitious to do as he had proposed; and being pretty comfortably seated close beside the counter, yielded to the boyish whim, as much to gratify the youth as for any other reason.

Charlie went to work according to directions, weighed out the articles with great nicety, and prepared to put them in papers.

"That's done nicely, only you have'nt given quite down weight enough; just put a pinch more tea in that scale—there—that is it; well, I guess I shall have to get up and put it in the paper, for you see my bags is all out and that fellow that pretends to help me, he is too lazy to live, or he would have made some."

"I can do it, sir, I can do it; sit still, Mr. Thompson, you'll see."

And in a few moments it was done, and in a remarkably neat manner.

"Where did you learn to do that?"

"Oh, sir, I never learned, but I've seen it done often."

"Well, well, well, some folks take to things easier than others. Now, my boy, or man, or whatever he is, he ain't neither the one nor the other, and not much of anything, he would have been as long agin, and he'd taken as much paper agin and then he'd have strewed it all over the counter, and wanted more than the down weight would have come to."

"Here is a bill, Mr. Thompson: I must trouble you for the change."

"Well, now, I want to see if you know figures; just put that note in the till there, and take out the change and let me see if it's all right; I've telled you the prices."

With much readiness the change was counted and placed in Mr. Thompson's hand.

"All right, all right to a penny."

"Good morning, Mr. Thompson."

"What! are you going off so soon? just stop a minute—I want to talk a bit with you: you have been off to school? ain't I right? I ain't seen you this long time."

"Yes, sir, I have."

"Going back?"

"No, sir."

"What are you going to do with yourself? play ball, I s'pose—or go fishing, or sailing—or may be, shooting? tho' that's dangerous work."

"Oh, no, sir, I don't think I shall do much of either if I can find any thing better to do."

"Do you like to work?"

"I don't know sir, I never tried it, but I think I should like it, that is, some kinds of work."

"How should you like to tend store?"

"I think I should like it very much."

"Not sich a store as this!"

"Yes, sir."

"Why it's all molasses and dirt; and my things is all higgledy piggledy in a mess together."

"Oh, well, sir, if I should be here, you know, and you would allow me, I could straighten things up and put them in order."

"Now, suppose I should be in airnest, and your pa and ma should be willing! *do* you think you should like to come here and do all that had to be done, that is, all you was able to do?"

"I should *dearly* like it, sir; I don't know much about keeping books yet, sir, but I think I could soon learn."

"Don't be alarmed about that, sonny; there ain't much book keepin' to be done here; *I* keep a book; and my *customers* keep a book; and when they pay, which ain't often, I just scratch it out, and that's the end of it; but now just hear to me one minute; just hush up, and don't say nothin' afore that long-legged clerk of mine; he's all legs, I think, and seems to have but little body, and no brains; he's comin' down the street there; but you just hush up, and I will call in a day or two, may be to-morrow; it just depends upon how this rheumatiz is, and I will have a talk with your pa and ma about it, but you see and hush up."

Mr. Thompson's rheumatism was not so bad as to prevent him from finding his way the next morning to the house of Mr. Leslie. Mr. Leslie was not at home, but Mrs. Leslie and Carrie were ready to receive him, and Mr. Thompson soon found himself in their company, and seated in a very large and easy chair.

He had a great many questions to ask, and a great deal to say upon many topics quite foreign to the business upon which he had come; until Carrie opened the way by saying:

"Our Charlie has been almost crazy, Mr. Thompson, ever since he came home from your store yesterday. He seems to think you were in earnest in your conversation with him about store-keeping."

"Well, Miss Car'line, I *was* in true airnest. No, no, I never trifle with a boy's feelings that way: I know what boys are; I ain't forgot when I was a boy, though it was a good long while ago. No, no, and it's the very thing I've come about this morning. The boy would really like it then?"

"He has talked about nothing else ever since, Mr. Thompson, and thinks he would like to go to work and clean things up, and so on. Boys, you know, are very sanguine, and Charlie is peculiarly so."

"Well, madam," turning to Mrs. Leslie, who had just addressed him, "somehow I took a notion to him at the very first, he came up in such a prompt and gentlemanly way, and spoke so respectfully, and you see, Mrs. Leslie, I'm but a plain body myself, and never made no pretensions to be any thing more than a shoemaker, which you know was my trade at the first. But I can tell when a man, or a boy, knows manners. Now that boy, the moment he came in, takes his hat off, and outs with his hand, and says, 'Good morning Mr. Thompson.' 'Good morning sir,' says I, but I didn't know who it could be, though I thought I see a little of Miss Car'line's look about the mouth; and then he did his errand in such a prompt pretty manner, and seemed to want to help me that I thought just to please him, I'd let him try. And you never see how handy he took hold and fixed up the things, and made the change and all just right, as if he'd been brought up to it."

"Charlie is very handy at almost any thing he undertakes, and very quick."

"Quick! why Miss Car'line he did the whole thing in less time than my great tall bungler would have taken to get ready to do it in. Well, I was looking on; thinks I to myself, what would n't I give for such a lad as that; you see, Mrs. Leslie, boys round here ain't to be got, that is good for any thing. I hired Tom Crow—you know him, may-be; well, he had no more manners than a goose; he would keep sitting on the barrels, and lounging about with his hat on, and never thought about doin' a thing but jist what I told him to do, and then he would look at me with a saucy stare, as much as to say, 'may-be he would, and may-be he would n't;' and then when I got rid of *him* I took one of Martin's boys, and he was n't no better, and so I sent *him* off, and so I've tried round; but you see the most on 'em ain't brought up, no how; and then I hired this man, or boy, or whatever he is, I don't hardly know which; but he is a poor scullion of a thing, and I'm afeer'd he ain't any too honest, in the bargain. But all this ain't nothin' to the point, nor what I came to talk about; but may-be it would be clean against your notions of what the boy ought to be doing; and I hope you won't take offense at my proposing such a thing."

"By no means, sir. Mr. Leslie and myself, Mr. Thompson,

are very desirous now to have our boys learning some useful occupation. We have taken some severe lessons in life that have taught us to estimate things very differently from what perhaps we once did. We now think an honest occupation infinitely better, even though it involves severe labor, than a life of dependance and idleness."

"I believe that is true, madam, though I, for one, am sadly grieved that any thing should have happened to your family to make it necessary; I am heartily sorry."

"We are well convinced of that, Mr. Thompson; and your generous conduct toward my husband, in an hour of severe trial, will, I trust, never be forgotten by us."

"Don't speak of that, my lady, I beg of you. I did n't do nothin' more than jist what was square and right between man and man; nothin' more."

"Charles is a very active boy, and very anxious to get into a situation where he can be learning to take care of himself. He is but a boy yet, and it will be some time, no doubt, before he can expect to receive any compensation."

"Well, madam, if you and your good husband are a mind to let the lad just come and try how he likes it, I don't know as you will think it much by way of pay, but I will engage to give him the first year one hundred dollars and his board. We are plain folks, you know, and don't do much by way of show, but we have enough to eat and drink, and that, if I say it myself, as good as is goin'.

Carrie and her mother looked at each other in surprise. Mrs. Leslie replied:

"I fear, Mr. Thompson, your generous disposition carries you too far. I fear my little son would scarcely be of sufficient service to you to earn so much. Remember, he has every thing to learn. He knows how to write, to be sure, and is pretty well acquainted with figures, but he must be quite a novice in most things pertaining to business, and can know nothing about keeping books."

"He don't need to know much about that, madam; it is but little we do in that way; so there need n't be nothin' more said about it. If you are only willing and he is willing, that's enough."

"Charles is not only willing, but very anxious to go; and Mr. Leslie has no objections, and I am sure I have none, Mr.

Thompson, although I should prefer, if it should answer you as well, that he should sleep at home."

"Certainly, madam, by all means; and I am glad you spoke of it. Boys are always better to have a father or a mother knowin' where they be in the evenings; and then, too, if he is here every night you can still have a care of him; boys, the best on 'em, want a mother or a sister to keep a watch on 'em: they do a deal better for it I'm glad you spoke of it; and now, if you please, madam, jist hush up about this matter, and say nothin' to nobody about it, till I go home and give my good-for-nothin' his pay, and leave to be trottin' after some other business; and in the morning, to-morrow morning, why jist let the boy come down and go to work, and I'll try to do my best by him. And now, Miss Car'line, I want to have jist a word with you about your school."

"Well, Mr. Thompson, I am ready to hear any thing you have to say about it."

"What I wanted to know was, how soon you would be ready to begin?"

"Immediately; you told me, I believe, that the room would need some cleaning."

"Yes; and a good deal of cleaning, too. But bless your heart, that has been done, and we have got the benches all ready, and a long desk for the girls to do their writing and ciphering on; and a chair and a table for the teacher. But what we've been a wanting, is, a little strip of carpet just to go under the chair and table, and so around it; so that Miss Car'line should n't have to stand or sit with her little feet on the cold floor."

"Oh, but Mr. Thompson, I can do well enough without any such luxury. I can stand the cold floor as well as the little children."

"No, you can't, nor you sha'n't; you 've never been used to it, and besides we 're agoin to show some folks that if you *do* teach poor folks's children, there is those among us that know how a lady ought to be treated; you see there is those that kind a look shy at the thing. You know, may-be, who I mean?"

"I am quite ignorant, I am sure, Mr. Thompson, that any one has objections to my making an attempt, in an honest way, to help myself, and, I hope, benefit others. No one has hinted such a thing to me; some of my acquaintance have, indeed in a friendly way, endeavored to dissuade me from it. But their reasons had no weight with me; indeed, I should be almost ashamed to mention them."

"No doubt, no doubt, Miss Car'line; very friendly to your face; but the world, in a general way of speaking, has two sides to 'em; you'll find that out, may-be, one of these days; and some sides on 'em is so crooked, you can't hardly tell what to make on 'em. You know, some folks, among the quality I mean, can't bear the thought that one who has always been one of them, and the highest among 'em too, should come down, and degrade herself by teaching school. You know, among our high folks, a teacher, unless may-be he's a preacher too, ain't at all set by, ain't in no wise respected by 'em."

"It may be that some indulge such views, but their opinion would not in the least affect me. The more I think of it, the more fixed I am in my purpose."

"Glad to hear you say that. But when you first spoke to me about it, my blood all riz up at the thought; and if it had n't a been that you talked about it as straight as you did, I should a been at a dead set agin it. But I know you are right, and there's others that know you are right; and their blood is all up when they hear a word agin it, or agin you; and that's the reason why they've fixed things up so; and that's the reason why they say we must put the carpet under the table; we want to show 'em all that we know how to treat a lady, and we'll have it, if we have to send to York to get it. Carpets, you know, ain't plenty in these parts, only among them as we don't choose to ask them for 'em."

Mrs. Leslie now interposed and said, that she would take the responsibility of providing that article, upon herself, and was sure she could spare something that would answer the purpose.

"Many thanks to you, madam; and then, Miss Car'line, shall I give out that you will begin next Monday morning?"

"You may, if you please, sir."

The first thing that Charlie did after his sister had informed him that Mr. Thompson had been there, and the business had been talked over, and of the offer Mr. Thompson had made, and that it was concluded he should begin the next morning, was to make sundry caracoles round the room, which from his peculiar agility threatened destruction to some of the more fragile articles about; and the next thing was to take his sister round the neck, and bestow some hearty kisses on her fair cheek.

"Dear, dear sister Carrie! I know this is all your doing."

"By no means, Charlie! I have had nothing to do with it."

"Yes, you have; don't you remember the day we came home from school, and Harry and I felt so bad when we heard of all the trouble here, how you took us into the northern room, and talked so to us?"

"Yes, I remember, Charlie; but what of that?"

"You see I felt clear down-hearted. I never before had a thought that we should, any of us, have to contrive for ourselves. You know how it was always said that, as soon as we were of age, each of us was to have a large estate to go upon. There was all ma's property at Hazleton, and pa's west farms, all so valuable! You know how we used to talk! Well, when you told us how it was, and that these were all gone, did n't I feel bad? But your talk 'cured me up.' I soon began to see that a man or boy ought to learn how to take care of himself; and to do that, must be acquainted with some useful calling; something that he should make himself master of. I then began to think how pleasant it would be to feel that my life was of consequence to some one; that my services in the world were needed; and how happy I should be to look at the money I had earned myself, and how different I should feel when I spent it."

"That is if you spent it in a proper way."

"And how do you think I should spend it, Carrie? Every dollar of it should go to helping pa along, or to get things for mother or you; I would n't let you do any thing; nor I sha'n't the moment I get so as to earn enough. Oh, you do n't know how I shall work, Carrie! I feel just like it; I know nothing will ever tire me."

The sister smiled at the ardor of her brother, and gave him another kiss. She would not say a word to damp his generous and fervent zeal.

"One thing I must tell you, Charlie. Do you know that it was your own prompt and gentlemanly behavior that won favor with Mr. Thompson? and your readiness in doing what you thought would be a kindness to him; and I hope you will remember what mother has so often talked to you about —politeness is a cheap commodity—it costs you but a little kind feeling, and a little sacrifice of selfishness, and it will help to make all about you feel more at ease, and make for you, among strangers, a favorable first impression, which is often of great consequence. You see already what you have gained by it."

Mr. Thompson's store was not just the place which Mr. and Mrs. Leslie would *once* have thought of, for a moment, as a situation for one of their sons. He was not a man of any education himself, and not by any means calculated to train a youth to proper habits of business. He had not much idea of the systematic arrangement of things; and, in consequence, there was in his establishment about as much confusion as the heterogeneous variety he kept for sale could well make. And it would have been a great mystery to a stranger on entering his store, how the good man could tell whether he had any particular article or not, or where to find it. The town's-people, however, had been so long accustomed to this state of things, that probably it seemed all right to them. How it was that he maintained his stock of goods, and managed as he did, would also have been as great a mystery to men of regular business habits; for he kept no books, that is, no set of books. He had a large folio in which he put down the names of those who purchased on credit, with the articles attached. And then he made each of his credit customers keep a small book in which whatever they purchased was put down, so that they might be sure that all was right, and might know how much they owed him. He always purchased for cash, and would go in debt for nothing. He lived in a very plain manner, although comfortably; and as he had no ambition to make a show, felt quite contented so long as he had on hand wherewith to supply his need. How much he was worth, neither he nor any one else knew, and probably it was a circumstance he thought little about. The greatest trial he encountered in the way of business, was the necessity he was under, at times, of replenishing his stock, and, of course, calling upon his customers for payment. He would turn over in his mind, again and again, the names of those indebted to him, before he could decide upon which of them to call

"This one, he feared, had n't any money just then; and that one had been sick; and the other had such hard work to make a living, he hated to ask for any thing from him; and another he had asked so often he felt ashamed to dun him any more." But money he must have from some of them, or the goods could not be purchased; and so he would make a desperate effort, and put down the names most likely to have the means, leaving the others until some time when it might "may-be," be more convenient for *them*.

It is, therefore, not to be wondered at, if Mr. Leslie had entertained doubts as to the propriety of committing a son to influences so unfavorable to his learning the right way of doing things. But he knew Mr. Thompson to be a man of strict integrity and of a benevolent disposition; and he also knew that loungers were never encouraged around the premises. He never sold by the glass, and, of course, such customers found other places of resort. Charles might learn some things, probably, that would be of use to him in a better establishment. The boy was very desirous of going, and as Mr. Thompson also seemed so anxious for it, Mr. Leslie felt no little desire to gratify *him*. We can not, however, follow Charlie into the establishment just now, as other parts of our story need attention.

CHAPTER XI.

Six years have brought Clarence Ralston from boyhood into the station and responsibilities of a man. He has finished his collegiate course, and spent a few years in the study of law; rather, however, as an accomplishment than with a view to its practice as a profession for life. During this period he spent but short seasons at home. There were few things to attract him there, and he was ready to protract his studies to form an apology sufficiently satisfactory to his own mind; to the friends at home none was needed, for his presence to most of the members of the family seemed of little consequence. But having completed the course he had marked out for himself, there was no longer a reason for his absence, and his parents having expressed a wish that he might be more with them, he resolved to make one more attempt to break down all opposing barriers to his union with his family, if any sacrifice or endurance on his part could accomplish such a desirable end.

It was early in July that Clarence once more beheld the beautiful valley in which his home was situated. It seemed more pleasant to him than ever before. It did not, indeed, bring to his mind those rich ideas which his birthplace and his home should have inspired. It had been too cold a place for his warm heart; it was not interwoven with his young affections; he had not spent his days of boyhood among its noble woods and rich fields; he had not sat with young brothers or sisters beneath the shadows of its large household trees, and enjoyed the cool breezes in the summer days; he had not played with them in the moonlight upon the smooth rich lawn before the door; nor clustered with them in the old wide hall on winter evenings. It was not associated with fond embraces and kind words from loving parents; nor even with the frolics of an old faithful dog. And yet he looked upon the noble structure where his parents lived, and upon the majestic trees that shaded it, and upon the thick woods that rose from the valley to the hill-tops on either side, with more of home feeling than he had ever been conscious of before. And perhaps it was because in his sanguine heart the thought predominated that he "could heal the troubled waters," and bind his brothers to him by an act that would prove how much he valued an interest in their confidence and affection above his own pecuniary advantage.

Mrs. Ralston received her son with a courtesy unusual for her; and Mr. Ralston with very evident tokens that his pride was not a little gratified with the manly form, the handsome face, and gentlemanly bearing of one who called him father.

"The fatted calf was killed," and a hearty welcome for the first few days did much to obliterate from the mind of Clarence all that had been before. His brothers (Richard had also broken up his establishment, and with his imbecile wife taken up his residence at his paternal home) were indeed reserved, and were sparing in tokens of affection. But he made due allowance for that. *They* had indeed wealth in prospect, with a certain allowance for the present, dependent, however, upon the good-will of their parents. *He* had wealth in his own hands, and need fear no man's frown on that account; and no contingency could deprive him of a large addition on his mother's death. He, therefore, could easily account for their feelings toward him; he did not lay their coldness "to heart," and was very sure that when his plans should be unfolded, and they be made satisfied that he cared more for their love than for the wealth bequeathed to him, all would be well.

It was the third day after his arrival, that Clarence invited his brothers to meet him in the family library. That was the usual sitting-place of his father, but Mr. Ralston had gone from home for the day. They accepted the invitation with as much formality as they might have exercised toward a stranger. As they entered the room, Ralph threw himself with much nonchalance into the old arm-chair of his father, exclaiming as he did so:

"The old fellow has got a pretty easy seat, has n't he, Dick?

Mr. Richard Ralston did not think probably that the question needed a reply, and being very busy with a segar just then, gave one or two extra puffs, at the same time leaning back his chair and planting his feet upon the table.

Clarence was shocked at the indignity offered to his father's name; but restrained the reply which his heart dictated, from motives of policy. He felt anxious at first to gain their good-will, as the best way to attempt the correction of their errors. He drew a seat near the table, and addressing himself to his elder brother,

"Brother Ralph, I have asked you and brother Richard to meet me—"

"Do stop with that kind of palavar, Clarence; it sounds too much like child's play. Why can't you say Ralph and Dick at once. Brother Richard! ha, ha, Dick, what does it sound like?"

Richard smiled sarcastically as he threw off the ashes from his segar, but made no other reply.

"I have been so much a stranger at home, you know—"

"Never mind about all that; get on with your story: call me what you like, it is all one to me; we are a loving family, you know. We love the old man and woman, and they love us. Dick loves me, and I love him; all pretty much after the fashion of cats and dogs."

Had Clarence Ralston not been on just the errand he was —had his heart not been full of a noble purpose, his sensitive feelings must have given way, and he would have retired from their presence. But the color on his fine features alone betrayed any emotion at their rudeness. He again began—

"My purpose in asking this interview was, if possible, to do away with any cause for the indulgence of other feelings between us than such as children of the same parents should exercise toward each other. By the will of my grandfather I am possessed of an undue share of an inheritance to which you are equally entitled with me."

Ralph's eye turned with a fierce gaze at the speaker; he struck the table violently, at the same time uttering a tremendous oath.

"Why need you tell us that? we know that too well already."

"My object in alluding to it is merely for the purpose of letting you know that I am ready to correct that wrong. I am ready to share with you equally, all I have thus acquired."

Clarence was so excited both with the harsh manner of his brothers, and with his own haste to set their minds at rest on the matter, that it was with difficulty he uttered the short sentence, by which, in the fewest words possible, he revealed his own noble purpose.

Ralph looked at Richard a moment, and smiled; and then turning to Clarence, remarked in quite a mild manner:

"I perceive, brother Clarence, that you are a true chick of the same brood with us. I perceive you did not 'brother' us for nothing—you have learned some of the lawyers' tricks pretty well. Don't you think he has, Dick?"

Richard again made no reply; he merely hitched his chair a little, and placed his feet further on the table.

"Do you suppose," said Clarence, now speaking with much energy, for his whole soul was aroused, "do you suppose I am not sincere in my offer? If you doubt me, here are my vouchers; here, under my own name and seal are the deeds of conveyance to you; read them for yourselves;" and he laid the documents which he had drawn from his bosom, down upon the table.

Richard looked with a very serious air at his brother Clarence for a moment, and then put out his hand toward the papers.

"Dick, don't you touch them."

"Where 's the harm? why not? if it's true what he says: a bird in the hand is worth two in the bush."

"Don't you touch them, I tell you."

Richard had ever feared his brother Ralph; he knew that his temper at times was terrible, so he settled back in his chair muttering to himself as he did so.

"And you suppose," said Ralph, turning again to Clarence, "that this soft manner of yours, and this pretended act of generosity on your part, will be a perfect quietus; will hush up matters, and leave you with a good slice now, and a large fortune at the old woman's death."

"I can not tell, brother Ralph, what you mean by supposing that my motives have any sinister end in view. As God is true, I have done this with a sincere desire that there may be nothing between us that shall have a tendency to hinder the indulgence of that love from my kindred which I have never yet enjoyed. I have done it to prove to you that I value a brother's heart more than I do my property, large as it has been."

"Perhaps that is all true, and perhaps you are quite innocent about the matter. One thing I can tell you, supposing it to be as you say: you will pay pretty dear for the whistle. Dick and I have got special little love to spare for any beside our own precious selves. But, upon honor, Clarence, just let the lawyer drop, and tell the truth: you have not heard, then, that a small lawsuit was in agitation about this snug little fortune of yours? a pretty little sum it is; and when the old woman steps off, as much more to be added to it; you have n't heard that it was about to be contested?"

"I have not, indeed! and by whom?"

"By myself and your worthy brother Richard; there 's news for you."

Clarence was indeed confounded; he could not at once reply.

"You see Dick and I have had our heads together about it for some time. It ain't often, or for small matters, that we *do* hitch horses together, but this is something of a haul, and not to be let slip. It can be pretty well proved that the will of old granddad was a little faulty—just a few cracks in it; and also that there was something of a crack in his brain when he made it. There must have been, no doubt, or the old fool would never have done as he did; so you may as well put up your papers and spare your soft speeches."

"And do our parents know your design? and do they concur in it?"

"They may, or they may not; we are not quite such fools as to have told them. We think it won't quite suit their convenience; but it will ours. And then when we come on the old folks for back pay, we rather think there will be some wry faces; we have been kept—that is Dick and I—hanging on their leavings long enough. If we break this will, you see, Master Clarence, the whole concern comes to us right off: or it will probably by the time the thing can be brought about. The old man can't have the use of it a single day, for he signed off all right to his wife's property before he married; she would not have him on any other conditions; cunning, was n't she?"

Clarence cared little for the threat; he knew they were in error as to the law, and he believed they would find they were in error as to the facts. But their cold treatment of himself, and especially the disrespectful manner in which his parents were spoken of, sensibly affected him.

"If it is your determination thus to deal with one who is anxious, above all other considerations, to have a true place in your hearts, I can only regret your sad choice; but allow me one moment to reason with you, and tell you all my views."

"Go on; I sha'n't stop you, for one, and Dick ain't very apt to be troublesome in the way of talking; go on."

"I have, in all truth, never before heard the least whisper that the will of our grandfather could by any means be disputed. I have thought, indeed, that it was not a wise measure, thus to distinguish one member of a family above the rest, and now, as I have returned to my home to make one among you, for a time at least, I resolved so far as was in my power, to remove that cause for any unkind feeling between us brothers. I have equally divided between us what is now in my possession, and there lie the deeds of conveyance. If you reject them, I can do no more. But I beg of you to pause before you take a step that may sunder forever the feeble ties which bind our family together.

"You may succeed, for I know not upon what grounds you are about to proceed. But think what it will involve! Brother arrayed against brother, and for a mere shadow, for you may lose what you are grasping at. Why not at once cease this unholy strife for gain? Has not the love of it already almost destroyed the harmony of our home? Has there not been enough of violent contention, of mere self-seeking? Why can we not be brothers in reality, and unite our efforts in soothing the last days of our parents into tranquillity? Are you willing to see them so near the grave, agitated by a contest between us.

"By all that is sacred in our relationship, I beg of you to listen to me. For heaven's sake let not the world any longer point at us as an example of domestic discord, where every noble feeling is swallowed up in the love of money, of which we all have enough, and more than enough, already."

Both brothers were silent for a moment: Richard seemed much moved, and looked earnestly at the countenance of Clarence through the whole address. But he said nothing, and turned toward Ralph as though he expected to see a marked change in *his* conduct. His own heart, cold as it had been, was evidently touched; Ralph, however, maintained the same unmoved aspect; he answered Richard's look with an angry scowl, and then, fixing his eye upon Clarence,

"It is all well, master Clarence, very prettily spoken. I think you will succeed in your profession, if you choose to pursue it. Very well said. But I must tell you, my boy, you have got men to deal with now who are not to be frightened by the world's opinion; we can do without their opinion, good or bad; and as to brotherly love, which you harp about so prettily, it is too late in the day to mend that matter; you must go to the old man and woman, and talk to them about that. They began with us pretty early in life to teach us the good lesson, 'that each one must take care of himself, and let the devil take care of the rest;' we have finished our education long ago, and don't care to go to school again. Perhaps, however, as you find us rather hard subjects, you had better go, as I have said, to the old folks, and see if you can not. 'convert them from the error of their ways.' Try if you can not persuade the old man to sign over some of his acres and bonds for the special benefit of his loving sons, or get the old woman to give up handling her own income to her beloved husband. Try your hand there, my boy. No, no, I tell you honestly, Clarence, you have got into the wrong nest for one of your training. Don't you think so, Dick?"

"I think perhaps it would have been better for us all to have been trained a little more as he has been."

"Ho, ho, my hearty! you have got dust in your eyes already, ha? Dick, you 're a fool."

"Perhaps I am; but I think there are other fools in this house besides me."

Ralph turned upon him a fierce and brutal scowl, and Richard immediately arose and left the room.

Clarence took up the papers which he had laid upon the table, and calmly replaced them in his pocket.

"That 's right—you had better keep those papers safely, and perhaps if we do not succeed in our present plan, why it will not be too late then to do the right thing, you know."

"I shall keep them, brother Ralph, to my dying day; and whenever that shall come, I will have them laid by my pillow as witnesses that in all sincerity of heart I once did what was in my power to win a brother's love. I would not part with them, Ralph, for any earthly consideration."

And thus saying, he was about to leave the room, when he was interrupted by the entrance of his mother. Mrs. Ralston, as we have said, was not, in youth, prepossessing in feature, although of commanding mien and figure. With her, as with many others, age had made great improvement. The face that was scarcely pleasing at twenty-one, was now, at three score and ten, if not attractive, at least comely at that age. The naturally stern and coarse features were mellowed by time. There was still fire in the eye and determination in the lip; but these only served to give character and life.

Dressed in the rich style of that day, with her hair crimped and powdered, and the flowing trail of her heavy satin dress sweeping beneath her tall person, there was not a little of majesty and grace in her appearance.

Clarence bowed reverently as she entered, and hastened to place a chair for her, while Ralph immediately arose, and with a look of derision at his brother, walked leisurely toward the door.

The mother turned her keen eye upon him.

"I hope I have not intruded; you need not leave on *my* account, Mr. Ralph Ralston; I have only a word to say to your brother."

"Say on, then, I don't care to hear it." And walking from the room, closed the door behind him, in no very gentle manner.

"Ah, he has got too much of the Ralston in him"—she might with more truth have said Williamson—"and the older he grows, the more it shows itself. Hasty, haughty, self-willed."

She then took the seat Clarence had placed for her.

"I came in, Mr. Clarence, to say that on the morrow I start for Maple Grove, and shall expect the pleasure of your company—I thus announce my intention early in the day that you may be able to make suitable arrangements. The Cranstouns are people of affluence, and I would that you made such preparations as become your circumstances and first introduction."

Clarence had received no intimation, previous to this announcement, that his mother had any such intentions, or that he would be expected to accompany her. He had made his plans for meeting his good old friends the Rices; but unwilling that a shadow of offense should be taken by his mother, he at once assented to her wish.

"I thank you, mother, for the honor you do me, and will prepare to attend you. Will your visit extend beyond a day or two?

"That is quite uncertain; in fact the length of my visit will not altogether depend upon my own feelings. I go not solely for my own pleasure, although Lady Cranstoun is an old friend, and I have great respect for her, as one who holds a very high station; and perhaps I may as well say to you at once that for special reasons on your account I make my visit. When we reach 'Maple Grove,' I can more fully reveal my intentions."

And the stately lady rose from her chair, and made a slight obeisance to her son, which he returned with as much formality as if she had been a stranger, and not entitled to call her mother.

As Mrs. Ralston had particular reasons for appearing "in state" at "Maple Grove," four horses were put in requisition, and the best coach was ordered, instead of their traveling-carriage. The coachman and waiter were in their finest livery, and the cortège would not have disgraced an embassador from an imperial court.

As this visit had been announced, and as Mrs. Cranstoun was well aware that her good friend expected all due formality in attention, her delegate, a gentleman who superintended her affairs, was dispatched, near the time when the arrival of her visitors might be expected, to the outer border of her estate, to meet and escort them to the mansion. This might have been done merely as an act of courtesy, or it might also have been designed to mark the line where the Cranstoun Estate commenced, and from which some three miles had to be traversed before the homestead could be reached. Mrs. Ralston received this mark of attention with due consideration.

"This is all very proper in Lady Cranstoun," said Mrs. Ralston to her son, after receiving the salutation of the gentleman who had announced his mission, and was then riding in advance.

"All very proper. She knows how to pay due deference to her guests; but what a noble estate! I am told it is four miles in extent either way; and do you know, my son, that there is only the Hazleton property interveuing between it and your farm of Chestnut Hill? Have you ever thought of that?"

"I have not, mother; nor, in fact, can I say that I know exactly where the Chestnut Hill farm lies."

"It is a valuable estate, and if you should purchase the Hazleton property, which adjoins it, and which, I understand, is about being sold, the owner, Mrs. Leslie, once Miss Hazleton having very foolishly signed off her right to it, has now the mortification of knowing that her lands are in the hands of mere speculators. She was a very foolish woman. I say, if you should purchase that, it would then connect your property along the whole border of the Cranstoun Estate."

As Clarence could not clearly comprehend what special advantage it would be to his property to be thus bounded, and the mention of the name of Leslie having probably awakened recollections of a peculiar nature, he did not immediately make any reply to her suggestion; and Mrs. Ralston continued:

"It would, I say, be a great thing to have the two estates thus adjoining—more closely allied—a very splendid affair indeed! and one that it would be my wish to see accomplished. They are a family of high station, and Miss Emma Cranstoun a very estimable young lady; and do you know that she is sole heiress to all these lands?"

"I did not; indeed I have not thought about such matters." Clarence could not pretend, he knew, without offense, to misunderstand his mother's allusions.

"That is all very proper; you have done very right in abstaining from all thoughts about connecting yourself, or taking any steps thereto without first consulting with those who are particularly concerned in any such arrangement. Young people know very little what is for their good, and are very apt to have foolish notions. I am glad, then, that there is nothing in the way of my wishes concerning you."

Clarence would have made further explanation, even at the terrible risk of an outbreak on the part of his mother, but just then the carriage was turned from the highway, and he perceived that the dwelling was close at hand. So he forbore all remarks on that subject for the present.

The reception was attended with all that ceremony which was affected by some of those wealthy families, much to the gratification of Mrs. Ralston, as it seemed a token to her of the high consideration in which she was held by her hostess.

She felt also not a little pride in presenting her handsome son, and was quite satisfied with the pleasant manner in which Miss Emma received him.

A little attention to this young lady may not be out of place here.

She was, upon the whole, good looking. She had blue eyes, and brown hair, and a round face, and a small mouth, and rather pretty lips. She had a fair complexion, the red and white blending charmingly on her dimpled cheek, and her smile showed teeth of the purest white. Her hand was small and plump, and her fingers just the true taper; her foot, too, was a very pretty article of its kind, and her form of the right height and proportion; she walked with dignity; she conversed with ease; she danced gracefully, and sang with more than usual sweetness. She was without affectation, and did not appear to be conscious that she was an heiress to a large estate. There was no particular fault that a gentleman in search of a wife or a fortune could easily have noticed.

Her father had died when she was quite a child, and left her his sole inheritor after her mother's death, and the possession of Maple Grove immediately on her marriage, Mrs. Cranstoun having an abundant provision in her own right, and by her husband's bequest of other property.

On the morning of the third day after their arrival at Maple Grove, Mrs. Ralston requested her son to afford her a short interview, which he readily granted, although he feared it might not prove very satisfactory to either.

"I suppose," said Mrs. Ralston, "you understood my allusion, the other day, as to the purport of my visit here, and therefore it will be unnecessary for me to enter into particulars. But it is time now for some definite arrangement to be entered into. I think Miss Emma a very agreeable person, and I have been gratified to notice that you seem to think so too."

"Miss Cranstoun has certainly endeavored to make our visit agreeable to us."

"She certainly has, and I think has shown very clearly that Mr. Clarence Ralston's company is quite agreeable to her."

"I hope that I have done nothing of which Mrs. Cranstoun or her daughter can reasonably complain. I came for my mother's pleasure, and have endeavored to act the agreeable so far as I am able. You will, no doubt, make allowance for any discrepancy on my part, for the reason that you know my advantages for the enjoyment of ladies' society have been quite limited."

"I should not judge so from your success in the present instance; for I can tell you confidently that the young lady is quite well pleased at the prospect of the arrangement which has been so long contemplated; although had that not been the case, she would doubtless have yielded to her mother's wishes as in duty bound; but it is certainly more satisfactory to know that the parties immediately concerned are also well agreed in the matter."

As Clarence felt that the time had come when his own views must be explicitly unfolded, he, in as calm a manner as his feelings would permit, replied,

"I would ask you respectfully, mother, for an explanation of what you particularly intend, when you speak of 'my success' in connection 'with some arrangement long since contemplated?' I believe those are the words you used."

"They are the words I used; and I could have hoped they were sufficiently plain to be comprehended by a dutiful son, without any further explanation. You certainly must know that I allude to the arrangement between you and Miss Cranstoun, which both her mother and yours have contemplated with much satisfaction for some time, and which I hope to find you quite ready to complete."

"I feel certainly much obliged to you, mother, for the kind interest you take in me. I have no doubt you design it for my good, but I am sorry to be compelled to say that I think a union with Miss Cranstoun, even if not disagreeable to her, would not accomplish the end you have in view, which of course can be no other than my happiness."

"And why not, may I ask?"

"Simply because I feel no interest in that young lady of a nature that would lead me to desire the union you speak of. *I do not love her*, mother; and however estimable she may be, I could never choose her for my companion for life."

"You talk like a fool, Clarence; are you willing to throw away the chance for such an advantageous connection for a boy's whim? Think what an estate it would be with your own added to it! You would be, without doubt, the wealthiest man in the State."

"And of what advantage would that be to me, mother?"

"Of what advantage! I am truly surprised, I must say, to hear you speak thus lightly of a position in society! You have not adopted, I hope, the vulgar idea that the base laborer and the poor mechanic, and the low rabble that live from hand to mouth, are on a level with men of wealth and high position! If you have, I shall bitterly mourn that you are a son of mine."

Clarence knew enough of his mother's peculiarities to avoid an argument on such a theme; he therefore merely replied,

"I do by no means despise wealth, as you have suggested; but I must tell you frankly, mother, that when I marry it must be one whom I wish to be connected with for other reasons than because an estate, large or small, is attached to the lady; and therefore, I entreat you, mother, let us drop the present topic."

"And how, may I ask you, am I to answer to Mrs. Cranstoun for thus condescending to receive you as a suitor for her daughter's hand, and after all that has been already said and done in reference to the matter? Are you, Clarence Ralston, going to prove so recreant to honor and filial duty! Your brothers are indeed but poor patterns of the latter, but even they did not presume to resist a parent's dictates on such a subject, when the interest and character of our family are concerned."

"You will acquit me, certainly, mother, of any blame for having accompanied you in this visit; I came not, as you know, as a suitor for this lady's hand, but merely in compliance with my mother's request; and I should regret exceedingly if my name has ever been connected with that of Miss Cranstoun by one who has so strong a claim to my obedience in all things as my mother."

Mrs. Ralston had been excited to a point where in general her feelings took command of her judgment, and led to the most furious outbreak of passion. But the calm and respectful manner in which Clarence addressed her, did much to prevent the catastrophe. She feared to lose the influence she still had over him, and instead of heaping invectives upon him for resisting her wishes, very evidently moderated her tone.

"Perhaps I had been wiser to have spoken to you more explicitly ere we came upon this errand, but what possible objections can there be to such a connection?—a family of the highest respectability! and in every way suitable to be connected with our own—and surely you can have no objections to the young lady herself! her personal appearance, her accomplished manners, and her excellent disposition, must, it seems to me, be all-sufficient even for the most fastidious taste, to say nothing of the addition she would bring to your own handsome property."

"I acknowledge frankly that all you say of Miss Cranstoun is true, and doubtless, to one who loved her, she would prove a most desirable companion. But I must tell you, mother, that on the subject of marriage, I fear my views do not coincide with yours, nor with those of my family in general. I look upon it as a most solemn contract, only to be entered into by parties whose hearts are united by strong affection, whose interest in each other is independent of all external considerations, and whose views and feelings correspond on that subject most important of all others, *our relation to Him who is our Creator and Redeemer.*"

Mrs. Ralston looked at her son with the most profound astonishment; such ideas had never before been whispered to her ears by one in any way connected with her. Religion involving any obligations in such a matter as marriage, or having any thing to do with it beyond its connection with the ceremony, was a thought never before suggested by her own reflections, and had certainly never entered into any of her arrangements concerning it. She therefore replied according to her own views of what his meaning must be.

"Miss Cranstoun attends the Episcopal church, and her family have been the chief supporters of our order of worship at Maple Grove. You have yourself been an attendant upon the church service: how then can there be a want of correspondence in your feelings?"

"We might, no doubt, agree as to the externals of worship; but I am well satisfied, mother, that we do not feel alike on some important points. I do not *love* her enough to unite my destiny with her; and even if I had formed the strongest attachment for her that my heart is capable of, I would not dare trust my happiness with one who can allow herself to speak lightly of *a change of heart.*"

"Has Mr. Clarence Ralston then become a Methodist? I learn that the order is gaining ground rapidly in our country, but I had supposed their adherents were only from among the lower orders of society!"

"I have had no communications with any of that persuasion, mother, from the fact that there are none in our vicinity, nor where I have hitherto been located. My views have been derived from the teachings of our own church, and from the holy Scriptures. But such as they are, I am firmly persuaded of their truth, and my life hereafter must be regulated by them. One thing I learn from them, that my parents are entitled to my love, respect, and obedience; and only when your requests shall be inconsistent with my duty to God, will you find your son disposed to do aught in opposition to your will; and I feel very confident, mother, that you will never command me to do that which my conscience can not acquiesce in."

Mrs. Ralston was naturally a selfish woman, and her whole life hitherto had been spent in endeavoring in some way to accomplish her own ends. But she was still a *mother*, and never until that moment had she felt what it was to be acknowledged as such, in a spirit of love and obedience. She had indeed been obeyed, but she felt conscious it had only been from fear, or for a mercenary end. A place in her heart had now been touched which she herself knew not of before—a feeling new as the first flash of love in a maiden's breast, arose within, before which even her pride, and love of money, for the moment, had to give place. And as she looked upon her manly son, now of full age to act for himself, and independent in his own right, and heard him speak such words of submission and confidence, she felt more the true spirit of a mother, yea, even prouder than she had ever felt under any circumstance of her life before. She also felt an assurance that she had a stronger hold upon him than she had ever possessed over her other sons. Her reply was marked by a complete change in her whole manner.

"What you say, Clarence, is certainly in accordance with all propriety; and I hope your future conduct may prove your sincerity; for the present, as you wish it, we will waive the subject, hoping that, upon mature reflection, you may conclude to yield to my suggestion. At present, however, we will let the matter drop."

The parting at Maple Grove was marked with all the ceremony and attention that had distinguished the reception. Clarence would have been glad to know that all ideas respecting the Cranstoun property had left his mother's mind. But the remarks she was constantly making, as they were riding through it, and the very particular notice she took of its rich fields, and majestic woods, and fine streams, intermingled with suggestions of their value, and of improvements that might profitably be made, told plainly that "the matter was only waived for the present." It was quite a relief to him, therefore, when the boundary of the estate was passed; and the mountain scenery into which they immediately entered afforded some other topic of conversation.

Mr. Ralston, we have said, seemed proud of his younger son, and manifested a readiness to give him a cordial reception at his return for a permanent abode at home. It must not be supposed, however, that the interest aroused in this parent's heart was essentially different from that which might have been awakened by any circumstance that for the time gave an impulse to his feelings.

The feelings of the father had been so long merged in those of the manager or proprietor, they could not be expected to warm up into much fervor.

His children were his *heirs*, and that one idea cherished through many years of his life, and mingled with all his thoughts, and plans, concerning them, had indeed given them a prominent place in his mind and fastened them there by a strong chain. They were of great consequence, not because his heart yearned over them, but because *they* were to continue his hold on earth; when he could no longer ride over his immense estates, nor count up the interest on his securities *they* would do it in his stead, and all his teachings had been directed to that end. Far as the eye could reach to the hills which bounded the view, a beautiful scene spread out before and around, mountains in their soft blue far off in the distance, hills, and woods, and streams, and green fields, sloping lawns, and old shade trees, and clean groves, and picturesque rocks, with the fragrant cedar piercing their crevices, and hiding their roughness, a noble mansion, large in its dimensions, majestic in its strength, beautiful in its proportions, and elegantly adorned within and without. All was there that the heart of man could ask, with every external requisite to bind its owner to it as a home for him and his. But he only looked upon it as "*Clanmore Valley the estate of Randolph Ralston.*" Its beauties had never touched his heart, he had never enjoyed the fresh breezes beneath its spreading oaks, nor the bright sparkles of its limpid streams, nor the varied colors of its forests; the golden tints of morning as they glittered on the eastern hill-tops, nor the rich hues of evening had ever yielded one quickening thought, nor led his mind beyond the simple fact that the sun arose and set to him within the bounds of Clanmore. And to his elder sons, it was only Clanmore; and to inherit this estate, to walk, or ride throughout its length and breadth, its sole owner, when the father should be lying in his narrow bed within the church-yard wall, was the only thought of each concerning it; and to win this privilege, was the one idea to which in youth they had been trained, and now in manhood was the absorbing thought. For this, plots and counter-plots were devised, false characters assumed, arts practiced, obedience yielded, and the whole economy of the family, at times, thrown into confusion.

As Mr. Ralston held this property in his own right, it was well understood by the sons that he could will it to whom he pleased. His last testament was therefore an object of great interest. It had been made when his first child was born, and it had been altered many times already. But its changes were known to have been merely the substituting one name for another. Ralph and Richard had been alternately the acknowledged heirs. But of late a cloud of uncertainty hung over the matter; it was unknown to which of the two the inheritance would finally be given. The return of Clarence formed a new element of discord, a new occasion for jealousy in the minds of the rival candidates.

Ralph was by no means deficient in intellect; he was a shrewd observer of men and things, and made his calculations without interference from what is usually called natural affection. He could indeed, when he thought his interest required it, yield obsequious compliance with the request of his parents, and did not hesitate to adapt his conduct to what he saw was their whim for the time. But as his parents seldom acted in concert, and what pleased one was often displeasing to the other, it required no small amount of dissimulation to maintain with both that standing which he felt was for his interest. Richard had apparently as little affection for his parents as his elder brother, but he had less ability. He at times had been a favorite with the father, but rather for the reason that the mind of the parent was unfavorably impressed toward his elder brother, than for any new feeling of complacency towards *him*.

Old Mr. Ralston spent much of his time in the family library, called so rather by courtesy, than for the fact of its being an apartment where any large collection of books were assembled, or any amount of reading, or study, accomplished. There was indeed an old-fashioned book-case, highly polished, containing a few old volumes, but they [illegible] the most part permitted to remain in their stations, or [illegible] pent up within their dark closet. Mr. Ralston's literary labors were chiefly confined to old manuscript documents, having reference to various tracts of land, which he either owned, or had once been in possession of, or to other tracts, on the security of which he had loaned various sums of money. It was this species of literature that suited the taste of Mr. Ralston, and for which he had a special fondness.

Clarence found the atmosphere of his home so uncongenial, and the treatment of Ralph so marked with dislike to him, that soon after his return from Maple Grove he intimated to his mother a wish to spend a few months by the sea-side, and the respectful manner in which he requested her assent, together with the faultless deportment of his conduct toward her, drew from her an acquiescence in his request that was almost unexpected, at least in reference to its manner.

"It will be a drawback on my pleasure, master Clarence, to have you leave us; but as you have manifested such deference in all matters, to your parents' wishes, I can not say nay. Have you made mention of your desire to your father?"

"I have not as yet, mother, but shall do so immediately."

"It is highly proper that you should do so, and you will find him, just now, in the library. I say just now, for in a few hours he will be off to superintend the surveying of a line that is to be run between his Langdon estate and the Golding property."

Clarence immediately repaired to the library, and found his father busily engaged in perusing a large parchment manuscript. Mr. Ralston laid down the paper on his son's entrance.

"Good morning, good morning, sir, walk in."

Clarence made a low reverence, and without speaking, took the seat toward which his father pointed.

"Be seated; I am glad you have come in, as there are some matters of moment about which I wish to confer with you. I have just been reading a copy of your grandfather's will. I mean the will of your grandfather Williamson."

"I am very sorry, sir, that he left any will at all, or that he had not made a different bequest. I fear, sir, that the consequences resulting from it may prove disastrous to my own peace, as well as that [illegible]thers."

"Yes, yes, that ma[illegible]ther Richard has informed me about certain things [illegible]rred lately. I am not surprised, knowing as I do, the peculiarities of your elder brother. You need fear nothing, however, during my life, for I have expressly informed him that any such attempt as he has threatened, will cause me to make a complete change in my arrangements: you need fear nothing then, during my life. But should he outlive me, there is great danger that you will be put to trouble, and what I wish is, that you should be prepared against possible contingencies."

"But why should my brother wish to do that by violence, which I am willing to do of my own accord. If my brother Richard has told you the whole truth, he has doubtless told you, sir, my proposition to divide the property equally with them.

"I have been informed of that, too, and had you advised with me I could have told you that such a proposition would only be met as it has been; your brother Ralph is not one who would be very likely to submit to an obligation if there was any possibility of gaining his end by any other means. And there are other reasons; in fact, to be plain with you, he might think, in such a case, you would have a claim as a competitor for the Clanmore estate; and that, you know, he thinks more of than all else in the world."

"And I sincerely hope, sir, that my name may never be

mentioned in connection with that property. I have more than sufficient already; and should regret that such an additional obstacle should be thrown in the way of my brother's regard for me."

"Your brother's regard will doubtless be not at all affected should I think it best to appoint you a reversionary heir; he has no regard, I am sorry to say it, for any one but himself. However, let that matter go; as things are, it is highly necessary for you to be well aware of your situation in regard to that which you now hold in your own right. I do not think he can possibly break the will. But there is another point which he has not named to you, and by which he, as I have secretly learned, expects to accomplish his end; and that is, by denying your claim to be one of the children of this family."

Clarence looked at his father in amazement, but answered not.

"It was indeed very unfortunate that Mrs. Ralston so long denied your claim to be her son—very unfortunate indeed—and as that circumstance can be so well attested, it will be a strong argument in his favor. But there are those living now by whom a chain of evidence can be made out that will be all sufficient. If one link of that chain should be broken, it will be bad—the parties may or may not be all living now, but no time should be lost in searching them out, and getting their testimony. In the first place, there was present at the time of your birth but one living witness; that is, two others beside her who were present are now dead—this woman was a Mrs. Barstow, a respectable neighbor of ours at the time; she was with your mother, and remained out of kindness to take charge of you, until a person whom we had engaged for that purpose was able to get to us; this other person was a Mrs. Barton—Lucretia Barton, or Luckie, as she was most usually called; she came a few days after your birth, and it was she who carried you to Mrs. Rice, where you was brought up. You now can see that the testimony of these two persons is of the utmost consequence. Mrs. Barstow and her husband have removed from here some years since; where they have gone I can not say; I have inquired diligently, but can get no clew to them. They had a daughter, a very comely lass, that married, it was said, a rich man in the city of New York; his name I remember to have been Folger; the reason for my remembering it is, that I have heard it mentioned frequently with one Thorne, who lives some miles from here, and is something of a villain, as I believe; whether Folger is a good character, or a bad one, I can not say; but he has had much dealing with Thorne—and I hear has lately purchased from Thorne the whole Hazleton estate—there is some trickery there, I think—but that is nothing to our purpose; only as he seems to be known about, some clew might be obtained through him to the Barstows. The testimony of Mrs. Barstow will be absolutely necessary. Mrs. Barton has also left her place of former residence, and I can not hear whither she has gone. It is possible Mrs. Rice can inform you.

"My advice to you, is, that you at once make it your business to hunt these persons up. First, Mrs. Barstow, to prove that she delivered you to the care of Mrs. Barton; and Mrs. Barton to prove that she delivered you to Mrs. Rice; and the sooner you are about it, the better."

Clarence listened with fixed attention to the recital of his father, and then took notes, at his dictation; resolving, as his father had advised, to lose no time in making the inquiries so necessary to his interests.

"If I am not mistaken," said Mr. Ralston, as Clarence was about to leave the room, "Folger resides at Princesport."

"It was my purpose, sir," replied Clarence, "to have mentioned to you, that if you had no objections, I should be pleased to spend some months where I could have the benefit of sea air; and, as I learn that Princesport has that advantage, had thought of visiting it."

"You had better do so, then; you may by that means acquire the information you need. Another thing I would say to you. It may be as well not to inform your mother particularly what your object in going there may be. It is a subject she does not care to speak much about."

Mrs. Ralston, although much changed in her feelings toward her youngest son, and had acquiesced apparently with much willingness in his anticipated departure from home for a season, had not, it seems, quite given up all ideas of the Maple Grove property, for on the evening previous to his departure, she very adroitly renewed the subject, and, very unexpectedly to Clarence, reminded him that she held a conditional promise from him in reference to that matter.

"Have you not mistaken what I said to you at that time, mother?"

"I hope I have not—nor also mistaken the grounds of your very correct deportment, since then. Do your professions of obedience to your parents, as a duty, depend upon the fact that what we may wish shall be in every point perfectly agreeable to yourself?"

"By no means, mother; I hold that your commands are sacred to me, provided they do not conflict with my duty to God."

"And suppose I should request of you, as a favor peculiarly grateful to me, and for other very special reasons, that you should make no arrangement with any lady, other than the one to whom I have been alluding, without first notifying me. Would that, do you think, conflict with any superior duty?"

"I am willing, mother, in order to show you that my spirit of obedience is genuine, to say that I will not thus slight your wishes."

"That is enough; I have the most entire confidence in your word

CHAPTER XII.

IT was no easy matter for Mrs. Leslie and Carrie to come to the conclusion that it would be best for them, under all the circumstances, to accede to the request of Mr. Folger, in reference to his little motherless child. Their prejudices had been strangely excited against him, not knowing, perhaps, all the circumstances connected with the business transactions between him and their husband and father; and listening, as women are very apt to do, to the thousand rumors which were abroad concerning him, without making due allowance for the ease with which false rumors are floated along—the first suggestion to them of such a plan was met with surprise, and almost displeasure; surprise that a man who had acted such a part should make such a request; and displeasure, that he should suppose they were so lost to sensibility, as to be willingly on such terms of intimacy, as the arrangement would involve, with one who had, as they thought, brought upon them so much unnecessary trouble.

Mr. Leslie was obliged, without being able at first to controvert their opinions, to listen with much pain to the outpouring of their injured feelings. He knew that for *him* their hearts bled; it was the trial that pressed upon *him* that had awakened their feelings. It was the injustice done to the *father*, the *husband*, that caused those who had hitherto manifested such a spirit of love and forbearance now to indulge resentment.

It was, therefore, with great delicacy, and the utmost tenderness, that he undertook the difficult task of apologizing for what had appeared unkind and unnecessary in the dealings of Mr. Folger.

He found, however, when he came to make out a defense in words, a greater difficulty in doing so, than when, under the spell of Mr. Folger's plausible manner and smooth speeches, his thoughts had become so softened toward him and his views of his character so changed; and he therefore very soon relinquished the idea of establishing his case, especially before a mind so clear, and a tongue so ready in her parent's behalf, as Carrie could command. He therefore attempted to turn her shafts aside by assuming the part of an apologist.

"I can not deny, my darling, that what you say is correct. There may have been wrong done; Mr. Folger may not have acted just as he would have wished another to have dealt with him under the same circumstances; but we must make some allowances for him. There he is: a man living alone; no wife or daughter to direct his mind, or soften his character; with nothing, perhaps, to think of much, besides his business. Such a man would be very likely, at times, in brooding over his affairs, to look on the dark side of things, to become distrustful, and to have his fears excited unnecessarily. We are not all alike. He doubtless thinks more or less of money; he has made it honestly, we have reason to think, and perhaps like many others who have money, dreads to lose it. We ought not blame him for that; in fact he has acknowledged as much to me; that is, he has expressed regret, and has said he sometimes wishes the whole had been sunk before he had put me to so much trouble. He has, I think, too, a much kinder heart than the world is ready to give him credit for. He seems to have the genuine feelings of a parent, and manifests a great desire to have his little 'motherless child' under proper influence. He has been compelled hitherto, he tells me, to board her with strangers, and ought we to feel surprised at his desire to obtain a situation for her, where he has every confidence she will be treated with kindness?"

Mrs. Leslie and Carrie could indeed say little against such reasoning. They did not wish to be unjust; but Carrie in particular had some private objections that arose in her own mind. To her they were very forcible; she could not readily bring herself to be willing that an opportunity should be afforded for such intimacy as must exist between Mr. Folger and herself, if his request was acceded to; she could hardly tell why, but she *shrunk from it*. She had seen, indeed, but little of him, and had but upon one occasion an opportunity for introduction; then few words passed between them. He was quite polite, and exceedingly respectful in his manner toward her; and yet she could not resist an impression made upon her at the time, that he was "acting a part." It might have been well for her had she never driven that first impression from her mind.

But Carrie reserved entirely within her own breast whatever thoughts originated there from any thing personal. It might be that some advantage would accrue to her father should the arrangement be entered into; and for such an end she was ready to do many things not in themselves agreeable to her.

The compensation, too, was something to be taken into account; and it was not for her to be in the way of any providential relief to the family, if it was then to be afforded.

An event, however, that occurred a few days after the interview, which has been recorded, between Mr. Leslie and Mr. Folger, assisted very decidedly in turning the scale in favor of the latter.

Henry Leslie, the twin brother of Charles, was a youth of retiring habits, of a modest and unassuming disposition, and much disposed to avoid society. He presented quite a contrast to his sprightly and social brother. There had been, from his infancy, a tinge of sadness to his countenance. He loved to be alone, appeared to look on the dark side of life, did not easily make acquaintances, and seemed "to take the world hard."

What change had taken place in his mind since the development of his father's reduced circumstances, no one knew, not even Carrie, with whom he was the most intimate of all the members of his family. There had been no perceptible alteration in his feelings or habits.

But sometimes there is quite a process going on within, when the surface marks it not; and it was thus with Henry Leslie. The fact that he had no longer a parent to lean upon, because that parent was himself prostrate and helpless, at once caused him to take new views of his position and prospects; and although he made no professions of what he would do, nor spoke of any occupation in which he should endeavor to engage, yet his thoughts were continually employed upon the great subject of his life's business.

The project, of all others most congenial to his wishes, was to go abroad, to venture among new scenes, and try to force his way, as many others had done, in a foreign country. He had heard especially of fortunes made in India and China, those far-off corners of the earth, and by young men who had started with no capital besides their hands and head. His imagination, too, which his retiring habits had a tendency to cherish, roamed away amid fantasies of its own creation, and worked up a pleasing picture of fortunate adventures in a foreign country, and a joyous return to the home of his childhood, with an independence for himself and those he loved so well; There was also in the scenes of his native place much that was calculated to entice him abroad upon the wide, wide ocean. The beautiful bay, whose waters spread so placidly around; the vessels slightly bending to the inland breeze; the cheerful songs of the seamen, as they mingled with the lash of waves upon the sandy shore; the echo of the oars from the fisherman's boat, far off upon the mirrored water; all excited a magic power upon his heart, and threw around his thoughts, as they dwelt upon the mighty deep, a winning influence.

Princesport had of late been distinguished by the arrival there of several vessels of large size, employed in the China trade, for the reason that their owners could make arrangements for the payment of custom-house dues more agreeable to themselves, than with the more fastidious guardian of revenue rights in the large sea-port of New York.

For some successive months there had been almost constantly one or more of these leviathans of the deep, moored by the dock, or lying off in the stream, creating no small stir in a place so retired, and alluring many, not otherwise employed, to congregate about them. Henry Leslie had been attracted among the rest, and meeting with much civility from the hands on board, made frequent visits, and held at times long converse with one and another, as he found them unoccupied, or disposed to be communicative. It happened one day, as he was talking with the second mate of the ship, he overheard a conversation between the captain and a gentleman whom he did not know.

As the subject did not appear to be one which they wished to be secret, and as it was one in which Henry felt much interested, he turned and fixed his eye steadily on the speaker. In a few moments one of the gentlemen came up to him, and in a very pleasant manner asked,

"Are you not a son of Mr. Horatio Leslie?"

"I am, sir."

"How do you do, my young gentleman? glad to see you; perhaps you do not recognize me; my name is Folger; you have heard your father mention me, no doubt?"—at the same time giving Henry a very cordial shake of the hand. Henry was much confused when he found himself in such close contact with one of whom he had no very favorable opinion. But the winning smile, and the pleasant tones of the voice, together with the friendly grasp, had a wonderful effect in obliterating past impressions. The gentleman continued,

"Please excuse my boldness if I ask you a plain question; have you any permanent engagement for the present?"

"I have not, sir."

"Would you like to take a voyage? Now do n't look surprised, my dear young fellow, that I seem to know your thoughts! I am merely guessing that you have a notion that way. I have observed you round here of late, and have gathered from the earnest manner in which you talk to the sailors, that you are interested in sea matters; you would like to try the ocean? am I right?"

"You have guessed correctly, sir."

"That is the thing; right straight out. I like frank open dealing; nothing like it. And now just step one side, Master Leslie."

Henry followed him toward the stern of the ship.

"I do n't want to speak very loud, for as soon as it is known about, there will be a dozen applicants for the place; but if you want it, you shall have it. I do not own the ship, but the captain feels under some special obligations to me, and will not deny me a favor; and I feel—I feel, I say, very particularly desirous of doing any thing that will oblige any of your family. This vessel is bound for China; she will sail in a few weeks. The captain wants a clerk, a young man who can write well, and will be prompt and energetic, and a right-hand man to him. He will give you thirty dollars a month; it is no great pay; but as you will be gone a year, it will amount to something in that time. And as you will have a little privilege in the way of freight, you may find some small venture back, that will pay—either silks or teas—and then, too, you will have a chance to learn the tricks of the trade, which will be no small item, as I should view it. Now, as I have said, I have no personal interest in the matter, but I *do* feel a great interest for all the members of your family. And if I can do any of you a favor, I shall feel most happy."

Henry's prejudices had all flown away long before Mr. Fol-r had done speaking.

"I should be most happy to obtain the situation, sir, and will feel under great obligations to you."

"Never mind that; you and your family will never find me wanting when a friend is needed. You need say nothing about my interference in this matter—I mean to people in general. The captain has gone ashore now, but he is to dine with me to-day. You see your parents and friends, and get their consent, and call down here to-morrow about this time. I will introduce you particularly to the captain, and you can have it all arranged; so good-day, my dear young friend; I must be going now; be sure and be on hand to-morrow; my best respects to your parents, and—and your sister, Miss Leslie."

And after another warm shake of the hand, the gentleman went down the companion-ladder and walked up into the town. And Henry, almost beside himself with joy, hastened from the vessel toward his own home.

As he entered the sitting-room, Carrie and his mother were in full consultation on the subject just then most upon their mind, which was, the conclusion they should come to as to the proposal of Mr. Folger in reference to "his little motherless child."

They both observed the unusual animation in Henry's countenance, and simultaneously exclaimed,

"Why, Henry! what is it?"

It was some time before Henry could communicate what he had to say. There was such a tumult in his mind, such a rushing together of counter feelings: joy, at the tidings he was bringing, and fear lest the project which he had indulged, and which was in such a fair way to be accomplished, might meet with decided opposition. It came all out at last, but not until he saw the tears flowing freely from the eyes that had been gazing with intense earnestness upon him.

When he had finished, the mother's heart was too full to allow her troubled thoughts to find vent in words. Alas! the tidings which that son had brought, were like death-damps to her mother's feelings. Her thoughts concerning him as a venturer in the scenes of life, had never carried him beyond her maternal watch. That he should be engaged in some useful calling, she had concluded would be proper. She now wished it. But to cut him loose, and let him drift, far, fa away on the rough ocean, and with rougher men! To brave the dangers of a foreign clime where no friend could be about him in the hour of sickness, or to whom he could go for sympathy in an hour of trouble! Her Henry, whose retiring, sensitive spirit, had never breathed its trials to any ear but hers. Alas! for that mother's heart. Let her weep, and mingle her tears with her sad sisters in our sorrowing world. Pure tokens they are of that love which knows no change, no death.

Carrie, too, could have wished for some secret chamber where she might let go the floods that were gurgling at her heart; for never had this loved one appeared to her so sweet an object of tender interest as at this moment. He had started up suddenly before her in a new and nobler character, no longer the timid, bashful, dependent boy. There was courage in his eye, and strong determination and undaunted resolution in every word and tone. She admired him, she felt a pride in looking at him, even through her tears. She dared not say a word to encourage the plan, for she knew not yet how her parents might decide, and she could not bear to damp the ardor with which she saw he was inspired. So she rose, and with the tears yet resting on her fair cheeks, laid her hand affectionately upon his shoulder, and gave him a warm sister's kiss.

"Dear Henry, how excited you are! Come, sit down, and tell us more about this business; I can hardly comprehend it."

And Henry took his seat, and related the circumstances as calmly as could be expected.

"And you say Mr. Folger first made the proposal? Did he appear to do it in a friendly way?"

"You would have thought so, had you been present, sister! I think it may be, we have done injustice in feeling and expressing ourselves as we have of that man. He seems certainly to have a great regard for our family. His manner toward me was kind as possible, and he said he had no other interest in the matter, only he thought it a fine chance for a young man. I believe he thinks me older than I am."

Mrs. Leslie now left the room in haste, to commune with her husband on a subject of such deep interest to them both.

"And do you think, Henry, that you have resolution enough to go forward in this business? Have you thought what your feelings might be, when you should find yourself cut off from intercourse with friends, a stranger in a strange land?"

"I have not tried to think much about that, sister; it will be time enough when I get there."

"Yes, but you ought to look at the thing in all its bearings; you would not wish to take a step you might regret, and throw yourself into a position that might be too painful for your feelings."

"We can not, any of us, tell exactly how we should feel under circumstances entirely new; but as I now feel, sister Carrie, and as I have felt for some time past, there is no danger I dare not face; there is no hardship I am not willing to endure; I know I am but a boy in age, although my size is almost that of a man; I feel the strength of a man, and an ardent desire to do something for myself, and, above all, for—for—"

He dared not speak the name. His feelings, manly as they might be, were too tenderly alive to those he loved, just at such a time, to speak of them as usual. Already did there seem to be the sacredness of a farewell hour about him; and the name of father or mother could only dwell in his breast.

After a moment's silence he resumed,

"I have been in a new world, Carrie, ever since the day you talked so with Charlie and me, when we returned from school. My thoughts have been turned into a new channel. Before then I had no care, no thought about the future, except, perhaps, how I was to enjoy myself, how I could spend life most pleasantly. I never felt that this hand was to do any more in life than my ancestors had done—direct others to perform my will. Now I feel that there is something better for a man to do; that there is a part for me to act, as well as others; a living, at least, to earn, if nothing more. I have a fair education, much better than many of my age. I am not afraid to venture upon it; and as for sad feelings among strangers, God can take care of me on the ocean, or in a foreign land; and, dear sister, I think I am willing to trust myself to His care."

Carrie could make no reply. The last sentiment he uttered was so utterly unexpected—it revealed to her what, above all else she wished to know, and for which she had for many months been endeavoring, in her correspondence with him, to bring out—that she could only in silence admire the wisdom and love of that Being who was thus leading one so dear to her, by a way trying, indeed, to affection, but to result in his best good in future years. *He could trust in God.*

There had, indeed, been a change in Henry—a great change—and, to use his own words, "he saw things in a new light." How it had been brought about is of little consequence. It may have been gradually working in his heart from the first dawn of reason; it may have been aided in its development by many a word of truth dropped from the sacred desk, and but little thought of at the time; or by his sister's admonitions; or by the trials of his family—none can tell, for He who makes the change worketh in secret. And Carrie's heart was full of gladness, for she believed the work had been done. The dark cloud was not all for judgment; mercy-drops were sprinkling from it; and when its heavy folds should roll over, beneath would be revealed the clearing-up streak of blue sky, and the beautiful evening-star be seen sparkling in mild splendor.

We will not take the reader through all the trying scenes attendant upon the departure of Henry Leslie from his home. That his parents gave consent can hardly be said; and yet he left with their blessing and their aid. Willingly they could not let him go; and yet they did not feel at liberty, under all the circumstances, to say aught against it.

The remark which Henry had made in reference to Mr. Folger, "that perhaps their family had been unjust in their feelings toward him," was not lost upon Mrs. Leslie or Carrie. And how could they construe his conduct toward Henry otherwise than as an act of disinterested kindness? And so, womanlike, they began to think hardly of themselves for all they had thought or said amiss, and to speak of him as one who must have some excellent qualities, and to whom they were under great obligations.

"He has not a bad countenance, either," said Mrs. Leslie to her daughter, "when one has spoken with him a few moments.

His smile is peculiarly agreeable, and his manners are certainly faultless."

"I have never seen him but once—that is, close by—and then but for a few moments; and then, you know, too, that I was strongly prejudiced against him, and that hateful state of the mind perverts every thing. I sometimes wish—yes, I mean to try and keep prejudice from having any power over me; I will not indulge it; it is a hateful passion."

"It is, indeed, Carrie, and often leads us to form very wrong conclusions, and pursue an unjust course."

"The true way for us is, 'to think no evil,' to forget injuries, and to put the best construction upon the conduct of others when their motives are to us doubtful."

"Your father, who ought certainly to be the best judge, seems to feel kindly toward Mr. Folger; and if any thing was really so much out of the way in his conduct, he would be the one to know it. I think it would be his wish that we take the child, although he will say nothing to influence us."

"Well, mother, I will not say nay."

"And I am sure, dear Carrie, if you have overcome all objections, I feel no disposition to make any. Let it be so, then, and when Mr. Folger comes here, we will endeavor to make it as agreeable to him as possible. Your father says that when he was last here, he asked so particularly after you, and spoke so frequently about you, that if he had not known how you felt toward Mr. Folger, he should have asked you into the room."

"Well, mother, you tell father, then, that we are quite ready to comply with Mr. Folger's request, and that he can bring his little girl whenever he thinks best."

And thus the way was opened for the reception of the "little motherless thing," and for what Mr. Folger thought more of—an intimacy with a family where he had long wished to be on friendly terms; and in comparison with which, *the money he had loaned, or the fate of his child, were of small account.*

It was but a very short period, therefore, after consent had been given, before the carriage of Mr. Folger was at their door, and the little orphan, holding the hand of her father, was ushered into the parlor, where Mrs. Leslie was in waiting to receive them.

Carrie entered soon after, and being introduced formally by Mrs. Leslie, was received by a most profound obeisance on the part of the gentleman, who immediately took the little Lucy by the hand, as she was standing by the side of Mrs. Leslie, and led her toward the young lady.

"I have great pleasure, Miss Leslie, in handing over to your *special* charge my little motherless child."

Carrie took the little one by the hand, and kissed her sweetly, remarking almost at the instant,

"I dare hardly venture upon the sole responsibility; mother will no doubt feel that the *chief* burden rests upon her. I will, however, do my best as an assistant."

"I leave the matter, ladies, to your own arrangement. I feel it a great personal favor, that I am permitted to leave her in the hands of those in whom I have such perfect confidence —and I hope you will find her ready to yield to your requests in every thing. You will probably find her rather backward, I fear, Miss Leslie, as a scholar."

"She is very young to expect much from her in that way; and I am myself but a novice in teaching; it is my first attempt, and I may not succeed."

"If you succeed as well, Miss Leslie, in gaining the good will and esteem of your scholars, as you have of—of those who have had the pleasure of your acquaintance, there can be no doubt of their earnest endeavor to do whatever you request."

A short time was spent in conversation on minor matters, and Mr. Folger prepared to take his leave. He called his little Lucy to him, and bade her to be a good girl, to which she made no reply, and without any apparent reluctance to part with her father, went at once back to the chair where Mrs. Leslie was sitting, and placed her hand upon the lady's lap. Carrie could not but notice the strange conduct of the child, but accounted for it from the fact that she had been away from her father, and perhaps those who had the charge of her had not been careful to encourage filial feelings. The thought could find no place in her mind that the cause could possibly be—a want of proper feeling on the part of the parent.

The interview was much less embarrassing than Carrie had anticipated, her own mind having cast out every thing of an unfriendly nature that had been harbored there; and when Mr. Folger departed, the invitation, which Mrs. Leslie, in the honesty of her heart, gave him, to call as often as convenient, to see his little daughter, was sufficient to satisfy him for all he had done, in order to bring about a result so much desired.

And now, as the father has departed, we can take a look at the little one he has left behind. *She* is not acting a part, has no sinister end in view, and although the offspring of one who has abundant means to supply her wants, and surround her with every luxury, is really an object demanding sympathy. She is a little stranger in a wide, wide world; an orphan in all, except that there is one in the world with her, who will probably feel bound, for his own credit's sake, to see that her wants are well supplied; he will treat her with kindness—merely kindness; he has never yet taken the little one to his heart; he has not yearned over her, nor watched her little motions with a father's eye; he has not spent watchful hours at night beside her bed, when the fever was upon her, and her little pulse beat quick and hard; he has never pressed her to his bosom, and called her by endearing names, and made her feel that she was all the world to him; his heart has never throbbed with joy as he heard her little feet patting toward the room where he was sitting, nor spent an idle hour in thinking of her future, and what he could do to make her life one long bright day of happiness. Such things, such thoughts, he has never indulged. There was no room in his selfish heart for aught beside his own personal enjoyment; the gratification of his own ease, and his own will. He has the father's name, and the father's power; but the strong affection, the absorbing interest, the unselfish devotion, connected with that sacred name, he knows nothing of.

The personal appearance of little Lucy was prepossessing; her form was neat, her countenance pleasing, it had even strong marks of beauty, and, but for the want of sprightliness in the eye, would have been called a very handsome child; and yet, the eye did not seem to be deficient in natural luster; it was a fine dark blue eye, but it looked not at you with that life so natural in children; there was no earnestness to it, no heart beamed from it; it gave but a glance, and then drooped or passed to other objects, as though all was alike to it.

Both Mrs. Leslie and Carrie noticed this peculiarity, and the latter spoke of it when they were alone.

"I think, mother, the child will ot be likely to give us trouble from a spirit of disobedience; but she will be one whose confidence it will be difficult to gain. She seems to be so indifferent."

"Perhaps that is owing to the fact that she may have lived among those who have been indifferent to *her*. It is a great misfortune that she has been so long away from her father. I think if he comes here often, which, for the child's sake, I hope he may, that peculiarity will wear off. We must be particular also to treat her affectionately. Love, you know, begets love, especially in children."

She is now in faithful hands, and if she has indeed a trusting heart, it will be brought out; its affections will be aroused, for she will be made to feel that she is not traveling a weary world all by herself.

CHAPTER XIII.

"AUNT EUNICE" had not been seen out of her room since the eventful evening when she gave such a loose rein to her temper, and brought upon herself the severe rebuke of Mr. Leslie.

As she was one of that class whose imperfections can not be mended by advice, or even by their own bitter experience—and as she found from the changes which had taken place in the family, that she could no longer be the controlling spirit, and if she took any part in family affairs, it must be one that required the use of her hands, rather than her tongue, she made up her mind to seek other quarters, where, if she could not rule, she might at least be free from the embarrassments likely to surround her, in a home from which, as she emphatically said, "the glory had departed." There were no horses and carriage now, which she could command at pleasure, and no servants to do her bidding. As no objections were made to her departure, and as she had the same means to provide for herself she ever possessed, Mr. and Mrs. Leslie felt they were doing no wrong by allowing her to seek an asylum elsewhere. A cloud seemed to have passed from over them when her presence was withdrawn.

The departure of Henry was a severe stroke to the sensitive mind of his father; it seemed to be a token of his fall and helpless condition that affected him more deeply than any scene he had yet passed through. This perhaps was aggravated by strong sympathy with his loving wife. She had borne the trial well, for a mother—she had allowed no outbreak of grief, on her part, and even could speak words of consolation, to the ear of her husband—but the eye of love was keen to discern between the outward semblance and the anguish that was working within. The very effort too, which Carrie made to appear cheerful, to stay up the spirits of [illegible] parents; her bright smile; her words of encouragement and love; her untiring industry—he noticed them all; his heart blessed the lovely child, and then turned in upon itself, and brooded over the past; and bitter upbraidings and torturing remorse caused him to cry out in his agony, "Alas! there is no sorrow like unto my sorrow."

A few days after the bitter scene of separation, and Henry's step was no more heard about the house, Carrie found her father seated in a room but little frequented by the family, and apparently much cast down. He at first scarcely noticed her entrance, and when he did, answered her pleasant smile, and kind address, "Are you here all alone, father?" with such a look of sadness, and such a broken hollow tone of voice, that she was seriously alarmed, although afraid to express her fears by any outward sign.

"It is the best place for me, my child; I ought always to have been alone, for I have only brought a blight upon all I love."

"Now, dear father, I will not hear you say so; you *must* not say so; can you in truth not say that each one of us, mother and all, have clung to you with a closer grasp, ever since your trial? Have we not, father? Can you, do you doubt that we love you with a true and most tender love?"

"No, no, my child, I doubt not that you all love me. You are continually manifesting your faithfulness and affection, all of you. But, oh! you can not tell how every token of it pains my heart. Why should it not? I can not shut my eyes against the truth. I can not forget that my own imprudence, my own want of management, has brought all this suffering on my family."

"But, dear father, we are not suffering, we are not unhappy—only when we see the marks of sorrow on your face."

"Ah, my child! do you think I can forget, ever forget what I witnessed when that dear boy tore himself from us. Did I not see the agony that wrung your mother's heart as she clasped him in her arms and gave him her parting kiss—and but for me she might have been spared all that; and every tear you all shed was caused by *my* misconduct. And when that dear boy turned, and cast a look, the last one, toward us, as we all stood and watched his departure, do you think I can ever forget it—he seemed to say, "Father, for your account I suffer this!"

Carrie had borne up nobly under every trial hitherto—doubtless it had often required the whole strength of her physical and mental powers, and by the effort the former had become insensibly weakened. The point was reached at last where she could resist no longer. She threw herself upon her father's neck, and wept aloud. Alarmed at an outbreak so unusual, the father began to feel that he had been again grievously erring by having allowed so much expression to his inward trials. It was not manly, he knew it was not, and at once resolved within himself that it should be thus no more; and then he attempted to allay the storm. He used soothing words, and even words of encouragement; but they only seemed to increase the violence of her grief. At length as though all command of her spirit had been broken, she cried out with a loud and bitter wail—

"Oh my father! my father! my father! oh father! father!"

He saw that under the power of intense feeling, she was losing command of her limbs, as well as her consciousness. He caught her in his arms; he spoke kindly, beseechingly to her, but she made no reply, beyond that bitter wail, in which his name rang like the knell of death, around the room, and through the house.

As he bore her through the hall, the family, aroused by the outcry, rushed to the scene. And as he laid her on the bed in an adjoining room, he could only reply to the agonizing inquiry of the mother—

"That he knew not why it was; only he feared he had said something which had overcome her reason."

All the expedients which could be thought of, were immediately resorted to, but with little avail. She answered no questions, nor heeded all her mother's fondest epithets; but lay and sobbed out in fainter, and fainter accents, that beloved name, until all power of articulation and sense of external objects seemed to have departed.

The physician was at once sent for, and reached the scene of suffering with as little delay as possible. He was a kind-hearted man, of much experience, and a friend of the family. Mr. Leslie revealed to him, as correctly as he could, what had transpired, and watched with intense interest the doctor's countenance, as it changed from its naturally bland and smiling expression to that of stern thoughtfulness. He followed him to the bed-side. Alas! for the doings of one short hour. No smile met him as he fixed his eye in sad dismay upon that lovely face; her cheek was pale, the eye partly closed had no brightness; all consciousness appeared to have departed; her breathing was faint and short, and her pulse fitful.

Long and patiently the doctor watched every symptom, and at length left the room, beckoning Mr. Leslie after him. He took off his outer garment, and requested that his horse might be sent home, and his family informed that they must not expect him that night.

"I dare not leave her, Mr. Leslie; we must watch her closely."

"What can it be, doctor? what do you fear?"

"Oh, well, my dear sir, we must hope for the best. But she must have the most delicate attention—over-excitement, sir! the whole nervous system has in some way got out of gear."

"Can not you give her something at once, doctor? something that might restore her; she wants bracing up; she is very weak. Is she unconscious?"

"Not entirely, sir; but we must watch, and trust some to nature; we might do too much, just at this juncture. She must be kept, if possible, in perfect repose. I should advise you and Mrs. Leslie to exclude yourselves from the room; Luckie and I can do all that is needed, and let the most complete silence be observed in the house; any sudden alarm would be bad; we must endeavor to prevent any renewal of excitement: the consequences might be very unhappy. We must do what we can, my dear sir, and hope for the best."

The doctor immediately made all arrangements for the night, and the house was soon hushed to the stillness of death.

Mrs. Leslie retired to her room, and the husband and father was left alone; alone—except as busy thought surrounded him with visions too sadly real to be thrust aside as creations of the mind may sometimes be. An almighty hand seemed to be upon him, holding him in firm embrace; and now in his silent chamber bidding him to look with naked eye upon his true condition. And the past came up before him: all its scenes, with that most heart-rending of them all, the experience of the last few hours. The present, too, all hushed in silence. This lovely daughter lying on the verge of madness or of death; and a breathless house, waiting in fearful anxiety what each coming hour might reveal. It was more than he could bear. He tried to hush his thoughts, arose from his seat, and took the Bible. It lay on the stand where it had been used at the morning devotions, for this duty he had begun to perform. He had always reverenced the word of God, but he had never delighted in it. He had not studied it to find out God or his duty to Him. It had never been his counselor, his friend in the hour of adversity, from whose promises his soul had derived comfort and strength. To him it had only been a holy book—there was an awe about it that chilled, but did not attract; it was only associated in his mind with the dark things of life—with the dying bed—the funeral—and the grave.

He opened the sacred book, and without design turned to the twenty-seventh Psalm, and he read:

"The Lord is my light and my salvation, whom shall I fear? The Lord is the strength of my life, of whom shall I be afraid?"

He could not say this, but the writer of that psalm could; a human being like himself; a man in trouble filling his heart with encouraging thoughts, because Jehovah was his friend.

What would *he* not give for such a friend! to be able to sing such a song in this *his* hour of distress.

And then he read on, and paused again at the fifth verse.

"For in the time of trouble He shall hide me in His pavilion. In the secret of His tabernacle shall He hide me. He shall set me up upon a rock."

"What firm trust! what a safe hiding-place! what an everlasting foundation must the righteous have—can there be such a resting-place for my poor troubled heart?"

And as he thought, he turned over the sacred leaves, his mind apparently searching for some resting spot, some ray of hope—his eye fell upon the thirty-second psalm:

"Blessed is he whose transgression is forgiven, whose sin is covered! Blessed is the man unto whom the Lord imputeth not iniquity. When I kept silence, my bones waxed old through my roaring; for day and night thy hand was heavy upon me.

"I acknowledged my transgression unto Thee, and mine

iniquity have I not hid. I said, I will confess my transgressions unto the Lord, and Thou forgavest the iniquity of my sin."

Here, then, the great secret was revealed; the man whose trust was as a rock beneath his feet, whose hope was a strong pavilion round about him, was he who had acknowledged his transgressions unto the Lord, and to whom the scepter of mercy had been held out!

And why should not *he* do as that poor sinner had done? But what assurance was there that the same mercy would be shown in his case? He had so long refused to pray, so long shut the Lord out of his thoughts; and then there came into his mind a passage of Scripture which had been read by his dear Carrie that very morning, and with a trembling heart he turned to it, for it brought back thoughts of her. Carrie, he had noticed, always selected the very sayings of Christ himself. It was some time before he could find it. He was now like the man searching for hidden treasure. He was in earnest; page after page he turned, and many precious sayings met his eye, but they were not those which he had heard from the lips of his dear Carrie. At length they are before him. How glorious they seemed, just suited to his case.

"I am the bread of life. He that cometh to me shall never hunger, and he that believeth on me shall never thirst.

"All that the Father giveth me shall come to me; *and him that cometh to me, I will in no wise cast out.*"

Again and again he repeated that last precious sentence, the richest words that ever fell upon a sinner's ear—"In no wise—in no wise cast out." "Him that cometh to me I will in no wise cast out."

"It is enough! yes, come life, come death, come what may! from this hour my soul shall rest on the arm of my Redeemer. Sinner as I have been and am now, I cling to Thy cross. I rest on Thy love—Lord save me!"

To say that his mind was at once filled with that sweet peace and holy joy which many at such a time are conscious of, would not, perhaps, be saying the truth. He had, indeed, found rest; and that, to his tempest-tossed spirit was great relief. He could now sit calmly and review the past—not with remorse, but with a penitent and contrite heart—and he could resolve for the future, not indeed as the strong man conscious of his own power, but as one who has found a helper, by whose side he can walk, and on whose care he can repose.

The hours of the night passed without his taking note of them, and the day was breaking ere he was aware. The door of his room was gently opened, and the faithful physician with noiseless step entered and took his hand.

"She sleeps—she sleeps quite sweetly; her pulse is more regular, and her breathing less hurried; a few hours' repose, undisturbed quiet, I hope will prove greatly beneficial. But let there be no intrusion; keep the house still; nature will do the needful work, I think."

And noiseless as the night had been, passed the hours of the day, until the noon had come—the watchful doctor still sitting by her side, and the anxious parents encouraging each other as every hour passed, "that it was favorable she slept so long."

As the clock struck twelve the door of the parlor was again opened, and the doctor beckoned to Mrs. Leslie, and she followed him. In a short time she returned; her eyes were wet with tears.

"Horatio, dear, Carrie wishes to see you."

Not daring to ask how she was, but apprehending the worst, he immediately repaired to the chamber where his dear Carrie lay.

As he opened the door he met the glance of her bright eye; and as he came up to the bed-side, a sweet smile, the smile he loved so well, lightened her pale features.

He stooped over, and she put her arms about his neck, and pressed his face to hers.

"Dear father, I feel greatly refreshed."

He could not reply; his heart was too full of joy and gratitude. In a few moments he turned to the smiling doctor,

"Will conversation injure her, doctor?"

"Oh, no, sir; not now."

Again he leaned over and whispered a few words which none but herself could hear. She took his hand and pressed it to her lips.

"The Lord be praised for his mercies! The happiest moment of my life is this, dear father."

Not wishing to increase her excitement, the father soon retired, and no one remained in the room but Aunt Luckie.

8

"Aunt Luckie," said Carrie, "I have news to tell you—good news; I know it will make your heart leap for joy."

And Luckie came up close beside the bed, her hands folded together, and fixed her calm placid look on the speaker.

"You saw my father whisper to me a short time since?"

"I did, my darling; and I heard you say, 'Praise the Lord;' I knew it must be something good; but do tell me!"

"I will, Aunt Luckie. My dear father has come to the light at last; I trust he is a new creature in Christ Jesus."

Luckie raised her clasped hands to her breast. She was silent, and seemed lost in wonder and surprise; and then the tears began to fall, and she took a seat by the bed-side. Carrie did not look at her; she knew the white apron was up, and so she said nothing, but permitted the good woman to indulge her feelings in the way most natural for her.

After Luckie had thus remained for some time, she at length broke the silence.

"And now you see, my child, it is true what I told you all at the first; when your father was so cast down, and seemed to feel that the frown of the Almighty was upon him, and that there was a blast and a blight upon him and his, I told him then, that it was not a blast; it was a heavy trial, but a blessing would come out of it; and now you see it; only to think what has come about!—first, that your father should have started family prayers, a thing that has never been done in this house since it has been a house. I know, indeed, it was n't just as if he prayed himself, because he read from a book; but to my mind it was a great thing, and a very hard thing for his mind to do it."

"It was, indeed, Aunt Luckie, a very severe task; but I do believe he joined sincerely in the worship, for he has always had great reverence for sacred things; he never would trifle with holy words."

"No, no, not he; but as I was saying, that was the first start, and then I felt more sure than ever that there was a blessing to come, sooner or later; only to think! to have us all together, morning and evening, and you a reading from the Bible, and then all a bowing down together; I do n't care if he does read from a book, it does n't hinder none of us from joining in it. But, as I was saying, that was the first start; and then only think what came next! why, Miss Carrie, I could hardly believe my own ears to hear that dear boy, that's gone from us now, talk as he did, and so still as he has always been, and keeping his feelings to himself; depend on it, Henry has got the 'root of the matter in him.'"

"I hope so, Aunt Luckie."

"And now, this last thing! only to think of it! Oh, let us praise the Lord for His mercies! 'God has lured him into the wilderness.'"

"What do you mean by that, Aunt Luckie?"

"Why you know, dear, how it says, 'I will lure him into the wilderness, and speak comfortably unto him, and give him vineyards and oliveyards from thence.'"

"Where is that passage, Aunt Luckie?"

"Well, I can't tell you exactly the chapter and verse, but it is in 'Hosea' somewhere; but it always seems to me a most precious text."

"What do you understand by it, Aunt Luckie?"

"Why, it seems to me the meaning is very plain. When God designs mercy to some, there ain't no way but first to take 'em into the wilderness; you know the Jews looked to the wilderness as a terrible place; they had a deal of trouble and vexation there; you know it was a scorching hot, dreary kind of a place, all rocks, and sand, and desolation, full of fiery serpents, and all such critters, and plagues, and airthquakes, and flies, and but poor living at the best; they had a hard time on it, you know, all the forty years; and most on 'em died there; and they never forgot it. So to take one into the wilderness, seems to me, means to bring 'em into trouble, and sorrow, and distress. Well, what is it done for? Only just think of it! It ain't to kill 'em, or to worry 'em on purpose, but to give 'em comfort there—'to give 'em vineyards from thence;' that is, I suppose, the trouble is brought on to make us mend our ways and do right, and then out of that very trouble to give us peace and all good things. And now only to see; ain't God a speaking comfortably to this family; and may-be he will do a great many more things for 'em, and make you all a great deal happier than you've ever been before."

"I wish you would hand me my Bible, Aunt Luckie; I want to find that passage: I have never noticed it before."

"Oh dear, no! no! now, you won't be a doing any such a

thing! just you keep quiet now, dear; I've let you talk too much, a ready, and may be I've talked too much to you. Wait till you get a little stronger, or may be, when you've had another nap, then we'll find it; it won't get out of the way I'll warrant; it's there, somewhere in 'Hosea,' I know it is."

Repose, and the devoted attention of loving friends, soon accomplished the work of restoration, and when Carrie was able again to be employed in the round of duties she had taken upon her, she could not but admire the dealings of her kind and gracious Father. She had been "in the depths" only to have given her fresh tokens of eternal love.

Mr. Folger had not forgotten what he had said to Mr. Leslie about employment abroad. It would have suited his views very well could a twelvemonths' voyage have been procured for the father, as he had been enabled to do for the son. But as probably no such chance presented itself, he accomplished an end nearly as desirable, that is, as the reader will soon see, assisted him to a situation where he could do but little toward helping his family, be out of the way from all interfering with Mr. Folger's private views, and not be very likely to free himself from the bonds by which he was then held. It was not long after the scenes we have just described had taken place, when Mr. Folger made known to Mr. Leslie that an opening had presented for a situation in the city of New York. He could not state precisely the nature of the duties required of him; and Mr. Leslie suggested his fear that he might not be able to fill the station suitably, and meet the wishes of his employer.

"There need be no apprehension on that score, my dear sir, for I informed my friend that you had never been accustomed to business, and also told him what I knew of your qualifications; you need be under no apprehensions on that score, sir; my friend has a large establishment; he is engaged in the printing and publishing business. I mentioned your case to him, and asked, as a particular favor to me, that he would if possible find a place that you might be able to fill; and it has so happened that death has made a vacancy lately. The salary is not large, but as your board will of course be given in, I have thought that probably it might be an object to you, although if you have any other place in view, or know of any thing better, of course you are not under any obligations to accept this. But five hundred dollars a year might be to you, just now, better than nothing."

Five hundred dollars a year, just then, was indeed a very desirable acquisition to Mr. Leslie. It would enable him, with his reduced expenses, barely to live, and that was a great consideration, for his means were now very small indeed, and how they were to be replenished he knew not! Another consideration had great weight with him, and that was the fact that he would be in a situation to earn, by his own efforts, a support for his family. He wanted *once* to feel that his loved ones were eating the bread provided by his own labor.

He therefore accepted the proposal, with many thanks to Mr. Folger for his trouble in procuring the situation for him.

"I am entitled to no thanks, my dear sir, and am only too happy if you feel that the little I have endeavored to do is acceptable to you, and I will furthermore add that as both yourself and elder son are to be away from home, I hold myself in readiness to be called upon for any service your family may need, and that I can render." (Mr. Folger had fallen into the mistake, which strangers to the family always made, of supposing Henry to be the eldest son. He was indeed much taller, and had a much older look than his twin brother Charles.) "And now I think of it, Mr. Leslie, allow me to hand you a hundred dollars in advance for the board of my child; you can give it to Mrs. Leslie yourself. I should have done so but from motives of delicacy."

This new expression of Mr. Folger's fine feelings was received by Mr. Leslie, and of course by his family, as a token which could not be mistaken. He was a *friend* and *gentleman*.

Although the prospect of earning a bare support for his family was in itself pleasing, even under the trial of a separation from them, yet there were other circumstances connected with his affairs that weighed at times heavily upon him. A large debt was hanging over him, the interest upon which was daily accumulating. The home which sheltered his wife and children was pledged for its security; at any time it might be taken, and they and he cast upon the world without a refuge. The man, in whose power he was, had indeed of late evinced much kindness and feeling; yet it could not be expected that interest would be allowed to accumulate beyond the value of the estate; the time must come when it would be wholly absorbed. But he was helpless now, either to reduce the debt, or pay the interest; he could only do for the present "what his hands found to do," and leave the future with Him to whom he had endeavored to commit every interest.

CHAPTER XIV.

Charles Leslie had entered upon his duties as assistant to Mr. Samuel Thompson, with all the zeal so natural to a boy in any new undertaking.

His first business was to get things into some shape, so that he could be able to tell "which was which."

And it was no trifling matter for one with so little experience to do that; for a more jumbled mess of all sorts of things could scarcely have been mingled together, if they had been whirled into the place by some catastrophe of nature. The building itself was very respectable in appearance: a substantial stone edifice of one story in height with the gable end to the street, and a small projection from the roof in front, to which hung a pulley, doubtless designed for the purpose of hoisting heavy articles from the ground into the store; but either the ground had been elevated or the store lowered, since that contrivance had been attached, as there seemed to be no possible need for any such extra help in getting articles into the store, that could pass through the doorway, as it was nearly even with the ground.

Every thing externally, too, was in good order, that is, sound and strong; and for this, Mr. Thompson was noted. His dwelling, barns, etc., although of a plain fashion, were kept snug and tight, and presented the appearance of having a thrifty owner.

As you entered the store, a space presented itself before you of some twelve or fifteen feet of open country, within which were generally two or three chairs, one of them a large smooth-bottomed arm-chair, which Mr. Thompson always appropriated to himself, and which he never left without apparent reluctance.

One side of this space ran a counter of fair dimensions, with two or three pairs of scales hanging over it, and in general quite a variety of articles lying about on it, which seemed to have no special business there, except it might be that there was no other place for them.

On the other side of this space lay crowded in beautiful confusion, boxes, crates, hogsheads, barrels, bales, baskets, and kegs; and on the top of some of these were demijohns, jugs, bottles, wooden bowls, and large earthen milk-pans; while back of them all, upon a shelf, which seemed perfectly inaccessible, was arrayed quite an assortment of crockery ware, covered with dust and cobwebs; and on the three pillars which supported the ceiling, hung chains, ropes, ox-bows, brooms, hoe-handles, and heavy cowhide boots, with a few bunches of muffin-rings.

These are mentioned as mere samples: an invoice would not be credited. It was indeed a variety store and variously disposed. How Mr. Thompson managed to get at the articles thus quartered, would be incredible to one who might cast his eye over the place for the first time; but somehow he contrived to do the thing, by keeping various openings and stepping-places, through which he appeared without much difficulty to lay hands on what he wished.

Charles had been anxious from the first to have things differently arranged, and once or twice had hinted as much to his employer. The old gentleman, however, would merely give a glance at things without making any remark. He probably thought it would involve a longer absence from his arm-chair than might be agreeable.

Happily, however, for the accomplishment of Charlie's wishes, an assistant was at hand, who entered into his views, and stood ready to give efficient aid in putting a new face on that magazine of confusion, the store of Mr. Samuel Thompson.

There had been now for some time at Princesport, a young man who had come there ostensibly for recreation, and the benefit of sea-air. He had taken board at the house of a plain couple, who occupied a small but comfortable tenement near the water. He had furnished his own room and in a very neat style, and proposed to pay for his board the same price which was asked at the best hotel in the place, with the stipulation that the old people should treat him with the same fare to which they had been accustomed; his object being, he said, to change his manner of living, and have the full benefit of it, both as to air and diet. His manners were quite unobtrusive; he accommodated himself to the habits of the old people, was sure to be in at meal time, and never absented himself in the evening later than nine o'clock. He had purchased for himself a boat which he could use either with sail or oar, as suited the occasion; which, together with a fine double-barrel gun, afforded alternate recreation on the water or through the fields and woods. He had books in plenty, too, with which on stormy days he appeared to spend the time quite contentedly.

That he was a true gentleman, the old folks, Mr. and Mrs. Conway, felt fully assured. "He never showed off any airs," they said, "nor put on any condescending ways, nor talked about what he'd been used to, and all that."

The only thing that he was particular about, and as Mrs. Conway, said "notional," was, "that his linen should be very white, and very nicely plaited, and so long as he was willing to pay the very highest price to have it done, she did n't see but he had a right to *be* notional."

The quality, she said, "was the finest that her eyes had ever looked at, and had ought to be well done up."

His dress otherwise was not remarkable, except that whatever he wore seemed to fit him perfectly; whether it was his fishing suit, or hunting suit, or, as the old lady called it, his "Sunday suit," which, by the way, was scarcely to be distinguished from that he usually wore when not engaged in one or other of his sports.

His personal appearance would not have attracted any special attention from those who merely saw him pass their dwellings, except it might have been the manly proportions of his frame, and his easy, elastic step. But those who might converse with him for even a short time, could not help noticing the fine finish of his features, his fair open forehead, with his dark hair thrown carelessly from it; the bright eye that looked so clearly out upon the world, as though he had nothing to fear, or to conceal; the well-set nose and mouth, and the white, wholesome-looking teeth, which an occasional pleasant smile slightly displayed.

But he had given only rare opportunities for any in Princesport to take special notice of him in this way. He had not indeed shunned society, nor did there seem to be any thing of the recluse or ascetic in his habits. But coming without introduction into a strange place, and knowing that the better society there was rather exclusive and disposed to be particular on points of etiquette, he had not cared to thrust himself into notice, and seemed to feel at no loss for the occupation of his time.

As the wharf to which his boat was moored lay opposite the store of Mr. Thompson, he had asked the privilege of placing his oars in a small adjoining shed, that he might be sure they would be on hand when he needed them.

The pleasant manner of the young man, forbade Mr. Thompson to say no, if he had been accustomed to the use of that monosyllable, and the very pleasant manner in which he granted the request attracted the attention of the stranger, and he would occasionally, as he saw the old gentleman at leisure, step in, and have a social chat with him. This by degrees had become, at the time Charles entered Mr. Thompson's store, almost a daily event, and the old gentleman used to look for his visitor as regularly as he did for old "aunt Rutia's" snuff-box, which came every day, Sundays excepted, at about five o'clock in the afternoon.

Mr. Thompson had not the curiosity, so natural to our good folks further east, or he would doubtless have found out all that there was to know, about his young visitor, for there seemed to be no disposition on the part of the latter to conceal any thing. But Mr. Thompson was rather disposed to mind his own affairs, and let his neighbors mind theirs. He knew nothing further about his visitor than his own observation assured him of, and that was, as he said to Charles one day,

"He 's a right down clever young fellow; and he knows manners—he is no upstart, depend on it. He 's been brought up where folks know what 's what."

Not even the name did Mr. Thompson get correctly, for when the young man one day, at his request, gave it to him, either it was not spoken very plainly, or the ear of the old gentleman was in fault. But to him it sounded like Boylston, and Boylston, he called him ever after, and perhaps the young man thought the mistake not worth correcting, as no doubt he and Mr. Thompson would be to each other merely as travelers who have met upon the road, after a short conversation to separate for different and distant homes.

Charlie, influenced by the opinion of Mr. Thompson, or more probably by the kind manner of the young man to himself, was very attentive and polite in return, and there had sprang up quite an intimacy between them; and upon the subject of making a reformation in the arrangement of things, had entered heartily into Charlie's views; and offered, whenever he could get Mr. Thompson's permission, that he would assist him in the operation. A favorable opportunity soon presented for accomplishing the object, from a circumstance which seldom occurred. Mr. Thompson had some business abroad which would call him away for a whole day. He had foreseen it, and talked about it, and delayed the matter as long as he could; but go he must, there was no help for it.

On the morning of his departure, and while the old mare was standing before the door, harnessed to the yellow gig, Mr. Thompson lingered still about the store, as though loth to depart, giving directions to Charlie, and cautioning him against trusting certain individuals, whose bills had become quite ancient, and from whom he had little hopes of pay.

"Then if the Potters come for any thing to day, Mr. Thompson, I must say we can not let them have it?"

"No, tell 'em they sha'n't have a paper of tobacco, unless they pay some of their account. It's been a runnin' up now ever so long, and it's send, send, send, and no end to it. They had n't ought to be trusted no more, that 's certain." And the old gentleman upon saying this took his seat. "I s'pose they are poor, though! It's plaguey hard if they should send for a little meal, or molasses, or tea, or sugar, or such like for the family, not to let them have it, ain't it?"

"Just as you say, Mr. Thompson; I shall tell them what your orders are."

Mr. Thompson had to take his hat off, and smooth back his hair, and move his big chair from one side of the narrow space to the other, as though he was troubled to get things to his mind.

"And I must say the same to Mr. Rice's family, must I Mr. Thompson? You said the other day to me, that we ought not to trust them any more."

"That Rice is a bad fellow, a drinking ugly fellow, and he'll never pay a cent, if he can help it. No—*don't let him have a thing.* I may as well stop first as last · don't let him have a thing."

"Very well, sir; I shall do as you say."

"But I'm a thinking about the Potters. May-be, if they want a little flour, or tea, or sugar—may-be, Charlie, you' better just say nothin' about it. They owe so much a'ready—why, a little more won't make much odds, any how, one way or another; may-be you'd better hush up, just hush up, and I'll see Potter soon, and talk with him; they're poor, I know they are. And then, may-be, if Mrs. Rice should send her little gal for some little thing they're a wanting—why you see the mother's as nice a critter as ever lived—if she had n't got such a—such a consarned bad fellow for a husband. It ain't her fault they're so poor; just hush up, and let them have it. Oh dear! what a pity it is there is so many good for nothin' vagabonds that have got nice women for their wives. But it ain't the wives' fault—I guess you'd better upon the whole, sonny, just let things go as we commonly do."

And then Mr. Thompson made another start, and seemed to be fairly on his way, when Charlie arrested him, by another question.

"Will you have any objections, Mr. Thompson, to let me fix up things a little to-day, if I get time? Mr. Boylston says he will help me to clear out, and put things in order a little, if you will allow it to be done."

"Put things in order! Why, bless my soul, child, ain't you got things a'ready all as nice as a new pin! Ain't they been all cleared up, ever since you've been here? Ain't them scales all scoured bright? and that counter dusted clean? Why it used to be thick, all over it, with tea, and sugar, and starch, and snuff, and molasses, all mixed up together. Now look at it; there ain't no scales in town as bright as them. What upon earth, child, do you want more?"

"Well, sir, I thought, if you would be willing; just to arrange things a little, outside the counter, among the boxes and barrels there: I might make it all look more snug, and perhaps we could get at things a little better."

"Yes, well, that's true; may-be you might; you're a thinking, may-be, about the sugar hogshead (Mr. Thompson, had, a few days previous, been betrayed into one by stepping on its head, and was very unceremoniously let down to the bottom); that was a bad go, I know it was; I thought it was clean over with me then; but I'm so afeerd if you once git a moving things, you 'll never find the end on 'em, and I sha'n't never be able to tell where nothin' is. Howsomever, you say Mr. Boylston is goin' to help you: it's clever in him, ain't it? Well, well, sonny, you and he manage it somehow; only see and don't hurt yourself; and then remember and hush up about what I said about Rice and Potter—jist let things go on pretty much as they have done till I git back, and then I 'll try and git out of them what I can."

And having satisfied his scruples about the Rices and Potters, the old man got into his gig, and jogged along on his journey.

Charlie and his friend had indeed a very busy day of it, and were obliged to call in some extra help, when removing the heavier articles.

All the empty boxes, barrels, and hogsheads were cleared out of their long resting-places, and stowed away in the adjoining shed; while those that were still needed were so arranged as to take up no more room than their dimensions required. Articles of a like character were placed side by side, and a new face put upon old things, by rubbing and dusting. A clear space was opened, nearly the whole length of the store, and all the articles for sale could be approached with perfect ease without squeezing, or climbing. The windows were washed, the barrel-covers and counter scrubbed, and the floor mopped—for this, however, Charles procured extra help in the person of an old colored woman, living near at hand. And to finish the whole, the floor, which had certain spots upon it, not to be removed by a mop, was well covered with a thick sprinkling of white sea-sand; and when all was completed the store of Mr. Samuel Thompson would not have suffered in a comparison with any in the place.

"And now," said Charles, "if I could only get Mr. Thompson to let me keep a set of books, I would try to get some one to teach me book-keeping, and I would have every thing as straight and snug as the best of them."

"I think, Master Charles, when Mr. Thompson sees what a pleasant change has been made in his store by complying with your wishes, he will not object to any reasonable request you may make. And as to book-keeping, if you desire to learn the art, I think I can give you all the instruction you need."

"Oh, can you? will you? I would sit up at nights, if I could learn!"

"And I think if you say to Mr. Thompson that I am teaching you the principles, and it would be a great help to you to be enabled to carry them out in practice, you would find him very willing to comply. He is sensible that you have not quite the advantages you need to fit you to be a merchant."

Charles had worked hard that day, and, under ordinary circumstances, would have felt very much fatigued. But when the mind is elastic, and its energies excited, the body is forgotten. Charlie was a boy of thought and feeling, as well as action. He had entered deeply, young as he was, into all the trials of his family; he had wept in secret when he thought of the sad privations his father had been compelled to undergo; when he recalled the fond grasp of his hand, as he bade the long adieu; of Henry, far off on the ocean, bound to a foreign land, where none but strangers were to be his companions; of his dear Carrie, traveling day by day to her humble occupation, and already losing the bloom from her cheek in her toil and confinement, and he longed to be a man, to be acquainted with business, to take his place with those who were struggling in the busy world. How he would work! How saving he would be of every dollar he earned! How glorious would it be then, when he should be able, by his own honest industry, to pour into their laps a fulness that would place them above the fear of want! And even in his fond imaginings, how he would redeem the old homestead, and all its fair lands, and see his kind dear father again its owner and enjoying the bliss of freedom from debt, and the proud consciousness that it had been preserved by the efforts and love of his own son.

And now the first step was taken: he was earning something; above all he was about to learn something that would place him in the ranks of usefulness. And how could he think of being tired! Work was only a pastime.

"I suppose, Master Charles, you will hardly feel like taking a lesson this evening. You have done enough to-day."

"I am not in the least tired, sir, but I think you must be."

"Oh, it will be no labor for me; you know my part will be rather easy So if you feel like it, come to my room after supper, and we will make a beginning."

That night, as Charles returned home after the labors of the day and evening had passed, and he beheld the lights in his old home glistening through the thick foliage which surrounded it, he almost felt as if it had already been cleared from the bonds by which a stranger held it. "It shall be, yet," he said, "if energy and economy can do it."

"Oh Carrie, dear, what do you think!" Charles was so out of breath, as he entered the room where his sister was sitting alone by the table engaged in sewing, that he could say no more.

"What is it Charlie? Have you been frightened, that you have made such haste?"

"Oh, no! but what do you think! I've seen your likeness!"

Carrie was not troubled with superstitious feelings, but the color brightened a little on her cheek. She saw such unusual excitement in the countenance of her brother, that her first thought was, that he supposed he had seen something resembling her in his walk home. But that thought at once flew away, it was only a momentary flash.

"What makes you think so, Charlie?"

"I don't think so, *I know* it! I've seen your likeness! just as you used to look when you came home from school. I can remember exactly how you used to look; you know your hair was lighter than it is now, and it used to hang all in curls about your neck, and your cheeks used to be so red, and you had always such a bright laughing look, only when you was a little serious, and then your lip used to curl up so."

Carrie looked earnestly at her brother without as yet being at all able to comprehend the matter. She could not keep back a smile, however, at the very particular manner in which he described her appearance; or perhaps it was at the idea that he could so distinctly remember how she had looked some years ago.

"Your imagination has been playing you a trick, Charlie. But tell me where you saw the wonderful picture, and who has got it."

"Well, I must begin at the beginning, sister, you see: do you know I have begun to learn book-keeping?"

Carrie could not refrain from a hearty laugh.

"It's true, sister Carrie! You may laugh; I like to see you laugh: it seems so like old times. But it's true, I've begun to learn book-keeping."

"And what has that to do with the picture, pray?"

"A great deal, if you will only wait, just to hear me."

"Well, tell your story, I will listen patiently."

"Well, you see, I've been busy all day, Mr. Boylston and I, fixing up the store: now you're going to laugh again."

"No, no, go on."

"You don't know how nice we've made it look. Well, when we had finished, I happened to say something about book-keeping, and how I should like to learn it, and what do you think? Mr. Boylston says right away, 'I can teach you, Charles, and if you will come to my room this evening, we will begin.' Wasn't I glad, though! So after supper, off I started. But what a nice place he's got! Every thing in the room is as neat as wax. The furniture is nice and new; and he's got ever so many books, and a table in the middle of the room, with a beautiful cover on it, and every thing. Well, when I went in, he was busy writing, and getting things ready to give me a lesson; so I sat down by the table, and there was a book lying upon the table, full of drawings, and I suppose he saw me looking towards it, and so he said, 'Are you fond of pictures?' I said I was. 'You can amuse yourself a little then until I get ready for you,' and he pushed the book toward me, saying, 'They are some sketches I have taken of different places.' And, oh, you don't know how beautifully he draws! Well, as I turned over the leaves, all at once I came across a loose leaf, and as I turned it over there was a likeness of a young girl. I knew the moment I cast my eye upon it, it was somebody I knew, and then in a minute more I knew who it was, and without thinking, I said,

"'Oh my!' He stopped right away and looked at me, and then when he saw what I was looking at, he turned as red as any thing: you know he looks pale in general."

"I have never seen him?"

"Have n't you? Well, he's seen you then; but just let me tell. 'What is it, Charles?' said he. 'This picture,' I said, 'looks so much like my sister.'"

"Why Charlie, my dear brother, why did you say so?"

"Well it was just what I thought, sister Carrie; and I spoke right out, without reflecting whether it was proper or not. Then he remarked, 'Not as your sister looks now, does it?' 'As she used to look,' I said, and then he took it up, and looked steadily at it awhile, and oh, you don't know how seri ous he looked, and then he took it, and placed it a neat case, which laid in his desk, and then locked it up. 'I did not know,' he said, 'that it was among those sketches. It is the likeness of a good friend I met with years ago,' and then he sighed, and went to writing again. But no one will make me believe it is not your likeness, sister Carrie."

"It is probably a sketch, as he said, of some young person, perhaps a relation of his, and your fancy has imagined that it looks as I once did; there is nothing strange about it, Charlie."

"Well, I think it is strange, but only to think, sister Carrie. We have been calling him Boylston all the time, his name ain't Boylston."

"What is it, then, Charlie?"

"Why, it is Ralston."

"Ralston?"

"Why, you see I have often noticed that when I called his name, he would sometimes smile; and I could n't think what to make of it. But what ails you, sister Carrie, you are not well?"

Carrie had suddenly dropped her work, and sat with her head resting on her hand, looking with unwonted earnestness at her brother, and was quite pale.

"Nothing, Charlie—go on with your story—I wish to hear the end of it."

"Well, as I was saying, he sometimes looked strangely when I called his name; I began to think I had got it wrong; you see I heard Mr. Thompson call him so. But to-night I have found out all about it. You see, when I had looked through that book, and shut it up, I saw a name on the back of it, and looked, and saw that it was C. Ralston. I then looked at him, and he gave me one of those same smiling looks: 'You have found it out, have you?' said he. 'Is that your name?' I said to him. 'Yes, Charlie; I believe it must be a very uncommon one here, for I told Mr. Thompson, on two several occasions as plainly as I could speak, but the next day, he called me Boylston again, so I thought I would let it go.' I told him *I* should not forget it, for I liked Ralston a great deal better: I think it is a fine name. 'I hope,' said he, 'you may make the name of Leslie a much greater one; I have no reason to be very proud of mine. But let us both try, Charlie that our name gets no stain through our means: a "good name is rather to be chosen than precious ointment,"' and he said a good many other things. I do almost love him, he is so kind, and so gentlemanly, and I know he is *good* too."

"He is certainly very obliging and kind to you; you have great reason to speak well of him; but I would not say any thing further to him about that picture—that it resembles me —nor would I say any thing to any one else."

"Oh, dear me, now that makes me think; I am so sorry I said any thing to you about it, but I guess he won't care."

"Why, what is it, Charlie?"

"Oh, nothing, only after, you know, I told you, he looked at it so, and then went and put it away so carefully, he said to me, just as he sat down again, 'Perhaps you had better say nothing to your sister about this: she may think strangely of it?"

"Did he say that?"

"Yes, and I am sorry, but you will not speak of it, sister."

"Never, Charlie! but you ought to have been more particular; and now I think it is your bed-time, is it not?"

"It is, I suppose, but I don't feel the least sleepy; but good night, and don't you sit up and work so: you work hard enough all day in that school."

Six years have passed, since Carrie Leslie and Clarence Ralston had been strangely thrown together, spent a few pleasant hours in company with each other, and then as strangely and suddenly separated, apparently to meet no more. These six years have determined their characters, have carried them from amid the playful fancies and bright sparkles of that sunny period of life, where care has but light hold of the heart, and sorrow makes no lasting marks, into the full reality of all there is to do, to enjoy, to suffer, on this busy stage. It can hardly be supposed that Carrie yet retained the feelings which might have been excited during the short and peculiar interviews with Clarence Ralston years ago. At times, indeed, she may have looked back to the period, as one of the sunny spots in her past life. She may often have suffered her memory to recall the polite attentions of the youth, the earnest gaze with which his bright eye fastened upon her, the feelings which affected her when she saw him lying helpless from the shock of the thunderbolt, and through the whole scene there were doubtless many a look and word which at times came back in more or less vividness, and she may, especially in her earlier years, have dwelt much upon them, but if even this had taken place, years too had elapsed since she probably even so much as gave the subject a passing thought.

The revelation which her brother, in his artlessness had made, not only refreshed her memory, as to that particular scene in her life, but there were things which he had unwittingly let out, that were calculated to make impressions on the mind of a lady, even if that mind were peculiarly well balanced.

She had not yet seen the gentleman, although she heard whisperings from others that had reference to him: "That he shunned society in general; that his personal appearance was striking and attractive; that he had dark hair, and a pale complexion, and a bright eye, and a very graceful manner;" of these she had thought nothing, because they were the attributes of one to whom she was a perfect stranger; but now she brings to mind what she has heard, and comparing it with her remembrance of the boy, can well realize that he might be as attractive as some proclaimed him to be.

But there was more than this. She had evidently not been forgotten by him: she might indeed playfully pass over the idea which her brother so earnestly clung to, that the picture he had seen was a likeness of herself, but there must have been some truth in it, after all, or he would not have been so thoroughly impressed by it, and why had it been kept, and why should Mr. Ralston have expressed so much feeling? and, above all, why should he have cautioned her brother against mentioning the circumstance especially to her?

But there were other things, that, in connexion with the story she had just heard, seemed worthy of notice. This young man had taken a peculiar interest in her brother. He had at several times presented Charles with little tokens of regard: the articles were small, indeed, but very choice of their kind; and his offer to instruct him in a branch of knowledge likely to be of great benefit, was an exhibition of true kindness of feeling; and she remembered now, too, that Charles had told her of a letter Mr. Ralston gave him to hand his brother Henry when on board the ship, and about to sail; and had told him that if Henry presented the letter to the gentleman to whom it was directed, it might be of some consequence to him, when he should get to Canton. She had thought but little of the matter at the time, for the trial of the parting-scene had absorbed all other considerations; now, it came back to her, very much magnified in importance; it seemed an act of friendship on the part of a mere stranger, the more striking, because unsolicited and unexpected.

And Carrie's thoughts for a while were so engaging, that her work lay neglected on her lap; and she sat thus a long, long time; for other subjects somewhat connected and collateral, came up for consideration, and when she at length retired for the night, she durst not look at the clock to see how late it was.

But the reader will doubtless ask, "Was this indeed Clarence Ralston? and why has he not taken more pains to renew an acquaintance with Miss Carrie, if the interest he once felt still remains?" We are free to reply at once, that it was indeed our Clarence; and a few considerations, just hinted for the reader's benefit, will, we think, clear up all mystery.

The circumstances under which they had separated, gave him good grounds for supposing that both Miss Leslie and her family might not feel anxious for the renewal of an acquaintance which had once resulted in such an insult to them.

When he came to Princesport, it was at the time when the family were suffering under the trial of a public development of their circumstances; delicacy, if nothing else, would of course have kept him aloof at such an emergency.

He could not, he well knew, of his own accord, seek an intimacy with the family, without exciting the displeasure of his mother.

He had promised his mother that he would seek an intimacy with no lady, except the one she had selected for him, without first acquainting her.

With these hints to the reader, we must leave the matter at present, hoping they will prove satisfactory.

CHAPTER XV.

The departure of a master from his home, is perhaps in general a matter for self-gratulation on the part of servants. The eye which they fear is withdrawn from its watch, and they can go about their work in their own way, or leave it undone if not agreeable to their feelings.

But quite different from this was the mind of the faithful old negro, who attended to all the out-door work, and to many an inside job, too, in the family of Mr. Leslie : Bob had never feared the eye of his master. He did his work because he loved to do it, and needed no taskmaster to keep him employed ; and whenever he had nothing else to do, would take his axe and work away at a pile of logs which he had drawn together for the purpose of converting them into fire-wood.

One day, on Carrie's return from her school, she noticed that the old man was seated on his chopping-block, his axe lying on the ground beside him, and he apparently indulging in no very pleasing thoughts, for he was muttering to himself, and his countenance was quite downcast. She stepped into the yard and accosted him,

"What is the matter, daddy ? Are you not well ?"

"Oh yes, Miss Carrie ; me well nuff, tank e ; me bery well ; only me just tinkin' a leetle."

"Does any thing trouble you, daddy ?"

"Not much trouble, Miss Carrie ; only me mad, dat all. You see, Miss Carrie, me fine 'em out : *de world am all for himself.* Dat is a fact, Miss Carrie ; me never fine 'em out afore : de world am all for himself ; and me most wish de debil hab 'em all."

"Hush, hush, daddy ; do not have any bad wishes ; what has happened to make you feel so unpleasantly ?"

"Nuff, plenty I tell you, Miss Carrie, *bery bad world ;*

take my word for *dat*—bery bad—ain't good for nuttin' at all, and me wish they might—"

"Oh hush, daddy, and tell me what is the matter; have any of the neighbors troubled you?"

"No, no, not trouble me much, and me no trouble dem no more, *I 'sure you*, nebber no more, so long de bret is in my body. But since a you ask, Miss Carrie, what de matter, I jist tell you de whole livin' trute:

"You see, Miss Carrie, I been tinkin' about de wood: how me git him home for de winter. Winter no come yet, but he be creepin' along by and by. Well, de wood is all cut ready down in de gully to put into de cellar; and now we hab such champin' weather, me tink how nice he be to hab de wood in under cover afore de storm come and soak him; and so me tink how me do it; Bob Linkum haul de wood like nuttin', only me hab no wagon nor no sich ting, only de old gig; so me tink where me go and get yoke of oxen and de cart; and so me start right off to go see Massa Latrap. Me often and often lend Massa Latrap my cattle, many time, plowin' an harrowin' and de like; and me say to myself, 'Massa Latrap bery glad to lend 'em.' Well, Massa Latrap bery pleasant, bery; he say, 'How do, Bob? all well at home?' 'Bery well,' I say, 'Massa Latrap, bery well.' Den I say, 'Massa Latrap, you no lend me your oxen to-day? Me want to draw Massa Ratio wood from de gully; me want to git 'em in afore de storm come and wet him all.' Well, he cough like, two tree time, and den he say, 'My oxen, ha! I would be glad to lend you, Bob; but dey been hard to work dis fall, and I want to let 'em rest a little; can't you get along widout 'em?' 'Oh yes, Massa Latrap,' me say, 'me get along well nuff—me git oxen somewhere nudder; good-morning, Massa Latrap;' me no say nudder word to 'em."

"Well, perhaps he had pity on his creatures, daddy, and thought they had labored enough for the present."

"Me no tell what he tink; me no like dat man *no more;* he no gem'man, *dat man no gem'man*—me no ask him nuttin' more—me die first.

"Well, den me tink Massa Blossom, he got two, tree yoke of cattle doin' nuttin' under de sun but eatin' dere heads up; Massa Blossom me 'member well; great friend to Massa Ratio, dine wid him bery often, drink plenty Massa Ratio old Madeira

—me open many, many bottle wine for dat man; he great friend Massa Ratio. So me tink me get de oxen *dere*, no mistake dis time. Massa Blossom look bery queer when me ask him, 'Massa Blossom, you no lend me your oxen leetle while to draw Massa Ratio wood from the gully?' 'My oxen, hey, Bob! well, you must go and ask Jake!' Me look at him, but me no say nuttin', and Massa Blossom turn on the heel and go into de house."

"Did you speak to his man then, daddy?"

"*Me* speak to dat nigger! me no ask dat nigger, Miss Carrie, if me hab to bring all de wood on de wheel-barrow; dat nigger be a bery debil, Miss Carrie."

"Oh hush, hush, daddy!"

"He am, though, Miss Carrie. He bery bad, saucy nigger; dat nigger ask a me many times: 'Bob, where your carriage-horses?' Him be a Satan himself; me no ask him for nuttin' at all.

"Well, den me tink me try once more, and me sure me hab de oxen *dis time*, true nuff, spite dat nigger. So me go right up de lane to see Massa Ludlow. Massa Ludlow no refuse 'em me, sure a dat; and jist as me turn into the gate, Massa Ludlow comin' out in the gig. 'Good morning, Massa Ludlow,' 'Good morning, Bob; how is all at home? how is your Missus and Miss Carrie, and when you hear from Massa Ratio?' and me tell 'em all about it, and den me say, 'Massa Ludlow, you bery much oblige me you lend me your oxen for tree four hours, draw a leetle wood home.' 'Well, well, well,' he say, 'you want my oxen, do you, Bob?' 'Yes, Massa,' I say, 'only for leetle while, two tree hours.' 'I'm bery sorry, Bob, but I don't know how to spare 'em just now; can't you get a yoke at Mr. Blossom's? he got two tree yoke; I can't well spare mine just now.' 'Bery well,' I say, 'Mr. Ludlow, me git 'em somewhere;' and so he drive along. But me no tink *dat* a Massa Ludlow; you no 'member, Miss Carrie, when he first came to de place, how he hab Massa Ratio's horses night and day, and the whole family, children and all, come right to your house, and Massa Ratio do ebery ting for 'em. Me no think he forget dat so soon; he worser dan all de rest; he *bery* bad man."

"I should not have thought, indeed, that Mr. Ludlow would have refused you."

"Ah, Miss Carrie, me learn somepin' to-day me no learn afore. *De world am all for himself;* me no hab nuttin' more to do wid 'em—dey may go to de—de—grass for all Bob—me done wid 'em."

"You say, daddy, if you had a wagon, the old horse could draw the wood?"

"Bob Linkum? Bob Linkum draw dat wood like nuttin', if me had but de wagon."

"Don't you think Mr. Thompson would lend you his wagon? He has one, has he not, daddy?"

'Sam Thompson, de store-keeper! You no mean him, Miss Carrie?"

"Yes, Mr. Samuel Thompson, where Charlie is."

"Miss Carrie! me no tink you ask me sich a ting. Ain't dat man take all Massa Ratio's horses and carriages and ebery ting out ob de stable! Dat man, Miss Carrie, ain't got no more soul dan dat log. No—no—he *bery ugly man—bery!*"

Carrie now felt called upon to correct the old man's views, respecting Mr. Thompson, and therefore, as far as she could make him comprehend, explained how very kindly he had acted. It was, however, a hopeless task. The old man could not understand how there could be any thing good in a man who had committed such a sacrilege as to take away from his master's stables the noble beasts he used to tend and drive; but having great respect for his young mistress, he very reluctantly consented to make the experiment.

"Me go see Mr. Thompson—you say so, Miss Carrie—but you see—he no lend you one pin to save a your life; you see *dat*, Miss Carrie."

Carrie saw nothing more of Bob until the next morning, when, hearing the sound of wheels in the yard, she stepped upon the back piazza, and beheld the old man walking very sprightly by the side of Bob Lincoln, and a wagon, loaded with wood, behind them.

"Ha, ha, ha, Miss Carrie! Bob Linkum good yet; he draw dis here wood like nuttin'; he no puff one bit; see dere, Miss Carrie!" and the old horse, lopping his ears, turned his head round, as he received a hearty thump on his short ribs. Carrie, not comprehending exactly how Bob Lincoln's merits could be thus proved, turned the subject by asking,

"Is that Mr. Thompson's wagon?"

"Ha, ha, ha, Miss Carrie! me neber so beat afore; me no tink bad dat Mr. Sam Thompson, no more. Dat man more de gem'man den all de quality-folks put togedder; dat *bery good* man, *I'sure you*, Miss Carrie."

"He let you have it willingly, then?"

"I jist tell you, Miss Carrie, what he say. You see, me ask him *bery softly*, 'Mr. Thompson—Bob was very careful to give the title of master to none but such as he called "quality-folks"—you 'blige Miss Carrie wid a your wagon? me want to draw leetle wood two tree hours.' He look at me putty sharp, and den he put his han' on my shoulder: 'My wagon!' he say, 'yes, you heartily welcome to it, and the old mare too into the bargain, if you want her.' 'Tank 'e,' I say, 'Mr. Thompson, me no want de mare, but me be bery much oblige for the wagon leetle while.' 'Well,' he say, 'you go, old fellow, and git de wagon, and keep it jist as long as you like, and when you a want it, you need n't come and ask me, but jist go and git it.' I tank him very much; he say, 'Hush up, hush up,' and den he take up de box, and put two tree paper tobacco right in my pocket, and when me hand him de change, he push 'em right back: 'Hush up, hush up,' he say, 'keep a your money; won't you let a man give away a paper of tobacco?'

"I *'clare*, Miss Carrie, I learn somepin' ebery day: me don't know no more what to tink. Dis world am *bery quere*; me tink he turn upside down *bery much*."

Carrie had learned some new lessons in life, as well as old Bob. With her correct views of what should constitute true merit, and what course of conduct should entitle one to an honorable distinction in society, it was with great reluctance, that she began to admit the fact that her attempt to gain a subsistence for herself, and to aid her parents by opening a school for the instruction of little children, had, in a great measure, cut her off from the circle in which she had been brought up, and where she supposed she had many friends.

It was not done suddenly, nor, perhaps, rudely. She was still accosted with a pleasant smile, and, in private interviews with some of her old companions, was treated with much familiarity and apparent affection. But she found that whenever her school was alluded to by herself, it never was by them.

A shade seemed to pass over their countenance, and some other subject was immediately introduced.

On public occasions, too, she could not but be sensible that a great change had taken place, which left her one side of general notice. She was no longer the *one* sought after. She was by no means a necessary member of the circle: all arrangements were made without consulting her. She was not excluded, but it was very evident she was merely with them on suffrance.

Carrie was not wanting in true pri e of spirit. She did not think less of herself than she had eder done, but was very careful not to intrude.

She had a loving heart that could embrace a kindred spirit with the tenderest affection. And her confiding temper could have derived rich enjoyment in reposing, without a doubt, on the truth of a friend. It was, therefore, a bitter ingredient in her cup, that she felt obliged to keep in those warm emotions, to hold a severe check upon her frank, and generous feelings, and to walk along her lonely path, in sight of those she could have loved and been happy with, as though she saw them not.

It was well for her that she had but little time for the indulgence of vain regrets or moralizing reflections on the false lights of friendship. Her school occupied many hours of the day, and her duties in the house filled up the time not thus employed.

She was not unhappy. No one in the faithful discharge of duty can well be so. And yet the young heart needs the quickening influence of the pleasantries of life, the free interchange of social feelings with those of like age, and condition, and at times to unbend from the sterner duties amid the laughter-loving circle, and take its part in the prattle of the thoughtless.

It was not favorable for Carrie, that she was thus shut up to a round of duties, that there was so little variety in her social life. It exposed her to intimacies most dangerous to her peace.

The offer of Mr. Folger "to do what was in his power to supply the place of the absent father and brother," was not an unmeaning offer. He was a very frequent visitor, at first for the ostensible purpose of seeing "his little motherless one;"

he did not indeed always appear to be very anxious to see *her*. "If he only heard that she was well, it was all sufficient." "Do not call her," he would often say, "Miss Leslie; if you say she is well, that is enough. She is, no doubt, enjoying herself. I am not at all uneasy about her." And then in an adroit way, would bring up some topic to engage Miss Carrie; and as he could converse with fluency, did in fact often engage her interest until her school or some other duty compelled her to ask him to excuse her presence. And then the leave was given with such a pleasantness of manner, with perhaps the remark, "And we will remember, Miss Leslie, where we left off; you have given me new views of this matter. I shall certainly take the liberty of resuming it, the next time."

And thus cut off from the society of companions, and daily exposed to that of one who had the ability to interest her mind, and the tact of introducing subjects which were congenial to her, it must not be wondered at if the company of Mr. Folger, from being at first only allowed, became at length an agreeable interlude amid the routine of duty.

Little Lucy, too, had begun to wind herself about the heart of Carrie. Her little heart, shut up so long within itself, soon opened to the kind and gentle treatment she received; her eye would fix its steady gaze on the lovely face of her teacher, as she would be sitting beside her in the room at home, while busy with the needle; and Carrie would at times feel almost abashed when conscious that those soft, bright eyes were gazing upon her. One day she turned, and in her pleasant way asked the child,

"Lucy, dear, what are you thinking of?"

"Oh, I don't know; I was thinking may be you looked like my mother."

"What makes you think so, dear?"

"I don't know; may be it's because I love you so."

Carrie saw that her bright eyes were glistening, and she laid down her work and drew Lucy up by her side.

"You like to be loved, do you, Lucy?"

"I should like to be loved by you."

"Do you doubt that I do love you, Lucy?"

"Not if you say you do."

And Carrie pressed her close, and kissed her pretty cheek, already bedewed with a tear.

"I do love you, Lucy; and I hope you will be a good girl, and grow up to be a great comfort to your father."

"But they tell me that my father will marry again, and that I shall have a new mother, who will not care for me."

"Who has told you that, Lucy?"

Carrie was much alarmed; she feared that some imprudent persons had been saying to the child things which their own imaginations alone could have suggested.

"Oh, they have often said so to me."

"But who, Lucy, and when! No one in this house, surely?"

"Oh, no; not here! It was before I came here."

And the heart of Carrie at once grew lighter.

"I am glad, my dear, that your father has taken you away from persons who would talk so to you. Your father loves you, and you need not fear that he will ever do that—that he will ever—ever be regardless of your happiness."

"Do you think my father loves me?"

"Why should you doubt that, Lucy?"

"I don't know."

"I think you have no reason to doubt his love, my dear; he has no one else to love; he is very kind to you, and gives you all you want; and comes almost every day to see you."

"Yes, but—"

"But what, Lucy? Tell me all your thoughts, dear Lucy."

Lucy could not just then, for the feeling within had overpowered her, and she must have her cry out.

"If you will tell me, dear Lucy, what troubles you, perhaps I can help you; perhaps I can show you that you are wrong; and if you are wrong, you would wish to be set right. I know you would."

"My father never cried when he went away and left me all alone."

"Men do not show their feelings that way, dear Lucy; they do not show them as we do."

"Yes, but when your pa went away, he did not do so. Don't you remember when he put his arms around you, and kissed you—I know he did not cry—but I seen him wipe away great big tears—and I run right off to my room, and cried very hard. I knew he felt so bad."

This allusion to the parting-scene, which was still so fresh in Carrie's heart, awakened emotions which for the time prevented any further reference to exciting subjects, and with a few words calculated to correct what she believed to be a misapprehension on the part of the child, Carrie took her little charge by the hand and led her away to make preparations for school.

The subject thus brought to a close was not forgotten, and Carrie felt that a new duty was unfolded to her. There had no doubt been some unhappy impression made upon the mind of little Lucy, which she, as her friend and teacher, must endeavor to correct.

How often is it, that the discharge of what we esteem to be a duty, leads us insensibly to take a deeper interest, either in the person or subject, for which we labor. She could have no doubt that a father's heart must be a place where the warmest affections have their home; and fully believing that the father of Lucy was not an exception; that he could not be a monster in human form; that a peculiarity of manner alone, in connection with unfriendly influences, had been the cause of the evil she designed to cure, took every opportunity to impress the child with a belief in the faithfulness of his care, and the sincerity and strength of his affection, and without speaking to him directly on the subject, took much pains, when in his presence with the child, to engage her in playful sallies with him, and acting as a kind of mediator, allowed herself to be thus brought into more free and social intercourse than she could have thought of under other circumstances.

It is not in the heart of woman to indulge suspicion, or maintain the feeling of distrust, unless the subject of it be very manifestly unworthy of confidence, and it was not possible for Carrie Leslie, with her pure heart, where no guile dwelt, where every thought was ready for the open day, and every wish was generated of that love, which thinketh no evil, to be on the watch against those evils which lurk under the garb of friendly manifestations. Her former prejudices had long been laid aside, and there was nothing in all his treatment of her, or her family, but seemed the result of friendship; and there was nothing in his manner as a gentleman, that could arouse the least suspicion that he was not one in its true sense.

But there were other influences brought to bear upon her,

of a most dangerous character, if there be any truth in suspicions we have thrown out against the man who was thus winding a coil about her.

It is a great pity that women as well as men can not always be wise, especially those who from peculiar circumstances have opportunity to influence the young. Among those with whom the family of the Leslies still maintained an intimacy, was one by the name of Crampton—a fine social good-hearted person, was Mrs. Crampton, and a very warm friend, where she "took a liking." She had married a gentleman much older than herself; a very respectable person, too, was Mr. Crampton, a man of property, and one who managed his affairs with discretion. He was a good liver, and affected full as much style as any in the vicinity of Princesport. Mrs. Crampton seemed to enjoy her situation very much. She could command her carriage whenever she wished, could visit at her will, and entertain her guests to suit her own taste. Mr. Crampton was not particularly fond of visiting, nor receiving visits. He was not particularly fond of even riding as far as the house of worship on the Sabbath, and did not very often trouble his horses with the extra burden of his own particular person for that purpose. But he put no obstacle in the way of Mrs. Crampton's taking her pleasure, and Mrs. Crampton really did love to go to church. She said she did, and nobody doubted her word, for she was rarely absent from her seat on Sundays. Mr. Crampton, likewise, was very much given to minding his own business, and permitting the rest of the world the same privilege; but people in general gave Mrs. Crampton credit for being in this respect somewhat in advance of her husband, for Mrs. Crampton not only attended to her own affairs, and certainly they were well attended to, but she also took a lively interest in the affairs of others, especially her friends, and was on that account thought well of, and deservedly so—for her heart was full of kindness, and much of her happiness seemed to be derived from her strong sympathy with others.

Mrs. Crampton had always been very fond of Carrie; had never from any change in their circumstances remitted her attentions to the family; and had entered heartily into Carrie's project of opening a school, and trying to support herself. Having happily been born and brought up in New England, she had more just views on that subject than many of her present neighbors. In fact her love and respect for the whole family had increased, as she beheld them all so ready, as she termed it "to turn to, and help themselves." Carrie could not but appreciate such a friend, and there had, even, since the turn in the fortunes of her family, been a great increase in their intimacy.

Mrs. Crampton's failing, if it can be called such, was a propensity to make "good matches" for her young friends, and especially for those of her own sex. She seemed to think that this was the *summum bonum*, which they were all aspiring after. She was, no doubt, very much mistaken in the matter, but she was honest in the belief, and acted upon it with all her heart.

Mrs. Crampton's ideas, too, of what constituted "a good match," were, we must think, not very orthodox. She had no belief in what is commonly called "falling in love." She had not herself gone through any such experience, and we are all very apt to be governed, in our opinion, by what we "have seen and felt," or have not "seen or felt," as the case may be. A man who was "well to do in the world," of fair reputation, not bad to look at, whether widower or bachelor, was in her estimation "a good chance" for any young lady not yet disposed of.

True love, that enchanting power which binds in holy embrace two kindred spirits, that sheds around the path of life its sweetest flowers, that creates within its charmed atmosphere a new world in which the heart finds enjoyments that never cloy, that talisman which neutralizes the bitter ingredients in the cup of life, and lulls the spirit into sweet repose, even amid turmoil and tempest without—this, Mrs. Crampton believed not in; to her sober judgment it was all "a fiction, only fit to be put into books to make pretty stories out of; or to be talked about by little boys and girls, 'who did n't know any thing,' as she said, what the world was made of."

Mrs. Crampton laid great stress on the idea, a very favorite one with her, "of getting used to one another." Her theory was, that "happiness in the married state" depended almost entirely upon "getting used to one another's ways;" and so firm was her opinion in this matter, that she had been heard many times to say, "that she believed she could be happy with any man that was n't bad at heart, when she once got used to his ways."

It may be Mrs. Crampton was right; our business is not to argue against her theory; we are merely painting her character, and its more striking points must be delineated.

We have said that this good lady had a sincere regard for our friend Carrie Leslie, and in many ways had manifested it. Of late she had taken rather a more serious view of matters and things in reference to her young friend; and perhaps we can not unfold the views and feelings of the lady in any better way than by introducing our kind readers to an interview between Mrs. Crampton and Mr. Crampton, wherein the subject most upon her thoughts was by her more directly brought out.

Whenever Mrs. Crampton had any thing on her mind, it was very natural for her, not having any children, and no other person besides Mr. Crampton to whom she could talk, except the servants, to let out her feelings to him.

And for this reason he had to listen to a great many suggestions, which to all appearance, that is to a third person, did any such happen to be present, he cared very little about. Mr. Crampton was, as he himself expressed it, "a mite deaf." The term did not exactly convey to the mind of one not accustomed to converse with him, what perhaps Mr. Crampton intended, and a stranger might probably fail in his first, or even second attempt, in making his communication audible to Mr. Crampton, if he followed strictly the hint which Mr. Crampton had given. Mrs. Crampton had, however, "got used" to the right key, and almost always made him hear something that she was saying, especially if she was solicitous that he should hear. All this, however, is only by way of introduction.

Mr. Crampton had come in from a walk around his premises, and, as was his custom, planted himself immediately before the fire-place, with his feet resting on the top of the polished fender. It was not quite the time for fires yet, but Mr. Crampton would have one kindled in the earlier part of the day, whenever the weather happened to be wet under foot or in the season of fogs; and it happened just then to be the kind of weather in which, Mrs. Crampton knew, a fire would be wanted, and had ordered one to be kindled.

As Mr. Crampton's boots had been in some rather wet

places, Mrs. Crampton would have been very willing to have rung the bell and ordered a servant to get Mr. Crampton's slippers, but "being used to his ways," she knew this would not do, as he always preferred, as he said, "drying his boots on his legs." And so she sat very patiently, looking at the little puddle that was accumulating on the clean hearth from Mr. Crampton's dripping extremities; "she had also got used" to this habit of his, and knew very well that he was not to be broken of it. She could not, however, help wishing secretly to herself, that he would endeavor to use a little more care in reference to her brass andirons; they were very handsome, and had been highly polished that morning. But Mr. Crampton must get rid of the extra tobacco juice—it must go somewhere—and if the andirons were in the way, he could n't help it. She had tried very hard "to get used" to that habit of his, but the best she could do, was to keep quiet and try to think of something else; and so she got to thinking about her friend Carrie Leslie, and to let Mr. Crampton understand that she thought he was doing perfectly right in soiling her hearth, and spotting her brasses; she looked very complacently at him and asked,

Mr. Crampton, do you know Mr. Folger?"

Mr. Crampton turned his head toward her, and looked inquiringly without speaking.

"I say, do you know Mr. Folger?"

"Folger! Do I know him? No—yes—I know there's such a man."

"What I mean, is, do you *know* him?"

"I speak to him, when we meet."

"Well, do you *know* any thing about him?"

"Yes. He's got money. They say he's rich."

"I know they say he's rich, very rich, but what kind of a man is he?"

"Tall."

"I know that: I've seen him. He is tall and good-looking; but what I want to know, is he good-tempered?"

"Good-tempered! you'd better ask his wife."

"He has no wife, he's a widower; his little girl, you know, is living at the Leslie's."

"Well, you had better ask them, then. I don't know any thing about his temper: what of it?"

9*

"Oh, well, I merely wanted to know, for a particular reason."

"Temper! What can you know about a man's temper? I suppose he's like most men. What under heaven, wife, have you got into your head now? What is his temper to you, one way or another? There! by blazes, I've burnt my boot! What a hot fire you do keep!"

And Mr. Crampton stamped his feet alternately on the beautiful rug, and shook off the mud which had dried thereon, to the disadvantage of two little cherubs, that had been prettily worked on it. Mrs. Crampton's eye followed the boots. She gave a slight cough, but said nothing. She was "pretty well used" to that too.

She saw, however, that the accident to Mr. Crampton's boot had somewhat stirred up the good man; for the blood had rushed to his face, and what between the heat of the fire and the commotion within, it had become alarmingly colored. And "being used to his ways," she knew that the part of wisdom for her, just then, was to say nothing. She had accomplished something, however; she had found out that Mr. Crampton knew nothing bad about Mr. Folger, and if there had been any thing bad about him, Mr. Crampton would certainly have heard of it. And so she took it for granted, woman-like, if there was nothing bad about him, there was most likely something good, and if he was n't a good kind of a man, Mr. Crampton would certainly have known it, and spoken right out what he thought; for that was "his way," when he spoke at all. And now Mrs. Crampton had almost forgotten about her hearth, and her rug, in the multitude of her thoughts concerning certain plans in her mind, which had originated her questions at this time, and came near working up the mind of Mr. Crampton into an uncomfortable state, besides doing damage to his boot.

Whenever there is mischief going on, either designedly or not, it is said that a certain personage is always on hand to help it along.

Whether he sent Mr. Folger there that morning, or whether by the simple suggestion of his own mind, is not material. But to Mrs. Crampton's utter astonishment, and Mr. Crampton's bewilderment, just as the latter had stamped off all the mud he could get rid of in that way on Mrs. Crampton's rug, a carriage was seen driving up the avenue to the house. Mr

Crampton just scratched his head the "least mite," and stood up straight to see who and what it could be, while Mrs. Crampton dived after the hearth-brush and shovel, and began clearing up the scandal to her housewifery, which made such a glaring exhibition on the hearth and rug.

"Who upon earth can it be, Mr. Crampton?"

Mr. Crampton, still thinking, probably, of his burnt boot, and on that account not being in the most amiable mood, let off a few expletives not very acceptable to the ear of Mrs. Crampton, by way, probably, of getting rid of extra steam before his visitor should arrive, and then added,

"Folger."

"You don't say so! What can he want?"

Mr. Crampton very gently referred her to somebody Mrs. Crampton was not very likely to ask any questions of; and then resumed his seat.

In a very short time the sitting-room door was opened by a servant, and the visitor entered.

Mr. Crampton received him with all due courtesy, and Mrs. Crampton with some extra smiles and marks of attention, as being due to one who for the first time had honored their house with his presence.

Mr. Folger appeared more mild and subdued in manner than Mrs. Crampton had ever noticed before. She had met him at Mr. Leslie's more than once, and had made up her mind that he was stiff and reserved, and a little haughty.

There was nothing of all this at present. He was quite affable, and had so many little pleasant things to say that Mrs. Crampton could not but do her best in return; and the more so, because Mr. Crampton, she feared, was not in the best humor for showing off.

"I have taken a great liberty, madam," said Mr. Folger, turning toward the lady, and bowing to her, "in calling upon you this morning; but my errand must be my apology, and if you will allow me, I will at once state the business for which I have come."

"No apology, sir, is at all necessary. I am happy to see you, and have been thinking that we ought not to have been so long strangers."

"Thank you, madam. It would have given me great pleasure to have waited upon you long ere this. But situated as I am, you know, doubtless, madam, that my dwelling—I can not call it a home—is without a mistress; it is desolate"—and Mr. Folger heaved a deep sigh—"I can not invite visitors; all such pleasant things in life are at present denied me; and moreover, madam, a man who has—who has—as much business as I have, on his hands, has but little time to spare. If a man has means, you know, madam, he is obliged to be looking after his affairs. You find it so, I have no doubt, Mr. Crampton?"

Mr. Crampton bowed assent to the proposition, having a very confused notion, however, of its import.

"My business, this morning, madam, is not for any thing concerning myself personally; I believe I may not be charged with flattery, by saying that your character for kindness and benevolence to the poor is pretty generally known."

"Oh, dear, I hope they don't say so! I am sure—"

"Well, madam, I believe I fairly represent what is the general impression in that respect; and on the strength of that as being a correct opinion, I have ventured to call upon you this morning. The fact is, there is a family not far from my residence, which, I really believe, needs assistance. I suppose I might possibly go and offer them aid; but I am a stranger to them, and have refrained from doing so from motives of delicacy, which you, no doubt, madam, can appreciate; and moreover, I have thought that a lady would be more likely to —to know, just how to find out what they most need; and in fact, perhaps they would feel a little more ready to expose their necessities to you, madam, than to a man and a stranger like myself."

"What family have you reference to, sir?"

"Their name is Duncan; probably you know them, Mrs. Crampton?"

"What, Jonas Duncan's widow! She lives down the lane?"

"The same, madam."

"Oh yes, I am very glad that you have mentioned them, for I have been thinking whether they ought not to be seen to."

"I don't care to have my name mentioned in the matter, Mrs. Crampton; and if you will allow me to place a trifle in your hands to disburse for them as you think proper, I shall esteem it a favor; and you need not say where it came from."

And here Mr. Folger opened a very handsome purse, and drawing therefrom a twenty dollar bill, handed it with a low bow to the lady.

Mrs. Crampton's heart was now full to overflowing; no one need say any thing more *to her;* she knew him now—a good man—a Christian man—almost an angel.

"Indeed, Mr. Folger, you are very, very kind. But you must not ask me to say nothing to Mrs. Duncan; you must allow me to name her benefactor."

"You will do me a great favor, madam, if you will be perfectly mum. I am not careful to have it known when I do an act of charity. You know there is considerable trumpeting about such matters at the present day. If the good deed is done, that is all sufficient; that is *my* opinion of such matters, Mrs. Crampton; and now, madam, I must take my leave."

And Mr. Folger arose to depart, when Mrs. Crampton, as though willing to extend the conference, asked,

"Have you called at Mr. Leslie's this morning? How much your little girl improves! Do you not think so?"

Mr. Folger was much excited.

"My dear madam, don't speak of it; it seems such a wonderful event, that my poor 'little motherless thing' should have got under the protection of such a—such an angel! What else can I call that young lady! And there now! I have let my thoughts out without any reflection; you are her friend: her dear friend she calls you, I believe. You will not allow this hasty expression to reach her ears! You will not, Mrs. Crampton!"

And Mrs. Crampton smiled very knowingly.

"Oh, you know Mr. Folger, they say, 'murder will out.' But you need not fear that I shall say any thing to Miss Carrie that will make her think any worse of you."

"Thank you, madam, for that assurance. Mr. Crampton, good morning, sir; good morning, madam;" and the gentleman, after several bows, found himself at the door, and then, making a final one, departed.

"Well," said Mrs. Crampton. "He don't want to have it trumpeted? I guess I shall trumpet it into somebody's ears and I guess I know who? She shall hear it. That man ain't known as he ought to be, but no matter: only to think of it?"

Men are not in general troubled with curiosity, and Mr.

Crampton in particular, never manifested a prying disposition, but being "a mite deaf," had prevented his entering into the merits of the case, and not being at all deficient in sight, he could not help seeing Mr. Folger's purse, and Mrs. Crampton's flurried manner, as she received the bill, and crumpled it up in her hand. Mrs. Crampton, moreover, could not help observing that her husband's eyes twinkled a little more than usual; and "being used to his ways," recognized it as a sign that she had better explain matters.

It took some time, however, to do this, for Mrs. Crampton was so full of the new development, that she could not refrain from enlarging upon it, both as she commenced and finished her disclosure.

Mr. Crampton seemed not in the least moved by her enthusiasm, and after chewing awhile on the favorite morsel he always kept in the right place for that purpose, and taking two or three pinches of snuff, while he set apparently endeavoring to solve the phenomenon satisfactorily to his own mind, he turned his head at length towards Mrs. Crampton, and simply asked,

"Why, did n't he stop there, and give them the money himself?"

Mrs. Crampton could understand perfectly why he did not, and in a very forcible and clear manner laid the reasons before her good man. He listened very patiently until she had finished; and then without removing his steady gaze from the fire, merely said—

But we will not repeat all Mr. Crampton said. There were a great many useless words, that were mere embellishments, and seemed to be only intended to relieve his mind of some unpleasant ideas, that had been gendering there for a little while past. He closed, however, with saying, in a very emphatic manner,

"It's all a piece of—humbug;" and then he arose, and left the room.

Mrs. Crampton could only say to herself,

"Men will be men; they are so incredulous."

A close observer might have noticed upon Mr. Folger's countenance, as he took his seat in his carriage, and bade his servant drive on, a peculiar gleam, as if the inner man was in quite a happy state. There might also have been noticed, very evidently a smile, but whether it was that lighting up of the countenance when one is highly gratified, or that expression which plays about the lips, when one has acted successfully the deceiver's part, it might not have been very easy to distinguish.

As one of the privileges which Mrs. Crampton earned, by accommodating herself to Mr. Crampton's ways, was the command of a carriage and horses, whenever it was her will to go abroad, she gave an order at once to the coachman to be ready at an early hour in the afternoon, as it was a holiday afternoon at Carrie's school. Mrs. Crampton sent word immediately to her also, that she should call for her to take a ride. The invitation was accepted, and as Mrs. Crampton designed to call at the widow Duncan's, she wished Carrie to participate with her in the joy which her visit would doubtless afford the poor woman.

It was indeed a place where the hand of charity was needed The widow had been left penniless, and four young children, too young to afford any assistance to their mother, were thrown upon her sole care. Sickness among her children prevented her from doing any thing for their support, and she was obliged to depend upon such things as neighbors in their kindness might send in.

Mrs. Crampton had a very kind way with her at such a scene, and she soon obtained the confidence of the person she had come to aid, and it was quite a feast of the heart to Carrie Leslie to listen to the kind words Mrs. Crampton spoke, to hear her tell the widow that such and such things should be sent to her as she then immediately needed, and to give herself no uneasiness about the coming winter, for that as long as she was thus helpless, she should be provided for, and to see the tear of gratitude on the cheek of the poor woman as she tried to express her thanks to Mrs. Crampton.

But Mrs. Crampton was not the person to take thanks which were not due to her.

"Your thanks are not due to me, Mrs. Duncan, for what I now do for you, although I mean to do something too. A gentleman, whose name I am not allowed to mention, has thought of you, and given me some means to aid you, and I shall tell him, shall I, that his bounty has come in the right time—that you needed it?"

"Oh, yes, my dear madam, tell him may God bless him, and his, and all that belongs to him, but I should like to thank him to his face too."

"He is one that does not care to have his good deeds known. He don't care, as many do, to trumpet out his charities. It will be sufficient satisfaction to him to learn that what he has given has done good."

As Mrs. Crampton and Carrie again took their seats in the carriage, the latter remarked,

"I should like much to know for whom you have been the almoner to that poor woman; I wish he could have witnessed her expression of thankfulness."

"I wish so too, my dear, and I mean to tell him, for although he don't seem to care to be thanked, yet it is no more than right that he should know how acceptable his bounty was.

"You say you wish to know who it is: can not you guess? Think among all your acquaintances. He is one that you know, and one that thinks very highly of you, that I can tell you; I wish you could have heard—but no matter; I'll tell you as much as this, he's a rich man, and a widower."

Carrie did not care to press the matter any further. She was pretty certain now to what individual her friend alluded, and for some reason she could hardly define, did not care to speak the name. Perhaps it was that Mrs. Crampton had on different occasions rather playfully hinted in her presence the possibility that a certain person had serious views in reference to her. This fact was enough, for one so sensitive as Carrie Leslie, to create an unwillingness even to mention the name.

But Mrs. Crampton had no scruples about such matters. And probably noticing that Carrie's countenance was slightly flushed, she took courage.

"And now I tell you what it is, Carrie, I must out with my feelings! I can't keep them in no longer. You know I love you; and I want to see you do well, and I don't want to see you wasting your life away in drudgery you have never been used to."

"Oh, my dear Mrs. Crampton, do not say so! I do not feel my daily duties to be drudgery, by any means. They are indeed fatiguing sometimes. But a night's rest makes full amends for all that: I really feel happy that I have work to do."

"Yes, that may all be, Carrie, and you know I have always upheld you in your plan, of 'taking hold and helping yourself.' There is no disgrace in that, according to my notion, however other people may view it. But that is not the thing; you have got to consider what can a woman do after all! You may, by teaching, do a little toward clothing yourself, and may be throw in a few dollars toward helping the family along. But what will it all. amount to? Would you not be able to do a great deal more, if you were the wife of a rich man?"

"Oh do please, Mrs. Crampton, say nothing further about that! I never could marry any man, with the expectation that his property was to be used for the support or aid of my dear parents—I had rather labor, even at menial service—and I never will."

"Oh, Carrie, you talk dreadfully! You are not willing to hear to reason at all! Now would you, rather than marry a nice, good man, who, may be, might be dying in love with you, and who was willing to make you a rich lady, and give you plenty of means to do what you pleased with, and ask no questions, and be able to keep your family all together in the old home! I say, would you, rather than do that, see every thing all broken up, the place sold, and may be all of you scattered about, and no house to cover you. You see, I've looked the thing all around. I know all about it; and I have watched him too. He is interested in you, take my word for it. And now if he proposes, you won't refuse, will you?"

"Why, Mrs. Crampton!" And Carrie could do no better than break into a hearty laugh.

"I know; I've seen girls laugh before. I have laughed myself, in my day. Why I laughed in Crampton's face, and had like to have spilled my dish entirely, when he first made proposals. 'I was n't used to his ways.' But I tell you, Carrie, do n't you ever do so. There is nothing that will kill a man so quick. Why, I had the dreadfullest time that ever was. You see he went right off, Crampton did, just as if he'd been shot, and there I was, you see, all my plans knocked in the head; and what to do I did n't know! But as good luck would have it, I happened next day to be in the house of a good friend of mine, and we were talking it all over, and I was telling what a fool I had been, when who should come in but Crampton! So I looked sober enough, and he just said, 'Good morning, Mary,' and I burst right out into a good cry, and ran out of the room. And that, you see, brought things all round to the right point again. But I got a dreadful fright and I've been almost afraid to laugh in his presence ever since and I hope you will remember it, and whatever you do, don't laugh, I beg of you."

Carrie, however, could not help laughing at the earnestness of her friend, on a subject that appeared so supremely ridiculous to her. Mrs. Crampton construed it into a good sign, and had great hopes of being able to bring the thing about yet.

"And you will promise me, dear, won't you? You *will* promise me not to laugh if he should offer?"

Carrie saw that Mrs. Crampton was really in earnest, and not wishing that the subject should be continued, restrained her lighter feelings, and with much seriousness of manner, endeavored to make her friend understand what were her peculiar views of the marriage relation, and closed by saying,

"And now, dear Mrs. Crampton, you can understand from what I have declared to be my true views, my sober, determined views, that the event you have hinted at, can never take place. I do not love him; *I never can love him!*"

The carriage was now drawing near the house of Carrie, and Mrs. Crampton saw that the conference must come to an end for the present. She was disappointed but not discouraged; and as she kissed the lovely girl when they were about to separate, she said in a low tone,

"Parents make great sacrifices for their children sometimes; *ought not children to be willing to do the same?*"

Had Mrs. Crampton known what a peculiar mind she was dealing with, had she been able to comprehend the depth of that filial love which warmed the heart of Carrie Leslie, she would not have ventured, much as she desired the accomplishment of the object which had been the subject of conversation, to have thrown such an element of disturbance into her friend's heart, as the idea which she had just thrown out. The opinion of Mrs. Crampton, much as Carrie loved her, as a kind-hearted friend, was not in general calculated to exert an influence over her. She was not refined either in feeling or manner, and Carrie was well aware of her peculiarities.

but influence is a word that stands for a mighty power, and it works at times by means which to all human views are inadequate to the end. It is like the working of animalculæ beneath the ocean's depths; it is like the rain-drop that falls into the crevice of the rock; it is like the vapor that rises unnoticed from the earth, and is only seen and felt when the dark cloud spreads above us and the storm bursts [illegible] secret chambers.

CHAPTER XVI.

Charles Leslie worked so faithfully, and made himself so useful, that Mr. Thompson could indulge himself with much longer sittings in his arm-chair, than he had ever been able to do; and as the area in his store, within which customers could assemble to be waited on, was so much enlarged, he could find room enough for his feet, without the danger of their being intruded upon. His usual sitting-place was now far back in the store beyond the counter, where he could keep his eye, however, upon all that was going on, and have a pleasant chat with a neighbor or customer, without in the least interfering with business.

And he enjoyed his retreat so much, and felt so much pleased with the new arrangement of things, and with the pleasant ways and constant diligence of his assistant, that he was quite in haste for the quarter-day to arrive, when, according to agreement, his first payment was to be made. He felt that the twenty-five dollars had been well earned, and the old man took as much pleasure in paying such an obligation, as he did in receiving what was due to himself.

One morning, it was just as the old gentleman was about to leave the store for breakfast, he called Charlie to him, and as he approached, held out toward him quite a handful of bills.

"There, sonney, is twenty-five dollars. It's just three months to-day since you begun. Take it, and welcome; you've well earned it."

Charles had hardly time to express his thanks in a becoming manner, before Mr. Thompson was far on his way through the back part of the store, making for the door which led into the yard, and across which was his dwelling.

Charlie stood a moment looking at the handful of bills he held, and then walked behind the counter to his desk, where he very deliberately spread out each bill by itself. They consisted chiefly of ones with a few scattering twos and threes— in order to magnify as much as possible the amount which he could call his own; and then he put each denomination in a separate pile, and finally gathered the whole into one bundle and laid it carefully in a corner of his desk; and then, as if he had some business on hand which must be attended to at once, ran to the other end of the store, and rolled a barrel of flour to the outer door, as in readiness to be carted off; and then he began dipping sugar out of barrels, and emptying tea out of canisters, and coffee out of bags, and weighing them with extra care, and tying them up in large paper covers, and placing them beside the barrel at the door; and then he had jugs to fill with molasses and oil, and a great many little extras to get, first from one part of the store, and then from the other; gathering them all in a heap together at the door around the barrel, as though they belonged to the same concern. And when he had finished, there seemed to be a collection of necessaries sufficient to last a small family for some months; and then taking the slate, upon which he had carefully noted down each article as he put it up, he walked to the desk and began making out a regular bill.

This was but just completed as Mr. Thompson was seen approaching from the rear of his store; and attracted by the pile of goods at the front door, he continued his progress past his arm-chair, and for a moment stood contemplating the sale his clerk had been making, and perhaps troubled with some thoughts as to the propriety of allowing so much of his stock to go forth, without knowing whether it was to be added to the account of Mr. Rice, or Mr. Potter, or some others already large enough. But before he had time to ask any questions, Charlie was by his side, holding up a regular bill, neatly made out and receipted. Mr. Thompson very deliberately put on his glasses, and looked steadily upon the paper. He saw Mr. Leslie's name at the head of it, and his own at the bottom, by his proxy, acknowledging receipt in full.

"I have put the money into the drawer, Mr. Thompson, and taken out the change: two dollars and sixty-two cents."

"What money?"

"The money, sir, for that bill. You will see it is receipted."

Mr. Thompson walked back as far as his chair, and, taking his seat very deliberately,

"You just come here, Charlie."

Charles promptly obeyed, and looked into the flushed face of his employer with his sparkling eye, and his whole countenance in a glow of delight.

"What have you been a doing now? Have you been a takin' that money I jist give you, and layin' it all out in this way! Tell me true now, have you?"

"Not all of it, sir; I have got some change left: over two dollars."

The old man tried to say something, or he appeared to be trying; but only succeeded so far as to make some motion with his under lip.

The truth, as it broke upon him, had taken hold of a tender spot. Mr. Thompson had a peculiar weakness of the heart, and when affected there, he found great difficulty in saying just what he wished to. Under such circumstances he was often affected with coughing and sneezing, and some such operation, until the tears would begin to run over his rough face, and he would be compelled to use his handkerchief; and rub and blow for some time until the fit was over. Charles began to be somewhat alarmed at the long silence; but, thinking that he had done nothing wrong designedly, and not knowing exactly what to do or say, stood perfectly still, intending as soon as possible to explain matters.

At length Mr. Thompson made out to say,

"I sha'n't do it; I sha'n't do it, no how."

Charles still made no reply, for it was out of his power to say what it was Mr. Thompson would not do.

"Do you think I am a going to do such a thing? No, I sha'n't! I see it all now. You 've been getting these things, and gone and taken your own money."

Mr. Thompson had to cough several times: "And do you think I'm agoin to let you pay for 'em at store price? I sha'n't do it, no how—now you just take this bill, you know what they cost as well as I do, and better too, and take it right off, every bit of it; don't let there be one cent profit on it, not one cent; and then, I don't believe you've done it right in the weight; I don't believe you 've given good down weight."

"Oh, I have weighed every thing correctly, Mr. Thompson; I know I have."

"I know you have n't, so hush up, hush up, and take off a

dollar for down weight; I know you ain't done it right; hush up now and do as I say, and figure it up now before the folks come in."

Charles did as he was directed, and then handed the account to Mr. Thompson, who, in his excitement, had left his chair, and was standing behind the counter.

"And the down weight, you ain't got that—but no matter, here, you take this."

And Mr. Thompson took a bill out of the drawer and handed to him: Charles saw it was five dollars.

"Oh, Mr. Thompson, you will wrong yourself."

"Hush up, hush up, and don't you say one word about it to home, to your house, do you hear? not a word; but how are you goin' to get 'em home?"

"I thought, sir, perhaps you would let me take the old mare and wagon, and I would run up with them, and get back before the folks begin to come in."

"That's it, and now sonney run in and get your breakfast, and then harness the crittur, and we'll have you off. But stop—did you tell 'em to home what you was goin' to do?"

"Oh no, sir, they know nothing about it."

"Well, well, well, go quick, and git 'em there—do—oh dear, oh dear, I wish I was young again."

This wish Mr. Thompson expressed after Charles was beyond hearing. The reason for the wish, he did not explain. Perhaps he saw there were some sunny sides to this life after all, and, under certain circumstances, there might be a great deal to enjoy in it.

Charles was not long delayed by the matter of breakfast, and the old mare and he were soon on their way with the precious load. Charles might have remembered the time when he would have thought slightingly of a ride behind an animal of the description he was then driving, or of being conveyed in just such a carriage.

Now, however, the bright and pleasant thoughts that quickened his young heart, shed their beautiful influence even over these, and he never rode before when he was better pleased with himself and all about him.

He had of necessity been acquainted with all the peculiarities of their situation at home, and had sympathized, as boys seldom do in the cares, and anxieties attendant upon their straitened circumstances.

He knew when necessary articles were nearly exhausted, and many a sad hour he had passed in thinking of the extremities to which the dear ones at home were at times driven.

He saw how downcast was his mother's looks, and how often the flush would mantle her cheek, as some new exigency came up; and he had noticed, too, the settled marks of care which his dear Carrie bore upon her sweet face. Oh, how he had longed to be a man: what wonders he would do.

And this was a beginning. He was on his way now with comforts that they needed, and purchased, too, by his own industry. It was his first gift of love, and his heart rioted in the joy he would have in their surprise. "Come along, old mare, amble as fast as you can, it will soon be Carrie's school time, and Charlie wants to make her heart feel lighter at her task to-day—come, come, old horse, hurry along, you have never before carried such a precious load behind you. That boy with his beating heart, and those tokens of filial love, are a richer treasure than if you were staggering beneath a weight of diamonds."

As Charlie drove into the yard by the side of the house no one saw him but old Bob, who was standing by the pile of logs.

"Oh, daddy, how glad I am you are here: just help me unload as quick as you can."

"What dat you got dare, Charlie?"

"Oh, never mind, daddy, something good; only just help me quick to get them in, before any of them see us. Let us take them right down into the store-room."

The old man hardly knew what to make of Charlie's haste, and turned out his under-lip, as he was wont to do, when not quite satisfied with any thing, but he complied with Charlie's request, and in a few moments they were all lying together on the floor of the store-room.

"I am so glad, daddy, we have got them in here before any of them saw us; ain't there a good sight of them, daddy?"

The old man laid his hand on the shoulder of the boy, and held him off at arm's length, looking at him sternly.

"Charlie, what fur you in such hurry 'bout dese tings: whare you git 'em?"

"Bought them, daddy!"

"Who pay for dem tings?"

"I did, daddy, with my own money."

"Charlie, where you git so much money, buy so many tings?"

"Earned it, daddy. Mr. Thompson, you see, paid me my wages this morning, and I thought how pleased ma and Carrie, and all of you would be, to find enough things in the store-room to last ever so long. Won't they feel glad?"

And as Charlie's bright eyes, sparkling with pleasure, looked at the old man, he saw that he was winking very hard, and that a tear was ready to drop.

"Charlie! Charlie! God Almighty bless a you for dis ting; you be great man yet, Charlie! min' my word. God bless a you, sure as de sun shines. Miss Carrie—Bob had heard her step—Miss Carrie! won't a you call missus and come here?"

But Charles had stepped off, and the old mare was conveying him back to the store at a good jog, before Carrie and her mother could obey the summons.

"What is it, daddy?"

"Jist see dare, missus!"

"Where have they come from?"

"Oh missus, I live long nuff, now; you no neber want while you got sich chillen. Dat—dat boy!"

"Did Charlie bring these, daddy?" said Carrie, coming close beside him, and looking with intense interest up into his old honest face.

"Only to tink a dat boy! Miss Carrie, dat Charlie buy dem tings wid his own money. You see, missus, when he drive up to the door wid Misser Thompson old mare, he say, 'Quick, quick, daddy! help wid de tings, git 'em to de store-room afore nobody can see 'em.' I tell you, Miss Carrie, he make my heart jump; me no tink what he bout. But it 's livin' trute, he buyed 'em wid his own money. Missus, dat boy be great man; he make a your heart glad yet. God Almighty bless dat boy, sartain as de sun shines."

Carrie and her mother looked at the precious tokens as they lay in all the confusion in which they had so hastily been thrown together; and what they thought and felt can not be so easily described, for the heart's richest feelings go not forth in words; it has its own deep secret joy, whence thoughts spring up like sparkling bubbles from the living fountain, silently, but radiant with beauty. Again and again we quaff the cool sweet draught and are refreshed.

"Oh, daddy!" said Aunt Luckie, raising both her hands, "He is giving them vineyards and oliveyards out of the wilderness!"

"Me no understan about dat, Miss Luckie; me no see 'em. But *dare* is plenty meal, and sugar, and molasses, and ebery ting, for last a good long while; no mistake about *dat;* dem oder tings what a you talk about, me no see 'em 'tall."

When Charles drove away from the store, Mr. Thompson stood at his door watching for some time the receding wagon, and uttering occasionally certain expressions for the relief of his own mind, as there was no one present to hear the purport of them, or to sympathize with him; and so absorbed was he in the thoughts which arose as he kept looking after the boy and the mare, that he was not aware that a gentleman was approaching his premises from the opposite direction, until he was accosted with

"Good morning, Mr. Thompson! you have sent off a load early this morning, sir."

"Ah, it's you, is it! Good morning, Mr. Ralston—I believe I've got the name at last, but I should n't never have larned it, if Charlie had n't a put me right so often—good morning. A load, yes; we've sent off a load, but it ain't often sich a load as that goes traveling along the road. Oh dear, oh dear! this rheumatiz! Come, come in, and I'll tell you something that will do your heart good, if you have got any heart, and I am much mistaken in you if you ha'nt; just come in, and take a seat. I see he makes the old mare's legs fly pretty fast; I guess it won't hurt her, though. Ah me! this chair feels good; I've been standing round so much, and all stirred up so by that boy."

By the time Mr. Thompson had finished his remarks, he had become quietly settled in his arm-chair, and his visitor had taken the one appropriated to common use. Mr. Ralston looked quite concerned, as he replied:

"I hope Charlie has not been doing any thing out of the way, this morning, to trouble you!"

"Oh, la, no; it is n't that. Charlie trouble me? you don't

know him, or you would n't talk so. But I 've been a thinking how queer things is fixed in this world! There's good all the time a comin' out of evil."

"And there is more or less evil coming out of good, or mixed with it."

"That 's true; sartain it is. But somehow it seems to do a body more good when they see things that have been working, as it were, clear agin a family, turnin' out for the best, and all for their advantage in the end. You know you and I have had two or three private talks, all between ourselves, about the Leslies; and you have said how you admired Miss Car'line, because she had independence enough to take right hold and help her family. You need n't be afeared of me, nor it need n't make you turn red, because I happen to mention particular names, for I take you to be a man that ain't afeared to hold to what you say; and when I heard you talk as you did about —about—somebody the other day, I thought all the better on you for it. But that ain't what I was goin' to say jist now; my mind was full of that there boy. To think what he 's been a doin', and how glad and happy he was after he had done it! happier ten times than if he 'd had fifty dollars in his pocket, and goin' off to have a week's holiday in the city."

Mr. Ralston could not say why Charlie ought or ought not to be happy, for Mr. Thompson had not as yet enlightened him on the subject.

"But I hav n't yet telled you about it!"

And then Mr. Thompson, in as short a space as he could, recounted the affair that had made such an impression on his own mind, and then looked at young Ralston to see how the case affected him. The countenance of the latter manifested no change in its expression, and in a very calm way he replied:

"It was well in him; but can it be that the family need such assistance? are they really so reduced?"

"There ain't no mistake about that, friend, I tell you;" and again Mr. Thompson had to recount many particulars of which he had knowledge; and before he had finished had let Mr. Ralston into some secrets in regard to the property of Mr. Leslie, and the manner in which it had melted away.

In the course of his narrative, he incidentally mentioned

the estate which Mr. Leslie had inherited, and the way in which that had been lost to them. To this part of the story the young man listened with peculiar interest, and after the old gentleman had finished, referred again to it, and made memoranda of a few things which he thought of more or less consequence. He then inquired,

"Are you much acquainted with this Mr. Folger? He seems to be a man of considerable consequence here."

"I ain't much acquainted with him—and—I don't want to be."

"He is thought well of by the family of Mr. Leslie—is he not?"

"Well, sir, there's no tellin'; things works very strange, sometimes, and folks talks very strange. I don't know, but I'm most afeared sometimes things will get into worse ways than ever they have done yet. You see jist how it is: I've told you how that man managed matters, and tripped up poor Leslie, who is as honest and noble-hearted a crittur as ever breathed the breath of life. But he was n't—he was n't what we call a good calculator; and he was n't in no wise a match for that fellow Folger. I tell you—between you and me—he's a deep one."

"I should have thought his early treatment would have caused Mr. Leslie to be on his guard, and created some suspicion, that his after kindnesses were for some dangerous intent."

"That is just my mind, my young friend; you 've hit the nail on the head now. But you see, I suppose the case is this: When a man gits into sich a fix that he can't see no way to turn to git out of it, he's very apt to catch hold of the first thing that offers, and it's my mind that Horatio Leslie feels so in the power of that man, and no way to turn for help, that he has jist done as he has. It's a thousand pities he was n't brought up to any regular business. It's my mind that since there is so many twists and turns in the world, and money slips through a man's hand so easy, that a man ought to have something to turn his hands to, if worst comes to the worst."

The very significant look with which Mr. Thompson accompanied this last remark, was so manifestly designed as a home thrust, that young Ralston colored a little more than he did at the reference made to Miss Carrie a few moments before. And as Mr. Thompson seemed to have finished just then what he had to say, he felt called upon to make a reply to it.

"You are right, Mr. Thompson; a man ought to be trained to some regular business. He ought to have some employment that he can pursue systematically, and to which he feels bound to give his attention. He should fill some station among his fellow-men that may be useful to them and himself too. No man has a right so to live, that when taken away, his loss would not be felt."

"You have said the right thing this time, my young friend, that's sartain; and you'll excuse me for being plain spoken. I wish you well, and I believe you 've got that in you that won't take offense where there's no offense meant. But you see I've somehow taken a notion to you, and it makes me uneasy when I see a young man of your abilities—a—a—"

"Spending his time in fishing, gunning, and sauntering about."

"Well, now you 've said it; but I hope you won't lay it to heart; you see I 've an old body, and maybe I've forgot how I used to feel when I was young. I hope you won't lay it to heart, for I did n't mean no harm, no how."

"I shall lay it to heart, Mr. Thompson, and I hope I shall profit by it, too. And I thank you most truly, not only for your present frankness, but for all I have learned from you, since you have allowed me to be so intimate."

"Larned from me!" And the old man shook his head. "There ain't much that any one can larn at my hands, sir. No, no. I am but a plain sort of a man. My boy Charlie knows more larnin' than I ever got. But I am glad you ain't taken no offense."

"I have learned from you, Mr. Thompson, what probably I should never have learned from books. And as I am about to leave this place, and may not see you again, you must allow me to say, that the spirit of kindness you manifest toward all about you, your consideration for the poor and unfortunate, your honesty of purpose, and your charity toward those who occupy a different sphere of life, have not only created in my heart an interest for you that I shall ever cherish, but have also taught me a secret of life, upon which, I believe our own happiness, as well as the happiness of others materially depends."

The old man laid his hand on the arm of Ralston.

"But you ain't agoin'?"

"In a few days; and I came in this morning for the purpose of talking over some matters in reference to others, and also to make some explanation in regard to myself, for I have felt satisfied I ought to do so. I must say, therefore, in justice to my own character in your opinion, that my time, although apparently spent to little purpose, has not, I hope, been all wasted. I have had an object in view of some consequence, by my stay at Princesport—and have in part accomplished it. I have not been altogether idle, although not actively engaged in my profession."

"What, profession! Then after all you have got a trade?"

"I have studied law, and have a license to practice, but have not as yet entered upon it as a business."

"I wish you had a better trade; but I don't know, maybe I am wrong. And maybe there ain't no need why a man may n't be honest if he is bred up to so many tricks, as they say they are. You'll pardon me, though, but I ain't no opinion of 'em. There seems to me to be deviltry enough in the world naturally, without taking pains to larn the trade."

"We must not judge a whole profession, my dear sir, by what may have been our experience with a few of its members."

"That's true, no doubt; but it's been my luck then, if there is any good among 'em, not to come across 'em. Don't they take the side of every scamp that has money enough to give 'em a fee! and don't they try to make out his case to be a right one! and don't they, with their consarned crooked writings, and long palavers, and oily, slippery ways, keep the people all the time in a brile! I tell you it ain't no good trade that lives upon the mistakes and quarrels of others, and you ain't in no wise fitted for it. You 'll pardon me for the liberty."

"But you seem to forget, my dear sir, that we live in a world where the selfish feeling is predominant; and that where so many are trying to grasp what is not their own, it is very difficult so to frame our laws, that men who only seek their own selfish ends, can not take advantage of them; and it is well that some are so trained that they are able to counteract the designs of the grasping. Now, for instance, there is no doubt in my mind that Mr. Leslie has been wronged out of all his wife's property by a man, or set of men, who have taken advantage of his confidence. I think there is a process of law or equity, by which he has a good chance to set that matter right, and perhaps punish the evil doers; and if I can assist in doing this, or have influence with those who can do it, and from my own knowledge of law accomplish the end, would you think it a wrong use of one's talents—or a waste of time?"

"The Lord forbid! Well, well, I am an old body, as I said, and maybe I don't see things all round; but do you think there's a chance?"

"I think, sir, it may be proved that there has been a conspiracy to deprive Mrs. Leslie of her rights, and I think it may yet come to light that the gentleman who is now so intimate with that family is a party to it. He is, as I understand, the owner of that estate now."

"You don't say!"

"I have learned this lately, but I fear he is trying to get a stronger hold there than the mere possession of their estates. Have you never thought of that?"

"Don't talk about it—don't mention it, I beg on you. It's too bad to think on for a minute. But I *have* heered sich things, and it's most bewildered my brain sometimes when I think on it. Why, she's an—she's an angel a' most, so good; and sich a beautiful young crittur. Did you ever see sich a picture as she is?"

"I have not seen her, sir, since she was a young girl, at least I have had merely a glance at her."

"Why don't you go there then, right off? They'd welcome you, I know they would; ain't you been so clever to the boy, and all that—why not?"

"I should hardly dare to intrude myself merely on the strength of such a claim to their notice; I might find myself in the way of others, or meet there with company with which I could not be very congenial. Mr. Folger looks with rather a suspicious eye on me already."

"For what? what have you done to him, pray?"

"It has been necessary for me to make some inquiries of him in reference to former relatives of his. He did not see fit to give me the information but I have, I believe, procured it elsewhere. I think it most likely that my name is not in very good repute at Mr. Leslie's, if Mr. Folger's opinions are as current there as report affirms."

"Well, well; things will go wrong, do the best you can. But if any decent body could just step in, and git that blessed young innocent thing out of that—that—what shall I call him?"

"Better call him no hard names, sir; but I must tell you frankly Mr. Thompson, I take a deep interest in that family, and one reason for my departure from here, is for the purpose of making more particular examination of matters in relation to the conveyance of their property. I have my heart set upon procuring relief for them, if it can be done; but, sir, I must rely upon your retaining within your own breast whatever I have said to you on this subject. It might prevent my being able to get information of great moment, should it be known what my object is. I have told you, Mr. Thompson, because I know you are deeply interested for their good, and because I wish you to be on the watch for all information that may throw light on the transaction which we have referred to, and whenever, you learn any thing important, here is my address, by which you can direct a line immediately to me."

"What! what! you ain't a son of the great Ralston! Ralston of Clanmore?"

"I never heard my father called great before. I am, however, a son of Randolph Ralston of Clanmore valley."

"Did I ever! well, then, it ain't no wonder you don't have to work for your living!"

"I do not mean to lead the idle life I have here, Mr. Thompson, I assure you. I have no need to labor for the purpose of a support, but I have a work to do in life for others, if not for myself, and I know you can understand how a man may engage with all his heart in labors for his fellow-man, where the only reward he has in view, is the approbation of his own conscience and another's benefit."

"I don't know, sir, but I can say that sich a thing might be. I ain't to be sure never done much for myself, or any body else, but I believe it does make me feel a little better when I lay down at night, or sit in my chair here all alone, to think I have n't never to my knowin' harmed any one, and maybe sometimes, in a small way, done one and another a kindness, but it's only been in a small way."

CHAPTER XVII.

As Princesport, in consequence of its beautiful water scenery, was a desirable place for those who wished for a few months the advantages of sea-air, or were fond of aquatic sports, a company had been formed for the purpose of establishing a splendid hotel, after the fashion of English houses of that description, of which at that day but very few could be found in our country. An elegant site had been purchased—the mansion of a man of property, who, tempted by a high price, was induced to sell his homestead, and although advanced in life, seek another resting-place.

The building itself was a fine structure, and the grounds around it well laid out. But additions were made to the size of the house, and changes internally and externally, to suit the views of those who had the management of the affair.

Large sums of money were expended, whether judiciously or not, is of no consequence to us now. At the time, it was thought well of, and many looked upon it as the great lever which was to raise Princesport to distinction, and impart that life and energy which it had seemed always to lack.

The affair having been completed, it was concluded by the managers, probably as a judicious way of advertising, and giving éclât to their establishment, to celebrate the opening of it by a ball. It was designed to be a splendid affair, and no expense was spared to make it so. Upholsterers as well as waiters and cooks, together with a band of musicians, were imported from the city of New York for the occasion, and to crown the whole, the very accomplished manager of the old "city assembly," had accepted an invitation to take the direction for the evening—a circumstance in itself sufficient to assure all who might attend, that the utmost decorum would be observed, and nothing allowed inconsistent with the strictest rules of polite intercourse.

Cards of invitation had been freely circulated even into remote districts of the State, and especially among the notables of the great city; as from thence, it was anticipated, its most profitable customers would be found.

The élite of Princesport were also among the favored ones, as a matter of course; and a great stir it made among the old satins and silks which had already seen more than one generation; and all the dress-makers far and near were put in requisition, for the purpose of remodeling, and trimming, and otherwise arranging, these costly, but old-fashioned garments, into some shape suitable for the present occasion.

The commotion, indeed, was felt by the whole community; for in some way almost all had an interest in it, or were affected by it. Carrie Leslie, by some oversight, or blunder, as the managers afterward proclaimed, was not honored with a ticket. She had not expected one. She had in fact scarcely thought of the occasion, except as on some account it was forced upon her notice. Her mind was too much occupied with the sterner things of life, just then, to be able to enter heartily into any such scene. And perhaps the reader may start at the suggestion, that Carrie, our Carrie Leslie! could, under any circumstances, have sympathy with a scene so nearly allied, as many think, to the territory which the great enemy claims as his! or which others claim for him. A ball is, to many minds, a synonym for all that is extravagant and improper in attire, and all that is dangerous to physical and moral health. We shall not attempt an argument on the other side; nor would we express the belief that like other things in life, which for the time entrance the senses, there may not be danger.

May there not be danger too, when care, that nightmare of life, presses heavily on the young heart? When the bounding spirit loses its elasticity; and the imagination pictures no pleasant scenes; and the ideal world has no quickening influence; and the youthful feelings droop and shiver within the cold dark shadow of life's sad realities?

It would be well, if the "sunny hours" of childhood and youth could pass unclouded, and all the storms that rage across the path of life be avoided until age has fitted those who must bear their fury for the stern encounter. But as this can not be; as the most assiduous care on the part of those who watch over their younglings, can not always guard them against the aching heart, it should be the duty of those whose age fits them to bear the heat and burden of the day, to afford such recreation for the youthful mind as will in some measure counterbalance its earthly tendencies. At least they should not knit the brow, nor shake the head, and say "naught, naught," when they hear the merry laugh, or see the bright glow upon the cheek of youth, which music and dancing inspire. And he who would deny to budding youth such pastime; and has no sympathy with the grace of motion, or the quickening sounds of music; manifests more of the ascetic than the Christian. Had *he* been intrusted with the garnishing of earth, he would have left out the flowers and the fruits, reared no mountain-tops; nor dug out one sweet vale. It would have been a vast clean prairie with no rocks to turn aside his plowshare, and no trees to keep the sunshine from his grain.

But Carrie had no wish to attend the ball. It had no allurement for her that could excite the slightest wish concerning it.

The appointed day at length had come, and strangers were hourly arriving, and quite a stir was manifest in the usually quiet town.

Carrie had labored through the day, at her usual task, and when her school was dismissed, hastened home to engage in other duties there.

As she entered the door of their wide hall, her hand was immediately seized, and the smiling countenance of an old friend beamed upon her.

"Carrie Leslie! my old schoolmate, how glad I am to see you!"

"Why, William! or I suppose I ought to say Mr. Dalton now; how *do* you do?"

"Call me mister if you dare! I shall Miss Leslie you right off."

"But you have grown so!"

"And so have you; that is, I can not say that you have grown in height. But you look older, Carrie! almost matronly!"

"And why should I not; for you must know that I am a 'school-marm, now; and have a good right to a matron's sober face."

These few words were passed as they walked, arm-in-arm, through the hall, and into the back sitting-room.

"I have been waiting for you so long that I was just about starting for your school-house, that I might have a talk on our way home. I have so much to say, and must be off again to-morrow morning."

"Not so soon, surely?"

"I must be back to my recitations by ten to-morrow morning, or be obliged to give some excuse, and hurt my conscience. You see I heard about this ball, which is to take place this evening, and thinks I to myself, What a grand chance for a trip over the floor with my old friend Carrie; unless by this time she should have some nearer friend whom she might prefer to dance with. But if she has, thinks I, he shall let me have one round with her, at any rate."

Carrie could not but smile at the earnestness of her old companion, as she replied:

"I am afraid, William, I shall be compelled to disappoint you, but not for the reasons you have named. There is no one yet would be so acceptable a partner as yourself were I to be one of a cotillion. But I have no idea—not the most distant—of attending the ball, and for several reasons."

"I know all about your reasons, Carrie; I have had a long talk with your good mother, so you can not tell me any thing new. Your mother has also informed me that no ticket has been sent to your family; but that is of no account, except as it shows the mean spirit of the managers of the concern. The fact is, the whole affair is a mere ruse on the part of the company who own the hotel to bring it into notice. But as to the ticket, I have prepared myself with one, which will be just as good as if you had one of your own. Come now I want you to say yes; you have often given me good sisterly counsel, and I as a younger brother have always taken it."

"I know you have—or you did—and I should very much enjoy a few hours with you, talking about old times; although I would not wish to deprive *you* of the enjoyment of the evening. I expect it will be quite a brilliant affair."

"I don't care a straw about that—and there will be nobody there that I know or care for beside yourself. I thought it would be a little change from Homer and Euclid—and also to have a little time with you. If you do not go, I shall not; and the ticket may go into the fire for all me."

Carrie now felt that she must decide the question without reference to her own selfish feelings. She did not care for the amusement on her own account. But she would by refusing to go, disappoint William Dalton of whatever pleasure he might have anticipated. She had no religious scruples as to the propriety of such amusements under proper circumstances. Such assemblies had not then the objectionable features of those of the present day. Young ladies, pure as the flowers which adorned their persons, did not then throw themselves into the arms of any voluptuous debauchee who might be able with éclât to bear them whirling round in the giddy waltz. Parents and grandparents were there; and those whose station in society commanded the highest respect; and there was on every side a watchful eye over any breach of propriety and politeness.

Carrie had her reasons why she would have preferred not to mingle in the pleasure-seeking circle; but they were not such as affected her conscience. She therefore replied, after a moment's reflection:

"Well, William, if mother approves I will no longer say nay; please excuse me until I see her."

Carrie found her mother and Aunt Luckie consulting very earnestly about some little preparation necessary for Carrie's respectable appearance in public. She waited a moment and exclaimed:

"And you, Aunt Luckie! you do not surely think that I ought to go!"

"And why should n't you, dear Miss Carrie; ain't it just the very thing that your mother and me have been saying all along that you needed; that you ought to have a change; you're getting all sagged down, and fagged out with care and trouble, and you must have a change."

"Why, I thought surely Aunt Luckie, if I should conclude to go, I must expect a reproof from you, you are so hard upon all light things."

"Oh! well, dear, you know there's reason in all things. I never set by such things myself; and then there is a great difference too, in the way such things is managed; and when all things is managed properly, as I've heard your ma, tell on, why

I can't see where there is any more harm it it, than in young girls playing Blind-man's-Buff; or in the boys playing ball. Things must be looked at with reason, child."

Although Carrie had really no desire for amusement, and would have much preferred to have spent the evening at home with William Dalton, yet no sooner did she find herself in the midst of the brilliant circle, than her spirits at once recovered the spring of past joyous scenes. She was Carrie Leslie again, the bright star amid a constellation of beauties. To say that she was the most beautiful among all the fair ones that graced the assembly, would perhaps not be saying just the truth. But in addition to her comely face and graceful form, was a perfect self-possession that enabled her to act with the same ease she might have manifested in her own domestic circle. She seemed to have no consciousness of her own loveliness, and no thought as to the impression she made upon others. She was simply but suitably dressed. One single jewel sparkled on her person; that was a neat brooch confining a sprig of white jasmin to her breast. Her hair, after the fashion of that day, lay in curls upon her back, bound by a broad pearl clasp, and exposing to full view her fair forehead and finely molded features; and the long tight boddice and full-flowing skirt exhibited in perfection her faultless form. As William Dalton led her across the room to a seat among the dancers, he must not be blamed if he felt some little pride on hearing the buzz of approbation that many, in the excitement of the moment, were not careful to restrain. We will not weary our readers with a minute description of a scene which most have in their day witnessed often, and the impression of which still lingers in their memory, if their dancing days have gone by. We admire the parterre when dazzling in the luxurious glow of nature's fairest flowers; our hearts melt in tenderness when amid the chastened hues of autumn, and we look with rapture at the golden tints which fringe the horizon, or paint the fleecy cloud, as the sun sends his parting rays from behind the western hills. And is not youth, in all its freshness, a more glorious sight than either? are our hearts so indurated by the sterner things of life, that the joyous smile, the flashing eye, the light spring, and the graceful motion of the young in the heyday of existence, can only draw from us a frown or a sneer?

While the party on the floor were going through the mazes of the first cotillion, there were standing among the spectators two gentlemen who were looking with fixed eyes upon the changing groups, and if it could have been noticed by those who observed those gentlemen, it would have been seen that their gaze was fixed alone on the easy movement and winning grace of one and the same individual, whom each had singled out as to their eye more attractive than aught else in the room. Both of the gentlemen were tall and distinguished for good personal appearance. There was quite a difference in their ages; one, the younger, a little past the age of majority, and the other, in what might be called the middle period of life. The latter was dressed apparently with the design of engaging in the pleasure of the evening, while the former was only sufficiently so to honor the occasion as a spectator. Although these gentlemen, as has been said, were both intently gazing upon one and the same lovely being, the feelings which affected them in reference to her, were vastly different. One saw only a graceful form, a beautiful face, and a faultless dancer. The other, while perhaps not altogether insensible to these external attractions, was much more absorbed in contemplating a richer galaxy of inward graces. Years had passed since he had enjoyed so fair a view of her—changes had those years made in her appearance, but not so material as to obliterate the lineaments which distinguished those sunny features that, from the first hour he saw them, had made a deep impression on his heart. She appeared more lovely to him now, because he thought that he could see more clearly marked upon the outer form those attributes which had entranced him at the first.

The two gentlemen were Tobias Folger and Clarence Ralston. The latter had come with no expectation of seeing any that he knew, much less of beholding her who had been—we may as well say it now as at any future period of our story—the idol of his heart, from which never for one moment had his affections swayed. He had come merely as a matter of curiosity, to witness a scene of which he had no desire to be an actual participant.

Tobias Folger was there, too, we may almost say, by accident; but as he has been described as arrayed in "full dress," we must give the reader an insight into the way bv which it happened.

For several days previous to that on the evening of which the affair was to take place, Mr. Folger had been out of town, or at least he was not seen at Mr. Leslie's, and of course he was very excusable for saying nothing about the ball. But the ball would be an excellent apology for a style of costume which Mr. Folger thought was to himself peculiarly becoming, and in which he felt exceedingly anxious to present himself before Miss Leslie. That Miss Carrie could have been induced to accept a ticket from him, and attend the festivity, he did not for a moment believe. But if he could make her the offer, and save his character for gallantry, and at the same time have an opportunity to appear before her in a peculiarly attractive attitude—a great point would be gained.

He had now for some time been very assiduous in his attention—carefully so, however, lest he should offend. He had engaged, as we have seen, a powerful aid in his attempts to win favor with the object of his attention. And she—Mrs. Crampton—had lost no opportunity to further his views. He had even gone so far as to make Mrs. Crampton a confidante of the true nature of his feelings for Miss Carrie; and Mrs. Crampton had at last communicated to him the intelligence that the time had arrived when he might fairly hope that his proposals would be accepted. And Mr. Folger had resolved to bring matters at once to a close. He had therefore arranged all his plans, as he supposed, in the happiest manner. He designed to call at Mr. Leslie's, properly equipped, and with his carriage—all in readiness to convey them to the hotel. Of course she could not accept at so late an hour; but "he had been out of town," "had made all the haste possible," "and if she could not go with him, he would remain with her." And a fine opportunity would be afforded him, and under the best circumstances, to make his intended proposals.

The unexpected tidings which greeted his ear on arriving at the Leslies', did indeed fill him with dismay. His plans were defeated, and his fears aroused, for he had not the most distant idea who the happy individual was that had borne off the prize he was just then so eager for—and he dared not inquire. To the ball, however, he was resolved to go, and if possible, yet have the honor of being her partner a portion of the evening.

And now, as we have said, he was among the spectators,

gazing intently at the lovely girl—drinking in her beauties as though they were rightfully his, and resolving with all the determination of his will that he would yet possess her as his own.

After the first cotillion was over, Carrie, not caring to engage with the next set, was seated beside her partner, pleasantly conversing about scenes of like interest which they had enjoyed while at school, when young Dalton asked her to excuse him for a moment, as he thought he saw a person that he knew at a distant corner of the room. He was away from her, however, but a few minutes, when Carrie saw him approach, leaning on the arm of a gentleman taller than himself, and whose countenance at once affected her with a peculiar sensation. He was a stranger, and yet the features were familiar. That open brow, the dark hair, the pale complexion, above all that clear full eye, so animated with thought and feeling, all flashed at once upon her. She knew him—it could be none else—and as William Dalton presented Clarence Ralston, without the least hesitation Carrie extended her hand, and with that smile so full of meaning to those her heart made welcome, said,

"It is a long time since we have met, Mr. Ralston."

"So long," and the face of Clarence was highly flushed as he spoke, "that I have not dared to hope I should have been remembered by you." Carrie might have been troubled for a reply, if William Dalton had not just then interfered,

"Why, what does all this mean? Here have I been dragging along this gentleman out of the obscure corner where he was ensconsed, for the purpose of introducing him to a friend of mine, to whom, of course, I supposed he was a perfect stranger, and lo and behold, the first thing I hear is a recognition of old acquaintanceship—what does it mean?"

"Since Miss Leslie has been so kind as to make the acknowledgment, I am very happy to tell you that we were once for a short period on quite intimate terms; but years have passed since."

"And why is it," said young Dalton, "that you have been here, Mr. Clarence Ralston, some months, and have allowed a mere accident to be the means of bringing you in contact with this young lady? Clarence, I almost am ready to call your judgment in question."

Young Dalton was naturally of a lively turn, and the excitement of the evening had increased the playfulness of his mind. But he was quick to discern when he was going too far; his two friends, he now saw, for some inexplicable reason, were both suffering under deep embarrassment; and he was about to say something by way of changing the subject, when an interruption was occasioned by the sudden intrusion into their circle of no less a personage than Mr. Tobias Folger. He took no notice of either gentleman standing beside her, but made a low reverence to the lady, and respectfully requested the favor of her hand for the next cotillion. Carrie at once turned toward Mr. Dalton, intimating thereby that she considered him as having a peculiar claim to her hand that evening, and that she must refer the petitioner to him.

Before, however, any further progress could be made in the proceedings, Mr. Folger was touched gently upon the arm by a gentleman from behind, and his attention arrested.

The reason for it will require a little explanation.

Mr. Folger had entered the room during the progress of the first cotillion, and as we have intimated stood among the spectators, and watched with glitering eyes the light and graceful manner in which one of the beauties of the circle bore herself through the various figures of the dance.

As soon as the performance was over. and during the general tête-à-tête, that followed, two or three gentlemen from the city, and well known to the manager, stepped up to him, and leading him a little one side, were for a moment earnestly engaged in conversation on some subject in which he at once seemed to take a deep interest. No sooner had the manager fully comprehended what they had to say, than he straightened himself to his usual commanding height, and, speaking in a decided tone,

"He must leave the room instantly." A gentleman who had overheard the nature of the communication, and also the name of the person, thought it necessary to interfere.

"I hope, captain, you are not in earnest. The gentleman you speak of, is a man of great wealth and respectability; in fact, captain, he may be called the boss here, for he owns a good share of the concern. I hope, sir, you will think what you do; it might be a serious matter."

Those who remember Captain F——, the gentleman who so

long stood as manager of the old "city assembly," need not be told that he was the very soul of honor. A gentleman of most polite address, unblemished reputation, and a great remove from any thing mean and low; of fine personal appearance, and possessed of a more than usual amount of physical strength. In those days a fair character was an essential requisite to any who wished to unite with that polished circle, and Captain F—— had ever guarded with a very jealous eye against intrusion by any who bore a sullied name.

Perhaps not well pleased with the manner of the last gentleman's address to him, he fixed upon the speaker his keen eye.

"I am here, sir, by the special invitation of gentlemen of known character and respectability, and the fact *that I am here*, sir, is a guaranty, to this company, that, no person of blemished reputation shall be allowed to mingle with them. If you are a friend of the person in question, I advise you to get him away as quietly and quickly as possible; for if he does not leave this room *instanter*, I shall show him the door before this whole assembly, be he as rich as Crœsus, or as strong as Goliah."

This was said, indeed, in a low voice, for it was not intended for any ears but his to whom it was spoken; but the tone of determination, the flashing eye, and the compressed lips, gave significant tokens that there was to be no further parley.

What the gentleman said to Mr. Folger, after attracting his notice, or what arguments he used, we know not, but they were all sufficient to induce him to leave the room without any delay, and he was no more seen that evening.

"Mr. Bevault," said the manager, after this little episode had passed, "can you tell me the name of the young lady who sits on the right there, conversing with those two young gentlemen?"

"I can, sir, she was formerly a pupil of mine; Miss Leslie of Princesport."

"May I ask the favor, of an introduction?"

"By all means, sir."

Carrie had scarcely recovered from the confusion which Mr. Folger's proposition had caused her, when she was again the subject of much greater surprise, for Mr. Bevault was bowing to her, with all the grace for which he was so distinguished, and by his side was the elegant person of the manager.

"Miss Leslie, allow me to introduce you to Captain F——."

"I have taken the liberty to ask the favor of your hand, Miss Leslie, in leading the next party; that is, if the gentleman attending you, can be persuaded to waive his claim."

Young Dalton knew too well what a high compliment was paid to Carrie by such a request not to reply at once,

"With great pleasure, sir," and the look he gave Carrie, told her that it would not answer for her to refuse.

In a moment more, she was the "observed of all observers;" and moving about the room, the admiration of many, the envy of some; and to the utter astonishment and dismay of those who had kept aloof from her society, lest the taint of her honorable endeavors to earn her daily bread should injure their respectability.

We have remained, however, long enough at this evening's entertainment, and must leave the gay party to its enjoyment, for Carrie had exacted a promise from William Dalton, that he would return with her at an early hour; and he was quite ready to keep his engagement, at the first intimation of her wish to depart. Very unlike persons who have just renewed an acquaintance after a lapse of some years, neither Carrie nor Clarence seemed to have much to communicate—there was evidently embarrassment on the part of each, and the little that was said by either, had no reference to any thing connected with the past.

Carrie had, indeed, expressed her gratitude for his kindness to her little brother; and he in a very easy manner, passed it over lightly, as though all he had done was merely a matter of pastime.

They had left the room, and in the wide hall of the hotel were about to separate. It was very evident that the interview, thus far, had afforded but little satisfaction to either. Carrie had none of the vivacity which distinguished her at the early part of the evening; and Clarence appeared more like one who had lost rather than renewed an acquaintance with an old friend.

As if she felt unwilling thus to separate, and perhaps impressed by the thought, that something was due from her, to one who was a stranger in their place, and also on account of civilities he had paid to her brothers, Carrie, just as they were parting from each other, at length said:

"I have not forgotten Mr. Ralston, that I once invited you to visit my house at Princesport. But great changes have taken place since then. My father is no longer there to welcome you, and my brothers, as you know, are also away. If you will come, however, at any time that I may not be engaged in my school, I shall be happy to point out to you the beautiful views from our place, which you may remember I once talked so much about."

"I shall be obliged to deny myself that pleasure now. I expect to leave Princesport on the morrow. But it may be that I shall take the liberty at some future time, before long, to call at your house. I may have some special business with Mrs. Barton that will make it very desirable that I should see *her*."

"Oh, indeed! I remember you were quite a favorite with Aunt Luckie. She, no doubt, will be glad to see you: for she does not readily forget old friendships."

"I have reason, always to remember her with gratitude. She was a faithful friend, in many ways. May I ask you to tell her that I have never forgotten her, nor her good counsels? And although somewhat altered by age, in personal appearance, have not *lost any of the feelings which the boy Clarence expressed to her when we last saw each other*."

A deep flush suffused the face of the lovely girl as he uttered the last sentence. She had long known what those feelings had been; for Aunt Luckie often playfully alluded to them as one of the instances where young love, so very ardent at the time, soon wears out.

Clarence noticed the effect his words had produced, but could only construe it as an indication that the scene so strongly impressed on his mind, and so cherished as the one lovely spot in his past life, was not recalled by her without pain. Some reply Carrie made, but in the confusion of departing, Clarence did not hear it; and perhaps she herself was hardly conscious whether she engaged to deliver the message or not.

Again they are cast asunder by influences neither could control. We can not make the record without heaving a sigh over the necessity which compels us. It would suit our feelings much better to see all the barriers removed, which keep apart two hearts so constituted for mutual sympathy, and to our apprehension, fitted to enjoy the highest earthly bliss, in their union. But the more we learn of life, the more reconciled we ought to be with allotments which run counter to our own short-sighted views; we should make sad work with the social state, as well as with the natural world, were it left to our management.

CHAPTER XVIII.

Clarence Ralston had not been as idle at Princesport as appearances indicated. He was not indeed, as yet, a wrestler on the field of active life; but had turned aside from the busy multitude that he might adjust his plans for the future. In general, the great question to be decided, is, what will prove the most lucrative employment? or lead to the highest honors? Necessity at first, gives energy to the thought, and urges on to steady toil, until the stimulus derived from success, or the habit which has been formed, are of sufficient strength, to keep the mind active in its calling, even after the main object has been attained.

But on those who by some providential arrangement have been born to a fortune, a great evil is entailed. They feel no pressing need for action. All their demands have been supplied from their earliest days, without care or thought on their part; and as they look forward to the future, the same abundance appears spread out before them. To a mind not accustomed to weigh in just balances the fortunes of this life, it seems no doubt a most desirable thing, that from the commencement to the close of life's journey, a sufficient supply of means, to gratify every reasonable wish, would be a most desirable attainment. But to those who take pains to look over the list, as the travelers of life are journeying on, and allow their judgment to be regulated by what they see; a very different conclusion is arrived at. They behold the heart drooping in the midst of abundance, satiety settling in moody bitterness on the children of affluence, debility of mind and body, and too often, dissipation, cutting short the life that had begun with promise. They see the toiling men, who started with no other provision than strong resolution, and good courage, making their mark as they forced through the roughnesses of life, carving their names on high places, extending their hand for help to their fellow-laborers, and with energies unnerved, even to old age. They see all the mighty changes working on our globe, whereby man is elevated, and his comforts increased, and his wants relieved; wrought out by the stern hand of diligence.

And they learn this lesson:

"The hand of the diligent maketh rich; idleness clothes a man with rags."

Clarence had not seen much of the world, but he had jotted down some items, in his small experience, and they had done much to assist him in his conclusions as to the path of duty. He had no need to labor for his own support; he could choose his place of residence, and the way in which he would spend his time; he could gather around him every luxury, for his means were ample, and by common prudence he could pass through life with no care, or the fear of want.

But when life should have been passed, and the end should come, would the retrospect be one that could satisfy a rational mind? would it be enough to reflect, that he had fared sumptuously, and lived without care?

But Clarence took a closer view than even this. How soon would a state of existence merely, with every wish gratified, begin to pall? How soon would every source of enjoyment begin to lose its zest, from the fact that it could be obtained without an effort? How soon would the common round of pleasure become wearisome? Or days succeeding days that had no great end in view, prove as insipid as an oft-repeated tale? And his mind shuddered at the specter which its own reasoning had raised.

Again another view of his situation presented itself.

He was in the midst of a changing, troubled world, traveling toward the same goal with those whose feelings were as sensitive as his own; and *their* journey was a long struggle with disappointment and care. Fathers were toiling through the long day, and spending sleepless nights in busy thought; because upon their skill and their strength depended the means by which dear ones were to have their daily bread. Children too, were agonizing in the troubled conflict; their hearts aching for those who gave them birth, because they saw the marks of care furrowing deeper and deeper, day by day; and the joy of youth was blighted, its morning dark with clouds, and its light step fell heavy and plodding upon the earth.

And all this for the want of a moiety of that which many a fellow-traveler had stored away; a super-abundance over all his largest demands, stored away beyond the reach of friend or foe. No need did it supply; it brought him neither food nor drink; it neither clothed nor sheltered him; it did not even purchase a single gewgaw to please his fancy. It had been locked away; he held the key which fastened it, and he could say and feel that it was *his;* and year by year he rolled its huge bulk over, and added to its size, and added to his own care, and called it *his own.* How many aching hearts it might have eased! How much of care and sorrow it might have alleviated! How like a heavenly chalice it might have proved to many a heart-sick, toiling, drooping, fellow-man! And will there be no reckoning for all this? can those who have walked side by side through this wilderness, so throw around each self a wall through which no human sympathy shall have a right to enter? Together they have been cast; to one spot in life assigned; this poor man was well known, and all could see the care-worn marks upon his brow; and though he never asked for aid, all knew he needed it; and when they meet before their common Father, will there be no reckoning? and will that treasure shut out from all the calls which suffering hearts are making in their agony, have no power then? will it be as useless as it has been here? will it not rather crush its wretched owner, and every dollar clutched and hoarded from his fellow's need, prove a scorpion to his soul?

And Clarence thought of all this, and the path of duty and happiness lay plain before him. "He was his brother's keeper;" and what their common Father had bestowed on *him*, must, he firmly resolved it should, be ever ready in the time of need. He had property—it should be used to comfort the sorrowing, to help the friendless, to stimulate the desponding, and to send joy and gladness into the social circle where it had the power to cheer.

He had an education—that was a talent too—he need not use it as a means of livelihood, or to add to his wealth. But by it he might be able to redress the wrongs of the injured, and to uphold the innocent, as in his path of life he might hear their cry for help.

One reason which hastened the departure of Clarence from Princesport, was the account which he had received concerning the health of his father. Randolph Ralston was evidently drawing near the end of his days. Without any apparent cause, life seemed all at once to be ebbing fast away. He was no longer able to go abroad, and for most of the time, reclined against the back of a large easy chair, with his bundles of papers on a table near at hand. What purpose they answered, or what he had in view by continually poring over them, it would have been difficult to determine, but it seemed a necessary part of his life. Those papers had a charm for him; they were the last link that bound him to earth. He could bargain no more—he could no longer go abroad, and ride over the immense tracts which he had called his own. He could no longer receive the obsequious homage to which for so many years he had been accustomed as the great landholder. All that remained to him now, was an extended view, from his window, of the beautiful estate of Clanmore, and these papers spread out upon the table before him.

Some days before the return of Clarence, it had been whispered in the family that a change was about to be made in the disposition of the property. Juba, the confidential servant of Mr. Ralston, had been ordered privately to go for Esquire Southard, and that gentleman had been there, and spent some time in conference with the sick man. For what purpose, none knew; but those immediately interested had their suspicions keenly aroused; and there were many whisperings about the house, and private consultations, for it was very evident that whatever alterations had been made, must now be final, for Randolph Ralston was fast closing all earthly business.

From his large easy chair, Mr. Ralston was at length obliged to retire to his bed. His papers, too, were removed from the table into his strong box for the last time. He could read them no longer; his trembling hands could no longer hold up the precious documents; so they were put under lock and key.

And now the bed upon which he has laid down, is to be his dying bed.

His long life was drawing to its close, and all its doings about to be sealed up against the last reckoning. But of that he could not now think. Earth had engrossed his heart so long! Lands, and houses, and bonds had been the favorite subjects upon which his mind dwelt, the chief objects for which his energies had been spent; and death is at hand, and about to make an eternal separation between him and all he has loved.

"How is my father?" was the first sentence Clarence uttered as he met his mother, who had advanced into the hall to welcome her son.

"And you have come, Clarence! I feared you would not be here in time. Your father is as well as can be expected; the doctors think that life is fast ebbing away, and that he can not last many days."

"I did not hear that he was so ill until within the last few hours, or I should have returned home sooner."

"It would not have availed any thing; nature must have its course. Please follow me;" and Mrs. Ralston led her son into a private parlor.

"As I was saying, nature must have its course: your father is quite advanced in life; his affairs are now all arranged—satisfactorily—so I think. But there are surmises by those who are interested in the matter, that he has made some changes, which may not be pleasing to them; you know who I mean; and from what I learn, there may be steps taken to—"

"My dear mother—" Clarence could no longer endure the pain of listening to such a theme, when an uncertainty oppressed his mind concerning matters of more consequence to his dying parent, than all the estates on earth; "pardon my interruption—but do tell me! does my father know he is about to die?"

"Doubtless he does—he must know it."

"What does he say, mother, in view of death? does he feel prepared to meet such an event?"

"Why as to that—a man of your father's prudence and foresight, would no doubt, if he felt any hesitation on that score, have taken proper measures in view thereof. He knows that the minister would come at any time if requested; on such matters every one must be their own judge."

Clarence knew well that such had always been his mother's views. But his own heart could not be at rest while uncertain how his dying parent felt in prospect of the great change.

"May I ask your permission, my dear mother, to see my father without delay?"

"Certainly; it would be highly proper that you should. But if you should be desired to unite in urging upon your father any changes in the disposition of his worldly matters, it is my injunction upon you, that you do it not."

"I can assure you, mother, no power on earth could induce me even to mention the interests of this world to him—at such an hour."

"You will need, then, to be very firm, for I fear there are, or there will be, desperate means resorted to—"

It is a solemn hour when the child stands by the bed of a dying parent. There may have been a cold and distant manner on the part of the latter; there may have been severity of treatment; and the keen eye of the father may have caused the son to quail before it. But these are all forgotten then; for the fire of the eye has been quenched, and the robust frame lies in its helplessness—beneath the withering touch of the great leveler.

Clarence had never feared his father, for he had never been treated with rigor by him. The failing on the part of the parent had been, that too little regard had been manifested, except for the security of worldly interest. But still the heart of the son clung to the fond idea of parent; and as he stood by his bedside, and beheld the pale and drooping visage, and felt the cold hand and the feeble pulse, a feeling of intense interest was awakened, and such as he had never realized before.

And in the most tender manner, he addressed him:

"You are quite feeble, father!"

The old man gazed at him a moment.

"Ah, Clarence! it is you! you have come! well, yes—I am quite weak; sit down—sit down by me."

Clarence drew his chair close to the bed, and again took hi father's hand.

"I want to talk with you about the Clanmore estate—you see—you see I am determined—they shan't have it—they have acted so—they never *shall* have it. Oh dear, dear! you don't know—they told me I was an old—" His trembling lip refused to utter the obnoxious word. "But they shall never have Clanmore—never—never. I'll tell you—but you must say nothing—nothing until—Southard has it—it's altered—you will—"

Clarence perceived that his father was becoming more and more agitated, and being desirous of diverting his mind to some subject more appropriate for a dying man,

"Dear father—try to let these matters go; do not suffer your mind to be disturbed by them now. Do you not feel, father, that you must soon leave the world?"

"Leave the world! Oh, yes. It is going—all going—I suppose it must be so—the doctor says so. But you must promise me one thing—now say it—you never will give up Clanmore, never give it up to them—it is yours—yours and your heirs forever."

Most heartily did Clarence grieve to hear these words; they sounded to him like the knell of all his future peace. Vexation, turmoil, contention, all arose before him a band of hideous specters—from which his soul shrunk in disgust.

But again he essayed to bring the mind of his father to the one great subject.

"Father, dear father!" his voice trembled so as scarcely to allow the words to come forth; "are you prepared to die?"

At that moment a loud ha! ha! burst upon his ear. He turned and perceived Ralph standing with the door ajar, and with the most contemptuous sneer upon his countenance.

Immediately the father grasped the arm of Clarence, and looked at him with intense interest, as he said, in a whisper,

"Promise me—promise me quick!" Almost overcome by the agitation caused by the brutal conduct of his brother, Clarence stammered out,

"I do—I do, promise you, father."

"What is that?" said Ralph, obtruding himself close by the bed.

"What is that? what has he promised?"

The father looked at him with an eye of anger, although the film of death was already beginning to gather over it.

"I have his promise—no—*never*—you shall never have—" The attention of Ralph was at that moment arrested by the entrance of Richard, who with much earnestness beckoned his brother from the room.

Again Clarence renewed the subject so much upon his own mind.

"Dear father, had you not better now let all these matters go? Turn your thoughts from earth; you have not long to live."

"Who told you so? But, yes, I suppose it is so; it is all going—what good—what good will it do me? yes, yes, yes;" and for a few moments he was silent, and then, with more strength than Clarence supposed he still possessed, he said, with deep emphasis on each word,

"Done—done—done with life!"

"But the next life, father; are you prepared for that?"

"No, they shall never have it; they shall never have Clanmore; they think I have not done it! remember your promise."

"Father—death is before you! Eternity! Father, think of that; are you prepared to go into eternity?"

The old man shook his head, and faintly articulcated,

"Oh dear, dear; I fear not."

"Shall I go for your minister?"

The father made no reply. Clarence then knew there had not been always the most pleasant feelings between the rector and his parent; he therefore asked,

"Or, perhaps, you would perfer to see Mr. Rice?"

"Yes, yes; he is a good honest man, tell him that I am—I am not long—maybe he can do something, or show me what to do. But, what makes it so dark? Oh life, life; where has it gone; and is this all? the end! Oh, how dark. Clarence, Clarence, it seems all night before me, dark and dismal; do feel my pulse; is it not strong yet? maybe I can live."

"Your pulse is stronger than I feared it was."

"It *is* strong then; maybe I shall not go yet for all—my father lived ten years longer, than I have yet. Ten years is a good long time yet, but if I should live to be a hundred, they shall never have Clanmore."

"Shall I go now father, and see Mr. Rice?"

"Well, yes; but don't you think my pulse is strong? you said so."

"I said, father, it was stronger than I feared it was; but you still are very feeble, and you have been growing more and more so for some time they tell me."

"Who tells you so? Ah, they would be glad to have it so. They want Clanmore; but they shall never have it. They are welcome to the rest; I have left them enough. Did you hear Ralph? did you hear him laugh; and all my care has come to this. Oh, dear, that darkness; it is coming again. Do you think that is death, and is it so cold, too? Do not leave me now; did you ever see any one die."

"I never did, father."

"I wonder if people all die so?"

Poor Clarence was in an agony. He knew not what to say; he dare not trust to his own skill in guiding a trembling spirit through the dark valley.

"Had I not better go at once, father, and bring your friend Mr. Rice He can tell you what you ought to do; you say that you do not feel prepared."

"Prepared, prepared to die; oh, it must take a long time! I never once thought it was to be so. They will say I have died very rich, and so it is: farms upon farms. Why, Clarence, Clanmore alone has three thousand acres. They shall never have it, you have promised me!"

"I will go now, father, and send some one to remain with you."

"Don't send Ralph or Richard, but stop—what can Mr. Rice do? Do you think he can help me; the doctor says *he* can't."

"Perhaps, father, he can direct your mind to something upon which to trust, that may make the way you are going more bright; you can not expect to get well, and, father, you must prepare to meet your God."

"Hush, hush; how can I? Oh, dear, how strange! what strange thoughts come over me. Is it so? do tell me, Clarence? shall I have to give an account? something tells me so: feel my pulse again. Oh, life, life; let me live. I must have life."

Clarence could bear no more; at once he left the room, and sent Juba, the favorite servant of his dying father, to remain by him, with strict orders to allow no person to disturb the sick chamber during his absence.

For some miles on either side of the road on which Clarence was driving, with the utmost speed, lay the vast estate of Clanmore, so much the object of his dying parent's thoughts;

and, he feared, destined to be a cause of strife and ill-feeling for years to come. It would have been beautiful to the eye of a stranger, but Clarence saw nothing desirable in all the marks of beauty and productiveness; his thoughts were entranced by the scene he had just left, and with all that he could remember of the past. To him, there was but one dark phase of contention, hard feelings, grasping, selfish ends. And now its owner was lying helpless, on the bed of death; clutching, with his palsied powers, still at this world, and shrinking with horror from that to which he was going. And these beauties which met the eye of Clarence had cheated his parent of all for which God had placed him in the world. These fields, and forests, and streams, had enchained his mind, and drawn the whole man away from all considerations of duty to Him, who "created him for his own glory," and Clarence could only read "vanity, and vexation of spirit," written in characters of blood upon every inch of soil over which he passed that belonged .o Clanmore.

He was received by his foster-parents with great cordiality, and although the summons was a very unexpected one to the good old man, he lost no time in preparing to obey it. From the representations, however, which Clarence made of the state of his father's mind, together with what Mr. Rice had known of him, during a long life, he anticipated little good from his visit.

"This matter of preparing for death," he said to Clarence, as they were approaching the end of their journey back, "is a very serious matter; and, when put off to the last hour, leaves but little to hope for."

"But you know, my dear sir, you have often mentioned the case of the penitent thief; he obtained mercy, and doubtless died in peace."

"Granted, my child; but that was a rare case; and the faith exercised then of a most peculiar nature, or rather I should say of peculiar strength. *He* believed when all others had lost their confidence; he believed when the very being upon whom his faith rested was undergoing, with himself, the tortures of death. He had not all his life been under Christian influence. He had not slighted the evidence of a risen Saviour, as we all must now do who turn our backs upon Him during our whole season of probation. But all things are possible with God.

all we can do is to hold up the Cross, and try to get the departing soul to put faith in it. Did you endeavor to lead the mind of your father to that refuge for the lost?"

Clarence hesitated to reply for a moment, for his conscience reproved him.

"I did not, sir; I felt as if I hardly dared trust to my own skill; and I found it so difficult to fix my father's mind on the subject of death at all; his mind was so absorbed with temporal matters."

"It requires but little skill, my son, to point a soul to the cross of Christ; you should have done it. There is a power in it, which affects when nothing else will. It holds out a hope; it offers a resting-place for the mind tossed in the conflicting waves which beat about the spirit in its last struggle."

Clarence felt sadly condemned, and knew not what to say, and the rest of the journey was passed in silence.

At the door of the mansion, Clarence was met by his mother, who, not knowing the errand upon which he had gone, was much surprised at the presence of Mr. Rice, and after receiving him with cold civility, and requesting him to be seated, asked her son to step with her into the adjoining room.

"Upon what errand has that reverend gentleman come this morning, Clarence?"

"I went for Mr. Rice, at the request of my father; he wishes to converse with him."

"And why so? Have we not our own clergyman? It seems highly improper to go beyond our own clerical bounds! what will be thought of it?"

"I have done, mother, what I have, at the request of my dying father; he wishes the counsel of Mr. Rice, and we know him to be a truly good man, and I only regret that it has not been done before."

"And do you design to have the same person perform the funeral service? I suppose that, now, must be as you direct. You know, doubtless, that your father has made you sole inheritor of Clanmore."

The very name of Clanmore now filled the mind of Clarence with intense disgust, and he was ready to let out the fullness of his thoughts, but he forbore.

"My dear mother! I entreat of you, do not let us talk about such paltry matters when father is just about to leave the world, and, I fear, not prepared for his exit. Of what consequence is all his wealth, or who inherits it, compared with the value of his soul? may I not hasten to him?"

Suddenly there was a call in the passage, by a servant, and Mrs. Ralston and her son hastened thither. They were met there by Mr. Rice.

"My dear madam," said Mr. Rice, "there seems to be some unusual disturbance in the upper chamber. In which room is Mr. Ralston?"

Clarence waited not for an answer, but beckoning to Mr. Rice, both hastened toward the room of the dying man. Scarcely had they reached the upper hall of the house, before the sound of loud and angry voices fell upon their ears. Maggie, the old friend of Clarence, was rushing from the room with her hands clasped in agony.

"Oh, Mr. Clarence, Mr. Clarence! hasten, hasten—gin ther'll be bluid spilt."

Clarence rushed impetuously into the room where his father lay, and for an instant his self-possession had almost left him.

Several persons were there; but the objects which riveted his attention were his brother Ralph, and the faithful Juba, the latter standing beside his master's bed, with his fists tightly clenched, and facing Ralph, who stood with his arm extended, holding a large pistol in deadly aim at the heart of the old negro. The words which Clarence heard as he entered the door were from the lips of the latter.

"You may shoote a me if you please, Master Ralph, but no man shall come near dis bed, only over my dead body."

Horror-stricken an instant, Clarence gazed at the scene, and then rushed forward, and by his strong grasp wrested the deadly weapon from the hand of Ralph. The latter, absorbed in his vile purpose, had not noticed his brother's entrance. At once he turned upon him a face marked with the most fiendish passion, and uttering a horrid oath, sprang at him with maniac violence. Passing the weapon to the faithful Maggie, who had followed him back to the room, he seized the arms of his enraged brother, but not before he received a violent blow that had nearly felled him to the floor. He was, however, possessed of great muscular strength, and was enabled by a powerful effort, to prevent further injury to himself.

"Richard why is this!" as Clarence now for the first noticed his presence and that of two others, apparently low characters, standing near him. "Why is this! and why are strangers, at such a time, allowed to intrude here!"

"Answer your own questions, and fight your own battles, for all me!"

"I can tell you," said Ralph; "they are here by my orders; and here they shall stay until that old man that you have enticed to alter his will, to suit your purposes, shall undo what he has done. Unhand me, sir! unhand me, or I will be the death of you!"

Clarence now understood matters. He was in general forbearing, to an extreme. But now the whole spirit of the man and the son was fully aroused.

"Mr. Rice,"—the reverend gentleman had indeed followed Clarence to the door, but being a man of delicate frame and very nervous withal, he was so overcome by the scene he then witnessed, that he forbore to enter; but stood almost petrified with grief and astonishment.

"Mr. Rice, will you request one of the servants to go immediately for the sheriff, and I will see who dares thus to disturb the last moments of a dying man."

The determined tone in which Clarence spoke appalled at once the vile wretches, and Richard with the two accomplices, in a hurried manner left the room, while Ralph increased his clamor.

"Unhand me, sir! unhand me! you shall pay for this with your life!"

"I will unhand you when proper authority shall be here to take you in charge. Juba remain by your master!" and with a violent effort Clarence forced his brother from the room, and the door was closed, just as his mother came up to the scene of trouble.

"Who is this, who has presumed in my house to make this disturbance!

Ralph ceased stuggling, and fixed his ferocious eyes upon his mother.

"Ask yourself, if you want to know! ask yourself! *you* are the mischief, maker you and your——son here as you call him, Yes, you have worked your cards to feather your own nest. But mind me, woman! hear me! I *curse* you!"

"Ralph stop! hold! you know not what you do! do not, I beg of you, bring the vengeance of heaven upon yourself."

"You unhand me sir, and save your advice for them that ask it. I do curse her! I curse you all! I curse this house! It has always been a hell, but I will make it a worse hell for you all than it has ever been yet. Unhand me sir!" and with a sudden and violent effort he broke loose, and bounded at his mother. Probably the violent blow he aimed at her would have proved her death, had it not been turned aside by the effort of Clarence to throw himself before her sacred person; at that moment a cry was made from the sick chamber, "That Mr. Ralston was dying, he was breathing his last breath." As though it had been a voice from heaven, a sudden stop was put to all violence. Ralph, perhaps exhausted somewhat by his fierce struggle and fierce passion, grew deadly pale. Mrs. Ralston, leaning upon Maggie, hurried to her own room, while Clarence, seeing his mother out of danger, hastened to the dying bed.

There could be no mistaking the sad signs he witnessed on the countenance of his father, and at once he issued orders that his mother and brother be informed if they wished to see the last they must come without delay.

Mrs. Ralston had never witnessed a dying scene, and said she never wished to; and as she could do no good now, preferred to remain in her own room.

In a short time Ralph and Richard entered, and approached the bed, as Clarence stepped aside to let them have a clear view of their dying parent. Ralph retained still the same fierce look. He fixed his eye steadily on the helpless form which he had but a short time before forced, by main strength, to sustain an erect posture, and endeavored, by threats of violence, to compel his signature to an instrument he had prepared, and from which outrage he was only driven by the courage and strength of the faithful slave.

He looked steadily at the sunken, pale cheek, the beamless eye, and the quivering muscles of the drooping jaw. He saw the death-damp gathering on the brow, as the struggle within the heaving chest grew more and more intense. He saw there before him, lying in all the helplessness of expiring nature, the father whom he had never respected, upon whose bounty he had lived, and whom he had now, by his own violent conduct, hastened from the world. Long years of unhappy dissensions came up before him, and all his hard thoughts, and hard speeches, flashed back upon his tortured mind with lightning speed and vividness. It was too late to ask forgiveness now; the past could not now be forgotten; no years of time could obliterate, no after-scene of life could cover, with its brightness or its dark mantle, the forbidding past; his torment from that dread hour had begun.

And his eye moved not from that pallid, quivering face; he could not have removed it had an avenging sword been sweeping for his execution. There was the stillness of the grave within the walls of that room save the low, faint rattle, as the fleeting breath flew back and forth. Suddenly there was a slight quiver, and the rattle ceased. Clarence stepped up gently to the bed and with a sad look, gazed a moment, and then in a low and soft tone, with his eye turned calmly toward his brother.

" Brother Ralph, it is your privilege, as the eldest-born, to close the eyes of your parent."

Ralph started as if awakened from a trance.

"Oh God!" he uttered, in a frantic tone, and rushed from the room.

The funeral ceremonies, with all the pageantry attendant upon the obsequies of the wealthy, had been performed, and some weeks had elapsed since the little mound had been raised in the church-yard over the mortal remains of Randolph Ralston. The ceremony of opening and reading the will had also been attended to, and whatever anxieties and disquietudes had for so many years been caused by the hopes and fears concerning it, they had all now been put to rest. There was no more doubt now, who were to be the happy owners of those various possessions which had been so long at the control of one.

Ralph Ralston was not at the funeral scene; and his children alone represented their father in the long procession. And when the will was opened he was not there.

No tidings had been heard from him since the hour when, in the agony of a guilty conscience, he rushed from the bedside of his dead father. He was not seen when he left the house, and no mortal eye, so far as could be ascertained, had beheld him since. Inquiries had been made among all with whom he had ever been acquainted, and at all the places to which he had ever been known to resort. The woods and fields too had been searched, but all in vain. Then large rewards were offered, and with no better effect. He had in some mysterious way eluded observation: and whether still an inhabitant of earth, or at rest in the grave, none could tell. Richard had become much softened by the dying scene; and although he shunned in general the society of Clarence, there was no bitterness manifested in his words or conduct.

Mrs. Ralston was, however, apparently about to follow him who had been so long her life's partner. The blow which Ralph had aimed at her was indeed warded off, but the violent shock her mind received from that terrible event had probably excited a naturally nervous temperament until a slight shock of paralysis gave her warning that the tabernacle of earth was beginning to crumble.

In a few days another intimation was given, and she was laid helpless upon her bed, one half of her frame without the power of motion, or the sense of feeling. Clarence was about her bed, soothing her troubled mind, and doing what he could to quiet her spirit, which now having lost much of its natural strength, manifested almost the weakness of childhood.

It was near the close of the day, about four weeks from the time the unhappy Ralph had been missed from among men, that Richard came into the room, where Clarence was sitting by the side of his mother and beckoned him out.

"Can you walk with me a short distance?"

Clarence saw at once that his brother was deeply affected for some cause, for his countenance bore the marks of a mind in agony, and his whole frame was in a tremor.

"What is it, Richard?"

"Come with me; I can not tell you now."

They walked from the house together, Richard a little in advance—for he seemed urged on by some desperate necessity.

Very soon Clarence perceived, by the path he was taking, that his brother was leading him toward the church; and the thought came into his mind that probably there had been some disturbance of their father's grave; perhaps by vile creatures who, tempted by the costly silver plate and trimmings, had laid sacrilegious hands upon it. As Richard had not yet spoken, he again asked,

"The grave has not been disturbed, has it?"

"No; you will soon see."

They entered the gate into the yard, and wound their way through the graves. The spot belonging to the Ralston family, and in which their dead lay, was in a distant corner of the burial-ground. It was much the largest space, of any that had portions in that field of the dead. Weeping-willows had been planted there, and were now trees of some size; and as the ground sloped down from the general level, the branches of the willows, with their long sweep, sheltered it from observation, so that the monuments erected there could only be seen on a very near approach.

Richard stopped suddenly as they entered through the leafy screen, and, without speaking, pointed with his hand to an object just beyond the little pile of earth beneath which the body of their father was laid. Clarence proceeded a few paces, and then, clasping his hands, stood transfixed with horror.

There, in the very clothes he had worn when he tore away from the death-bed of his parent, lay the body of the wretched Ralph. His face, what of it could be seen, was emaciated to an extreme; and the horrible aspect it presented caused Clarence to utter a cry of agony. Covering his face, he gave vent to the full feelings of his heart. For some time no other sound was heard but the deep groans and the stifled sobs that told what warm emotions glowed within that manly heart. Richard moved not from the spot where first he had stayed his step, until Clarence, when the spasm of grief had subsided, beckoned his brother to his side. "Richard, this is the hand of God! we must be still; he has no doubt come here to die; we can not tell what agony he has suffered, nor what thoughts of penitence he may have had. It looks as if it might have been so; let us hope it was, and that the poor wretched wanderer was made at last to feel repentance for the past! And now, Richard! by our father's grave, and with that token which lies there by its side, shall we not pledge to each other, forever from this hour, a brother's love?"

Richard could only cover his face and weep in bitterness of soul.

"Richard, do you believe it has ever been in my heart to wrong you or him whose body lies before us?"

"No; never, never!" And he put forth his hands; and the brothers stood thus clasped hand in hand for some moments.

"Richard, let us have a full understanding. I have never, as God is my witness, desired this property which has been such a source of disquiet."

"I believe you never have."

"But in my father's distress, and to quiet his mind, I hastily promised not to relinquish my claim to it. But why can not we enjoy it together? and if your provision is not satisfactory to you, I have abundance of my own, which I now offer again freely to divide with you."

"There is no need, Clarence, that more should be said on that point. I have more already than is of any use to me. Of what value to *me*, do you think, would this estate be? You know my wretched condition; with a wife whose mind has sunk almost into idiocy! No, I see clearly now, 'The curse of the Lord is on the house of the wicked.' That hideous corpse, whose features are so disfigured by the birds, or beasts of prey, needs no explanation to *me*. *God's curse! God's curse!* Oh, it is dreadful!"

CHAPTER XIX.

Tobias Folger had felt his way very carefully, had acted with great discretion, had set all the springs in motion which he thought necessary, even to hiring a pew near to that in which Carrie sat in church, and reading the responses in an audible voice. But his keen observation enabled him to see that as yet he had made no lodgement in the heart of Carrie Leslie. Or, what to him was the same thing, had no reason to hope that any proposal on his part would be accepted by her. It would be a useless detention for the reader, to state all the causes for this belief on his part. He was dealing, he knew, with a heart free from all guile, disposed to the strictest rules of honesty in all things, and a few replies she had made on certain occasions, when he was feeling his way "very softly," assured him, as well as would an open rebuff, that the time had not yet come, if it ever would.

But Tobias Folger was not the man to give up, for a trifling obstacle, an object upon which his heart was set. He had never hesitated at the use of any means calculated to accomplish his ends, and hitherto he had never failed. To gain wealth had been the great object of his life, and wealth he had. How much, none knew but himself, and how obtained, had been in the earlier part of his history a great mystery to many. That an opinion was held concerning him by no means favorable, he was conscious; and for that reason had chosen a new and retired place of residence. Here, however, from an unfortunate occurrence, the eye of "envy and malice" has at last discerned him, and but for timely interference, he would have been exposed to public insult; nor was exposure alone the only evil accompanying that affair. He had learned, to his dismay, that some particulars in reference to past events, and which he supposed, were forever hushed in the silence of the grave, had, in a mysterious way, got abroad into the busy circle of life. How, need not be asked. There are many ways by which an overruling hand, brings to light the "hidden things of dishonesty." It was to him, therefore, a time when all things about him began to tremble with uncertainty; whatever plans he designed to accomplish, wherein a fair reputation would be of indispensable importance, must therefore be carried into execution without delay.

But keen and selfish as he was, he could love. His heart had yet passions that were beyond his control. When he first allowed himself to be pleased with Carrie Leslie, it was merely because he was fascinated by her beauty of person, and from a desire to form a connection with a family of such high respectability. But his interest in her began by degrees to strengthen; her image followed him to his lone seat within his own dwelling. He would fancy her reclining in all her loveliness upon his Grecian couch, or walking with queenly grace through his well furnished rooms, or smiling upon him as she sat by his side and looked unto him as the lord of her affections. It was fancy, to be sure, nothing more—an idle dallying with the mind's vagaries. But fancy all this while was winding a chain about him, and the fetters, though but a silken cord, became too strong for even his heart to break.

Although capable of being fascinated himself, he had no correct idea how a heart like that he wished to gain could be won. He knew nothing about that *affinity of the social affections* which draws by its holy, unintelligible influence, two beings into a oneness, mysterious, though real, subtle, as the fluid which gives sensation to the physical man, yet powerful to bring the whole moral being into obeisance.

He thought only of what might be done through more tangible means. His object was not to gain the heart, he merely wanted the assent; a written contract would have been as valuable, in his estimation, as to have known that he possessed the whole affections. His belief in the power of money, was like the faith of Archimedes in the power of his lever. The latter, however, could not test his grandest theories for want of a suitable fulcrum. But Tobias Folger believed that in the strength of filial affection he had a fulcrum upon which he could apply the strong arm of pecuniary power. His hold upon the father might, if properly exerted, *bind the daughter to his will.* His first plan was to make him a bankrupt: this he had accomplished, and then, when his victim was helpless, came forward with professions of kindness, and by smooth words, and an insinuating manner, and some trifling acts of generosity, gained a footing in the family, and even a consideration that was dangerous to their peace.

Thus far he has failed, or thinks he has; but what Carrie Leslie might do in an extremity that involved the degradation and distress of her father, it would be difficult to decide. Her heart clung to him with a strength of affection which was superior to all calculations of her own happiness, and so completely was her mind absorbed in the one idea of seeing him released from the oppressive load under which he labored, and again in the full possession of his old home, and master of his own estate, that it became the one great theme out of which her imagination wrought bright golden visions, and around which her thoughts, by day or night, when not completely occupied by demands of duty, continually played, and all thoughts about what happiness might be in store for *her*, or what this world could give her of its most bounteous allotments, were entirely laid aside.

It was, indeed, a lovely trait, thus to lose sight of self in one absorbing thought for a dear parent. But like all earthly affections, when cherished by a warm imagination, and without due reference to Almighty wisdom, may but lead astray.

It was well for Carrie that she loved her parent, that his comfort was so dear to her, that she was ready to labor for his aid, that her own enjoyment should be lost sight of in her eager desire to shed light and peace around his path. But she could not take the rod out of the hand of Him who held it; nor could she say when its design had been accomplished. It might, indeed, appear to her worth the happiness of her whole life to see her parent released from his burdens, and his heart at rest. But she could not know that Infinite wisdom designed it thus to be.

Perhaps, had she been as submissive for her parent's trials, as for her own, there would have been but little danger that she could ever be insnared by the wily hunter who had marked her as his prey.

Mr. Shipley was a man of several occupations. He was a little read in the law; a little acquainted with farming; he was also constable by appointment, although in the quiet town of

Princesport there was very little for any such officer to do. He was a constant visitor at the two taverns—the place maintained two, quite decently—and at other places where people were in the habit of congregating. He was fond of talking, and of being talked to; and knew a little about every one's business and circumstances, or thought he did. But it was said few knew about his. Mr. Folger had found Mr. Shipley very convenient for his purposes, and had more or less business for him most of the time. And Mr. Shipley rather congratulated himself on being thus employed, and on terms of intimacy with one so wealthy. It seems necessary, in all schemes, either for the accomplishment of good or evil, that man should have an accessory. Folger, however, in all his confidential communications, to any whose aid for the time he needed, had the peculiar tact, while he made great show of privacy, and of trust, in the second person, of keeping number one alone in the secret of his true intent, and also of so arranging matters that his end would be accomplished, and the evil design kept out of view.

Mr. Shipley had received an intimation that his presence was desired at the respectable mansion of Mr. Folger, and very soon thereafter he was entering the office, and bowing obsequiously to the great man of the house.

"Ah! good afternoon, Mr. Shipley—glad to see you, sir; sit down sir, and amuse yourself with the paper; I shall be ready to wait upon you in a moment."

Mr. Folger was busily employed at his desk, or appeared to be so. It saved him, however, the formality of giving his hand to Mr. Shipley.

In a very few minutes Mr. Folger had finished his task, took the chair he usually occupied—a large well-cushioned concern—and as he seated himself, asked:

"Any news stirring to-day?"

"Nothing much, sir; nothing at all. But you mentioned yesterday that you would like to see me soon, and I thought I'd just step in, as I had not much on hand this afternoon."

"Yes, I did, and I am glad you have happened in. I want to commit a little private matter to you, and I have confidence that you will be mum on the subject and perhaps you can be of some little service to me, just now, and I will endeavor to make it all right with you."

"Any thing I can do, Mr. Folger, you may depend upon it,

I shall do, without asking questions, or answering them; and I guess I can keep a secret as well as most folks. You have never heard, I guess, any thing that has come out of my lips that you have n't wanted me to tell. I did, to be sure, hint round a little about Leslie's mortgage, but I rather took it at the time that you did n't care if that was known."

"Ah, yes, yes; that's all past; and it was about as well it happened as it did."

"So I think; he was clear up, and it might as well be known as not. He may thank old Sam Thompson, though, that he was n't torn all to bits. Old Sam took a good many dollars out of my pocket."

"Yes, yes; well let that go. Leslie means well enough, but he is a poor manager, and the fact is, I have a matter against him yet, and I have no security for it."

"Much?"

"Well, no great matter; it is a little more than a thousand dollars."

"As much as that? how happened it? I thought you would have taken care of that; a thousand dollars ain't no small sum!"

"I ought to have done so; but after I had supposed all our matters included in the mortgage, I found, upon looking over, a note of his that had been somehow mislaid, and I agreed with him to let it run along until maybe something would turn up and he might be able to pay it."

"I know how you can get it."

"How?"

"Clap on to the furniture."

"Oh, well, yes; that might be done, that's true. But it would be unpleasant, you know, just as things are. No, I should rather not do that under present cirumstances. In fact I feel very reluctant to have my name concerned in the thing at all; I am on visiting terms with the family, my child boarding there and all that; no, I wish in some way the thing could be done without my name being known in the matter"

"Transfer it to some one else, then."

"Say you so? that is a new thought;" and Mr. Folger assumed a very serious look, as if the idea had never before occurred to him; or, as if Mr. Shipley had not been expected to make this very proposition. And Mr. Folger was for some minutes in quite an abstracted condition, very much troubled with his thoughts; at length he seemed to see his way a little clearer.

"That might be done, I think, but I should much prefer, if any such arrangement was made, that the note should be presented to Mr. Leslie; and—and in case he could do nothing about it, he might, by proper management, be induced to confess judgment there, where he now resides; that would enable any one, you know, at any time, to levy either on his property in New York, if he has any, or for want of that, to take his person."

"Has he any property there?"

"Well, there is no telling. I can not say certainly that he has, and yet it is not impossible. In fact I don't care to say all I know about that. Such a course as I have indicated would no doubt test that matter."

"It would so; I should try it pretty quick."

"It is a very unpleasant affair, any how. He has, you know, a very agreeable family; very much so; to go and seize the furniture and turn them all upside down would make a great talk, and, under the circumstances, I can not bring myself to do it. The note, though, for that matter, need not appear as my property at all; and in fact Leslie knows that I paid it away, and although I told him the man would no doubt let it lay—for of course my name was on it, and I must stand between him and all harm—yet you know the holder could if he chose prosecute the drawer."

"Then you have not got the note?"

"About that I wish you to be very mum."

"No fear of me."

"Well, the fact is, I have the note; and it has got the name of Thorne on the back, the name of the person to whom I passed it. He and I, you know, have had a good deal of business together, and in the course of some of our trades, I took this piece of paper back. Now, it just strikes me what might be done. This note might go into your hands as the property of Thorne, or even as a transfer from him to you; in either case you could prosecute in New York. That is, for a suitable compensation. But perhaps you might feel some delicacy about it?"

"Not I; I have got pretty well used to such matters"

"Then if I hand this to you, you think you understand, Shipley, how to manage it?"

"I do; I understand all about it."

"And how soon could you attend to this matter?"

"Right off, whenever you say."

"Well, in general, such things are as well attended to with promptness. But remember, my name, for various reasons, as I have stated to you, must be kept entirely one side; you receive it from Thorne, and that's enough."

"I understand; you will see it will be managed right, and no mistake."

And Mr. Shipley left Mr. Folger, with an idea that he had been made a confidant, and for the purpose of securing a debt which Mr. Folger felt some delicacy in prosecuting in his own name.

But Mr. Folger, much as he loved money, cared but little, comparatively, for the amount in question; in fact, he knew well that in all justice there was no validity to the claim; and should Mr. Shipley succeed on presentation of the note in receiving payment in full, it would be a great disappointment to Folger. He was playing for a higher game than dollars and cents. He was about to take advantage of the helpless condition of Mr. Leslie, and of his unsuspicious, honorable spirit; and by process of law, in a place where he was a perfect stranger, bring him down to the degradation of an imprisoned debtor; thereby shutting him away from his family, tying his hands from an effort to do aught for support; and throwing those who loved him into the depths of despondency and sorrow. It was in fact the cool unfeeling effort of a desperate man to accomplish, at a cruel sacrifice, an object on which his heart was set, and which he wished to accomplish without delay.

The establishment to which Mr. Leslie carried his letter of introduction was situated in Cliff street, then, a very narrow and unsightly place, the buildings in a dilapidated state, and for the most part tenanted by the poorer class of inhabitants. He looked up as he read the name of the firm over the door, and saw that it was a four-story brick building, and from its appearance had long been erected. Signs, indicative of the business carried on there, were hung out even as far as the third story; and the whole front, which was very narrow, presented a forbidding aspect. As he looked over the way, a row of old frame buildings met his view; the windows broken and stuffed with garments of various patterns, or what had been such, and the open doors exposing comfortless interiors, with inmates as filthy and dilapidated as the houses they occupied.

On entering the store, he was obliged to thread his way through a confused mass of boxes, piles of paper, and unbound books, far back into a small office in the rear of the building. On inquiring, he was directed to the principal of the establishment, or to one of them, and handed his letter to an elderly gentleman, rather small, and thin, with green spectacles, and a very dry visage, who sat on a high stool, perched before a small desk, busily employed turning over the leaves of an old book. The gentleman laid the letter upon the ink-stained cover of his desk, and continued without interruption to turn over the leaves of his book. At length, having satisfied his curiosity, or ascertained what he was looking for, he handed the book to another gentleman behind him, occupied in writing at a double desk, which stood between the windows, making some remark as he did so. He then very deliberately took up the letter, and casting a glance toward Mr. Leslie, commenced reading it, which he did apparently more than once. After he had completed the perusal, he carefully folded it again, and laid it in one of the pigeon-holes before him; and dropping himself to the floor, walked up to Mr. Leslie, and looked up at him. He had to do that, for his visitor was of full medium height.

"You have brought a letter from Mr. Folger?"

"I have, sir."

"Yes, well, I wrote to him that we had a place vacant; one of our readers died lately. I suppose he stated the terms?"

"Mr. Folger informed me, sir, of the amount of salary you could pay, but he was not able to say what part of the business I was to be employed in."

Without noticing the reply of Mr. Leslie, he turned his head one side, with rather a waggish air, and putting his spectacles up on his forehead, asked,

"Have you been long acquainted with Mr. Folger? do you know him?"

"Yes, sir, I know him well."

"You do? Well, that is more than I can say, although I have done more or less business with him for many years. If you *do* know him, you know more than a good many folks; I can tell you that, neighbor."

"Why, sir, I say I know Mr. Folger; I have been acquainted with him for five or six years past. I can not say that I have been on very intimate terms all that time. But I have had business transactions with him. But I have been more intimate with him of late; and he has treated me, I must say, with kindness."

"You remember, perhaps, an old saying of Dr. Johnson, 'When a Scotchman smiles, look out for mischief.' And you may depend on it, when Mr. Folger does a man a kindness—he means—he means something by it; but that is nothing between us. He has spoken, sir, I must say, in high terms of you, and he is a man that can spell out a man's character pretty correctly. There ain't many men that can deceive Tobias Folger.

"He tells me likewise that you have been unfortunate: sorry for it! a great many, sir, just now, in your case. There is one man now in the room you will occupy—a very worthy man—once a favorite of fortune—all gone to the dogs, poor as Job's turkey, and glad of a place to do any thing he can do. You say Mr. Folger did n't tell you what I wanted a man for? Well if I did n't tell *him*, it must have been a great mistake of mine. But I am very sure I did. However, that is it, sir: I want a proof-reader; we are getting out some discount tables, and some mathematical works, and a few such things. Simple enough the business is, but it wants care, great care. A man must n't be thinking of something else, while he is examining such things, for a mistake will not be so well; but it's simple. Have you a boarding place?"

Mr. Leslie looked at him with astonishment. "I have not thought of that, sir, as I was not aware what provision you made for those you employed."

"We make no provision at all, my dear sir, except for the payment of salary; and *that* you can have weekly, or monthly, just as you please."

"The terms, sir, which Mr. Folger stated to me, were—five hundred dollars a year and my board."

"He stated to you then, sir, what he had no authority for doing. Five hundred dollars is the most we ever pay. I am very sorry, sir, if you have come so far, with such a misunderstanding, and although I should like to have your services just now, would by no means have them, unless you are satisfied with the terms. Good board can be procured for three and a half to four dollars per week. But you must decide for yourself. I must only ask you to say at once what you will do; as I must look elsewhere for help."

Mr. Leslie was greatly at a loss. The salary would leave, after paying his necessary expenses, but a pittance for his family. If he should decline, it might offend Mr. Folger, or prevent any effort on his part to aid him. He was in his power. He had already begun to feel that a chain was about him. The best he could do under present circumstances, so far as he could judge, was to accept the offer; and after a few minutes' delay the matter was settled.

"Very well, sir; our reading-room is up-stairs. Here James," speaking to a young man who had just entered, "show this gentleman up into the reading-room—Leslie, I think your name is, sir."

Mr. Leslie bowed assent.

"Then, James, show Mr. Leslie up-stairs. He will go on with Roulett's Tables and Simpson's Euclid. There must be quite a batch on hand at present. You will see where Colmar left off. Poor fellow, he worked to the last minute. Weekly or monthly, your pay will be ready for you, Mr. Leslie."

And the little man went up to his perch again, and Mr. Leslie followed James up stairs.

"Take care of this second flight of stairs, sir; it is very crooked, and it's plaguey dark."

It was indeed both crooked and dark, being completely boxed in. The only light that could get there, must come from the top or bottom; and there was very little of that article in any of the premises. As they reached the top, James remarked again—he seemed to be a very considerate young man,

"You will mind, sir, that trap-door, as you come down—they leave it open sometimes."

"Do we ascend higher?"

"Oh yes, sir; the printing is done on this floor."

And James went on, followed by Mr. Leslie; both treading in the dark until arriving at a passage formed by the wall of the store on one side, and piles of boxes on the other, through which they marched into a back room of small dimensions where sat two men busily engaged, but in what way, Mr. Leslie did not notice. After a suitable introduction by James, and a request on his part that one of them would initiate Mr. Leslie into the arcana of his duties, the young man politely bade him adieu.

The gentlemen were truly polite, and seemed in every way disposed to aid the new-comer, and although the room was small, and the view from its one window not very inviting, nor very extended, and the appearance of things about him not calculated to interest a stranger, Mr. Leslie was so taken with their kindness of manner, that he forgot other things, and was grieved to learn after some conversation with them, that they were only expecting to be there for a short time; in a few weeks he would have the room to himself.

By the assistance of one of the gentlemen, a situation was found in the outskirts of the city, which was then not very large, and within a reasonable walk to his place of labor, where he could lodge, and have partial board for a reasonable sum; and by certain ways of managing, into the secrets of which these inmates of his room instructed him, he found that he would be able probably to devote a little more than one half his income to the service of his family. It was indeed a small sum, yet it would be better than nothing. But how small the remuneration he received, or how slender his diet, or what means he used to enable him to send on to their aid, what he did—he would for no consideration have divulged to them.

It was, however, a violent change for one at his time of life. His habits had not been sedentary, and especially had he never been accustomed to regular confinement, at one thing. To sit from day to day, poring over dry and uninteresting details, with the necessity of keeping his mind intently occupied, and with nothing in the employment itself that was either quickening or instructive; with no objects of sympathy about him to whom he could unbend his thoughts, or whose smiles might enliven the tedium of his round, was enough to affect one unfavorably.

It was also a great change to leave the open air of the country, the fresh beauty of nature, and the inspiration she yields, even to her unconscious recipients, for the narrow bounds of a small upper room, in a confined portion of the city, where nothing met the eye without, but rough, unsightly walls; and nothing within, but piles of old manuscripts, boxes, books, and dust. To see the sun shining but in streaks, and lighting up that which reflected no beauty; to hear the constant rumble of the busy world around, and realize that he had naught to do with it, nothing but to sit and perform his daily task, and at night walk his regular track to a hired resting-place!—it was a mighty change from the scenes of life to him hitherto! But there was no repining in his heart, not at least on his own account; no thought that his lot was hard, or that he had been, or was then, unkindly dealt with, by Him whose providence had appointed this discipline. He had become like a weaned child, and ready to do or suffer manfully whatever should be laid upon him.

And yet, when not bound closely to his work, his thoughts would go back to the past, and then forward to the future: regret and penitence for the former, but the latter full of dark forebodings, and often filling him with dismay.

His family was now sheltered, but in what way? Only at the sufferance of one whom he could not, after all he knew of him, quite comprehend. His conduct had manifested a strange mixture of harshness and kind feeling. He was, however, in his power. A large amount of interest was accumulating daily—there was no possible way by which any part of it could be met. A bare subsistence was all that he could earn. How long should this remain? and how soon would the climax be reached, and his family be driven homeless upon the world?

The heart of man is strong to endure for those it cherishes, and the severest toil is but pastime when by it they, who are entwined with its warm affections, are sustained and comforted. But *hope* must mingle with the daily labor, or at least that blessed stimulus must not be wholly withheld. To toil for mere subsistence, with a load of debt weighing down the spirit, is like the labor of the criminal who hears at every step the clank of the chain, and feels the galling weight impeding every motion, and can only look forward to the hour of death as a release from his drudgery.

Mr. Leslie was not conscious that any change was working in his physical system. He could not perceive from day to day that his powers of body were sinking under accumulated trials. At times indeed, when he arose in the morning from his sleepless bed, there was a sense of langor that caused him to dread the duties that were before him; but by a strong effort he would throw it off, attributing it rather to the close air of the city than to any real decay of strength. He said nothing of all this, however, in any of his communications to his family, or of any unpleasant attendants upon his daily course. They knew not but he was as well and happy as a separation from them would allow.

But the change in his personal appearance, although not noticed by himself, was often a subject of conversation with the kind-hearted people who had received him as a lodger.

Mr. and Mrs. Barstow lived in a very plain way at the western end of Spring-street. In that day Spring-street was a very unpretending street indeed. The houses were two story frame buildings, with brick fronts, and high wooden stoops, and not very many even of them; for a large part of the street ran through the vacant lots on which no houses of any description were erected. Rents were low there: but the locality had a respectable character, and withal, quite a country air about it. For some distance along the south border of the street lay the large pond called Lispenard meadows, extending from thence to Canal-street, and whose waters formed a convénient reservoir for many things which were not so sightly in the public streets. The atmosphere of that vicinity was in consequence not thought quite so salubrious as in some other parts of the city, and many on that account shunned it as a place of residence.

Straitened circumstances will not, however, allow of too nice a choice, either by taste or apprehension, and Mr. Barstow was contented to overlook some minor objections to a location, for the sake of a small rent and a decent neighborhood. It had, however, been rather a trial to him that Mrs. Barstow was so troubled with the idea of its being an unhealthy situation. They had been accustomed, in their early life, to the pure air of the country, and it had always been against the wishes of his good wife to have any thing to do with the city. But the fact that their daughter, an only child, had married a man in the city supposed to be wealthy, and the inducements held out by him to change their residence for the sake of a situation in the counting-room of that gentleman, and the further inducement that Mrs. Barton could be near her child, decided them to remove. But Mrs. Barstow always insisted upon it "that the air was bad, and that wasn't the worst on it, there wasn't enough to be got, bad as it was—such a tight, confined sort of place! a body never could take a good long breath, and full of pisen too."

Mrs. Barstow, however, would probably have suffered more or less with her breathing apparatus, even in the country; for as she advanced in years her flesh had increased likewise, and being short of stature, and having become what some would have called "a fat lady," the lungs probably found their precinct rather crowded there was not room for "easy working."

She was, however, an excellent wife, and had been a kind mother, and was really ready to do the best she could for every body. Mr. Barstow, as it very commonly happens, took a turn in a direction the reverse of his good lady; that is, in the matter of flesh: as she began to thicken up and spread out, he began to shrink up and draw nearer the bones, until he had become a very spare person indeed. Mrs. Barstow always insisted upon it that the cause was to be laid to nothing else but "chewing and smoking;" "he had taken to it," she said, "ever since their troubles had been coming on, and he'd got so wedded to the 'stuff' that what between that and his low spirits, and his groanin, and sighin, he'd put himself in the grave yet."

Mr. Barstow, however, did not relinquish the habit either for fear of the grave or the loss of his flesh, and as he had been now for some years just about so, Mrs. Barstow concluded that her fears, perhaps, were groundless, and that after all he got along as comfortably without his flesh, as with it.

The fact probably was that he had lost what could well be spared, and things be kept at all together. What was left, was in a state of preservation. He certainly appeared like it.

The two, however, lived very happily together, for they had a sincere regard for each other, and the trials they had gone through, being equal sufferers, had tended to unite them more closely.

Mr. Leslie had been introduced there, as we have seen, by

one of the gentlemen who were engaged in the same room with himself; and he found it a place well suited for his purpose. They were kind, and agreeable, and cleanly; and the terms were reasonable, which to him was a great consideration. Mr. Barstow was naturally reserved, and seldom joined much in conversation; that, he left almost entirely to Mrs. Barstow. It was very easy work for her, being never at a loss for something to say. There was, however, one peculiarity, which may as well be noticed here. They never, or very seldom recurred to the past. Occasionally a word might be dropped, that indicated a feeling of sadness, in contrasting the present with that which had been. But no particulars were referred to; they seemed, by common consent, to cast a vail over whatever had been trying in their past lot, at least, before others. So that Mr. Leslie, although an inmate for many months, had become acquainted with some mere outlines of their history. All he had learned was, that they had been once comfortably settled on a farm; that they had sold it and removed to the city for the sake of their daughter, and other reasons; that the daughter had died, and from things which they had intimated occasionally, Mr. Leslie had drawn the conclusion that much of their trouble had grown out of her loss.

But the particulars he never heard. They did not seem to care to dwell upon it, and he had too much feeling to question them. They were poor, their only support depending upon the daily labors of Mr. Barstow in an office for which he received a small salary.

Another peculiarity of theirs was, that they never seemed curious to know the secrets of others, and had not troubled Mr. Leslie with any questions in reference to his history, so that, with the exception that he had told them he had a wife and children, and where they lived, did they know any thing of his private affairs. That he was in straitened circumstances of course they could not help knowing, from the fact of his present employment, and that too, away from his family.

But Mrs. Barstow had noticed now, for some time, that a great change had taken place in the appearance of their boarder since they first saw him; and as she could not account for this change for the same reason that had taken away the flesh of her husband, as Mr. Leslie, to her knowledge, made no use of the "nasty weed," as she was pleased to designate that popular luxury, she attributed it to the bad air of his sleeping apartment; and her anxiety was not only a constant source of worry to her own mind, but more or less so she made it a cause of trouble to her good husband, until, at length, he was compelled to speak plainly on the subject.

"I think, Lucy,"—Mr. and Mrs. Barstow always called each other, especially when alone, by the name which had been most dear to them in youth—"you give yourself unnecessary trouble about things which we can not help; the man knows about the pond as well as we do, and if he has a mind to sleep with his window open, how can we help it?"

"Yes, but Timothy, you don't consider how thoughtless men are. He has been used, no doubt, for he has got a wife, to leave all such matters to her. You know yourself, if I wa'nt to think for you, what a condition you would be in sometimes; men don't think—they 're heedless and careless. Suppose now I did n't watch you, and see that your things was well dried and aired, what would become of you? I know its the pisen air from that pond that's a killing him, inch by inch; you know he sleeps to the back side of the house, and I hear him every night hoisting the window. I s'pose he wants air, he's been used to have air, but he don't think nothin' how dreadful the night air is, all comin' up from that nasty pond."

"Well, what would you do? you have spoken to him, you say—you can't go and shut it down, can you?"

"I know that, Timothy. But something ought to be done. I've been a thinkin', sometimes, you ought to write to his family, or I had ought to write: you see how he looks! why, when he first came, you know you said yourself, what a handsome man he was; and now his cheeks is all sunk in, and so sallow, and his eyes look heavy, and he stoops when he walks, and he don't eat nothin', only jist sips his coffee, and eats a bit of toast, and maybe a mite of fish. Sometimes I think maybe its trouble that ails him. It *does* kill people. It had like to have been the death of you—you knew it did; and trouble you know, laid our poor Lucy in the grave—but we won't talk about that. Oh, dear! Well, I don't know as we can mend matters. Things is dreadfully out of kilter in this world, and there is no help for it!"

Mrs. Barstow's views were not so much out of the way in reference to the last reason by which to account for the change in the appearance of their lodger. "Sorrow in the heart of man maketh it to stoop."

The heavy pressure of that burden which weighed upon him amid the labors of the day, and in the quiet of his own room, which haunted his dreams by night, and rested on his heart as he awoke to consciousness on each new morning, was greater than he could bear, and his physical powers were gradually wasting, and his mind losing its elasticity.

Mechanically he arose with the breaking light of each new day, and ate his slight repast, and walked off to his usual drudgery. Beside him in the lively thoroughfare of the great city, moved, with sprightly step and animated looks, the multitudes hastening to their daily duties. But he was among them as one that "listeneth to music with a heavy heart," and as he returned at evening how they outstriped him in their haste to mingle in the scenes of home, and tell to loved ones the joys or trials of the day. He had no need to hasten; no loved ones were expecting him, no cheerful board awaited him; he had taken his frugal supper ere he left the room in which he had labored through the day, it was simple enough, and he had dined on the same fare.

At first, the sacrifice he made of personal comfort for the sake of those he loved, was stimulus enough. It sustained him for a time, and it would have carried him triumphantly through even worse privations, could he have seen that his efforts would yet result for their permanent benefit. For such an end he would manfully have endured, and even gone rejoicing to the grave.

He tried to trust, and at times a flush of comfort would warm up his heart, as he was enabled to look up to God. But his faith was weak and fitful. He was yet only a new scholar. He had not experience of the ways of Providence, and his failing health seemed to affect even his faith in a heavenly Father's love. The world had a sickly look to him, a shadow rested upon it like the somber hue which nature puts on when the sun's bright beams are eclipsed at mid-day. But he has not yet reached the abyss of sorrow where, hopeless and helpless, the sufferer can only, as a last resort, hang in mute resignation on an Almighty arm. He is fast approaching it.

Mr. Leslie was much surprised, one day—it was some months

after he had been in the city—at the appearance of a person whom he had known as a townsman, but with whom he had never been on terms of intimacy, and in fact whom he had never respected.

It was Mr. Shipley—and the mention of his name will doubtless suggest to the reader the purport of his visit.

There was, at first, on the part of the visitor, quite an attempt to be very social; but as Mr. Leslie was now in general much more reserved than he had formerly been, it was not so easy for him to put on a pleasant manner, especially in the presence of one whon he fancied as little as he did Mr. Shipley. It was not very long, therefore, ere the object of the visit was made known.

"I have called to see you, Mr. Leslie, about a note that has come into my hands."

And Mr. Leslie took the piece of paper which Mr. Shipley, thus saying, presented for his perusal.

"Did Mr. Folger send you with this?"

"Folger! oh, you see it's not Folger's—you can see by the endorsement on the back."

Mr. Leslie did see that the name of Thorne was on it, and he was about to express surprise; at the audacity of a man who had so cruelly wronged him, but his opinion of the one who stood by him caused him to refrain from the expression of his feelings. He therefore simply inquired,

"And what do you want me to do, Mr. Shipley?"

"Why, I suppose he expects payment, Mr. Leslie, or he would not have sent me; if you can't pay it right off in full, perhaps a part might answer."

"I can not pay it, Mr. Shipley."

"Can't you pay a little, sir, just to make Thorne a little easy? It is nothing to me, you see, Mr. Leslie, but he has sent me here with it, and says I must get the pay somehow."

"I can not do it, Mr. Shipley; it is utterly out of my power."

"Well, what shall I do now? I don't want to go and put you to a course of law about it. That will only, you know, cost a good deal of money to both parties."

"I can see no good to be obtained by such means, Mr. Shipley. I acknowledge I owe the money, or at least I have given the note; I am bound for it."

Shipley was silent a moment—he seemed to be thinking hard.

"I declare I wish I knew what to do! I don't want to go and put this into a lawyer's hands. Had you not better just go and confess judgment upon it? That will satisfy Thorne, because if you have property in the city, why, you know it will be a claim upon it; it will save a deal of expense and trouble. You know he can get judgment, for you have acknowledged to me that it is your note, and that you felt bound to pay it."

"I will do that, sir, although I can see no good which can result from it. I have no property here that can be secured to the owner of the note by any such process. But I will confess judgment, if you think it will be more satisfactory."

"Then let us go and have it done."

And without much reflection upon the propriety of the step he was about to take, Mr. Leslie accompanied the wily man for the purpose of doing the business in proper form.

That evening Mr. Leslie threaded his solitary way home—solitary in the midst of the jostling crowd—with a heart more sad than it had yet been. Whether it was any thing in his experience that day, which had recalled past scenes of harrowing distress, or that strange doubts were flitting through his mind as to the character of the man in whose power he was, or whether it was that shadow which coming events sometimes cast before them as tokens of evil, we can not say. But his step was never more heartless, and the little room at the end of his tedious walk never appeared so desolate. And yet he almost wished he could shut himself in it, and make an eternal separation between himself and the outer world.

CHAPTER XX.

CHARLES had been, for some time, urging Mr. Thompson to allow him to open a set of books. He felt quite confident in his ability, and was ambitious to see how neatly he could keep them.

The old gentleman, probably from a reluctance to try any new ways, had, for various reasons, not very clear to Charles, put him off from time to time. At length, one day, after Charles had almost given up all hope that his wishes in this matter would ever be complied with, he saw Mr. Thompson come in with quite a bundle under his arm.

"There, sonny, see if that will do for you!"

Charles soon released the paper cover.

"Oh, Mr. Thompson, thank you, sir!"

"Is that all you want? I've got jist what you telled me—but what upon earth you 're agoin' to do with so many, it's beyond me to see."

"Here's a day-book, journal, and ledger! Oh, yes, sir; thank you, sir; these are all we want. I mean to go right to work now and take stock."

The old gentleman looked at him a moment very significantly as though he did not exactly comprehend what was said, but he asked no questions, and went into the house, it being about the time when he usually left the store for the day. Charlie came in as usual to his supper, after the store had been closed, and very soon thereafter, as Mr. Thompson supposed, went to his home. About the middle of the evening, Mr. Thompson was startled more than once by what he thought was some disturbance in the store, and finally concluded he would step to the back door and listen a moment; it might be that the old mare was in some trouble, for the stable was near at hand.

He saw, however, that there must be something going on

in the store, for a light was there; he could see that plainly through the small panes of glass, which were inserted at the top of the door, and stepping out rather softly, listened as he approached the door for the sounds which had attracted his notice. They were very distinct; indeed, quite a commotion was going on there, but what the cause of it, or what it could be, was a great marvel. With the same care he had used in treading through the yard, he turned the latch, and as the door opened without noise, he had a fair opportunity to take an observation without disturbing the persons, whoever they were, in their operations. There was but one person, however, within sight. Mr. Thompson knew him well. It was "hopping Johnny," as they used to call him; a useless sort of a being, who spent his time, for the most part, sitting on a tar-barrel near the store of Mr. Thompson, looking at the sailors climbing the shrouds, or the fishermen mending their nets, or working their little boats. He was now busily engaged rolling barrels of sugar, coffee, rice, etc., in a heap near the front door, by the side of which hung the big scales. As Mr. Thompson cast a glance toward the counter, he saw it filled with the cannisters, boxes, and jars, which had been taken from their places on the shelves, and which now presented a very naked appearance, indeed; they were literally stripped.

Mr. Thompson saw all that he wished to satisfy himself that there was a "screw loose" somewhere; for such a state of confusion he had not witnessed, even in the worst of times in days past. So he walked very deliberately up toward "hopping Johnny," and thus addressed him:

"What, what, what are you about, Johnny?"

When Mr. Thompson was excited, he was more or less given to stammering.

Johnny had a pipe in his mouth, or the stump of one, which, being held firmly between his teeth, he did not care to remove just then, especially as his hands were otherwise employed. He merely gave a squint with one eye, and nodded his head toward the door. This, however, did not give any light to Mr. Thompson's mind; so he put it to him again,

"I say, what, what, what are you about, moving these casks, and making sich a hubbub! Hush up, quick, and tell me what you're *about!*"

Johnny hearing such a strong emphasis laid on the last word, straightened himself up, took the pipe out of his mouth, and looked around as though searching for Charles; but not seeing him, turned his face up to Mr. Thompson, and smiled.

"You, you, you old simpleton, if you don't tell me what you're about, I'll lay this chair over your head."

Johnny thinking that matters were beginning to look serious, thought best to say something.

"I rather guess he's goin' to ship 'em."

Johnny looked round again.

"He must be stepped out. I rather guess he's gone for a cart."

Mr. Thompson's face was now very much flushed; and Johnny saw that he was getting into a state of bewilderment, and was very much excited; he, therefore, in his own way, tried to clear up matters.

"What makes me think as how he has gone to git some one to fetch 'em away, is, because when he axed me to come and help him to-night, I remember now very well, he says to me, 'I want you, Johnny, to come and help me git out the big casks; I'm agoin' to take the stock, and I can't move the biggest things.' That's just what he said, Mr. Thompson, and I don't want to tell no lie about it."

Just then Charles made his appearance—it seems he had gone into the house to speak with Mr. Thompson in reference to some of the articles of which he knew not the first cost; and he and his master had been playing hide and seek.

He came up with much assurance toward the old gentleman who looked very sternly, and appeared to be much more excited than Charles ever remembered to have seen him.

"What, what are you about, Charlie? Heavens and earth, see what a muss. The whole counter is full, and there ain't a thing on the shelves."

"You know, Mr. Thompson, I told you that I should go right to doing it—as fast as I could."

"To doin' what?"

"Taking the stock, sir."

"Taking the stock! I see that—that's plain enough—but how much?"

"The whole of it—every thing that's here."

"You are, ha?—that's plain speaking—just come back here,

Charlie!" and Mr. Thompson walked as far as his chair, and taking his seat very deliberately, went to wiping the perspiration from his forehead. He had no doubt of Charlie's honesty, for his fine open countenance looked as bright as ever. But it was the most unaccountable occurrence he had ever met with, and he began to fear the boy had lost his reason.

"Charlie, come here—you don't feel well, do you?"

"Oh, yes, sir, perfectly well."

"Hush up, then, and jist tell me what you're about—turning things all up helter-skelter, and what that lame old crittur y u' e got there is a doin', rolling them casks and things to the door—and this time o' night, too—it's all onaccountable to me."

"Why, I know, Mr. Thompson, it makes a little confusion just now; but we can soon put them back again. I suppose I've been too much in a hurry, but I thought I could do a good deal of it to-night, when there would be no customers to disturb us.

"I will soon have the counter clear again, for I have taken every thing that's there. See here, sir, what a list."

Mr. Thompson took the paper, glad to get any thing that would throw light upon the puzzling subject. He found, indeed, a long list of teas, spices, fruits, and all the etceteras, which his shelves had once contained, the weight of each, and its cost price attached, but what it meant he could not divine.

"I see you've been a weighin' all these odds and ends, and you've put down the prices what they cost—that's plain enough; but what are you disturbin' on 'em at all for?"

"I can not take them, Mr. Thompson, until I know how much there is of each article. You know we want to find out how much stock you have on hand, and we can not do that until every thing is weighed and counted; and when I know just what stock we have on hand, then I can begin the books."

Mr. Thompson's mind began to be a little more at rest.

"And is that the reason why that old crittur is there overhauling them barrels, and turning things heels over head?"

"Yes sir."

"And are you goin' to take down every thing, and make a count on it?"

"Yes sir."

"Well, now, jist tell me, Charlie, what earthly good is to come of it?"

"Why, sir—when I get a correct account of all the stock, and what it has cost, and what is owing to you, and what you owe, then next year, by doing the same thing over again, we can tell exactly what has been made."

"That's it, is it? Well, well, you are taking a deal of trouble to little purpose, for I'm afeared you'll find there won't be much difference between this end of the year, and t' other end. But if it 's any satisfaction to you, child, you are welcome to do it."

"And will you, if you please, Mr. Thompson, let me have an account of what you owe for any of the stock? I can't find nothing about it in the old book."

"You can't, ha! Well, I guess you'll find it hard work. That's one good thing about it. It is bad enough to have so many people a owin' me, without my owin' other folks. No, no; if there must be any owin' at all, I had rather folks should owe me than I should owe them. Where do you think I should have landed long before now, if I should a gone and got in debt to other people just as they do to me? we might have gone on to doomsday, runnin' in debt both ways, and all landed in limbo together."

"Then, sir, you do not owe any thing for the stock?"

'Bless your young heart, no—nor for nothin' else. How should you think I was goin' to sleep quietly o' nights, and a thinkin' all the time of *this* one I owed, and *that* one I owed. I've begun so, and I've kept on so, and I mean to go through so, and if you mean to keep a light heart all through life, sonny, just mind what I say: *Pay as you go.*"

"I mean to, sir."

"Stick to that; you' ll find it hard pinchin' sometimes, maybe; and maybe you'll have to do without a good many fine things which your neighbors may have. But you can sleep o' nights, and you can look any one in the face without a fear that he is a goin' to dun you, and you can sit down quietly in your chair by the fireside, and if it *is* a plain wooden chair it will be easier without a cushion on it than the finest stuffed sofa that ain't paid for."

"I mean to do just as you have said, Mr. Thompson; but I

should think a great many people ought to pay you that don't. I have been looking over the old book, and I find some accounts running on for several years."

"What people ought to do, and what they *do* do is two different things. And you'll find that out too, one of these days."

"I intend, Mr. Thompson, so soon as I have opened the new books, to make out a list of debts, and then if you will let me, I will go round and try to collect them."

"You'll find it hard tryin' with some on 'em; they seem to think it's been standin' so long that it's like payin' for a dead horse; but I have nothin' agin your tryin'. I've tried till I'm ashamed to see *them*, and they're ashamed to see *me*, and so between us both the bills is like to remain in '*statter quo*.' But don't let me hinder you no more, for if you are goin' to do what you have been a talkin' about, you've got a job before you."

Charles, however, did not get through his job that evening. Every thing had to be replaced, which took more time than he had anticipated. For, boy like, he had by his haste put himself to much unnecessary trouble. He learned better by his experience of that night, and the next morning without making any confusion, as opportunity offered, he went on quietly weighing and marking down one thing at a time, while Mr. Thompson sat in his chair admiring the diligence of the boy, and sometimes indulging thoughts in reference to him, which if Charlie had known at the time, would, we fear, have caused great confusion in many of his calculations. He will know of them however one of these days.

A sudden interruption was made upon the reveries of the old gentleman by the stopping of a horse and gig before the door.

"There is Mr. Crampton's horse and gig," said Charles, who immediately stepped out, and offered to take charge of tying the horse. Mr. Crampton got out very leisurely, and as he did so, remarked to Charlie, who was holding the horse by the head, "I am not so spry as I once was; this rheumatism makes a man stiff."

But Mr. Crampton, in all probability, would not have been very spry, even without the rheumatism; for he was past the period of sprightliness, and had reached an age when sobriety of movement, as well as of conduct, are peculiarly appropriate.

Mr. Thompson, contrary to his usual custom, arose from his chair to meet his visitor.

"A good morning to you, Mr. Thompson; hope I see you well, sir." It may as well be said here that Mr. Crampton had what some would call "a pompous way with him," and it affected even his manner of conversation; every word was uttered in a slow and distinct manner, and in somewhat of a loud tone, for being a "mite deaf" he seemed to think every one else affected in the same way.

"Your sarvant, sir; glad to see you; take a seat."

Mr. Crampton did not take the seat offered to him, but signified to Mr. Thompson that he would be glad of an opportunity to have a little private conversation with him. This was readily assented to, and immediately the two gentlemen repaired to a small back room in the store, the door of which Mr. Crampton requested might be carefully closed. Mr. Thompson likewise had the precaution to drag along his chair, knowing, as he did, that there was usually but one in the room, and if there should be any long communication to listen to, he could attend to it much more to his own satisfaction, while maintaining an easy posture.

"I have called, Mr. Thompson, to have a little conversation with you, as I said. I suppose you know that, in general, I am not apt to meddle myself with other people's business; I am a 'mite deaf,'" putting his finger significantly up to his ear; "and I have a bad cold, which makes it worse." This was doubtless said in order to prepare Mr. Thompson in the matter of giving the right pitch to his voice, in whatever responses he might be called upon to make.

"Are you acquainted with Tobias Folger?"

"I am not."

"You are not! well, you know there is such a man?"

"I know him by sight, and that's all the acquaintance I want with him."

"Indeed! yes; well, perhaps you are right. I believe he is a deep one, and I just want to tell you now what I have lately been informed of, and then you can judge for yourself, and form your own opinion of matters. As I have said to you, I am not very apt to meddle with other people's affairs, but for some reasons I have thought best to vary a little from my usual habit. You know Folger has a mortgage on the property of Horatio Leslie. I believe it is said to be fifteen thousand dollars."

Mr. Thompson nodded assent.

"You know also, perhaps, that Folger has come into possession of all that handsome property which Mrs. Leslie inherited through her mother, the Hazleton property, as it is called?"

"I have lately heard such a report."

"And do you know how he came into possession?"

"Never heard."

"Well, sir, it is a queer story all round. It seems that Horatio Leslie and his wife gave a deed of that estate to a man in the neighborhood there, of the name of Thorne. The story is that Mr. Leslie wished, to dispose of it—you know it is woodland, very fine timber, the finest timber lot, perhaps, in New Jersey. Well, as he lived—that is, Leslie—at a great distance from the property, and as the lot had to be sold off in small parcels, it being too large to be disposed of advantageously otherwise, and it is said by the advice and persuasion of Mr. Folger, Leslie, as I have said, and his wife, gave a warranty deed to this Mr. Thorne. This Thorne, from what I can learn, once had a fair name, very fair indeed; he is one of your fair-faced, smooth-tongued men, very plausible, and a very active stirring fellow; but as things have turned up, and as I hear—but it must be between you and me—I should rather be inclined to the opinion that he is a great rogue. Well, Leslie gave him the deed, and he went to selling; whether he ever accounted to Leslie or not, I can not say. Well, he began to sell, when all at once a document turned up on the records which led him to think he might not be very safe in making sales under his deed; at least he found it impossible to make any sale in that vicinity. People felt shy, and did not like to venture their money on it. The document I allude to is the will of Mrs. Leslie's grandfather, who, like a great many of our old landed proprietors, wanted to keep the property in the family as long as possible, and entailed it as far as he could."

Mr. Thompson now put his hand on the arm of the gentleman, as a sign for him to stop one moment. For what with his slow and measured way of speaking, and the parentheses he was continually putting in, the patience of Mr. Thompson was about exhausted, and his mind was getting into a state of confusion.

"What has Folger to do with it?"

"Folger?"

"Yes, what has Folger to do with it?"

"Do with it! He has n't done it yet, but he will—he's a cute one."

Mr. Thompson only found things getting more confused, so he concluded to let the gentleman go on.

"You see, Mr. Thompson, the thing is this. The will, as I was saying, devised this property, and a handsome property it is—there are five hundred acres of the choicest timber land in the whole State, and what is more, being on the very border of the Delaware river, it can be floated straight to market; why, sir, they say it is worth, for timber, from one hundred and fifty, to two hundred dollars per acre—only think of that, sir, think of that!"

Mr. Thompson nodded assent.

"A very handsome property indeed, sir; but it can only be disposed of in fee, by the heirs to whom it has been entailed; one proviso, however, allows, that there can be cut from the property, five hundred cords of wood annually, and no more, until the property shall have reached the heirs at law. This no doubt, was a saving clause, designed to preserve it intact from all serious damage, so that those for whom it was ultimately designed might become possessed of a handsome property."

Mr. Thompson made a movement, as though designing to say something.

"In a moment, sir, in a moment; just hear me through. You see, sir, further than this, that those who might be heirs *ad interim* having the right of use, but not the power to dispose in fee; I say, that they might receive a certain benefit therefrom, and not be merely inheritors *in nomine*, it was provided, that a certain amount of the timber could be annually cut, and I think, if I am not mistaken—and I am pretty sure I am not—the clause in the will specifies five hundred cords, that is annually—you understand?"

Mr. Thompson had given up trying to understand; fearing, however, that the explanation would be repeated, he concluded to nod assent again.

"Well, sir, things being thus and so, you plainly perceive that any further depredation, beyond the five hundred cords specified, would subject the person thus trespassing to an action for damages in a court of chancery, which court, you know, takes special cognizance of all matters relating to the rights or wrongs of minors, or heirs of entail.

"How much Thorne has disposed of is probably not exactly known; but perhaps not more than he is entitled to as tenant in occupancy—you understand?"

"You are right, no doubt, sir."

"Now, it comes to this. Had Horatio Leslie any power to give a deed in fee?" Mr. Crampton here looked earnestly in the face of Mr. Thompson, but as the latter gentleman had a very indistinct idea of what had been said, and seemed very much at a loss how to reply, Mr. Crampton answered for him,

"I think not, sir. He doubtless supposed he had, but, sir, it is as certain as that you are sitting in that chair he had not. The entail ended with his children—don't you see that, sir. His children only have the power to do that, and they must be of age too, before they can do it."

Mr. Thompson's face brightened up now. The last assertion he clearly comprehended.

"The property is safe, then, for all!"

"I have n't told you all yet, sir. You have asked me what had Folger to do with it? I will answer that question *instanter*. This Thorne, who had a deed from Leslie, it seems, has been for some years, more or less, linked with Tobias Folger. He has been some sort of agent or go-between in the matter of selling lands for him, etc. Folger, you know, claims large tracts, which have come in his possession by hook and by crook, in a great many odd ways, and there are many hard stories about him in that region; it is said he does not care to trust his head up that way. But this Thorne has been his agent, and I am now coming at the gist of the thing: I am credibly informed that there is now on record in the town of Corrnwerll, Hunterdon county, a deed from Curtis Thorne to Tobias Folger of all that property."

"You don't say! But—but—but what use can it be to any one on 'em—Folger, or any one on 'em? So long as the deed ain't good for nothin' it can't be of no earthly use to 'em."

"Not so sure of that, sir. You see, Mr. Thompson, Folger has got Leslie under his thumb; you understand?"

"I understand."

"He has got him in his power in such a way that, you see, the man can not move even to help himself. He holds his property here, house and all, by a heavy mortgage; he holds over him a floating debt for interest; he has wormed every thing out of him. Mr. Leslie, being as you know, a very honest man, and of high and honorable feelings, has scorned to keep back any thing, even to the last dollar. He can at any moment throw him out of house and home, and can at any time, as I understand matters, prosecute him for the floating debt, where he is, in the city of New York, and clap him in jail. Now, under such circumstances, you see a man can stand but a poor chance, should he be ever so much disposed to make resistance against his oppressor."

Mr. Thompson began to be quite oppressed with the heat, and had to wipe his forehead, and open his vest; he could not, however, help saying,

"Howsomever, if as you say the right to that property you've been speakin' on is in the children, no earthly power can take it from them; they must have it at the end, come what will."

"But supposing, Mr. Thompson, that in the mean time Mr. Folger, being a moneyed man, and having the plausible right by a deed from Mr. Leslie, as to the occupancy, at any rate, supposing he should get a large number of hands, say a hundred men, he has money enough to pay them, and should set them to work, cutting the timber, and floating it off to market. How long would it take, do you think, to make such a clearing as would leave the property of but little value?"

"But you don't think the serpent would do such a thing."

"That brings me, Mr. Thompson, to the very thing for which I came to see you. A day or two since my man came to me and gave me notice that as his month was nearly up, he should leave me, as he had let himself for some months to go away out of the place. I said nothing to him at the time, but when his month was up, and while I was in the act of paying him his money, I suppose he felt rather awkward at leaving me, as I had paid him fair wages, and his money was always ready when he asked for it; so he says,.

"'Mr. Crampton, I don't like to leave a good place, but as I am a poor man, I want to get all I can, and I am offered double what you give me.'

"'What,' says I, 'Joseph! to do the same work?'

"'Oh, no, sir; it's harder work, no doubt; but Sam Shipley has engaged me, and I guess he's got fifty more from the country round about, to go to Hunterdon and cut timber."

"'Does Shipley own any timber land?' I said.

"'I don't know, sir,' Joseph replied; 'I rather think he is hiring them for some one else up there.' I paid him, and there it ended. Now you know Shipley, Mr. Thompson, and I know him. He never owned a stick of live timber in his life. Well, sir, the knowledge of one fact sometimes enables one to comprehend several others. As I was walking down town the other day, I passed Mr. Folger, as he was in earnest conversation with Shipley; you know that Shipley does a great many jobs for Folger, which he don't like to dirty his own fingers with. Just as I passed, I heard Shipley say to him, 'How many more hands will you want?' I did n't hear Mr. Folger's reply, for being a 'mite deaf,' his reply escaped me. But Shipley spoke out quite loud, and I heard very distinctly, 'How many more hands will you want?' and so I could not help putting these things together: Shipley was hiring men to cut timber in Hunterdon county; he could not be hiring for himself, for he had no timber to cut. He was hiring men for Folger, for I heard him very distinctly say, 'How many more hands will you want?' I knew that Folger had a deed of the Hazleton property, and putting these things together, and knowing, or believing, that Folger is not too good for such a trick, I have worked it all out; and to cut the matter short, Mr. Thompson, as you are, I know, a well-wisher of Mr. Leslie, I thought I would for once break through my rule, that is, to let every man take care of his own affairs and I take care of mine, and just come and let you know the whole thing."

Mr. Thompson felt somewhat relieved, to be sure, to hear that the budget was emptied at last; but he was by no means in an agreeable state of mind, and looking very earnestly at Mr. Crampton, he asked:

"What is best for us to do about it?"

Mr. Crampton put his hand behind his ear, and Mr. Thompson spoke a little louder.

"What had we better do about it?"

"You must do what you think best, Mr. Thompson; I have told you all I know; you had better consult with some judicious lawyer; and now sir, I must bid you good day."

And with the same pompous manner in which he had entered, although very polite, Mr. Crampton departed.

Not understanding very clearly all his visitor had said, Mr. Thompson for some time remained in the little room by himself, trying to get the sum and substance of it.

Two principal items he remembered: one was, that the property, which had been supposed to be lost to Mr. Leslie, was after all secured to his children; and the other was, that Folger had a claim upon it, which, under the circumstances, might be the occasion of rendering it of no value; and now the question for him to decide was, "How should he act? What had he best do?" He could not take the matter coolly, as Mr. Crampton appeared to. His kind old heart could no more be satisfied with such apathy than it could have justified him in giving short weight or measure; he felt it as much his business to see about these matters as if the interests of his own family were concerned; but what must he do? One thing he felt sure he must not do; he must not let Folger know that any of these secret doings are known or guessed at.

Sometimes the harder we think, the further we get from any conclusion that satisfies us; and thus it proved with Mr. Thompson. Tired at length with turning over in his mind the various projects which presented themselves, he suddenly arose and proceeded to the outer world to take cognizance of what his young clerk was busy at, and he noticed, as he walked up by the counter, that there was quite an array of empty boxes and barrels outside the door.

"And what are you doing with them things to the door Charlie? empty are they?"

"Oh, yes sir, and Mr. Thompson, you don't know how many things we are out of. We want sugar, and rice, and molasses, and tea! We are almost out of all these things, and you know it will not answer to be without them if they are called for; what shall we do?"

Mr. Thompson very deliberately walked back to his chair.

"Come here, Charley; you say we are most out of all these

things. Oh, dear, dear!—then I've got to go to the city again—Oh, dear, dear!"

"I wish I could go for you sir."

"You do! well, maybe afore long you will, for I'm clean tired of trampussing there and running around them dirty streets—may be afore long"—Mr. Thompson suddenly checked himself, he seemed to be about to say something very much upon his mind, but which it occurred to him just then had better not be said. "But that makes me think, I believe we are a most out of money too, that's the plagueyest thing of all; money, money, money; when that's out we're up-a-tree! you will have to go to some of the folks and tell 'em how we are situated, and that we shall have to come to a dead stand if they don't pay up. But who you'll go to is more than I can say."

"Suppose, then, Mr. Thompson, I should go right to work and make out a list of debts; I know I can get money from some of them; may I try, sir?"

"Well, well, I'll tell you what you can do. Just put down some of the names, and then let me see 'em. I can tell you pretty nigh who among 'em is likely to pay. There won't be no earthly use in goin to many on 'em. It's a pity they don't feel as I do about things, it would save a world of trouble; why, I couldn't no more sit down and eat my victuals if they wasn't paid for afore hand—they'd choke me—the coffee and the tea would all go down the wrong way, and how they sleep a nights, I don't see!"

It was no trifling job, for Charlie had to turn over every leaf of the old book to make out such a list as satisfied his own mind. He spent the rest of the day at it, and when it was finished he found it a much more formidable article than he had anticipated.

The next morning Mr. Thompson was presented with the paper; it was just after he had come out from breakfast and had taken his usual seat.

"There, Mr. Thompson, is the list, and what do you think it foots up?"

"Hush up, hush up, no matter about the footing up. Oh, dear! Oh dear! It makes me qualmish to look at it. But you've got clean too many names down—a dozen on 'em is enough at one time; you'd have to keep footing it to dooms-

13

day, and then you wouldn't get enough out of the most of 'em to buy shoe leather; you just put this away, we'll see about 'em some other time. Here's a paper that has got some names on it, that maybe you can do something with; just let this long thing go; I ain't no time, and I ain't no inclination to look over it now, and it makes me most sick to read some to the names. I've seen e'm so long that I'm most a mind of scratch e'm off and be done with it. You just go, now, and give my compliments to these folks, and tell 'em we're clean out o' money, and if they can spare me a little, I shall be exceedinly obliged. Go now, that's a man."

About the middle of the afternoon, Charles returned and prepared to give an account of his success.

"And did they all pay you, boy?"

"They all paid me some sir, except Mr. Shipley, and he said he would be glad to give you some money, but he was going right off in the boat to New York, and he wanted all he had to take with him."

"Going to York, is he?"

"Yes, sir, and he asked me very particularly the number and the street where my father lived."

"Hush up! now hush up! You're sure he did?"

"He certainly did, sir. I wonder if he can have any business with him?

"And did you tell him?"

"I did, sir."

Mr. Thompson settled back in his chair, and for a few moments seemed to be thinking hard, at length he asked; Charles.

"Is your sister, Miss Caroline, to home do you think?"

"I think she is by this time, sir?"

Mr. Thompson said nothing further, but went off into the house, and in a short time thereafter was walking quite fast for him, toward the house of Mr. Leslie. He was dressed in his best, and more than one person turned round to look, after he had passed, and wonder whether there was a funeral that afternoon, for which he had thus prepared himself.

There was no affectation in Carrie's smile and cordial greeting as he entered the house, for she was truly glad to see him. But why he had come was rather a startling question. She almost feared something had gone wrong with Charlie!

"I am so glad you have come, Mr. Thompson, for I was just hinking that I must go and see you; I want to say something about the school."

"Then I'm sorry I hadn't waited a little, for the folks to home would be so glad. But as I'm about going to the city, I didn't know but you might have some message, or something or another you might want to send."

"You will see father, then, Mr. Thompson?"

"That's what I'm expecting to do; and I thought I would just call and see if there was any errand you had to send by me."

"I have no errand, Mr. Thompson, but I am very anxious to see my father, and to tell the truth, I have been thinking to close my school for a few days, and go to the city. But you know it is a long ride alone. How do you go, Mr. Thompson?"

"I am goin' in the mornin' to take the stage. This time a year I don't fancy the water much—the less I have to do with it the better."

"What should you say if I should conclude to go with you, Mr. Thompson? or perhaps you would not care to be troubled with the charge of a lady, although I feel pretty well qualified to take charge of myself; but it would be rather more agreeable to be with some one I know."

"Bless your young heart! it won't be no trouble to me; I'm but an old body myself, but I should like to see a young one or an old one that would dare to say an uncivil word to you in my hearin'; it would n't be best for 'em."

"Oh, thank you—I hope there will be no need for your protection so far as that. I think I shall go; if I do, we shall meet at the stage-house."

CHAPTER XXI.

"My dear Carrie, is this you? How glad I am to see you!"

"My dear Ellen!"

And the two friends were locked in each other's arms, in the hall of the large mansion of Langdon Douglass, while the kind old guardian of Carrie was standing on the stoop and admiring the bright lamp which hung in the center of the hall, and not a little gratified at the warm reception his young charge was receiving.

"And will not this gentleman walk in? Do come in, sir!" and the warm-hearted Ellen walked to the door, and even out on the stoop in her urgency to welcome the attendant of her friend.

"Many thanks to you, madam; but I have seen her safe, and that's what I promised to do. I must be jogging to my own quarters."

"And you will call in the morning for me, Mr. Thompson?"

"Sartain, and I will; and we will take a hack; for it's too long a walk for you. Spring-street is clear up town, ever so fur."

And the old gentleman made a polite reverence to the ladies, and stepped off, quite lively for him.

Words flew fast between the two young ladies, as they walked through the hall into the back parlor.

"It can not be!" said Mrs. Douglass, as Ellen introduced Carrie to her mother. "Is it possible this is the Carrie I have heard you speak so much about!" and giving her a hearty kiss, "you are truly a welcome visitor."

The reception by Mr. Douglass was full as cordial as that by his lady, and in a few moments Carrie felt quite at home in a family she had never before visited.

Carrie and Ellen had been companions at school for several years. They had been room-mates during all the time; they had been confidantes of each other's thoughts and feelings; there had never been a jar in all their intimacy—no coldness, or distrust, or jealousy, had ever troubled them. They had been true friends, and seemed to have become essential to each other's happiness. They were not alike in some characteristics. Ellen was somewhat impetuous and inclined to chafe under restraint, while Carrie was calm, her feelings under control, and disposed to yield readily to the requirements of her teacher. Both had warm affections and great sincerity of character. They were not alike, either, in personal appearance; for Carrie was distinguished even among those who could lay claim to beautiful form and features; and Ellen was merely a fair, good-looking girl.

Their intimacy had not been broken off on leaving school. At first, they corresponded frequently, and thus kept alive the warm feelings which they had indulged when together. For some time, however, Carrie had been remiss in her part of this duty, for the reason that her time was much occupied, and perhaps because she did not wish to trouble her friend with the particulars of her own trials.

Langdon Douglass, the father of Ellen, was a wealthy merchant in New York, engaged in the shipping business. He had been wise and fortunate in the management of his affairs, and had attained a position beyond the chances and changes of a mercantile life, but still pursued his avocations as regularly, and with as much attention to details, as he had ever done.

But Langdon Douglass was not merely a successful merchant, he was a liberal and useful member of society. He felt that the wealth of which he was possessed, was a trust committed to him not solely for his own benefit. He did not scatter his bounty with a reckless hand, nor openly parade his name before the world in large bequests. He rather embraced such cases as were brought, as he judged, providentially to his immediate notice. These he would examine into with as much care, and exercise for them the same discriminating judgment as he gave to any department of his business.

It was, as he viewed it, one of the most responsible, as well as difficult duties which devolved upon him, requiring as much care and prompt action as though planning a voyage, or preparing an outfit for his vessel.

At home he was a kind parent and husband, but not remarkably indulgent to his children, at least the older ones said he had not been so to them, when they were young. Ellen had, however, no cause for any such complaint; she was the youngest, and the only one unmarried at home.

Ellen had visited Carrie at her home during one of their vacations, and had long been urging her friend to let her have the pleasure of introducing one she loved so much to her own parents, and home, in the city. And Carrie, thinking it might not probably be convenient for the family where her father boarded, to receive her, had ventured upon the many invitations which had been given her, to go at once to the house of her friend; and as it was evening when they reached the city, concluded to defer calling upon her father until the next morning.

It was sometime after breakfast; Mrs. Barstow had cleared up things, and was just about settling down to her knitting, when she became conscious that a carriage had stopped at her door; and giving things a few touches about her person, she stood waiting for a summons from the knocker. As it did not come in the time it might have been expected, she was just on the point of going into the front room, for the purpose of observation, when three loud raps, that made the house ring, checked further progress in that direction, and she lost no time in gaining the front door.

On opening it, her eye met the portly form of a man somewhat advanced in life, plain in his appearance, but yet with quite an air of respectability. From the knock, as well as the outfit of the stranger, she judged at once that he was from the country.

"Your sarvant, madam: can you tell me does Mr. Leslie live here?"

"Well, sir—yes; he is here part of the time. He sleeps here, and takes breakfast, and then he goes down town, and we don't see him again till night."

"Oh, dear, dear!" The gentleman said this in a low tone, as merely expressing to himself some disappointment or difficulty. But Mrs. Barstow heard it.

"Maybe if you want to see him afore evening you had better go to his place down town. It's in Cliff-street."

"I have been there, you see, madam; but the man telled me he'd been there and had gone away, and he guessed he'd gone home again, for he was n't no 'wise well."

"Have you a lady with you in the carriage?"

"It's his darter, madam; and what to do I don't know."

"Won't you just ask her to come in, and then walk in yourself; and we will see—maybe he'll be along presently." And extending the invitation herself to the lady in the carriage, Mrs. Barstow was in a few minutes leading Carrie Leslie and Mr. Samuel Thompson into her sitting-room; and giving them seats, she looked at the former in a kind, motherly way.

"You are Mr. Leslie's daughter, then. I have heard him speak of you, but now I see you, I don't wonder he's grown so thin and pines away so, if all his family is like you. Parents' hearts can't be separated from their children, though their bodies may."

And as Carrie looked at the good lady, she noticed a tear already gathering.

"Is my father not well, madam?"

"Well, I think he is n't. But you have n't seen him lately?"

"Not for many months; but he has said nothing of his being unwell, and we have thought from his letters that his health had been good."

"Well, maybe he ain't conscious of it. I know it was just so with Mr. Barstow; I kept a telling him that there was certain something or another the matter, for he kept a losing flesh, and growing thinner and thinner, and I says to him, Mr. Barstow you ain't well, and you can't be well; for your victuals don't seem to do you no good. But he would n't hear to it, and said he was well enough. But I tell you what it is, my dear young lady, men have their troubles; they have to take the rough of the world, you know, and sometimes it's hard gitting along. What, with close people, and dishonest people, and hard-hearted people, and hard work all the day, and hard thinkin' a nights, it's a wonder to me how they stand it at all."

How long Mrs. Barstow might have gone on with the sub

ject, it would be difficult to say, for it w . . . that often troubled her. But she was suddenly cut sh . . by the opening of the street door.

"There is your pa, now! I'll bet any th' ng. But you stay here, and I'll go and see."

Carrie was much excited, and could with difficulty restrain herself from rushing into the hall, so impatient was she to get a glimpse of her dear parent, and yet full of apprehension.

Mrs. Barstow led the persons, for there was more than one, into the adjoining room, and was for a little while earnestly engaged in conversation with them, although in a low tone. At length the door was opened—Carrie gave one long earnest look, and then ran into the arms of her father. Mr. Thompson rose and stood with his hat in his hand, wiping his face occasionally, but saying nothing, when Mr. Leslie, after leading Carrie to a seat, stepped up to him.

"My good old friend! I am glad to see you!"

Mr. Thompson grasped the offered hand, and tried to say something, but it amounted to very little, beside the motion of the lips. He saw Carrie giving vent to her feelings, and the kind-hearted old man was very near joining in with her.

"Mr. Thompson," said Mr. Leslie, after a moment's pause, "I must ask you to step in with me to the other room, as I wish to have a few words with you in private." And as they entered, Mrs. Barstow arose and went into the room where Carrie was seated.

"I may as well tell you at once, Mr. Thompson, how I am situated, and I must leave it to you to break the intelligence to my daughter. It is a sad thing for the poor child that she has come to see me just at this emergency. I have been arrested for an old debt, and am now in the hands of the officer, and on my way to jail. Get the dear child home as soon as you can—I had better not see her again."

"Mr. Leslie," said the officer, "I have learned that your daughter has just come on to see you; I regret exceedingly that you are thus situated. If you will say that I shall find you here this afternoon at three o'clock, I will take the responsibility of leaving matters until then. I take you for a gentleman, sir, who will not allow a poor man to suffer for an act of kindness."

He was, indeed, an officer of the law, but his unpleasant duties had not spoiled a generous heart. Mr. Leslie replied, with evident emotion,

"You are very generous, sir. It would, indeed, be a great favor, and I pledge my word that I shall take no advantage of your gentlemanly offer."

"I will be here then, sir, by three o'clock."

"And I will be ready to accompany you."

The officer rose to depart, and Mr. Thompson followed him to the door, while Mr. Leslie hastened to his daughter, desirous of spending with her the short time allotted to him.

"And now tell me, friend, just the upshot of this thing—what has got to be done?"

Mr. Thompson asked this, standing on the pavement outside the house, with one hand fast to the lappel of the officer's coat, and the other holding on to the wooden railing of the front stoop.

"The upshot of it is, he has to go to jail. It's plaguey hard, he seems a nice, gentlemanly kind of a man—I don't know as ever I felt so bad on taking any one before. But you see I've done all I could. I'm but a poor man, and have to do a good deal of hard and ugly work too for my living, but I thought I'd risk it, just leaving him a few hours. Safe, ain't I? His word is good, ain't it?"

"You needn't be at all consarned about that—he'll stick to his word, come of it what will; but he ain't really, in earnest got to go to jail!"

"The jail, and nothing else! I asked him, you see, 'Certainly,' says I, 'you'll give bail, and go on the liberties?' 'I can't do it,' says he, 'I have no one to ask such a favor of?' So you see, friend, what can I do?—my orders are positive."

"I'll tell you what it is, neighbor, this can't be, *no how!* That man go into their nasty old prison! Hush up, hush up; no! no!"

And the old man took off his hat and wiped away the profuse perspiration that was starting from his forehead. "No, no! I say, that can't be done! I'll go there first myself."

"I am sorry, sir, sorry; but you see the law is strict, and there's no getting away from the thing—your going there won't answer the turn no how."

"Ain't you a mind, neighbor, jist to get into this hack and

ride down town with me? But tell me, first, how much is it? how much is he took for?"

"The execution is for a thousand and over—say a thousand and fifty."

"Well, you jist git in and go with me, and let that man take us to No. — Old-slip."

"I will, sir, certainly."

When Mr. Thompson reached the store of Blossom & Co., Old-slip, he was informed that a gentleman was waiting for him in a back office of the store.

"Waiting for me! well, I guess he must wait a bit longer. Mr. Blossom, I want a word with you; just step out here one minute;" and Mr. Thompson walked into the open store and seated himself on a barrel of sugar that was lying on its side ready to be carted off.

"I must sit down, for I get so worried a goin about this big city a yourn, I'm a most tuckered out."

"So you had to hire a carriage! I don't know that I ever saw you in a carriage before."

"It ain't often I trouble 'em, any how; but I'm getting old and bulky, and what with one thing, and what with another, my own troubles and other people's troubles, their ain't much rest for a man in this world."

"I thought you never had any trouble; you always pay as you go; money makes all our trouble here in the city, or rather the want of it. You have n't been getting in debt have you?"

"No, no, neighbor—no fear o' that; I've got too many debts owin' to me, and I see too well how plaguey hard it is to pay 'em, for me ever to go and do sich a thing as that. But I'm clean worried out for a neighbor of mine, a real honest man, and a gentleman who's been took for an old debt, and they're goin' to clap him right into your nasty stone jail; ours is bad enough, but it's only a wooden one, and plenty of air-holes in it; there 's plenty of breathin' room, but it makes my heart sick to look at the great stone iron-grated consarn you've got here; I should think it's enough to frighten folks, so that a sight of it would keep you all from runnin' into debt. But that ain't here nor there. I ain't a goin' to let this man go there if there's any body in this city that knows old Sam Thompson well enough just to tell the folks to the court that I am a responsible man for a thousand, at any rate—just so that they'll take me for bail, that's all."

"I don't know as that can be done, Mr. Thompson, you not living in the State. But I know what can be done, if it is going to oblige you: they will take Jo Blossom for a thousand, I guess, or a little more maybe, and if you say I am safe, it shall be done."

"Bless your soul for that; you've taken a load off my mind, neighbor—and just make out any writing you please, I'll sign it, and hold you harmless."

"Done, sir; shall I go with you now?"

"Yes, to rights—; just let me see what that man you tell on wants with me in the back room; but first I must speak to my man in the carriage."

Mr. Thompson soon made satisfactory arrangements with his carriage companion, requesting him, at the same time, "to hold on a bit," and have a little more patience, and he would go with him, and finish the job "to onst." He then, with as much expedition as he was accustomed to make, hastened to the back office. Had Mr. Thompson seen a being from the spirit-land, he could not certainly have been more astounded than he was when, on opening the door, he beheld Tobias Folger, sitting very composedly at a small green table reading the paper. That he was in town Mr. Thompson knew, or thought was likely to be the case, for he had come on with them in the stage the day before. But what he could be wanting with him! what business Tobias Folger could have with Samuel Thompson, was the mystery—it must be some other Mr. Thompson—he was very sure there never had been, and it was not very likely there ever would be, any thing in the shape of business between them. Mr. Samuel Thompson was not, in general, afraid of the face of man: he owed no man, and if folks owed him, he was not to blame for that. But Folger he feared, that is, he would no more have had any business transaction with him than a mouse would willingly unite with puss at the same bone. He was prejudiced, strongly prejudiced, and he "could not tell why, but he did n't never want to have nothin to do with the critter." Things, he said, "between him and that man would, he guessed, remain in *statter quo*."

But Mr. Thompson was now in his presence: he must say

something. That trouble, however, was saved, for Mr. Folger had no sooner lifted his eyes from the paper, than he rose and hastened toward Mr. Thompson, and before the latter gentleman had recovered from his surprise, was holding out his hand for salutation.

"Ah, my good sir, I am glad to see you this morning. Well, after your long ride, sir? And how is Miss Leslie this morning? Have you seen her to-day? You have been quite a favored one, Mr. Thompson; come, take a seat, sir."

Mr. Thompson made reply only to the last proposition.

"Your sarvent, sir; I am somewhat in a hurry just now; can't sit no how. Mr. Blossom tell'd me there was a gentleman wanted to see me in the back room, and so I thought I would just step along; can't sit no how, sir"—seeing Mr. Folger had placed a seat in readiness for him.

"But I wish to speak to you a little in private, Mr. Thompson. I will detain you but a moment; sit down, my good sir, sit down."

Thus urged, the old gentleman, with apparent reluctance, sat down; and taking off his hat began very leisurely to smooth down his foretop.

"I believe, Mr. Thompson, it is pretty generally known that you are a good friend of Mr. Leslie."

"I wish him well, sir; I wish him well, with all my heart."

"I know you do—at least I have every reason to think so. Well, sir, I have heard, very much to my sorrow, since I have been in town, that he is in trouble, very great trouble."

"It is even so, sir."

"He has been sued, I hear."

"He has; and he's been took, and—and—"

"About to be incarcerated."

"I don't know about *that*: it's a part of the diviltry I ain't heerd of. I thought it was bad enough to put a man into their stone jail without a doin' that other thing you talk about. If they can 'carcerate a man into the bargain, dear, dear! I don't know but I've had all my trouble for nothing then. I was just a goin' to have him bailed out."

"You—you have stood bail for him then?"

"Yes, sir, or them have stood it as are well known."

Mr. Thompson did not notice the countenance of Mr. Folger just then, or he would have seen that it had suddenly become quite pale. The former personage was too much taken up with thoughts about that *other thing* Mr. Folger had suggested. Mr. Thompson had heard the word before, but somehow he had in his mind connected with it State Prison recreations. Mr. Folger had certainly been baffled in some of his plans. Things had taken a turn which he had not anticipated. There was no way now but to make the most out of a wicked plan which had thus, as he thought, been sadly frustrated. It was not long, however, before he was ready with a proposal—it was quite different from that for which he had sought the interview.

"Well, Mr. Thompson, you have shown yourself a good friend to Mr. Leslie, and now I can freely communicate to you my wishes. I am also Mr. Leslie's *friend*. He owes me money, no doubt—a good deal of money. But between you and me, he is too fine a man to be dealt with in such a way. He must not go to jail, sir, nor on the limits either. You see, Mr. Thompson, I found out about this thing before I left home. I said nothing, but I have been on the watch. Now, what I want is this, I want that note taken up."

"Who is to pay it?"

"I will pay it."

Mr. Thompson began to doubt his own senses.

"I will pay it, Mr. Thompson. I must do it, however, through you; you can very well realize that under the circumstances it would not be so well to be known that I had interfered. To be sure *you* will know it, and Mr. Leslie and his family will know it; but for no consideration would I that such a thing should get abroad. There are a great many reasons why it would be highly improper. I need not state them now, but having various dealings with many different people, I am obliged to do things at times *sub rosa;* you understand?"

Mr. Thompson did not pretend to understand any thing just then; his mind was very much clouded. He merely nodded his head.

"I am aware, Mr. Thompson, that it may appear very strange to you that I should thus add to Mr. Leslie's indebtedness to me. But, sir, consider for one moment: what can he do in jail? or even on the limits? How would his family feel? How would *he* feel? No, sir, I may lose the money, but he shall not suffer in that way while Tobias Folger has the means to aid him. People think I love money—perhaps I do, Mr. Thompson, but I for one can not see a man like Leslie, or a family such as he has got, suffer, and stand by with hands in pocket and do nothing."

"Glad to hear you say so, sir—glad to hear you say so."

"And now, Mr. Thompson, here is the money." And Mr. Folger drew from his pocket-book a roll of bills.

"By the way, do you know the exact amount, Mr. Thompson?"

"I can't tell the precise sum, but the man who has got the warrant is now a waiting at the door; he can tell."

"The officer! Is he with you?"

"Sartain—I've kept close to him till I could see what was for to be done."

"Well, now, do not, for the world, say one word to him. Let it all go as coming from you. You are known as a man of property. It will not appear at all strange that you should thus interfere. Just take the money, pay up the note, clear off the whole concern. You do it, and then you can hand me the note."

"I will do your bidding, sir, with a right good will, and thank you into the bargain."

"And you can see Mr. Leslie as soon as you please, and let him know that the thing is all settled; but remember and keep mum."

Mr. Thompson took the money and went on his way, occasionally rubbing his eyes, and once or twice giving his arm a good pinch—he was not quite sure that he was awake.

Mr. Leslie had designed, if possible, to keep from Carrie the sad condition into which he was now plunged. But the eye of his lovely daughter could discern, even through the wreck which change of place, and care, and toil had made of her father's fine countenance, that there was some deeper cause of grief then weighing on his heart. It was in vain that he endeavored to put aside her earnest inquiries. Her love was stronger than his resolution. He could not resist that pleading child. By little and little the truth came forth, until the terrible reality lay unvailed before her.

It was indeed a point in poverty that Carrie, in all her imaginings, had never before brought up. The vision of a father, whose love had been the light of her life, fast inclosed within the walls of a prison, had never, for a moment, flitted before her mind. She had fondly supposed that the specter, which to many looked so horrible, had, by just reasoning on the good and ill of life, been disarmed of all terror, and that she could boldly face it and dare its worst.

A humble cottage, rude furniture, plain apparel, scanty fare, ceaseless labor, and the sneer of the world—all these she had looked at as possibilities; she did not fear them. With those she loved, all these could not take away one real joy from her heart.

She had never before supposed that poverty was so nearly allied to crime that it might involve a degradation of the being around whose tender sympathies her own were entwined with a grasp stronger than the love of life.

Her purpose in this visit to her father had been to use her influence in persuading him to anticipate at once the reality of their situation; to relinquish the home they were inhabiting, and which was only adding to future difficulty, and come down at once to the humble circumstances which seemed now to her most suitable, and on many accounts most desirable.

There was still, as she thought, an inconsistency between their ability and the style in which they were living. And this had been the subject of conversation during which Carrie had finally brought out the true state of things.

Her plans were at once swept from her mind. One idea alone absorbed every other. How she might release her parent from the grasp of the law! Her thoughts flew with lightning speed; suggestions which before she had cast away from her as the unwise thoughts of a friend, came back, "*Ought not children to be willing to make sacrifices for a parent?*" Little did Mrs. Crampton imagine, in her urgency to win the mind of her friend to her own way of thinking, what a power the words she uttered might, under certain circumstances, be permitted to exert. Yes, the truth must be told: she thought now with an interest at which her mind would once have been justly alarmed, of all that had been said and done in reference to a matter that involved her destiny for life. But what was life to her now? a blank—a wilderness—a tempest—a dreary winter night—yea, worse than all these—a living death—where all that was beautiful had fled—and the heart bereft of all but its power to suffer.

Folger had no doubt anticipated that the extremity which his own wily measures were about to accomplish, might make his aid so necessary that an application to him for assistance would be no impossible event. He had, on entering the stage, where he found Carrie on her way to the city, made the remark "that he had been very unexpectedly summoned there," and seemed to be highly gratified that he was to have such good company. He was, however, by no means forward in his attentions. He made himself agreeable, and seemed to take more pains to do so than was usual. In fact, the delicacy of his behavior, and the happy manner in which he introduced subjects of conversation, and the just views he expressed on matters of importanee, did really beguile the tedium of the day's ride, and gave Carrie a more pleasing view of his character than she had ever as yet entertained. Before separating from her he had, as though by mere accident, mentioned the number and street where he expected to remain during his stay in the city. She thought lightly of the fact at the time, but in her extremity now, it was a relief to her that she remembered it. It was no time for too nice attention to the conventional rules of social life.

To save her own life she would not have ventured to thrust herself into obligations to Mr. Folger; but *to save a parent from disgrace* she could not hesitate to ask aid from one who had manifested the feelings of a friend. She could not have supposed that a man of honor would take advantage of such an opportunity to urge a personal suit.

Any thing which was not a breach of God's commandments appeared to her, under present circumstances, right and proper to be done.

With a slight apology to her father for leaving him for a short time, she at once left the house and proceeded toward the lower part of the city.

CHAPTER XXII.

CARRIE was seated in the front parlor at the house of her friend Ellen Douglass—or rather she had stationed herself there; she could not sit, her mind was too highly excited. To and fro about the spacious room she walked in silent agony—in constant expectation of a visit from one to whom, in an hour of extreme distress, she had sent a message requesting an interview. The bell rings, and with all the effort she was capable of making, she has seated herself and awaits his entrance.

"Ah! this is a most unexpected pleasure, Miss Leslie! I hope I see you well—you are not, I fear!" And the countenance of Mr. Folger changed at once from its bright appearance, assumed on entering the room, into an aspect of marked concern.

"I am well, I thank you, sir; but—but I am in great trouble, Mr. Folger. I have ventured to take a great liberty in sending for you—I know not to whom else to go—we have no claim upon you, Mr. Folger—but you have wealth—and my father has been arrested for debt, and is about to be thrust into a loathsome prison. Oh, sir! how can I see this evil come upon him?"

"Miss Leslie, I feel, more than I can well describe, the great favor you have done me! I only could have wished you had said that you came to me as to *the friend* most likely to aid your father or to do your bidding. I have wealth, to be sure—but do you think—"

"Pardon me, Mr. Folger, my mind is so intent on one idea alone, that of aid for my parent, that perhaps I have said what I ought not! The fact of my applying to you, sir, must be your assurance that I esteem you my father's friend."

"Miss Leslie, I know well what a loving heart you have, and I would not allow one pang to pierce it that I have the power to ward off. I therefore hasten to inform you that I have heard of your father's difficulty; I feared it even before I left my home, as I had received a letter from a person who held some of your father's responsibilities, in which he mentioned that orders had been given to prosecute. For that reason I came to the city. I have already interfered for your father's rescue. The note has been taken up, the execution satisfied, and your father is a free man. I hold now the claim which has given him so much trouble, and now I ask you Miss Leslie, to add one item to your last acknowledgment; you have said you regard me as your father's friend, have I no claim to be called yours too?"

Carrie arose and stretched forth her hand, while tears of joy at the news of her father's deliverance were bedewing her lovely cheek.

"Mr. Folger, he who has manifested such an interest for the father, and in an hour of extremity has proved himself a friend in deed, has a claim upon the child which I must frankly acknowledge. If my kindest feelings, my best wishes, my ardent prayers, can be of any avail to you, be assured you have them all. Oh, sir! you have relieved my heart from a burden too heavy to be borne."

There was a smile upon the lip of Folger, blended with the expression of serious feeling which predominated in his countenance, as he listened to the outpouring of that truthful heart. Carrie did not notice it, or, if she did, thought not that it expressed any sinister meaning.

It was the lighting up of joy on the face of the fowler as he sees the bird of his prey perching within range of his gun.

"Sit down, Miss Leslie, I see you are much excited." And Carrie resumed her seat, while Folger drew his chair into close proximity to hers.

"You must be under no apprehension on your father's account. His present trial is at an end. But I wish to have a few words with you about the future, and I wish to talk in all frankness with you. Circumstances, you are aware, have thrown your father's property into my hands, or at least given me a power over it that controls it. I do not know that I am to blame for this, and I think your father acquits me of censure." He paused and looked at Carrie for a reply.

"He does not censure you, Mr. Folger--far from it."

"I thought as much. Sure am I he has no reason so to do. But let the past go, the future must be looked at; interest is daily accumulating—I presume already a sale would hardly realize the amount due to me."

"I have thought of that, Mr. Folger, and the principal reason for visiting my father at present was to use my influence with him to relinquish our home at once, make a change in our whole style of living, and come down to the reality of our actual condition. We are poor—let us live in accordance with our circumstances!"

Ah! the bird has again flown, and the wily hunter is despoiled of his prey. Those five sentences Carrie had uttered filled Folger with dismay; the prize is lost if the plan upon which her mind is intent should be carried out.

"Dear Miss Leslie, believe me, you can have no idea what such a change as you speak of would involve. Remember you have always lived in a condition that has procured for your family a certain consideration in society; to lose that would be a source of deeper trial than you can now well imagine."

"It would be much better, however, Mr. Folger, to lose the acquaintance of those who value us merely for our station in society, than to endeavor to maintain a standing beyond our means; I am very certain we should be much happier to live as our circumstances indicate we should. Poverty is only to be dreaded in anticipation."

"I will readily grant, Miss Leslie, that there is much happiness among that class of society which we denominate as poor. But there is a vast difference between the views and feelings of those who have always been accustomed to toil for their daily bread and those who, like yourself and family, have lived upon the labors of others. There would be privations and trials to you which the first-named class have never experienced. It is no small matter to change all our social relations, to step down into a lower sphere; you can have no present conception what the trial would be. But, my dear Miss Leslie, allow me to be plain with you, and ask you to look at things as they really exist, and not as your imagination may fancy them. How long do you think your father can live in his present circumstances? I have not yet seen him, but I am told he looks wretchedly, and has every symptom of decline!"

Carrie could not reply. The selfish wretch had touched the tender point in her heart. He knew it well. He saw the color fly from her blooming cheek, he knew her heart was in agony, and resolved to profit by the torment he was inflicting.

"Depend upon it, the change which he is obliged to endure in his present separation from his family, in his daily confinement to uninteresting duties, and, I almost hesitate to speak of it, his poor manner of living, which, perhaps, you know nothing of—"

Carrie clasped her hands, and pressed them to her breast in silence.

"Now I am well convinced that some change must be made or he will sink! and upon yourself it now depends, my dear Miss Leslie, whether this burden shall be removed, your home retained, your father released from his responsibilities, his life prolonged, and his future happiness secured."

"Upon me! Oh, do tell me, Mr. Folger; my life itself I will give for such an end. Do tell me, Mr. Folger!"

Folger was himself astounded with the earnestness of her manner and the readiness she expressed to make any sacrifice.

"My dear Miss Leslie, be calm. Hear me patiently. You have it not only in your power to secure your father's happiness and that of your family, but there is also another whose fate rests upon your will."

As Carrie spoke not, he continued: "This is no sudden emotion on my part, you have long held the supreme dominion over my affections. I now throw myself, my child, my wealth, at your feet. I ask you to seal my happiness, and your father's future welfare."

Had such a proposal been made to Carrie Leslie but a few hours previous, she would, no doubt, have answered with a prompt refusal. Life, within that short period, had presented a new aspect to her. It had in fact become concentrated into one ardent wish, one absorbing care—the relief of her father, and the preservation of his life All else connected with her earthly existence had vanished. Folger, too, had appeared in the character of a friend in need: he had not made promises, he had contributed *essential aid*, and that in an hour of her dire necessity. "*And ought not children to be willing to make sacrifices for their parents?*" That question, at such a moment, was full of meaning. Its power at once scattered all arguments her reason, feeble as it then was, could urge. Her tortured mind, weakened, distracted, in a whirl of contending emotions, could only express itself in a flood of tears.

Calm and unmoved, the heartless being who had thus by his art wrought up her sensitive spirit, and overpowered its better judgment, looked on in silence for a while, and then, in tones of the utmost tenderness, resumed,

"My dear Miss Leslie, I see I have been too presumptuous. I have caused you needless anguish; my proposal displeases you—forget that I have made it, and forgive the offense."

Carrie could keep silence no longer.

"Mr. Folger, I have nothing to forgive."

He took her hand, to which she made no resistance, and he raised the priceless treasure to his lips.

The hour of joy is often shaded by the cloud of misfortune. Folger had consummated a project for which he had labored long. He felt that his great end had been gained, and youth and beauty were again to be added to his gifts from fortune. Carrie and he have parted, she to the privacy of her chamber, there to compose her mind and prepare to mingle again in the family circle, if not with a glad heart, at least with a cheerful countenance. And Mr. Folger to make preparations to carry out to its completion the plan he so artfully devised. He had proceeded but a few steps from the dwelling of Mr. Douglass when, as he was passing a gentleman, he became conscious that the eye of the stranger was fixed intently upon him; as was natural, he unconsciously returned the gaze; in a moment the countenance of one he had not seen for years was recalled. But it would not be for his interest to renew the acquaintance. He passed on, but the stranger paused, and as Folger turned the corner of the street he could plainly discern that he had been recognized, for the gentleman was retracing his steps, and as he went with quickened speed to gain the crowded thoroughfare, he was conscious that an eye was upon him, and that footsteps were keeping time with his. And even in the throng that crowded the great highway of the city, he had the same consciousness of being followed for some distance. A band of soldiers, however, fortunately for him, with music and a mass of sight-seers, were just then crossing the street he was in. A rush through their ranks enabled him to place an obstacle between him and his pursuer, and he saw him no more. But the game of his life he felt must be played fast now; whatever plans he meant to accomplish by the maintenance of a fair character, must be accomplished without delay.

CHAPTER XXIII.

Mr. Samuel Thompson, having finished the business of the day—and a busy day it had been to him—was seated quietly in the back room of a very respectable hotel in Courtlandt-street. He was alone, as the boarders had all gone out for the evening, either for business or amusement, and was engaged in pondering upon the strange incidents of the day, and trying to unravel, or account satisfactorily to his own mind, for the remarkable conduct of one individual, at least, with whom he had dealings, when a young gentleman very leisurely walked into the room, and bowing slightly to Mr. Thompson, without speaking, took a seat by a table in quite a distant corner, and commenced reading the papers of the day which lay scattered upon it. As the back of the young man was toward him, Mr. Thompson could take note of his appearance without rudeness, and as he had become tired of thinking, where thought only grew more obscure the more it was indulged, was glad of any thing to divert himself with. He noticed that he was a young man of very fine form, and genteelly dressed, in a rich suit of black. He was in mourning, and that doubtless for near relatives, for his hat, which lay upon the table, was trimmed with crape, and the long black band hung down over its edge. Occasionally a glimpse was had of his side-face, and then the old gentleman began to be impressed with the idea that the countenance was one that he had seen before, but when, and where, he could not recall. The lights in the room were not brilliant. Gas had not then been invented, and tallow-candles were more generally used than oil. And Mr. Thompson's sight was not very keen, even with his glasses on.

Presently the young gentleman arose, and approaching the table by which Mr. Thompson was seated, was about to lay his hand on a pair of snuffers, with a remark about the dimness of the lights, when he suddenly paused, and looking with much earnestness,

"Why, can it be! Surely I am not mistaken! This is Mr. Thompson?"

The old gentleman arose, and holding out his hand,

"I thought it was somebody I knew, but I dare n't speak, for fear it might n't be, after all. But I am glad to see you, Mr. Ralston, mighty glad to see you, sir."

"And I am to see you, for I am on my way to Princesport for that very purpose. How are they all doing there, sir?"

"Tolerably well, sir, what is left on 'em there. The most on 'em, however, seem to be on here just now."

"Ah! is it so? for what purpose?"

"That's beyond me to tell; I 've been a puzzling my head all the evening; but I'll take my chair again, for what between a riding in hacks, and a walking on my legs, and a worrying of my mind, I feel clean tuckered out to-night. It 's a plaguey hard place to get about in. You see I began to say as how I'd been a puzzling my head all the evenin' afore you came in, to try and put things together, and see what to make on 'em. But the more I think, the thicker it gits, and I've about giv it up."

And then Mr. Thompson, with as much brevity as possible, went over the scenes of the day, and more particularly the strange occurrence in connection with Mr. Folger. "I tell you, friend, it puzzles me the more I think on it. There is that Shipley hand in glove with him, doin' all his bidding, as every body says, come on here, and making such a 'to-do' with poor Leslie, and Folger a knowin' on it, for he telled me himself he had heered about it afore he left home. Why did n't he go to Shipley and settle matters with him? No, but he must come to me, and make me promise to be whist as a mouse, and not say any thing to any body, and I ain't—I ain't said a word to a livin' soul, only to Mr. Leslie, but I can't help tellin' you of it, but don't say a word good or bad. Only if you can jist tell me what it means. Your law larnin' maybe will help you to see the diviltry of it. For that there's somethin' or other crooked about it, I 'm sartain."

"Perhaps he only wished to make Mr. Leslie feel under greater obligations to him, for the purpose of accomplishing an end which you once suggested to me, that you thought he had in view."

"Well, I don't know that I can just tell what eend you're a thinkin' on. That man always seemed to me to have as many eends as an eel out of water—a squirmin all ways to onst."

"Perhaps, if Mr. Folger is enamoured of the daughter he may think it worth while to appear especially kind to the family; and you being known as friendly to them, it would be for his interest to have a good word from you."

Mr. Thompson fixed his eye steadily for some time on young Ralston, and seemed to be thinking very hard.

"I'm most afeared friend, that I've been caught in that trap. Hush up, hush up—you don't think the wily sarpent could have had sich a trick in his head?"

"I can not say, Mr. Thompson, but from your representation of the whole case it appears a very strange proceeding."

"I tell you what, friend, I've been clean bamboozled—I begin to think he's got round me for all. There I've been and telled Mr. Leslie what a kind and good man Folger was, and how he seemed to feel so cut up because Mr. Leslie had been put to trouble, and how kind he talked about him, and all that. I don't know but I've drove the nail clean in, for Leslie was all took with Folger, and thinks now he's one of the nicest men that ever was. The old cunning sarpent!"

"I mentioned to you, Mr. Thompson, that I was on my way to Princesport for the purpose of seeing you; I have ascertained some things which are of moment to Mr. Leslie, and of which he ought to be informed, and that speedily. I am a stranger to him, and he might think my interference quite uncalled for, and perhaps put a wrong construction upon it. He is, as I understand, peculiarly sensitive about having those not immediately interested even speaking to him on the situation of his affairs. It might accomplish no good purpose therefore, should I seek an introduction, and make any communication I have it in my power to make. I therefore had concluded to see you, and from your intimacy, perhaps, a good deed might be done for him, or an evil prevented."

And Clarence at some length explained to Mr. Thompson the situation of the property, and confirmed all that Mr. Crampton had previously revealed.

"I understand it all now, neighbor; I've heered the same story afore, but not quite so plain as you 've made it."

"Have you mentioned the matter to Mr. Leslie?"

"Well, to tell you the truth, that was one of the things that helped to bring me up here. I s'pose I might have sent my money up and got all I wanted most as well as comin' all this way myself. But I heered of this matter, and, thinks I, it will be a neighborly kindness jist for me to come up and let Mr. Leslie know all what I had heered; but you see when I got here this other thing came right up and knocked all my thoughts clean into confusion. You see, friend, I ain't never been used to any kind of disturbance. Things in my own way have always been jist about so—they keep pretty much in 'statter quo,' and the moment any trouble gets a buzzin' about me, it turns me all clean up; I ain't got no sense nor nothin'."

"It would, I think, be a great act of kindness, however, to inform Mr. Leslie as soon as possible. He has no doubt acted under a wrong impression, and the matter ought to be attended to at once; for Folger has a very large number of hands busily engaged in cutting off the timber and hauling it to the banks of the Delaware."

"Well then, old Crampton was right about that too. He is a cunning old fox; but he ain't got no feelin', or he 'd have done somethin' himself, just to help a neighbor. Oh, dear, dear! Some folks had ought to be hung. They are always a contrivin' how to work their own ways, right or wrong, but I'm most afeered it's too late now. You see, neighbor, how things stand. Here is Folger a holding all his property at Princesport, right or wrong; I don't know; folks say, though, that they guess there ain't much right about it. Then he has got a deed of that other property you've been a speakin' about, and he holds that—then he 's got this new grip on him for the note he's paid to day. Now jist s'posing, I goes and tells Mr. Leslie about this crook in the thing, what is he to do? turn right round and go to fightin' the man who has got sich a grip on him? You see the man is tied neck and heels; he can't stir no how, without gittin stung, and I believe it's sartain truth the imp has been a contrivin' to git it so; and this last caper jist caps the whole, don't you see?"

Clarence did see, and moreover he knew that an attempt

to eject Folger, might not only bring Mr. Leslie into immediate trouble, but that he was liable also for prosecution, on account of the warranty deed he had given, should Folger be disposed to take that step. Mr. Leslie had no doubt acted in good faith, although he had committed an illegal act, and as Clarence had made up his mind to do all in his power to have things set right, difficulties only increased his zeal in the cause.

"It can do no harm, however, Mr. Thompson, to mention the matter to Mr. Leslie, and to apprise him of the fact that unless some measures are at once taken, that property, which rightfully belongs to his children, will soon be stripped of all its value. I think an injunction might be obtained to stop the plunder at once. And you may tell him that you know a person who will undertake to manage the whole concern for him without any cost, that is, it shall cost him nothing if we do not succeed. And moreover, that there is good ground for believing Mr. Folger could be prosecuted, in connection with others, for a conspiracy to deprive him of that property."

"You don't say!"

"I believe it can be done, sir; and rather than see an honest man thus dealt with, I am ready to spend time and money to obtain justice."

The old man seized the hand of Clarence.

"Bless your young heart! I'll do your bidding with a right good will."

"But I must have authority from Mr. Leslie to act. I must see him, and we must confer together. You unfold the subject to him, Mr. Thompson, and if he expresses a willingness to have any thing done, and to see me, I shall remain here for a few days, and shall be glad to call upon him."

"I will do your bidding—come of it what will."

"And now, Mr. Thompson, I must bid you good evening. I have a call to make upon some friends. We will see each other on the morrow."

Carrie Leslie had enjoyed a pleasant interview with her father during the early part of the evening. That is, she had an opportunity for a long private communication with him. There was, however, nothing said by her, either in reference to the business for which she had come to the city, nor to any of the scenes of the past day. There were so many

without repining, and rather thought of the journey's end than of what she might pass through on her way. But as yet Carrie had not clearly defined the state of her own feelings—and we have merely given their general impression. She had not yet had time to look out from amid the tempest by which she had been betrayed into a step of such moment, and take a calm survey of its whole moral aspect. At present a mist is around her. A chill occasionally shoots across her sensitive spirit; she is not happy, but her resolution is strong—duty has been her watchword, and she shrinks not from the way that she thinks has been indicated as *her way* through life.

Was she conscious, too, that he who had thus again so unexpectedly been brought into communion with her felt any interest beyond that which every man of sensibility might be expected to have for one of the opposite sex whose sympathies were in unison with his own? Was there nothing in the tone of the voice, or the gaze of the eye, when she was addressed, that spoke to her heart? and were not the words which he last spoke in her hearing intended as a revelation to her especially? *He had lost none of the feelings which then had such power over him.* She had delivered the message to Mrs. Barton, but had she no interest in its meaning? Thoughts similar to these would come in spite of all her efforts to keep them off, and no wonder then if when Clarence Ralston first entered the room, and many times through the evening, she heartily wished he had not come, or that she had not been there.

A severer trial, however, awaited her during the latter part of his stay; a lady and gentleman, neighbors of the family, called in, and Mrs. Douglass and Ellen were for the time more particularly taken up in entertaining them. It afforded Clarence an opportunity to place his chair more immediately in the neighborhood of Carrie, and confine his attention to her, and he could not resist the temptation which so happily presented to bring up past reminiscences. The first interview, and all the little events connected with it; not the most trifling circumstance seemed to have been forgotten, and how could Carrie but listen? How could she do otherwise than respond to his earnest inquiries whether she remembered this and that? Carrie had not forgotten.

"You may think it strange, Miss Leslie, that I should appear to lay so much stress upon an accidental meeting, or should so minutely recount the incidents of a scene so far back in our history but to me it was the most important event of my life." Carrie began to be really alarmed, and Clarence could hardly have failed to notice her agitation.

"You remember the thoughts suggested by you while we were seated on the rock? how you enforced our obligation to the performance of filial duty by reference to the word of God?"

Carrie blushed deeply, and her embarrassment but heightened the beauty of her countenance. Never before had Clarence seen any thing that so thrilled his breast as when, on making her reply, she fixed her eye calmly upon him.

"There is no other source from whence we can draw our rules of duty that can be safely relied upon. And when we draw them thence we can trust to him who points the way to give us strength to walk in it. I do not remember all I said; you know I was then quite young I only wonder at my own presumption."

"Oh, say not so! It was not presumption' you pitied me, you saw the rock on which I might have been wrecked, your warning took hold of my heart, your words were spoken in due season, and they were the means of changing the whole current of my thoughts and feelings—to you I owe more than I can express in words."

The tone in which he spoke, was soft and low, but the emotion which he manifested did not escape the notice of Carrie; her whole heart was convulsed with a rush of feeling; she longed for a secret place where the full fountain might have vent. She could not reply. She dared not trust herself in the attempt. She had begun to realize what to her now, was a fearful truth, that the *feelings of the heart* are stronger than the *power of the will.* She had a fitful glimpse of the terrible trials which the step she had taken might entail upon her.

Clarence, like most ardent lovers, was ready to construe every manifestation of feeling in his own favor; and in the presumption of the moment ventured to say,

"Our intercourse has been, from circumstances beyond my control, merely occasional—I may say accidental. I should be very happy if you will allow me an opportunity to explain the reasons. Am I presuming too far to ask the privilege of an interview on the morrow?"

"I expect to be particularly engaged, and perhaps the less reference to the past the better. My reason for saying so, is one that admits not of argument. You must not ask it now. Time will make it plain to you."

Ellen Douglass now arose and joined their circle. Both endeavored to put on a cheerful countenance, but it required a strong effort, for both were really unhappy. Clarence sat for a few moments, and then arose to depart. He shook hands with Ellen, but merely bowed low to Carrie, and as he fixed his eye upon her lovely countenance, its beauty enhanced by a sad expression, he felt that it was a last look upon all that his heart coveted on earth.

CHAPTER XXIV.

TOBIAS FOLGER had no idea, when he left his home at Princesport for the purpose of accomplishing his selfish ends, even at the expense of terrible trial to others, that he would so soon be called to exercise all his ingenuity in order to escape the toils which justice was preparing for him. Rumors have reached his ears which, with other circumstances, have combined to convince him that whatever he has to do, that may be accomplished under the cover of a fair name, must be done without delay.

There had been, in the early part of Mr. Folger's life, some unpleasant mystery in reference to the sale of a vessel and cargo which it was supposed had been consigned to him by the owners at Port-au-Prince.

Rumors were afloat—but no one could well say from whence they originated, after the sale of the vessel—that false oaths had been taken by the captain and consignee, and that the proceeds of neither vessel nor cargo had ever been accounted for. The report was that the real owner had, with his family, been cut off, during the bloody scenes of a revolution in St. Domingo, and that a conspiracy between the captain and consignee had been entered into, whereby a great wrong had been perpetrated against persons in Port-au-Prince to whom the estate of the deceased owner was indebted.

The loss of account-books there, and the vessel having put to sea at night, and without any entry at the Custom house, had made it very difficult to ascertain facts in the case, and more easy for the conspirators to accomplish an evil purpose. Years had rolled by, most of the active merchants of that day had retired from business, or had departed this life. But the rumor against Folger had not entirely been forgotten.

The captain, who, it was said, had been a sharer in the scheme, had also died. There was, however, one person living who knew some facts in reference to the matter, that might have been of great consequence, if his testimony could have been corroborated by some reliable statement from Port-au-Prince. This person was indebted to Folger, and in such a way that he was completely in the power of his creditor. His testimony alone could answer no very definite end, and to divulge what he knew, would only bring himself into trouble, without benefiting others. Thus had things remained until the period we are now considering, when Folger's fears became somewhat excited by the fact that a portion of the money due to him by this individual had been paid but a day or two before he left his house. He had not asked for the money and probably never designed to, and it was a matter of some curiosity to him why his debtor should have thus of his own accord come forward to liquidate the debt. On the day of his arrival in the city, and after he had the interview we have recorded with Miss Carrie Leslie, the reader will remember that he suddenly came in contact with one whom he declined to recognize, and whom he endeavored, in as quiet a way as possible, to elude, and in which he finally succeeded. Years had passed since he had seen that countenance, but at once he recognized it as one he had been familiar with at some long time ago, and his thoughts soon carried him to Port-au-Prince, where he had occasionally visited, and he recalled him as one he had formerly known there. There was no business between them that Folger knew, they never had any transactions together. Why, then, should the stranger have dogged his steps? And as guilt is ever wakeful in the breast where it inhabits, and ready to start up imaginary fears, Folger at once began to connect the circumstance of the unexpected payment with that of the stranger trying to track him through the crowd. And he came to the conclusion that there was danger on hand. The sum due to him now by the person whom of all others he feared the most was but trifling, not enough to prevent any man who did not care to keep an unpleasant secret, from letting it go abroad.

And Mr. Folger's fears were by no means groundless. He had judged correctly, although he knew not yet how far matters had gone, nor what need he had to get his affairs into a movable condition. With a caution, however, and energy worthy of a better end, he had already begun the preparations necessary for a sudden exit, should that be unavoidable.

The determination with which he had carried on his plot to gain the consent of her whose heart he never expected to win, had lost none of its force, even in view of personal difficulties which he might have to encounter. But he felt that unless he could bring matters to a speedy conclusion, all his past labor might be useless; he was therefore resolved to venture upon the bold policy of at once opening the subject to her father. He had ever found him yielding where he had before tested him, and he doubted not he should be able not only to gain the father, but even to persuade him to join in a united effort to obtain the daughter's consent to an immediate marriage.

Mr. Leslie had but just entered upon his duties of the day when he was arrested by a gentle knock at the door, and immediately the bland countenance of Mr. Folger was beaming upon him, as the latter, with a quick step, advanced to greet his friend, even before he had time to rise from his seat.

"Do not rise, Mr. Leslie, do not rise, my dear sir; I am very happy to see you—but," and Mr. Folger assumed at once a most serious air, "I am very sorry, my dear sir, to see you so much altered in appearance. You are not well, Mr. Leslie; you can not be well?"

"I am in usual health, sir—perhaps, not quite in as good flesh as formerly; sit down, Mr. Folger."

And Mr. Folger sat down, maintaining the same look of deep anxiety.

"Indeed I fear, my dear sir, that you are not aware of the change which has taken place since we last met—I mean in your appearance. It must be that the confinement is too severe for one accustomed, as you have been, to exercise in the pure open air of the country."

"I have probably suffered a little from the change, sir but that is not of much consequence. It was not pleasure, but duty, which brought me here, Mr. Folger—my only regret has been that I have been able to accomplish nothing as to freeing myself from debt. The confinement, sir, would be even pleasanter to me than the largest liberty I ever enjoyed, if by means of it I could see any prospect of paying my obligations. It is the burden of debt that affects me more than aught else; I can bear being poor, but—"

"Stop, stop, Mr. Leslie! In thus speaking, you seem to intimate an oppression on the part of him who is your chief, almost your only creditor. Surely, sir, I do not deserve the censure your words imply."

"By no means, Mr. Folger. I am too much your debtor, for acts of kindness in days past, and for your recent interference in my behalf. You have acted generously toward me, I must even say nobly; I am fully sensible of you kind acts; but I still am your debtor. By your interference on my behalf, I am consequently able to be at my post to-day. But my mind is not free. The clog still hangs heavily there. It dampens my energy—it takes away my resolution—it follows me at any moment when I am not actually engaged, and like a hideous specter, plays before me—it disturbs my dreams, and makes my bed any thing but a place of repose—it comes with my first waking thoughts—it is an evil I can bear no longer, and, sir, I am fully resolved to dispose of every thing, and go down with my family to the very lowest condition. Why, sir! a hut—a bed of straw, bread and water, with freedom from this hideous monster that haunts my spirit, would be a sweet exchange.

"I am not a man, sir, I am not my own master. What pleasure can I enjoy? What is nature to me in all her beauty? What is even the love of my wife and children? The world is spoiled to me. Every tie that binds me to life is poisoned. I can suffer it no longer, Mr. Folger; I can not live with shackles upon my mind and heart, if there is any possible way to break them, and free myself."

Mr. Folger was not prepared for such an outbreak of feeling on the part of Mr. Leslie. He had, hitherto, found the latter peculiarly mild and yielding, and disposed to look on the hopeful side of his affairs. He had therefore formed the opinion, that if kept along in circumstances of outward respectability, almost any demand might be exacted from him; but he had misjudged the man. Leslie had indeed yielded to his demands, often extortionary and unreasonable, without cavil. He had been extremely sensitive in regard to his wife and children. He could not bear the thought that they should be deprived of the comforts they had ever enjoyed, and he had allowed this feeling too much sway. But he was not less sensitive in regard to his own personal obligations. He felt most keenly. His spirit was just. He would not have defrauded his fellow, to have saved his own life, and the fire which has been burning within has at last burst forth. It will spoil Mr. Folger's plans if he can not manage to quench the flame.

"My dear, sir, I fear you look at things in a wrong light this morning; come, sit down."

Mr. Leslie had arisen under the excitement of his strong feelings, and was walking the room. "Come, take a seat, Mr. Leslie, and let us talk over matters calmly." And Mr. Leslie resumed his seat, almost displeased with himself that he had allowed such an exposure of feeling.

"Now, Mr. Leslie, just look at things as they are. It is one thing to feel a burden which oppresses us, and another thing to take a step that may involve trials, which we have never experienced, and whose force it may be harder to endure than our imagination can conceive. You can not alter the fact, Mr. Leslie, that both yourself and family have been born and brought up amid the higher walks of life. You and they have ever been accustomed to a genteel style, you have been surrounded with the luxuries of life, and although of late many of those have been dispensed with, yet the comforts of life you have still enjoyed. Your house has been despoiled of nothing material. It remains as it ever has been. It is a noble mansion, and every thing about it in good keeping. Do you imagine that you can have the least conception what your feeling would be on leaving a spot where every association is so sacred? To see it in the hands of others, and to feel that all your right to it had gone forever?"

"But I have for some time, Mr. Folger, looked upon it, as having passed from my ownership."

"Not so, my dear sir. It has not passed from you, and I trust never will. But I was going to say; granted that your own mind had become reconciled to the idea of giving up your home, and coming down to the bare necessaries of existence, have you thought how you might feel to see your wife, delicate as she is, and your lovely daughter, with all their refinement and sensibility, and even your little sons, enduring the privations, and suffering the mortification, which must be theirs if reduced to a low condition?"

Folger could plainly perceive that he had again placed himself upon vantage-ground. The change in Leslie was too evident to escape his notice. The whole aspect of the man was affected. His countenance fell, his head drooped, and he seemed like one yielding to a pressure too heavy to be borne.

"Mr. Leslie, I hope that the trifling matter of my interference yesterday on your behalf, has not been without some effect in convincing you that I am not an indifferent spectator of your concerns; and furthermore, Mr. Leslie, have I ever pressed you for payment of interest? Have I ever mentioned that matter to you?"

"You have not, I acknowledge, sir; but the interest is accumulating—accumulating fast. I can not reduce it by any effort I can make, and I see no way by which I can do it at any future time. The fact is, Mr. Folger, I am like one cast upon a distant island, who has never learned how to do any thing whereby life can be sustained. I am even in a worse condition than such a man. I find myself in the midst of a busy multitude, all pursuing some occupation for which they have been trained, and by which they are making their way to independence—at least supporting themselves and families in respectability. They have learned the art of making money in some way; they have a purpose before them, and know how to go to work to accomplish it. But to me, their business is a mystery. My habits of life have unfitted me for making money; I can neither be useful here to myself or others. No, sir, my training has been most unfortunate, and the most I can hope for is a mere subsistence under the plainest circumstances. I must go down to the grave in poverty. My children, I trust, profiting by my experience, may rise to a state of independence founded on their own exertions. They must and will learn to make their own way, to stand up as men in their own strength; and never, never suffer, as their helpless father has, from a sense of his own inefficiency."

Had Folger possessed any sensibility, had his heart been capable of one generous emotion, he could not have listened to the words of Leslie without a feeling of commiseration, at least. But one only thought possessed him: how to take most advantage of this state of mind to further his own ends. He cared not what suffering the father endured—nor whether the daughter ever enjoyed one hour of happiness after she had passed the rubicon and was linked to him legally for life. But to gain that possession of her was now almost with him an infatuation.

It was not love that influenced him—not love in its true sense. There was probably as much of that passion as his selfish heart was capable of. But he was *resolved to have her.* His mind had never before been so completely absorbed—not even in the pursuit of gain. And poor Carrie would have trembled with alarm could she have been aware of the intensity of his feeling. The artless girl and the unsuspicious father were dealing with one of whose peculiarities they were not aware.

"Do you not think, Mr. Leslie, that a man—say a husband and father—to be more particular, I may as well say—instance yourself, sir; do you not think, under all the circumstances in which you are placed, it is your duty to do all you can to maintain your position in society? I mean more especially in reference to those dependent upon you."

"Doubtless, sir, I ought; and every man should wish so to do, and even to gain a higher position, if he can do it honorably."

"And now, then, Mr. Leslie, I come to the proposition which I have to make. I feel some delicacy in so doing." There was quite a pause, and Mr. Folger manifested a state of excitement Mr. Leslie had never witnessed in all his dealings with him before.

"I have a request to make of you, Mr. Leslie—and that is —*to ask your consent to a union between myself and your daughter!*"

Mr. Leslie fixed his eye firmly upon him, and sat for a moment speechless. He was either in doubt as to the reality of the proposition made to him, or too much astounded to be able to answer.

"You comprehend my request, Mr. Leslie?"

"I believe I do, sir. But I must ask you, Mr. Folger, a plain question—Have you authority from my daughter, to make this request?"

"Why, sir, to speak plainly—I did not receive a special sanction to apply thus soon to you, Mr. Leslie, in reference to the matter. Circumstances have transpired since I last saw your daughter which will make it desirable for—in fact for all concerned, that a consummation of the arrangement should take place at once. There is an understanding, however, between Miss Leslie and myself, I believe, perfectly satisfactory to us both. She has not mentioned it to you, then?"

"She has never lisped such a thing to me, sir."

"Ah, well—you know, sir, young ladies feel great delicacy about such matters. It is as I tell you, however, sir. The fact is, Mr. Leslie, ladies can sometimes see into the propriety of things more quickly and more justly than men. Matters, you see yourself, sir—in fact you have just stated the truth in regard to your affairs. Things are with you at an extremity; you are, as you say, helpless. Your life, and the comfort of your family, are all at present at a crisis. My union with your daughter at once gives me a claim, as one of your family, to relieve you and them. You must be satisfied of my kind feelings. All that is needed for your deliverance, Mr. Leslie, is, that you grant the request I have made of you."

"Mr. Folger, if I was now within the four walls of a prison, and a certainty that I must end my days there unless I assented to your proposal, I should not listen to it for a moment without first an interview with my daughter, and a firm conviction of my mind, from the expression of her own wishes, that she has made the decision because her heart is interested, and from no other consideration.

"And hear me further, Mr. Folger: sooner than listen to any proposition for deliverance from my difficulties, based upon, or in any way connected with, the disposition of my daughter's hand, I tell you now, sir, that in the event of any such union, I would spurn your offer of aid as an insult; and I feel, sir, that you have not quite maintained the character of a gentleman by naming the two things in connection with each other. You have ventured rather boldly, sir, upon the fact of my poverty!"

"But, Mr. Leslie—"

"Not a word more, sir—not one word will I listen to until I have had an opportunity to know the truth from the lips of her whose name I consider to have been used by you, sir, very improperly."

Folger had never before fully understood the man he had so long dealt with. He was for a short time at fault. He could not go on, and he knew not very well how to retrace his steps and get calmly out of the dilemma. At once all hope of accomplishing his design by the usual and proper method passed away. He saw that he would be thwarted. His determination to pursue a course which had suggested itself to him within the last few hours, was now fixed. To accomplish that, however, he must smooth over matters, and so conduct as at least to keep on fair terms with the daughter. And to do this, if possible, the father must in some way be appeased. He arose, as about to depart,

"Mr. Leslie, I have been very unfortunate in my explanations to you. I am sure you have not fully apprehended my meaning; but I will say nothing further on the subject; I see that, under any circumstances, the connection would not be agreeable to you. Pardon my presumption—you shall not lose my friendship because you can not consent to my wishes. Good-day, sir!"

And Mr. Folger bowed very courteously, and retired.

When our feelings have been highly excited, especially if the passion of anger has had dominion over us, we are very apt to be let down to an opposite extreme—almost losing sight of the provoking cause, and ready to charge ourselves with undue haste and unnecessary zeal. Mr. Leslie, however, did not get quite so low as that. His feelings did indeed soon relax when once left to his own reflections, but only so far as to enable him to look at things with serious determination. He could scarcely believe what he had just heard—that his lovely Carrie could have yielded her heart to such a man as Folger; and yet there must have been some understanding between them, or Folger would never have ventured, under the circumstances, to make such a declaration.

He feared, however, that the same means had been resorted to in her case that had been attempted toward himself. And perhaps—yes, he had no doubt of it, to free her father from perplexity, she had made a sacrifice of herself. He would prevent it, if yet in his power so to do. His thoughts for the time were now interrupted by the approach of another visitor—there was heard the sound of a staff occasionally striking the floor, and a slow, measured step. Mr. Leslie knew well the tokens, and arose to open the door.

"Ah, my good friend! I'm glad to see you this morning;

walk in, Mr. Thompson, and take a seat. It is quite a journey for you up these long flights of stairs."

Mr. Thompson made no reply, but after shaking hands cordially, he took the seat placed for him, laid his hat on the table, and commenced wiping the perspiration from his forehead.

"I am afraid it is almost too much for you, Mr. Thompson."

"I am gittin' over it, I'll git over it to rights. But you see I got about half way up that last stretch—I was so put to it for breath that I thought it was clear up with me, and that I should have to remain in '*statter quo*' for all gittin' any higher—so I sat down and blowed a little, and then crawled slowly along up. But a little more sich up-hill work would put an end to *me*, that's sartain."

Mr. Leslie expressed much regret that he had not waited in the office below, and sent up word to him.

"I might have done so, I s'pose, but you see I wanted jist to see you alone for a few minutes, for it's business I've come about. But what they build sich pokery places for, and run their houses clean up into the sky for, I don't see, without it is to get a little breathin'-room; they want it badly. Oh, it's a nasty place, this city! and sich a hurry as every body is in, tearin' along, and looking as earnest and anxious as if heaven was at t'other end of the street, and they was trying to see who'd git there first! It ain't no way to live, my friend. This hurryin' and scurryin' through the world, pulling, and hauling, and scrambling, and worryin' their souls and bodies out, just to see who can git the biggest heap, and live in the biggest house, and make the biggest show. And what can they git, after all, in such a shut-up place, where there's no heaven, nor no green earth to be seen? Hardly air enough to keep a toad alive, and nothing but stones and bricks to look at or to walk on. And, to be plain with you, my friend, you ain't agoin' to stand it long in this place—you ain't the same man you was when you left home; and it makes me sad to look at you."

"Change of air, and change of our habits, sir, are apt to have some effect upon us, until we get used to them."

"But it is no easy matter, depend on it, gittin' used to such a change as you have made. It's bad enough to leave one's wife and children, let alone spending one's days up in a co.k-loft, where there ain't nothin' to be seen but a slate roof and a patch of sky no bigger than a pocket-handkerchief. But that ain't what I've come to talk about. You see, Mr. Leslie, I've got something to say for my own account, and then I've got some business which consarns you that had ought to be seen to. But I'm afeared to begin any of it, because I don't know that the first of it will be pleasin' to you, and the last of it you may think ain't none of my business."

"I hope, Mr. Thompson, you will feel at perfect liberty to speak your mind to me freely. I assure you, sir, that I look upon you as a firm and tried friend, whose kindness I shall never forget; and I esteem you also as a man of sound judgment, with a pure, unselfish heart. So speak freely to me, Mr. Thompson, just what you wish to say."

Mr. Thompson found it difficult just then to say any thing. He coughed a little, and wiped his forehead, and grew quite red in the face. It took some little time before things were settled.

"It is kind in you to say so; but since you have given me permission, I'll just say my say, and you can do as you think best after that.

"You see, Mr. Leslie, I'm getting to be an old man. I've been a working hard pretty much the best part of fifty years, and I'm getting along pretty far, as I take it, toward the end of my journey. I wish it had been a better one; that is, I wish I had n't worked quite so hard for this world, and done a little more about other things. I've done well for myself though—that is for this world. What with plain living, and saving the odds and ends, and going slow and sure, why, you see, I ain't no wise bad off. I owe no man any thing, and that is good to think on, when I lay down at nights, and I've got some owin' to me, and I've got some out to interest, and some little property, in land, here and there. To take it altogether, it ain't much matter for me to be a scratching any more, only just to have something to look after. It's my opinion that a man ain't no right to burrow; he ain't so happy as to keep stirrin' a little, till his time comes.

"I ain't no son of my own, and I've been a thinking that when I die, if there ain't no one to keep the old place again, the thing must be sold; and maybe the old place shut up or torn down; or, maybe strangers a comin' in, that never heared who old Sam Thompson was, nor how he did things; and maybe they'll be rogues, or hard and grinding upon the poor folks that ain't got much to buy with. And altogether I can't bear the thought of it. It has been an honest shop, so far, and a poor man has got his little things there a mite cheaper than the rich man; and it seems to me I shall die easier just to know that things is goin' to remain as they have always been, when I ain't above ground to see to 'em."

Mr. Thompson had to stop a moment to take breath and get a little calm; he was easily excited, even by his own thoughts, and the theme he was upon lay very near his heart.

"And I've been a thinking you see, Mr. Leslie, I've taken a great notion to your boy. He is a boy yet, I know, but he's amazin' smart, and what is more, he won't lie, I don't believe, to save his life. And he is willing: when I say what I want done it is done, and no questions asked. And the folks like him. He is bringing all the custom round. He is civil to rich and poor, and has pleasant ways that take with the towns-folk, and country folk, and he has got all the run of things, so that I don't have nothin' to do but look on and watch the motions. And it is my mind just to make a partner of him, and that is what I want to say concerning myself."

Mr. Thompson had not finished, but he was "put to it" again for breath.

"But, Mr. Thompson do I understand you? Did you speak of making a partner of my son? My little Charlie!"

"You ain't seen him for many months; you wouldn't hardly know your own boy, he's grown so, and there is more of the man in him than many a good deal older, I tell you. He has learned how to keep the books, and he's got every thing as straight as a die. And he knows all what is wanting, and what the folks fancy, and what will sell well, clean ahead of me. It's my opinion, if he keeps on, he will do a trade that will make the 'old Sam Thompson store,' as they call it, known further than it has ever been known yet.

"Yes, I did say, I was thinking, if you was willing to do the thing right off. But I ain't got through yet. I ain't told you all what I've got to tell. You maybe feel sometimes as though friends was scarce, and that maybe you had n't just such friends, as could, or would, give a helping hand in a time of need. Now I want to tell you it ain't so."

"You, Mr. Thompson, are the only man I can truly call a friend."

"Hush up, hush up! Pardon me for the liberty; but I must say you are wrong there. You have got friends, and one on 'em has a heart as big—as big as a bushel. He ain't one that cares to be known, and I ain't at liberty, for particular reasons, to tell his name. It ain't Folger, though!"

"I can not say but Mr. Folger has been friendly, Mr. Thompson."

"Don't trust too much to it, I beg on you; but we we will come to that point to rights, only I did n't want you to think that maybe he had done it, for he ain't. It is clean another sort of a person. But no matter who he is, just hear what he's gone and done. Oh, dear! it's hard breathing up here, I don't see how you stand it."

"I will open the door."

"No, no! keep all shut, there's so many folks a buzzin' round, like flies round the sugar pot, that there might be them a hearin that we don't want to hear. No, no, I'll get along, in time. But I was going to tell you what this man has done. He's put a thousand dollars in my hands, and I'm to take it and let Charlie put it on the books to his credit. It is to be his share of the capital to begin with, just as an encouragement to him to try and do his best. And I'm to give him this year one third of the gains and maybe next year a half. It ain't to be known to any living soul but Charlie, and me, and yourself, or your folks, maybe. That is if your mind is so agreed, and if that man ain't a friend then I ain't much acquainted with the thing no way."

"It is indeed a strange act of friendship, and manifested at a time which I can truly say has been the darkest period of my life. But why not let me know the name, that I may take the man by the hand and thank him in the name of my God as a friend of the friendless?"

"You see, friend, I've told a little bit of a lie a'ready. He wanted me to make believe it was come from me, and I let him talk on, and think maybe I should do so. But I can't, *no how*; so you see you have got friends yet, of the right sort, too."

"Well, Mr. Thompson, I can have no idea who this generous friend is; but this token of sympathy is worth more to me than I can find words to express."

"Yes, sir, I can tell him all, just what you would say; but I tell you, friend, you must n't no more keep a lookin' on the dark side. Things is a goin' to be brighter. I'm a thinkin' we see'd about the darkest time yesterday. It will be daybreak afore long, see if it ain't. And now that is all done with, I want to talk a little about t'other matters. They ain't quite so agreeable, but we've got to see after 'em, for all that. And may I ask you, friend, whether you are knowin' to the fact that Folger has got a deed of the Hazleton property?"

"Mr. Folger?"

"Sartain."

"A deed from whom?"

"From Thorne, the man you gave the deed to."

"You surprise me very much, Mr. Thompson." And Mr. Leslie, greatly excited, arose and walked the room.

"I thought I should—it has surprised a good many; though some seem to think it ain't nothin' strange, no more than was to be expected. He's a cute man, as I take it."

"Are you certain, Mr. Thompson, that this thing is so?"

"I am sartain of one thing, that I have heerd it from two different persons, and one on 'em has see'd the thing with his own eyes; and he's a man that won't lie to me, no how. And be you sure, Mr. Leslie, that you had a right to give a deed, after all?"

"Certainly sir, or Mrs. Leslie had. Why do you ask, Mr. Thompson?"

"Oh, well, maybe it ain't so, arter all; but I've been told that it was 'tailed property, and that the 'tail was n't out only with your children; but maybe they was mistaken."

"To tell the truth, Mr. Thompson, I have never read the will, by which Mrs. Leslie inherited that estate. We both always supposed the entail ended with her."

"No doubt; but if you ain't very sartain about it I should n't be surprised if, when you come to look, you should find it as I have said. It ought to be seen to, though, for Folger is making quick work with it. He's got all of a hundred men a cutting, and hauling; he'll make a hole in it, if he's let alone. It ain't according to my nature, in the general way, to think hard of my fellow-creatures; we are all on us with a hole in our coat, somewhere. But I've been a thinkin' about this man a good deal, and it seems to me hard to git at the natur' of him

One thing is sartain, there ain't nobody that thrives when once in his clutches. They all seem like flies in a spider's web; they are easy enough, for the web is very soft, but they can't git away from it: and the spider is easy enough, all curled up in the middle of it. He knows he can nab 'em when he's a mind to, and so he lets 'em buzz, or keep still, just as they please. And it's my candid advice to any man that can cut clear of the critter, to do it in short order. He ain't a safe man for an honest person to have any dealings with."

"And yet, Mr. Thompson, you know how kindly he has acted?"

"Sartain I do; but the more I think about it, the more I'm puzzled. There's a wheel within a wheel, working both ways to onst. Maybe I don't see straight through, for things is dreadfully blurred, and turned wrong end uppermost to me these few days."

"I begin very much to fear, Mr. Thompson, that Mr. Folger is not what he sometimes appears to be."

"I've been a fearin' it, sir, a great while; but I own to it, he did come clean over me about this last job. I was clean took with him; that was afore I had time to think of things all round, and try to make the tallies match. But the more I tried, the more they would n't."

"I am at present, as you know, Mr. Thompson, unable to extricate myself. I can think of but one course, and that I have made up my mind to pursue. But how can I, in my present circumstances, attempt to redress my wrongs? I am in his power. I have no means to enable me to have recourse to the law. I may only provoke his displeasure, and to do that, when he has the power at any moment to bind me in close confinement, seems almost madness."

"As to the means to go to law, that maybe might be got along with; but the other thing you mention, ain't so clever to think on. We must be wary; there's so many different ways they can do with a man, as I've heerd on, that it seems to me, if I was so unfortunate as to owe any body in this plaguey place, I should n't feel that my very in'ards was my own. And yet it's nothing but buy, buy, buy; charge, charge, charge; just as if they could n't put a man into prison, or 'carcerate him, and what not. But as I was sayin', 'gin you conclude that it will be best for you to stand to your rights, and to bring your matters to a tussle with the law, there need be no fear on account of the expense. I ain't no friend to lawyers in the general way, but I guess they ain't all alike, and some on 'em have got some bowels and mercies. I know a man that is ready, if you say the word, to take hold on the thing right off, and there needn't be a word said about pay, without you're righted. And if you are, you can then do the fair thing. And I want you to think of the matter, and we'll see one another to-night, maybe, and have it all fixed, if so it should be your mind. But I must be jogging now."

And the old man arose, and his hand was grasped with a power that needed no words to explain its meaning.

"My good old friend! may God reward you an hundred fold."

There was a slight motion of the lips on the part of Mr. Thompson, but nothing audible was uttered—his heart had its own reward.

Mr. Leslie accompanied him to the lower apartment, and saw him fairly into the street, and then returned to his usual labors.

CHAPTER XXV.

There may possibly be some who will read these pages, whose memory can recall the old tavern at Hoboken, opposite the city of New York, as it was the early part of the present century. If so, they will remember a long, low building, situated on a slight elevation above the river, and not far from the ferry stairs. Large trees sheltered it, and attached to it were a multitude of stables, around which could always be seen two or more old-fashioned, rakish-looking stages, and no small number of white and black hostlers and stage-drivers. It was the most popular stage-house of its day, being the starting-point and stopping-place for a great part of the travel through West Jersey, to and from the great cities of New York and Philadelphia. The matter of crossing the ferry was a very different affair then from what those of the present generation are accustomed to. Wind and weather had to be taken into the account, and if these would answer, the horse or horses must be untackled, and by coaxing, and pulling, and whipping, and sometimes even by hoisting bodily, were deposited in the open hold of the boat, and the carriage or wagon placed there likewise, while the passengers took care of themselves, for the most part, in the stern, ranged on seats each side of the helmsman. We say took care of themselves, that is, had to see to it that their heads were bobbed when the boom of the aft sail swept over them, and to screw themselves one side, out of the way somewhere, when the tiller had to be pressed hard up or hard down.

It was rough sailing there, too, sometimes, and great skill was required by the helmsman, who ventured to guide his open boat through the white caps, and against the surging blast of a stiff north-wester.

Those days are over now, never to return. There is no longer any romance in crossing that ferry. No chance to

have the pretty girl, whom you are escorting for an afternoon's ramble amid the richest scenes of nature, seize your arm for protection, as the careening boat lays its gunwale beneath the curling water, nor to hear the confiding tone in which she lets out unwittingly the secret of her heart's trust.

Thousands cross now where one crossed then. But we doubt whether, with all the safety and convenience of the present mode of transit, there is one thousandth part of the enjoyment to be had, either in the passage or the hours spent amid the enchanting scenery that distinguishes that beauty-spot of nature, assisted as it has been by the taste and art of man, as when it lay in all the simplicity of a common rural establishment.

Hoboken was then a lonely place. Besides the tavern, but one house of any note could be seen, and that was the mansion belonging to the owner of all the property in that vicinity. It was situated at some distance from the tavern, on a beautiful elevation, commanding one of the most extensive views which our country affords. The few tenements scattered at distant intervals for some miles around, were occupied, for the most part, by those who labored for the proprietor, or rented his farms.

At the stage-house or tavern, however, there was seldom any want of company. For in addition to its attractiveness as a place of meeting for the residents in the vicinity, it often happened that there would be quite a collection of travelers to spend the night. The stages for the west starting early in the morning of necessity compelled those who were leaving New York to be there over night; and many coming to the city preferred enjoying the good fare and clean beds they were certain of at Hoboken, to the uncertainties of New York hotels in those days.

As Mr. Samuel Thompson never liked to be hurried, and moreover was somewhat desirous of breathing the fresh country air as soon as possible, having already spent many more days in the city than had been agreeable to him, he fixed upon an early part of the afternoon for the passage of the river. He had taken his seat near the stern of the ferry-boat, and was apparently on the look-out for some one to come on board, as his head was almost continually dodging about, in attempts to distinguish, amid the moving mass upon the pier, some person or persons. He had also laid beside him, on the seat, quite a heap of bundles, as though he designed to save room, near to himself, for another passenger.

At length his countenance lighted up, as he perceived a gentleman, with a very fair and sprightly young lady clinging to his arm, trying to lead his charge across some barrels which intercepted the way into the boat.

"Don't rise, Mr. Thompson," said the lady, as she came tripping down over the side of the boat. "I'm going to take my seat close beside you."

"And I've been saving a seat for you—but where's your pa? I thought I see him with you."

"And so he was—but he has stepped back to pay the cartman. Oh, how pleasant the idea of going home! is it not, Mr. Thompson? and then to think that father is coming, too, in a few days!"

"He has really concluded to go, then?"

"He has—but I fear he will have a sad heart. We have no home any more, you know."

"Hush up, hush up, darling! Don't you be a talkin' so."

"I do not care, on my own account, Mr. Thompson, although I love the dear old place; but I fear my parents will almost sink under it. There was no other way, however; it is better to be poor than to be in bondage. But father is coming, I must put on a cheerful face, for I have urged him to do it."

Mr. Leslie now came up, and taking a farewell kiss of Carrie, gave his hand to the old gentleman.

"And you will take good care of my Carrie, Mr. Thompson?"

"I will watch her, sir, depend on it, like a mother by her baby in the cradle."

Mr. Thompson thought lightly of Mr. Leslie's request at the time, or of the reply he made to it; but they came up to his mind with terrible force before many hours had elapsed.

Although there were many things upon the mind of Carrie which under ordinary circumstances might have depressed the spirit of one so young and sensitive, yet there was a sprightliness in her countenance which it had not possessed for some time. Carrie had settled some doubtful matters in reference to the path of duty for herself. Her mind was clearly made up on a point of immense interest to her peace for life, and comparatively she was happy. And we must go back a few days in her history, to see how this has come to pass.

When Carrie retired to her room, after the interview with Clarence Ralston, as recorded in a previous chapter, her mind was agitated by a painful conflict—the cause we will endeavor to explain.

That the consent she had yielded to her artful suitor was not the consent of her heart, the reader need not be told. It was a sudden resolve, under circumstances of great pressure, to sacrifice affection to the demands of filial duty. But she had not taken into the account that in her assent was implied that which was not true. *That she loved the man* to whom she had consented to yield her hand.

When the stimulus which buoyed up her mind, caused by a sense of having gained a relief for her parent, had time to subside, clearer and juster views of all her obligations began to assume their power. She began to doubt whether she possessed the right to throw away for life those holy affections which God himself had planted in the heart, and which if not always certain directors as to the object for whom they were designed, and from whom they were to receive an interchange of sweet communion, yet, until they were drawn forth—until they were quickened into action, by that call upon the heart—that subtil charm at whose bidding they should flow forth—no bond which man can make, or has made, can to a virtuous mind appear aught beside a bargaining with sacred things, a base barter of God's holiest gifts for that which can purchase any gewgaw the world has to offer; and would not the vow to love, honor, and obey one on whom she was conscious the affections of her heart did not rest be a solemn mockery? a falsehood laid upon the altar of God! and her heart shrunk away from the terrible idea.

But a more glowing fact presented itself to Carrie's mind than even this. She not only had no proper love for him, whose hope she had encouraged, but shall we say it, and why not dear, reader? Was it a crime that her pure and gentle heart had warm affections? Or that they had been placed on one who had not yet made open confession of his interest for her? But right or wrong, the truth must be told, she *did love* Clarence Ralston.

She had never been able to banish from her mind the first impressions made there at their intercourse in early life. They revived in all their freshness when, after years of absence, again they have accidentally met. She had never before analyzed her feelings on this subject, but now the truth spoke to her consciousness, without the trouble of any long process of reasoning. She had done, as she thought, her duty, in checking all advances for intimacy which he had made; and had severed, even by a blow against her own heart, the cord which had, by an invisible power, hitherto connected them. He would never more be to her but as the bright image in a vision that had fled forever; but she could not, she dare not consent to give her hand to another, with the consciousness of her present feelings.

And her resolution was fixed. She would deal frankly by him whom she believed felt kindly toward her. He had not, indeed, as after-reflection convinced her, chosen the most delicate time to make known his intentions, nor had he urged his suit with the most delicate arguments. Yet she believed, he meant kindly by her. She would, therefore, deal justly by him. She would seek an interview as soon as she should reach her home at Princesport, if no opportunity presented sooner, and confess her error, and place things in such a position between them, as forever after to preclude the hope, on the part of Mr. Folger, that she could be his wife.

The afternoon was pleasant, and just wind enough to fill the sails, and ripple the blue water, and Carrie enjoyed the gentle motion by which they were wafted to the beautiful shore of New Jersey; and the lively song of the seamen, as they passed the huge travelers of the ocean, riding at their anchors, and the white sails of sloops and river craft, shooting in all directions across the long stretch of water.

While Mr. Thompson was engaged in watching over the baggage, and seeing that it was carefully stowed away, Carrie went at once into the tavern, and found her way into the pleasant, but old-fashioned parlor. No sooner had she entered, than a lady sprang forward to meet her.

"Why, Mrs. Crampton!"

"My dear Carrie! Oh, I am so glad to see you. But come right away to my room, I want to talk with you."

And without removing her things, Carrie hastened with her

friend, and when they reached the room, Mrs. Crampton turned the key, and before Carrie had time to ask any questions, began to pour out her burden.

"Oh, dear, I am so glad to see you, for I hardly knew where to go, and look for you in the city, and you see we have come on just on your account."

"Is Mr. Crampton here?"

"Crampton is here somewhere, and he is as mad as a hornet. You know he can not bear to stir a step away from home; but he has got so worked up about Folger. You see he has been suspecting for some time that something was going on. Folger is so dead in love, that I suppose he has let out something or other that has got to Crampton's ears. How he hears things I don't know; but I believe sometimes he guesses at them. But he has heard something, and what does he do but come right to me. 'Lucy,' says he, 'has that ——?' I dare not say what he calls him, for he is dreadful bitter at Folger—and he calls him dreadful wicked names. But no matter for that. It's his way when he is out of sorts. But he says, 'has Folger been a sneaking round you to get you to court that young girl for him?' 'Why Crampton', says I, 'what do you mean? What girl?' says I. But I saw he was getting high. I know his ways you see; and when he gets up on his high horse, there is no way for me, but just to keep as meek as a lamb, and try to let it work off. Says I, 'Do you mean Carrie Leslie?' 'I do,' says he, 'and I want to know whether you have had any hand in helping that scamp?' I tell you just what he said, that is, the substance of it; for he said a good many things not worth while repeating. 'Have you been helping that fellow to get hold of that young lady? has he talked with you about her? or have you done any thing to help him to gain her favor? I want you to tell me the truth, right straight out.' Well, what could I do? I never saw him in such earnest before, and I trembled so I was afraid he would see me shake, and I know his ways so well that if I had not told him the whole truth, just as it was, I don't know what the end of it might have been; so I told him the whole, just how it happened, and what I had said, and I says to him, 'I am sure, Crampton, Mr. Folger seems to be a very nice kind of a man, and very good to the poor, and he is very rich, and I believe will make a real good husband.' Well, he heard me through patiently with my story, until I began to talk about his goodness. When, oh, dear! it was dreadful to hear him, he went off like a madman, and such awful words as he used, it made me crawl all over. I am used to his ways, in general, but I never saw him in such a tantrum before. Well he let off all the bad words he could think of, and then says he, 'Do you get ready to-morrow morning, and go with me to the city, and do you see Carrie Leslie, and tell her if she marries that man she must do it at her own risk, and I,' says he, 'will go and see her father, and I mean to tell him all I know about the villain.' Oh, he talked dreadfully, and then says he, 'We will wash our hands of the business, and they can do as they like,' and out of the room he went. I knew it would be of no use to say any thing, I knew his ways so well, I must just do as he had said; and so in the morning early the carriage was at the door, and off we came; and I have been in such trouble all this blessed day, for I thought perhaps it might make trouble for you; and I did n't know but Folger might have got you to consent, for the last time I saw him, he seemed so set upon having you that I was sure he would propose right off, the first chance; and under all the circumstances, I did n't know but you might accept him, and then if you had, and Crampton should go and talk with your father as he said he would, why, it might make a dreadful muss all round. And then again I thought maybe Crampton did know something, after all, for you know men can find out some things about men better than women can. And if it should be that he is what Crampton says he is, and you should have gone and committed yourself, and then he not turned out well, why, that would be more dreadful still. One can get along with a man, say like Crampton, when you get used to his ways, but if Folger is what Crampton says he is, why, then he has got ways that one can't so well get along with. I know you could n't, and I know I could n't; but, oh, dear, do tell me quick, all about it, for you look so pale, dear Carrie, you most frighten me to death."

Carrie had, indeed, some very serious thoughts during the long harangue of her friend, and perhaps had a little of that feeling which one might very reasonably have on coming suddenly in contact with a venomous snake. The danger may be past, for perhaps the reptile has crawled away, or you have got beyond his reach, but there will remain some trepidation in the heart at the thought how near you had been to danger.

In a few words Carrie made a full revelation of what had occurred, and the recital caused Mrs. Crampton to exhibit quite as much feeling as the former had.

"Oh, the goodness me." And Mrs. Crampton pressed her own hands tightly together on her lap, and looked at Carrie.

"But, Mrs. Crampton, I have made up my mind the moment I get home to have an interview with Mr. Folger, and tell him candidly how I feel, and let him know that my mind is made up—it can never be."

"Oh, the goodness me! but if he should hold you to it now? You know they do sometimes. There was Kate Blauvelt—you have heard of that? She was only in fun, so she said, but there was some one by that heard her say she would have him, and he said he would have her. And what does he do but claims her as his wife. You know what a fuss there was about it. The father went to law, and all that. The judge decided it was a true bill, they were married and no mistake, and when Kate saw there was no way for her but to give in, or live single all her life, why, she concluded at last to let it go on."

"I do not feel any uneasiness on that account, Mrs. Crampton. There is nothing that I have said or done that a gentleman could construe in that way."

"But you gave him to understand that you was willing?"

"I suppose I did."

"Oh, dear! I do wish I was n't always such a fool to be meddling with such things. But I got such a blessing from Crampton last night, I guess it will cure me. It made the ceiling and all look blue about me. If I had n't been some used to him I should have gone clean off into hysterics. It was dreadful the way he took on, the names he called that man, and the places where he wished he was. Was there no chance, you think, for any one to be listening?"

Carrie could not refrain a hearty laugh at the earnestness of her friend.

"Oh, the goodness me! Carrie, don't laugh when there is any thing doing about such business! It is always bad luck, any way. Don't laugh, I beg of you! for I am all in a tremble. You see, if any thing should happen, and I having something to do with it, Crampton would go on like a crazy man. He would never forgive me—he is so dreadful particular about meddling with other people's business.

"But are you sure there was no chance for any one to be listening?"

"There was no one present, I assure you, Mrs. Crampton; you may set your mind perfectly at rest on that score. Are you designing to cross to the city this evening?"

"Oh, dear, no; I suppose not—there will be no use now, without Crampton should take it in his head to see your father at any rate."

"My father knows all the circumstances, Mrs. Crampton."

"Oh, Carrie, do, la—look here!" Mrs. Crampton was just then looking from the window. "Do, for goodness, look! there is Folger himself—and we thought he was in Princesport."

Carrie saw indeed that it was the very gentleman about whom they had been just holding such earnest converse. He was finely dressed, walking very deliberately toward the house, swinging a light gold-headed cane carelessly in his hand, and his countenance expressive of a mind rather happy than otherwise.

"I intend to see him at once, Mrs. Crampton, and have all this affair settled. I supposed he had returned home."

When Clarence Ralston took leave of Carrie Leslie at the house of his friends the Douglasses, he felt that all his fond hopes in reference to her, cherished so long, even against so many opposing obstacles, must now forever be relinquished. He had the most perfect confidence in her integrity; he felt certain that the few words of discouragement she had uttered, conveyed a meaning designed to check all advances, and there was a seriousness in her manner, mingled with such an expression of kind feeling, that his pride could take no offense.

He had not been aware until then how strong was the hold by which his heart had clung to one who had been rather a beautiful image to his imagination than a being of real life. The reality he found more captivating than that which his fancy had so long lived upon, but as unsubstantial to his yearning heart.

But his disappointment, in no way affected the deep interest he had taken in the affairs of her family. He had pledged himself to an active part in redressing what he believed to be a flagrant wrong committed against her parent, who, from circumstances now beyond his control, was powerless to relieve himself.

Through the good offices of Mr. Samuel Thompson, and the more efficient aid of Mr. Douglass, arrangements were at once made by which Clarence was enabled to take decided measures. The only great impediment had been the immediate power which Folger possessed over the ruined man. Circumstances, however, occurred to remedy that evil. How much Clarence had to do with them need not now be revealed.

Mr. Leslie had an application for the purchase of his homestead. It came at a critical juncture—when suspicions of Folger's honesty began to be indulged; and the plea of his daughter, that he would at any sacrifice free himself from the power of his creditor, became more urgent. These, united with the advice of Mr. Douglass, who had taken a friendly interest in his affairs, decided his action. Chelmsford was disposed of. Folger was paid in full, and although but a few hundred dollars remained to Mr. Leslie, after a settlement with his creditor, yet the chain by which he had been held was broken, and he felt free to take any course which prudence might dictate.

As it was felt to be of the utmost consequence that strict privacy should be maintained in regard to their proceedings, until ready for action; it was perfectly unknown to Carrie that Clarence Ralston had any agency in her father's affairs. All she knew was, that their old home had gone from their possession, and that her father, although nearly penniless, was a free man.

Clarence having made every necessary preparation, had gone to Princesport, having learned that Folger had returned thither, immediately after a settlement with Mr. Leslie. But he had not been there; and no information could be obtained as to when he might be expected. He therefore retraced his steps toward New York without delay. He knew that measures were about being taken there, for the purpose of bringing Folger to account for a high misdemeanor, committed years ago. This he had learned through his friend, Mr. Douglass, and also that the only cause of delay was in the non-arrival of a messenger from Port-au-Prince, who had been now for some time daily looked for. Should Folger hear of the designs against him, he would doubtless at once leave the country. This Clarence feared, he was therefore extremely anxious for a speedy interview. He had taken an officer with him to Princesport, and as has been said, not finding him there, watched closely on the road, as they retraced their way, for the object of pursuit. As they approached to Hoboken, the gentleman by his side drew his attention toward an object ahead, apparently on the same track with themselves, al though a clear view of it was intercepted by a bend in the road.

"You had better stop your horse a moment, Mr. Ralston."

And Clarence at once reined up. It was, however, out of their power to see distinctly, as the day was drawing to a close, and the twilight not sufficient to enable them to distinguish small objects at such a distance. But a carriage had stopped, and there seemed to be much confusion around it. Both gentlemen thought they saw a lady lifted into the carriage, apparently by force, and some one or two persons getting in with her; while others seemed to be engaged at a little distance from the carriage detaining a man who made no efforts to release himself.

"Ralston, drive on; drive as fast as you can! I do not like the looks of things! There is some villainy going on, depend upon it."

And Clarence urged on as fast as the tired beast could be driven, but it soon became evident that they were not to be overtaken, for the carriage in a few moments turned off into a narrow lane at a furious rate of speed, and was soon lost to their sight. Their first impulse was to follow the carriage, but perceiving, as they supposed, one of the persons who had been near the scene walking upon the road they were traveling, and apparently in a very unconcerned and leisurely manner, they concluded that the whole affair had been a matter of no moment, perhaps only a frolic on the part of some of the rude inhabitants in the vicinity to which the lane led, it being the direct route to a spot of no very good repute, some miles above Hoboken, called the "'long shore houses," a by-place where a few low taverns formed a convenient rendezvous for Sabbath profanation and low carousings beyond the inspection of prying neighbors.

It was their intention, however, to inquire into the circumstance from the individual ahead of them, and upon whom they were rapidly gaining. But it seemed contrary to the wishes of the gentleman that he should be questioned, for no sooner were they in full view of him than they saw him spring over the fence, and pass with rapid steps through the thick shrubbery which intervened between the road and the river.

"How much," said Clarence to his companion, "that man, even at this distance, reminds me of the one we are searching for."

"What, Folger!"

"Yes; I can not tell why, but his appearance impressed me at once with that idea."

"I never saw him, to my knowledge, so I can not say; and it would be difficult to distinguish an individual at such a distance without one was very familiar with his appearance. I should say, however, that the man we saw was rather tall, and by his walk, not a common working man. Whoever he is, he evidently don't want any company. I should like to have asked what had been the difficulty."

"The whole thing looks suspicious. I wish almost we had followed that carriage."

"It would have led us into a pretty wild place, and one where a man needs a weapon, or help enough to fend off; they are a rude set about there."

But the mind of Clarence was not at rest. He had a strong belief that the man who had so suddenly withdrawn from observation was Folger. He believed him capable of any vile act. And there flashed across his mind strange and terrible fancies. He dared not express his fears, nor even in his own thoughts allow full shape to them.

As it was not their purpose to make known at the stage-house the object of their mission, they made no inquiries on their arrival there, and after committing their horse to the stable-boy, walked quickly down to the ferry stairs, as they perceived that the boat was about to cross.

"I think," said Clarence, "we may as well take a look at the passengers. I feel so confident that the man we saw walking on the road was Folger, and that for some reason he did not wish to be recognized. He may have come by the path along shore, designing to take the boat for the city."

"At any rate, whether that man was Folger or not, should he be about to cross, I should like to mark him, for there may have been mischief going on, and we may hear of it yet."

There were no passengers, however, beside two market-men, with their baskets of produce; ascertaining that this was the last boat for the night, they felt assured that if their suspicions were correct, they would probably before long have an interview with the individual in question at the stage-house. As the boat slipped away from the ferry stairs, a rough-looking man called from the shore in some haste,

"Captain Stanley, may I take your yawl which lays up by the fish nets? Bob and I want it, to row a man off to a vessel in the stream."

"What man?"

"I don't know who he is. But he is in a stew to get to the vessel. It is the brig *Boxer*, he says, and she lies off Bedlow's Island."

"Yes, you can take it; be careful how you handle her."

Without passing a word to each other, Clarence and the officer, as if affected by a simultaneous impulse, followed the man who had thus obtained leave to use the boat, keeping the path which ran along on the top of the acclivity. The shrubbery which lined the path was at times so thick that the person they were following was completely hidden from their view. But they could hear his heavy tramp on the gravelly shore, even above the noise of the waves that were gently rolling their long crests upon the hard sand. Before reaching the spot, however, where the boat lay moored, the path they followed wound off in a curve away from the shore, and Clarence being well acquainted with the grounds, at once entered the thicket which intervened between them and the river.

It was not easy walking, for the rocks protruded constantly, and twilight had almost left them. At length they reached a rocky ledge which bounded the shore, and saw a boat lying at the edge of the water, a few rods ahead. The man they had followed had just reached it, and with his companion was shoving her off from the sand, upon which she had been partly left by the receding tide. A gentleman was standing by, apparently ready to jump in the moment she was released from her moorings. Clarence and his companion sprang quickly down from the ledge of rock, and hastened to the scene.

"Mr. Folger," said Clarence, for it was the gentleman himself, and he had already one foot on the bow of the boat, "one word with you, sir, if you please."

"With me, sir!"

"Yes, sir; Mr. Brooks, this is Mr. Folger."

Folger at once stepped a few feet from the boat, and the sheriff made a short communication to him. He spoke in a low voice, for he was willing to gratify what seemed to be the wish of Folger not to have the business, whatever it might be, exposed to the boatmen. The purport of his message, however, had a powerful effect; Folger merely made an exclamation of surprise, but in a low husky voice; he was evidently unprepared and alarmed.

"If you would be advised by me, sir," said Clarence, speaking in a calm, mild tone, "you will at once go with us, where matters can be discussed with more propriety than in this place."

"I am ready to follow you, sir."

The boatmen seeing the party about to leave, called out,

"Hullow, mister, are we to lose our job?"

"Perhaps, Mr. Folger," said Clarence, "an arrangement can be made that will prevent trouble; if so, I have no desire to injure you."

"You can wait, then," replied Folger to the men, in a firm voice. If an arrangement could be made, he felt there was a pressing necessity for his going in that boat.

"Ay, ay, well; we'll wait awhile, but don't be too long, the tide will soon change, and it will be a hard pull to the brig."

"Is there no house to which we can adjourn beside the tavern? I should prefer it if there is," said Folger, addressing himself to the officer.

"We are near the house of the proprietor. I am acquainted with him. He is also a justice of the peace, and if we have any writings to sign, it will be quite convenient."

"It will be agreeable to me, sir."

The party now ascended to the mansion, which, as before

described, stood on an eminence commanding an extended view of the river. They were near its more private inclosure, and they walked along through the smooth path without a word being spoke by either party.

The gentleman of the house received them with all that politeness of manner for which he was distinguished. A private room was readily granted. Lights were brought, and writing materials, and the door closed upon the company.

Clarence at once made known to Mr. Folger the steps which had been taken in reference to the case, and without hesitation produced the grounds upon which he had gone, and the evidence he could command. To all which Folger made no reply. He was a shrewd man, he thought quickly, and his conclusions were in general soon formed. He no doubt saw where he might make a good defense, and but for peculiar circumstances, would not for a moment have listened to a compromise. He was, however, anxiously absorbed just then, by matters of more consequence to him than the loss or gain of the Hazleton property.

"It is a false charge, sir! Every word of it is false, except the statement that I have a deed of the property. But, sir, I have made arrangements for a voyage to Europe, on special business. A great damage will result to me by any detention; I expect to sail early to-morrow morning. What arrangement, sir, do you propose? Let me hear it."

"I propose, Mr. Folger, that you at once give a quit claim deed to Mr. Leslie of all your right, title, and interest to the Hazleton estate."

"For what consideration?"

"In lieu of a prosecution which will end in your ruin. If you conclude to accept my proposition, the prosecution shall cease at once, and you may be at liberty to go where you please."

"And do you call that justice, sir! Thus to rob me of my rights! Is it the part of a gentleman thus to act, after having frankly disclosed the fact that I am under a necessity to go abroad, and that great pecuniary damage will result by my detention?"

"Call it what you please, and choose your own course. I shall not alter my terms one iota."

Folger now broke out into a violent tirade against the land,

and its former owner, and cursed the hour he had ever put forth his hand to aid him. "But make ready your paper, I will sign it—unjustly and unhandsomely as I am treated."

"You are so reluctant, Mr. Folger, I will let the matter drop. Perhaps it will be better for all parties, that things should ta e their proper course. Mr. Brooks, the business is in your hands."

And Clarence arose to depart.

"I have said I am ready to give the deed you ask for, sir. What more do you require? Surely, Mr. Ralston, you can pardon a few hasty expressions on the part of a man under my present circumstances."

"You will sign it, then, freely? and without feeling that you are under any compulsion on my part so to do?"

"I will, sir."

Clarence soon prepared the necessary paper.

"Your acknowledgment must be taken before a justice of the peace. Shall I call the gentleman of the house?"

"I am ready, Mr. Ralston, to make the acknowledgment of my free act and deed."

The gentleman was called, and the formula written, the paper signed and sealed; and as soon as it was delivered into the hands of Mr. Ralston, Folger rose.

"You have no further business with me, gentlemen?"

"Nothing further, sir."

"Then I wish you all good evening."

He bowed to the gentleman of the house, thanking him for his share of the accommodation so politely afforded, and then left; and his step was heard rapidly retracing his way back to the boat. Had Clarence known what circumstance contributed more than aught else to the conclusion of what he thought a most desirable end; had he known why Folger was in such haste to reach the boat, he would sooner have seen the property he had regained for his client forever lost, than allowed him to leave the strong hand of an officer of justice. And thus it is; we are ever working in the dark, and often when we have accomplished that upon which our hearts have been intent, ard rejoice that our end has been attained, we find, by after experience, that we were only laying a foundation for future woe.

CHAPTER XXVI.

Clarence returned to the stage-house with a light heart. He had accomplished a great work with much less difficulty than he had anticipated. He had regained a valuable property to its rightful owner, and he was anticipating the pleasure he should have on the morrow in placing in his hands the voucher that insured its redemption.

As he and his companion approached the stage-house, there seemed to be an unusual degree of confusion. Lights were moving about at the stable, and quite a concourse of people were gathered upon the piazza.

Stepping up into their midst, and about to ask what had happened, the arm of Clarence was seized by a stout hand, which he soon ascertained belonged to Mr. Thompson, and dragged along, *nolens volens*, into a back room, where he beheld a lady, apparently in great agony, walking to and fro, wringing her hands, shedding tears violently, and making exclamations of great distress. It was Mrs. Crampton, although Clarence knew not her name, and Mr. Thompson was too much occupied with internal troubles of his own to think of introducing any body. He had not said a word until he reached the room, and then, to the earnest entreaty of Clarence to tell him what the trouble was, merely replied:

"The Lord have mercy upon us."

"Can I be of any service to you, madam?" said Clarence, addressing the lady respectfully.

"Let him see the bit of paper," said Mr. Thompson; "maybe he can help some, for I know he will do it at the risk of his life."

"Oh, dear, yes! There it is—does he know her, Mr. Thompson?"

"Be sure he does; hush up, and let him read it; maybe he can tell what we 'd best do, for my mind is all like a whirligig, it goes round and round till I'm a most clear crazed out of my head."

Clarence read the note; it was a few lines on the blank leaf of a book:

"DEAR MRS. CRAMPTON—I am lost if help is not given me at once. The young woman will tell you!

"Yours,

"C. L."

"What does this mean?" said Clarence, in great agitation.

"The Lord only knows! but she's been took by some villains, and carried off!"

Mrs. Crampton saw, by the earnestness of his manner, that Clarence was highly excited, and she stepped up to him,

"Are you a friend or relation of Carrie Leslie? Do tell, quick!"

"I am a friend, and will lay down my life willingly to save her from any evil. But tell me the whole quickly! for by this note she must be in imminent danger!"

"Oh, dear, then I'll tell you; but you must wait a minute. I'll try to be as short as I can. Has any body gone up there, Mr. Thompson?"

"Yes, yes, yes; half a dozen on 'em! jist tell him as quick as you can!"

"Oh, dear, then I'll try to tell, but I am almost crazed; for Crampton is raving away like a madman. He says he never was in such a scrape before. I am most afraid he'll never get over it."

"The ——, woman! You'll make me swear next! Can't you hush up, and jist tell Mr. Ralston the hul upshot of it! Oh, dear! If my head ain't a turnin' round all ways to onst!"

"Well, I'll try; but you see, first you must know—but maybe you know it already! She is such a lovely creature! and Folger, you see, was so dead in love with her, and he's been trying all the ways that mortal man ever did try to get her, but Carrie had no mind to him. But Folger would n't give her up; so he came to me, and I, like a fool believed all he said, and he made me think he was such a kind, good-hearted man!"

"Oh, dear, dear! hush up. Can't you tell the upshot on it to onst?"

"Well, I will, Mr. Thompson. Where was I? Oh, well! You see I tried to persuade Carrie to have him; but I know I did wrong. Crampton is dreadful angry at me for it. But no matter for that; Carrie would not consent, she said she did not love him, and never could love him; but a few days ago—she never told me of it until this blessed day—you see, she went to New York."

Mr. Thompson now groaned aloud.

"She went to New York, and there was her father in dreadful trouble; and you know she doats on him; I believe she would die for him any time. There he was—took—and just going to jail. Only to think of it; no one to help him, nor nothing, and Carrie almost crazed. Well, what was to be done. Somehow or other, Folger come in her way, and she tells him her trouble, and asks him to help. Well, Folger worked his card so fairly, that what with his smooth speeches, and what with her father's troubles, why, you see, the poor thing, I expect at last consented that it might be so. But when she come to think of what she had done, that after all she did not love him, and never could, she felt that she had done wrong; and undo it she would, at the very first opportunity. So this afternoon as luck would have it, Folger came over, and she saw him and told him the whole truth."

"Was he displeased?"

"No, sir, not at all. He told her to think no more about it, and to let it all go, that they would be good friends, and he would never trouble her again on the subject. Well, Carrie was so happy when it was all over. But after tea—he had been off somewhere a good while—he comes back, and asks her right before me, 'If she was a mind to take a little walk?' She looked at me, as much as to say, 'will you go too?' But I thought of Crampton, and so I told her no; but that perhaps *she* had better, after what had happened. And so she went, but I believe it was much against her will; and that's the last we know of her, only when that young woman came with this note. Oh, dear! the goodness me; what shall we do?"

Clarence lost not a moment further; he had been almost entranced by the revelation Mrs. Crampton was making. But as soon as he comprehended the whole case, he rushed from the room, and made inquiries for the messenger who had brought the note. She had returned, and all he could learn was, that "a young lady, a most beautiful creature, had been brought in a carriage down Licket-lane, that she seemed in great trouble. That she got an opportunity for a few minutes alone with the young woman, when she wrote a few lines on a piece of paper torn from a book, and asked her, if she had any feeling, to run with it at once to the stage-house and hand it to the lady to whom it was directed. And he learned further, that several men had gone to the place from the tavern, with their horses on the full run.

"I now understand," said Clarence to Mr. Brooks, "why that man was in such haste. His design is evidently to force her into a marriage, and bear her off to a foreign country. Shall we not at once go to the place?"

"Had we not better first make inquiries to ascertain whether Folger has gone off in that boat?"

"I fear to lose a moment—the only hope is in our speed."

In a few moments the gentlemen were driving rapidly as the nature of the ground, and the darkness, would permit, down the lane which led to the river above Weehawken. Clarence was in an agony as they drew near the house, and beheld its lights. He never knew before how intensely he loved. What would a sacrifice of life be to save her? He now understood some things which before seemed mysterious in her conduct. What would he not give once more to see her!

The house was indeed well situated for dark and desperate deeds. It was in a lone place, on the bank of the river. A few rods of level land lay between it and a high bluff of almost perpendicular rock. One only road had access to it, except a winding path up the high bluff, very difficult of ascent, even for one on foot. The river spread out before, and a rude dock at which lay an old hulk formed a stopping-place for river craft. A chill of horror almost paralyzed the heart of Clarence when he found himself thus shut in, and thought of her who had been betrayed into such a den.

As they entered the house, quite a number of men, much the worse for the liquor they had been drinking, started up, to gaze on the new-comers; some from benches on which they were reclining, some from the floor, and others from a rude table, where they had been busy at a game of dominoes.

Mr. Brooks was no stranger to the keeper of the tavern, and perhaps not altogether to some of his customers, for they soon became sober enough to find their way out of his presence, and without waiting to be asked any questions.

Mr. Stubbs, upon being informed for what purpose the gentlemen had come, tried to make out a very plausible story. He said "there had been a young lady there, it was true; but they told him it was only a runaway scrape; he did n't concern himself about it. If young girls were such fools as to run away, let them do it. A boat had come there by a signal from the shore, some one put up, he did n't know who, but it was n't him nor none of his folks. The boat got there just after dark; the mate and four hands, and they took her off, and that's all he knew about it."

"Did she go willingly?"

"How should I know, Mr. Brooks? The galls, you know, always make believe they ain't willing, when they are, all the time. I did n't see her go. It was no business of mine."

"Perhaps you will find that it is your business, Mr. Stubbs; you have confessed to the fact of a young lady having been brought here, and violently taken away."

"I did n't say violently, Mr. Brooks."

"You said as near that as was necessary; you shall answer for this matter—you know me well enough to be sure I will keep my word with you; give me now, without the least equivocation, the names of the men who brought her here. I demand them at once."

Stubbs was now thoroughly alarmed. He took most sacred oaths that he did not know them; and had never seen them before. He even shed tears in testimony of the truth of what he said.

Clarence was too much excited to be willing to remain a moment longer.

"Mr. Brooks, you can attend to these people some other time. The villain has accomplished his end. She has been taken off, and she must be reclaimed, if I follow her to the ends of the earth; come, let us lose not a moment."

With a word or two more of admonition, Mr. Brooks followed Clarence from the house, and they were soon rapidly urging their way back toward the ferry.

The first effort of Clarence was to obtain the names of the men, who had carried Folger to the vessel. In this he soon succeeded, but they had not yet returned, and from what he learned would not, probably that night, as they frequently spent their nights in the city. He then immediately offered a large price to any four men who would carry him at once to the vessel; the name of which, and her position, he happily remembered. The four hands were readily obtained, for he had offered to pay any price they should ask. The boat was immediately manned, and Clarence was about to jump on board, when Mr. Brooks took him by the arm, and led him one side.

"What is your design, Mr. Ralston, after you have reached the vessel?"

"To go on board and rescue her; I will do it or die in the attempt."

"No doubt, sir, you would; but consider for a moment! Do you suppose such a scheme would have been devised by Folger without he knew well how he was to carry it out. He no doubt owns that vessel, and has a commander that will be ready, at the least, to wink at his doings. Do you suppose you will be allowed to enter the vessel? What would be your power, or that of the men you have with you, against a determined captain, and a crew under his command?"

Clarence was silent, for he saw clearly what difficulties he might encounter, and Mr. Brooks continued,

"The vessel does not lie in our waters, or I might do something in my official capacity to aid you. Take my advice, now, and do this. Cross to the city as soon as possible—make known the case to friends there—make an affidavit of what has taken place, and procure an officer from the police, with a warrant. I will go with you, if you wish, to aid you in the matter."

"Thank you, thank you; I believe you are right. Let us be off at once, then."

In a few moments more the little boat was speeding across the North river as rapidly as four stout rowers could urge her.

"My fear is," said Mr. Brooks, in a low voice, after they had got some distance on their way, "that the vessel may be put off to sea at once; you remember Folger said that he expected to sail early in the morning. If so, she is doubtless all ready for sea, and, under the circumstances, I think he would wish to get an offing as soon as possible. The wind is freshening up too, and fair for a run out."

The suggestion was no doubt the result of correct reasoning on the part of Mr. Brooks. Clarence, however, did not need it for the sake of stimulating him in his efforts. He would have gone with lightning speed, had that been possible; all he could do was to urge the men to greater exertion by the promise of a large compensation.

"No, no, sir," said a rough-looking tar, who seemed to be a leader among them, "fair play's the jewel—we are not a going to take advantage of a gentleman because he needs our help—we will do the best for you, and all we want is the just thing; come boys, pull away; she'll soon be over now, sir; head to the north a little, sir; the tide 's on the turn."

No sooner had the boat reached the ferry stairs, at the foot of Courtland-street, than one of the men stepped up to Mr. Ralston, and pointing to a small boat, with two men in it, remarked,

"You was inquiring on the other side, sir, for the men that borrowed Captain Stanley's yawl—there they are, sir."

Clarence was about to go to them, when Mr. Brooks again arrested him. "Let me manage this matter."

"Certainly I will, but had we not better at once see those men?"

"No, not we! Folger may have crossed with them. They are evidently waiting for some one." Mr. Brooks then spoke a few words to the man who had given him the information, when the latter sprang ashore, went round to the other side of the slip, where the yawl lay, and after a few moments returned.

"They are waiting, sir, for the man who they carried to the brig. He has come on shore to see the captain, as they want him on board at once."

"I told you so," said Brooks, turning to Clarence. "His design is no doubt to get the brig off without delay. If we do any thing we must be quick about it."

Clarence put some money into the hands of the men, and

received their pledge to wait for his return. He and his companion then sprang ashore, and walked rapidly on their way to the house of Mr. Douglass. He lived near by, and Clarence knew of no one who could so efficiently aid in an affair of such emergency.

CHAPTER XXVII.

Carrie, as Mrs. Crampton had said, did not by any means feel an inclination for a walk with Mr. Folger, after the interview she had with him that afternoon.

The interview itself had been more agreeable than she anticipated. She made a frank acknowledgment of her error in giving him the encouragement she had—and she also frankly stated the reasons why she felt under the necessity of asking him to relinquish all claim which her assent had allowed him.

If Folger felt at all disappointed, he manifested no displeasure. But to her great joy, yielded readily to her request. He only asked that he might have the favor of being considered her friend and well-wisher, and that he might be privileged occasionally with her society, under his promise never again to make any pretensions to her hand. This Carrie of course felt she could not deny.

The interview was a short one, for although Mr. Folger had appeared quite at leisure previous to it, no sooner had the affair been settled, than he pleaded a necessity for leaving her, as he had business of great consequence to attend to that afternoon.

What his business was, need not now be told: the reader can well understand. But it must not be supposed that the plans of Mr. Folger had not been laid before, or that the mere fact of the exposition which had been made was the cause of his subsequent conduct. He had given up all hope of a union with her from the hour when he unfolded his views to her father. And desperate now in his fortunes, he had resolved upon a bold stroke of villiany, and had completed his arrangements for placing the wide ocean between himself and those whom he had every reason to believe were laying a snare for him in New York. And he was fully resolved, willing or unwilling, to make her a partner with him in his flight. The vessel belonged to him, and the captain was so far let into the secret as to be informed that a young lady to whom he had been clandestinely married was to accompany him, and that a device had been contrived by both the lady and himself, whereby it was to appear that she had been forcibly taken away. But that the captain would be perfectly satisfied when once away from shore, and out of the reach of friends, that the lady fully sympathized in the matter.

Mr. Folger's business there that afternoon was merely to complete some part of the strategy.

Supper was over, and the evening approaching, when Folger, in his most winning manner, requested the company of Carrie for a short stroll. The beautiful scenery of that enchanting spot, and the pleasantness of the evening—it being just that season of the year—the opening spring—when nature puts on some of its most pleasing forms—all, afforded sufficient apology for the request. Although reluctant to go, Carrie felt unwilling to refuse so slight a request. She soon arrayed herself suitably, and they walked together from the house.

"I fear," said Folger, after they had reached some distance from the stage-house, "I have been thoughtless of your comfort in extending our walk so far; suppose we just step one side into this path which now crosses our track. I want to show you a natural curiosity, if you have not before seen it: a cave covering a delicious spring of water, and then we will retrace our steps."

Carrie had followed her conductor but a few steps—the path was so lined with bushes as to allow of only one passenger at a time—when two men at once seized her, and a thick covering was thrown over her face. She called for help, but felt conscious that the thick folds which enveloped her made her call of no avail, while a voice she had never heard before addressed her:

"You must go with us, miss. If you go peaceably no harm shall happen to you while in my power."

She heard a carriage, as she supposed, driving past, and again made a greater effort to be heard. But the vehicle stopped, and she soon found herself carried towards it; no violence seemed to be designed, for great care was manifested in placing her within it, although again she was warned that her only safety was in yielding to her fate. She soon felt herself borne rapidly away, but whither she knew not.

After riding, as she supposed, some miles, the carriage halted at the foot of a steep hill down which they had descended, and the covering was removed from her face. The men beside her were disguised, so that she could not have recognized them by their countenances, but that they were utter strangers she had no doubt. She looked from the carriage, and involuntarily shrunk back and clasping her hands in agony exclaimed,

"Oh, why is it? Why must I go there?"

The men, as she thought, seemed rather surprised at the apparent sincerity of her expression, and merely replied,

"The boat will be here soon."

"Oh, what boat! where! do tell me, if you have the feelings of men, tell me why I am brought here, and where I am to go!"

"Well, if you don't know it already, it is more than we can tell you. But it will be no use to make believe any longer. You are safe enough away from them now that would n't let you have your own way. And you will soon be away from this place. It is a rough concern, but we will try to get you a room by yourself, and we will keep watch that no harm comes to you."

Carrie caught a glimpse of hope from the idea thrown out that she was a voluntary prisoner. She might be watched less strictly. She would not undeceive them.

As there were many rude-looking persons gathered at the door of the house, Carrie endeavored, as she alighted from the carriage, to act with composure. It was indeed a dreary aspect for a lone female. The low and rough-looking house with the high bluff towering behind it, and the water coming within a few rods of its long low porch, seemed to shut it in from the notice of the world, while the bloated countenances of those who appeared to be its indwellers or visitors, gave sure token of what might be expected from their sympathy Her heart shuddered at the sight, and she felt her limbs to be losing their power, and only by a strong effort could she brace herself against the terrible scene. Her only hope was, in retaining the full power of her faculties. Her conductors led her through the open bar-room into a rough, unfurnished apartment. One of the men alone entered with her.

"I will leave you here for a few minutes, to look for some of the women, if there is any such a thing to be found here. My companions will watch the door to see that no one comes to molest you."

"Thank you," said Carrie; and for a moment she was almost tempted to fall on her knees and beg him, as he was a man, to rescue her. But the thought came to her that it might be better to intrust the secret of her real situation to a woman. She felt now convinced that the men who had brought her there had been informed that she connived at it.

In a short time a young woman came into the room. She was a rough specimen of the gentle sex, but she had not a bad countenance, although, had the skin been a little cleaner, it would have appeared, perhaps, to better advantage. Rough as her exterior was, Carrie felt some relief at her presence.

"Was you a wanting me?"

"I am very glad to see you, as I am a stranger here; are you the lady of the house?"

"Oh, la, no! what do you think? how old do you s'pose I be? Why, la! I ain't a smitchel over seventeen, and old Stubbs is all of fifty; no, I ain't no woman of the house—I'm only here a day or two to help 'em with their spinning. So you 're goin' to make a run of it, ha? Well, I pity you!"

"What do you mean by a run of it?"

"A run of it! why a run away! I've heered all about it; that man has told me jist how it is. But I think it's queer if it's all jist as he says, that he has given Stubbs such strict orders not to let you stir a foot out of the house till the boat comes for you. I guess they 're afeered you might change your mind."

"The men who brought me here have not gone, have they?"

"I guess you'd think so if you'd seen them put it up the hill. I've a notion there's something about the job they don't like, or they would n't be in sich a hurry to be off."

"Then, what prevents my going, too? Oh, my good girl! only help me once out of this place! into any decent house—do help me! you shall be handsomely rewarded—and you will do an act of kindness that I shall remember all my life. Oh, do help me! let us go at once!"

"Do, la! Well, then, it ain't your doings after all! Well, I thought just so. But you can't no more git out of this house than out of a jail. You see old Stubbs had promised them men, and he did it with a dreadful oath, that you should n't get out of his clutches till the boat come for you; and he's got men a watching all round the foot of the hill—that's the road you come; and there ain't no other way to git off. You could n't no more climb the hill behind the house, than you could fly—a cat can't climb it. And then, if you should try to git out, there's so many half drunk all around here, that it would be dreadful for you to be took by them. Do, dear lady, don't think of it! But maybe I could get off and call some help! but there ain't no place nearer than the stage-house, where one could git help enough."

"Oh, will you go there for me? Have you any paper? But stay!" and Carrie seized an old book that lay on the rude mantel-shelf, and found one leaf partly blank. She tore it out, and with her pencil wrote a few lines.

"I'm a thinking the boat 's come."

Carrie felt her strength giving way, and she threw herself on a bench by the side of the wall. It was a moment of intense anguish. Her whole life's well-being lay on the point of balance. Was she to be thus torn from home and friends, and be made the sport of vice and cruelty?

"They 've come, depend on it! I hear old Stubbs and his gang a coming for you. What, dear lady, can I do for you?"

"Here is all the money I have with me—take it—and take this paper, and run to the stage-house, and inquire for the name on the back of it. Oh, do! do! and be as quick as you can!"

"Hush—hush—be still! don't take on. Here, give me the paper—and don't mind if I take on, and laugh at you, and make believe I ain't a goin' to help you. But I won't touch the money; no—no—but here's Stubbs!"

A gruff voice accompanied a rough knock at the door

"Mag, I say!"

"Well, what you want?"

"Tell the young woman the boat 's ready, and the mate is swearing because she don't make haste."

When the door opened, and Carrie beheld the bloated, ill-looking being who stood there, and caught a glimpse of the miserable objects behind him, peering at her, around his person, she felt that even a boat with rough sailors would be preferable to exposure alone with such inmates of the dwelling. She arose from her seat, and with as much composure as she could possibly command, followed the girl who preceded her, walking rapidly through the outer room, and down to the sandy shore toward the boat. Four stout seamen sat holding their oars, while one, rather more comely in appearance, and better dressed, stood by the boat on the shore He was swearing furiously at somebody or something—he probably did not well know at what himself; he seemed to be in an ill humor.

Carrie had borne up to the last extremity. She had beheld no single countenance, with the exception of the young woman, that gave her the least encouragement that any sympathy could be expected. But there was something in the appearance of this man, rough as his language was, that it seemed to her a helpless female might appeal to. She fixed her eye on him as he held out his hand to help her into the boat.

"Oh, sir! I cry to you to help me! Oh, if you have the heart of a man—save me—save me!" and she burst out into an agony of tears, and would have fallen, had not the mate caught her in his arms and placed her carefully on the seat of the boat.

"Oh, sir, I call upon you as a man, not to take advantage of my helpless condition! Oh, tell me where you are taking me to—do tell me!"

"I have nothing to do with it, miss; I came here by the orders of Captain Marshall to bring off a young lady who was just married to the owner of the brig. All he said was, 'it was rather a sly business—that I must make haste, and get you off, or there might be trouble.'"

"Who is the owner of the brig you speak of?"

"The owner! Why, Folger—is he not the man you've married? Shove ahead, men—off with her—I wish people would do their own business of this kind; shove ahead, I tell you!" and his stern commands caused the men to spring to their oars, and the little boat shot out into the dark bosom of the river.

The full extent of the terrible snare into which she had been entrapped was now revealed to the poor trembling girl. She was to be introduced on board the vessel as already married! And what would her denial avail, against one whom she learned was the owner of the vessel, and of course upon whom all others on board were dependent. Her fears, too, were aggravated by the harsh language of the mate to the men under his command. He seemed to be enraged at them and all about him, for he swore at the water, whenever the spray flew on him, and at the wind, and at the men alternately. He had, however, some feeling for the poor girl, who was weeping bitterly beside him, for he took off his own pea-jacket and wrapped it carefully around her—for the night was chilly, and the wind and tide against them caused the spray at times to fly even over the stern of the boat, where she was seated. This act gave a thrill of hope to Carrie, even in spite of his rude language.

"Oh, sir—you will not give me into the power of that man! Oh, do be my helper! Have you a mother or sister?"

There was no reply other than a fierce order to the men to "pull away, or he would have them tied up and lashed for a set of lazy lubbers."

The sky was unobscured, except above the western horizon, where lay a mass of vapor that seemed to be spreading upward; near to it, and shining with unusual brightness, was the evening-star, which Carrie had always called her own, and her eye fastened upon it. Years came back in quick review. Her days of joy, and days of sorrow. Her friends! Alas! what agony did the thought of them awaken! and they were near her, too; on each side of the black water, over which she was hurrying a helpless victim. They would fly to her rescue—but were in fatal unconsciousness of her danger. Soon, she feared, a great gulf would intervene between them and her forever.

And now the brightness of the star is dimmed; the cloud is spreading upward—a shred from its dark bosom has vailed the beautiful planet; again she has emerged, and shines more brightly than ever—pure and brilliant like virtue's self. Alas! the rays tremble on the edge of the dark mantle—they die away—the cloud has wrapped its heavy folds about her, and every ray has vanished.

"Boat ahoy!"

"Ay, ay," was anwered by the mate, and poor Carrie beheld close at hand the large hull of a vessel, against which their little boat was hauling up. In the agony of that dreadful moment her heart rose in an urgent plea to Him on whom she had ever trusted. It was the cry for help amid the whelming billows.

With a kind and respectful manner, mingled with stern orders to the men, the officer assisted her to mount the vessel's side, and the moment they reached the deck, he asked,

"Is Captain Marshall on board?"

"He has gone ashore, but said he should be back at nine."

The officer who had brought her then stepped up to Carrie.

"Be as calm as you can, miss; I am not the master of this vessel, but she is under my charge until the captain returns. You shall have the whole cabin to yourself, and no human being shall enter it—while I command—unless at your request."

"Oh, bless you for those kind words."

He assisted her into the cabin, and then left it, closing the doors, and keeping a strict watch beside them. At length the trying moment came. A boat rowed by two men drew up alongside; she was hailed, but no answer returned. The mate stepped to the side of the vessel, and a man well dressed at that moment sprang upon deck.

"Ah, Mr. Decker! All safe? Is the lady on board?"

"There is a lady here, Mr. Folger, brought from the Jersey shore." And so saying, he stepped leisurely toward the cabin door.

"In the cabin, I suppose," said Folger, as he walked quickly up, with the intention of going down.

"I have given the lady possession of the cabin, Mr. Folger, with the promise that she shall not be disturbed by any one until Captain Marshall arrives."

"That is very strange, Mr. Decker, I must confess. The lady is my wife, and I demand admittance to her."

Decker had now placed himself immediately before the door.

"She has my promise, sir, that no one shall see her before

Captain Marshall comes on board. There is something wrong about the business, and I must see the commander of the brig before any one sees *her*."

"You know, I suppose, sir, that I am owner here, and no one has a right to command but myself; you forget your place, sir." And Folger made motions for a violent entrance.

"Don't lay a finger on me, sir, or I'll spatter the deck with your brains in an instant."

"You will, ha?" and Folger at once drew a sword from his cane. "Now, sir, give me entrance at the instant, or you are a dead man." And the deadly weapon glittered in the light upon deck, within a hand's-breadth of the brave sailor. In a moment it was flying in the air, and over the vessel's side.

Thus discomfited, Folger began to call upon the men for help.

"Hold—hold, sir! Another word in that style, and you leave the deck of this vessel, owner or no owner. I have given my word that no one shall enter this cabin until Captain Marshall comes, but over my dead body, and I shall keep it."

"Then, sir, I shall go at once for Captain Marshall, and your insolence shall receive its reward."

"When the captain comes, he can do as he pleases; and if he chooses to give up a helpless woman to your tender mercies he can do so. It will be his affair, not mine."

Folger jumped into the boat that still lay by the vessel's side, uttering threats that he would not only bring the captain but a warrant to arrest the mate for daring to keep a wife confined away from her husband. After a short parley with the men who had brought him, the boat shoved off, and was rowed rapidly toward New York.

With much anxiety the mate waited for the return of the captain. He had acted from dictates of manliness but he could not be sure that Folger had not the claim which he pretended to have. If so, he might indeed get himself into trouble, for he had taken an unnecessary stand against his rights.

An hour had thus passed when the sound of an approaching boat was distinctly heard, and in a few minutes the well-known voice of the captain calling out,

"Hold up."

"All well, Mr. Decker?" said Captain Marshall, as he sprang on deck.

"Not exactly, sir; there is like to be a row about that young lady. Folger has been here, and swears that she is his wife, and she denies it, and begs not to be given up to him. And I could n't find it in me to let the bloody villain, as I believe he is, go into the cabin. He then drew a sword-cane at me, and I sent his darning-needle over among the fishes. He then went to ordering the men to seize me. I gave him a small blessing on that head, and he went off swearing by heaven and earth that he would get you, and also a police warrant, that would give him his rights. I don't know but I have done wrong, sir, but I thought I knew you well enough to know that you was n't the man to be caught kidnapping a young girl away from her friends; and if it ain't a genuine case of kidnapping then I don't know what grog is, that 's all."

"Was n't she willing to come?"

"Willing? if ever there was a poor, frightened, broken-hearted creature, she is one. And she's the handsomest piece of flesh I ever laid my eyes on. I would have given my life first, Captain Marshall, before a finger should have been laid on her against her will. But now, sir, it's your business, not mine."

Captain Marshall was a short man, but he had an eye that told of determination and energy. He spoke quick to the point, and seemed to hate useless words.

"Let me see her."

The companion-way was opened at once, and he descended.

"Don't be alarmed, my lady, I am Captain Marshall. My first officer, Mr. Decker, thinks that you have come here against your will. Let me know the truth."

Thus encouraged, Carrie at once revealed the whole story of her wrongs.

"And you now wish to leave the brig?"

"O dear sir! only free me from that dreadful man, and I and my friends will bless your name as long as we live."

"Would you wish to be put on shore to-night, or would you prefer to stay until morning? You shall have this cabin to yourself, and sleep as safely as in your parents' house."

"If it would not be too much trouble, I should prefer to go to my friends at Hoboken: they know not what has become of me, and are no doubt in great distress."

"Please take my arm, miss, and let me help you up these stairs."

As they were ascending, the captain became aware that some persons had come on board; and to his chagrin, on reaching the deck, was confronted by Folger. His hope had been to get the young lady safe among her friends before his arrival. He now prepared his mind for trouble, for he saw two men with Folger, who he had no doubt were officers of police. He felt the shudder which passed through the frame of the helpless one by his side, as she grasped tightly to his arm, and heard her whisper of alarm, as she beheld the person of her betrayer.

"Don't be alarmed miss, I will not leave you until you and your friends have a fair chance for justice."

"Captain Marshall," said Folger, "did I hear aright? and do you also design any interference between me and my lawful rights?"

The captain was framing an answer which would have convinced the gentleman that he had indeed heard aright, when the attention of all was arrested by the addition of a few more visitors on board the brig *Boxer*. A call from a boat alongside, was made, to inquire, if "this was the brig *Boxer*?"

"Ay, ay," shouted the lusty voice of a sailor.

"Is Captain Marshall on board?"

Hearing his name called, the captain, with Carrie still clinging to his arm, walked to the side of the brig, and his hand was seize by a gentleman, who was just mounting the bulwarks. d

"Oh, Mr. Douglass, Mr. Douglass!" cried Carrie, in an ecstacy of delight.

He caught her in his arms.

"My dear child! thank God, we have found you."

The sight of a friend, and one in whom she could confide as a deliverer was so unexpected, and the change from a state of uncertainty to that of entire confidence was so overpowering, that for a few moments she was scarcely conscious of what was transpiring around her. Mr. Douglass helped her to a seat, telling her to fear nothing, and hastened to attend to some matters with Captain Marshall, leaving one of his company standing by her. Her face was covered, for she was giving vent to her overcharged feelings. Perhaps with a desire to make known his presence, or to allay the agitation of her mind, a voice in gentle tones addressed her.

"All danger is past, Miss Leslie." Carrie now started, she raised her tearful eye at the speaker.

"Oh, Mr. Ralston, and you too!"

Clasping the hand which she had extended toward him, he replied,

"This is the happiest moment of my life!"

During this time a great change had taken place in the circumstances of him who had thus sought her destruction.

When Clarence and Mr. Brooks entered the house of Mr. Douglass, and revealed to him privately, what had taken place, with a calmness of manner peculiar to him he very gently remarked, "The fox will be taken in his own trap." He then in a few words explained to Clarence how matters had been arranged. The evidence against Folger was complete, and the judge of the United States Admiralty Court had issued a warrant for his arrest, and nothing was necessary but to place it in the hands of an officer. It was to have been done on to-morrow, but the information he now received convinced Mr. Douglass that no time should be lost. The services of the high sheriff were obtained, and he, with an attendant officer, accompanied Mr. Douglass and his party on board the brig.

Folger was at once in the hands of a power from which there was no escape, and glad to hide his guilty head from one whom he had so basely injured, he made no delay in ensconsing himself within the boat that was ready to convey him to the city, and Carrie saw him no more.

Some little time elapsed in private arrangements between Mr. Douglass and Captain Marshall, for the brig had been also seized as the property of Folger.

"And now, my darling," said the former, stepping up to Carrie, "I am ready for your commands—what is your wish? To return to Hoboken, or go home with me?"

"Miss Leslie seems to prefer an immediate return to the former place, as her friends there will suffer great anxiety until they see her again."

"Be it so, then."

"And with her leave I will accompany her, and deliver her into safe keeping," said Clarence, looking earnestly at Carrie to see whether the proposition met her approval.

Carrie was still too much overcome with the joy of the present deliverance to be able, for the moment, to express her wishes in words, but the look of confidence which was marked upon her smiling countenance, as her tearful eye rested on Clarence, was all the assurance he wanted.

"And when you get over the present excitement, dear Carrie," said Mr. Douglass, "you may very properly spend a few words in thanks to this young gentleman, for his untiring efforts have this night, under God, been the sole means of your deliverance from the scheme of that villain.

"Do not speak of thanks, my dear friend!" taking the offered hand of Carrie, and addressing Mr. Douglass; "I am sufficiently rewarded. It is an hour in my life that will never be forgotten."

The captain now came up to know what were the gentlemen's wishes as to their return; as soon as they were communicated, he ordered the cutter to be manned.

"I will accompany the lady myself, for I want to see this matter well finished, and the lady and her friends assured that neither I nor my officers had any hand in this nefarious business; are you ready, miss?"

Carrie arose, and giving her hand to Captain Marshall,

"I assure you, sir, neither I nor my friends will ever regard you but with the greatest kindness. I thank you most heartily for your prompt and manly interference. I only wish it was in my power to reward you as your generosity deserves."

"I have seen to that," said Mr. Douglass. "Captain Marshall has lost his brig, but he will go out in a few days the master of one of the finest ships that sails from our port."

"But where is that generous, noble man, who at the risk of his life interposed for my safety?" and the captain immediately led her to his first officer, who was by the side of the brig, giving orders to those who were to man the boat.

As Carrie approached him, she took from her breast a pin of some value.

"I know not, dear sir, what other token to give you as an assurance how much I feel your kindness; I shall never see a sailor after this, but I shall think of a man to whom a female in distress may appeal with confidence. Keep this trifle as a memento of one whom your brave heart saved from the power of a bad man."

"Thank you, miss, and with your leave I will put it upon the breast of one who, although not quite so fair, has, I hope, a heart as generous and true as your own."

And again between her and Mr. Douglass farewells are exchanged. And Clarence holds her hand as she descends into the boat, and they sit side by side. And as though he feared some evil might befall her yet, he still retains the precious treasure in his grasp, while the boat cleaves her rapid way through the rough water. The night has no chill now, and the spray sprinkles them unheeded. She is delivered! and the spoiler caught in his own snare! No barrier rears its dark form now between her and the noble youth by her side, nor are words needed to express the feelings which now can pla untrammeled in each heart. Silently they sit, and Carrie fixes her eye in joyful rest on her sweet star, that shies far off above the western hills, more brightly than ever it has shone before. The cloud so threatening has risen and passed off quietly, and not a shred of its dark mantle is left to dim the brilliant planet. Is it indeed a token that the darkness which had been lowering about her own pure way is no longer to disturb its brightness?—we shall see.

Old Mr. Thompson and Mr. Crampton had kept together, all the evening. They were both in great distress. The former from his sincere regard to Carrie, and the latter from his sensitiveness on the score of meddling with other people's business.

"It's the last time I will ever be caught in such a scrape. If Mrs. Crampton can not keep her hands out of other people's dishes, I will quit."

"Hush up, hush up, you talk like a madman! Leave your wife for a fault that you know is as natural to a woman as to pin on a handkerchief? Hush up. Oh, dear! Oh, dear! That dreadful villian! I know it's him. There's deviltry in his very bones. I know there is. He's a clean underground sarpent. But ain't that a boat a comin'? Don't you hear it?"

"I'm a mite deaf to-night; speak louder."

"I'm tired on it. I sha'n't waste my strength no more a hollering to-night, for what with the wind, and the noise of the water, and the hullabaloo there's been all the evening, I'm clean done over."

So Mr. Thompson took a seat upon a spar that lay on the

dock, and Mr. Crampton, without saying any thing further, took a seat beside him. The former had no heart to go into the house, and the latter wished to keep clear of his wife. He wished to let her know how *indignant* he felt. But Mrs. Crampton, after walking up and down the room, and wringing her hands, and indulging in various exclamations over the fate of poor Carrie, and calling upon all the men who came in her way "to go and try to do something," at length began to be uneasy about her husband, and learning that he was not in the house she started off for the ferry-stairs. A light was visible there, and she made directly for it.

"Oh, Mr. Crampton, are you here? I've been so worried! you will get your death of cold! you can not do any good sitting here. Oh, I am so afraid they will never find her! Is it not dreadful to think of?"

"Dreadful?"

"Yes, ain't it dreadful!"

"I will tell you what, Mrs. Crampton!" ("Oh, dear, it's all up with me!" "He always called her Lucy)" "such disgrace as your conduct has brought upon me, *is not to be borne.* It is your doing, madam;" ("Oh, dear!" exclaimed Mrs. Crampton) "this has come of your match-making. I told you from the first that he was a—"

"Oh, dear! don't say such dreadful words. Do hear! Mr. Crampton, hear to reason! Did n't I do it for the best?"

"For the best?"—There was quite a pause. "The best thing you can do is to go right up to the house and go to bed, do you hear?"

"Hush up, hush up, there it is! It's coming! I can see it; look!"

And Mr. Thompson, taking Mr. Crampton by the shoulders, turned his face toward an object on the water.

All now hastened to the stairs, and in a moment more Carrie was in the arms of her old friend Mr. Thompson. He took her up bodily and carried her up the ferry-stairs, when Mrs. Crampton seized her, and then the old gentleman went and took his seat again on the spar, and had a quiet moment or two all by himself; what he was doing nobody knew, for it was quite dark, but somebody on the dock seemed to have taken a violent cold.

Mr. Crampton, without saying a word, walked straight up to the house and into the bar-room.

"Give me a punch—make it *strong*."

"Pretty sweet?"

"I'm a mite deaf."

"Shall I make it sweet?"

"Sweet! no, sour; I don't want any thing sweet to-night."

Mr. Crampton, after the punch, was no more seen until breakfast-time the next morning.

CHAPTER XXVIII.

As Clarence had some special business with Mr. Leslie, it was decided that he should return to New York the next morning, while Carrie pursued her journey homeward in company with her friends Mr. and Mrs. Crampton and Mr. Samuel Thompson, with the expectation that Clarence would accompany Mr. Leslie, who was about to return home for a few days in order to make arrangements for the removal of his family to some other place of abode, his homestead having been disposed of.

Mr. Thompson had gone through a variety of exciting scenes during his present journey, and he inwardly resolved, as he took his last look of the great city, in starting from Hoboken, "that they should never catch his carcass there again. It might do for young people, or for them that liked a hurry and worry, and to be in hurly burly all the time; but as for him he guessed they'd find him in 'statter quo' in his own home—he'd done with goin' to town onst for all."

Mr. Thompson's spirits were quite good all day, considering the wear and tear they had suffered. But they grew more elastic as the day was drawing near its close, and familiar scenes began to break upon his eye and ear, and when the top of the hill was reached which overlooked Princesport, and the beautiful bay spread out before him, all silvered with the rays of the setting sun, with here and there the white sails of the sloops caught in the calm, and apparently hanging in the air, and when he saw the boys driving their cows along from the commons, or the pasture-fields, and heard the tinkling bells echoing through the cedars, and the lively strains of the young men driving their teams home after their day's labor, and singing the tunes which perhaps reminded them of the girls they loved best. The old man was quite in an ecstacy.

"No, no," said he, speaking to Carrie, "they may talk till their tongues is tired about the beautiful city, and how grand they live, and what lively doin's they have there. I don't want nothin' to do with it. There ain't no peace nor rest there, day nor night. There ain't no sun to see, only just when he's over your head, and not much at that. I'd rather hear that cow-bell than all the noises they can git up."

And Carrie was by no means backward in expressing her sympathy with him in the more attractive scenes of their home.

Charlie had taken great liberties with Mr. Thompson's store during his absence, so that when the old gentleman came in, which he did very soon after seeing that all was well in the house, he took his hat off—a very unusual thing for him while in the store—and stood looking round in amazement.

"Where! where am I?"

Charles came up to him, with his bright eye sparkling with pleasure at beholding his old master again in his place. The old man shook his hand most cordially.

"Where am I, Charlie? What have you been a doing?"

"I thought I would fix up a little sir, as you gave me liberty to arrange matters as I pleased. So I have painted our barrel-covers, and all our standing casks. And I have put an oil cloth over the counter—you know it can be kept clean so much easier; and I have put, you see, a new baize on the desk, and painted the sides and legs, and given the cannisters a new coat over; and then I thought I would give the edges of the shelves a little trimming, and the posts you know, sir, were very much soiled; do you not think it looks better, sir? They say we have got the handsomest store for miles around; and it has only cost the value of the paint, I have done the work myself."

"Well, well, well; jist come here and let me sit down in my chair. I'm plaguey tired; what with one thing, and what with another, I'm clean tuckered out. And now come, tell me what's put this into your head? Who's been a putting you up to this?"

"No one, sir; but I thought it would give a more cheerful appearance to the store, and look more inviting to customers. And I believe it has had a good effect already; for we have had some of the best folks from the next town here, since you have been gone, sir. And they all said they should come soon again, when I told them you had gone to buy some new goods."

"They did, ha? Well, I hope the goods will please *them* better than they did *me* a buyin' on 'em. I see so many new-fangled patterns, and sich new-fangled stuffs, with such queer names, that my head was all in a blur, and I told 'em to give some on 'em all. So you'll see a sight, I guess; and maybe you can make out the names, and do something or another with 'em. If I had to manage 'em, I'd put the whole to auction, and let them buy what they liked best. But ain't you a most tired, Charlie, of this old dull place?"

"Oh, no, sir; why, it is not dull now, sir. You don't know how the customers come in. And I have sold more for *cash* than we commonly do. I make an allowance when they pay cash. It encourages them to bring the money, and that you know, sir, saves a good deal of trouble, and—"

Charlie rather hesitated to express what was upon his mind.

"What was you a goin' to say?"

"Why, sir, it is not my business, I know, but it seems to be a bad way for you and for them too, to have such long accounts."

"How are you goin' to help it, when they ain't got any money, and maybe nobody else won't trust 'em. Must the poor critters go a starving and we got plenty of the things? But if you can git the money out of 'em, well and good; but you must n't never let a poor body go away with a sorry heart, that wants maybe a little tea, or sugar, or molasses, or maybe a little flour, to make their short-cake. Don't you never do it."

"I will do as you say, sir."

"And you ain't lonesome, you say? and ain't a thinkin' all the time that you would like to go to the city and larn the ways there, and be a great merchant one of these days?"

"No, sir; I think we can make a great business here, sir, if we try. Why, Mr. Thompson, only think what a grand chance there is here to send off produce that the farmers raise; if we only could take it of them you know we could send every week by the sloop to New York, where it would bring a good price; and if we dealt liberally by the farmers we should have a great trade. Don't you think we might, sir?"

"I don't know what might be done in that way, I never tried it; I've gone on pretty much of a slow jog, and kept things just about so. But if you're a mind to try your new ways, and see what you can do, why you see I ain't a goin' to make no interference. But one thing you must n't never do while I'm above ground, Charlie—you must n't never go and buy any thing for credit."

"But you do all the buying, you know, Mr. Thompson."

"*You've* got to do it, arter this. You see, I've bid good-by to the city onst for all. Sich another trampus there, as I have had this time, would just, you see, make an eend of *me*. No, no, there's got to be so many folks there, and they're got so many new ways, and there's sich a hullabaloo there, all the time, it clean crazes me—no, no, you've got to do it all yourself. And that brings me to the pint I've been wanting to git at. You see, Charlie, I ain't got no boys, you know, of my own, and I'm gitting to be an old man. I feel just like getting my neck out of all the worry of business. I've been now five and forty years a standin' behind that counter and poking about the barrels and boxes, and what not, and now I'm a goin' to haul off."

"Oh, Mr. Thompson, you are not going to give up your business now when every thing is doing so well; you need have no trouble with it; I know if you will just be round here, to tell me sometimes what had best be done, I can do all the work, and take all the charge. Oh, sir, don't give it up now."

"Hush up, hush up; I ain't said I was goin' to give it up. Just hush up, and hear what I've got to say. You see I ain't got, as you know, any body of my name, and I've been a thinkin' that if I could git some nice young fellow that I could trust, and that would jist do as I say, and that would be kind to the poor folks, and that would be saving, and not be going ahead too fast, and spending more than he makes, and that would see and give good measure, and good weight, and pay as he went, and not be hurtin' the character of the store, why, I've been a thinkin' if I could find sich a one, it might do for me jist to take him in as a partner, and let him have say one third of the business the first year, and more afterward maybe. It might be a good thing, don't you think so?"

The countenance of Charles, as Mr. Thompson closed, had assumed a very sober expression, and was quite pale, and he looked down at his foot, which was making marks on the neatly sanded floor.

"What ails the boy, ain't you well? Maybe you don't like the thing."

"Oh, yes, sir; but I suppose, then, you would not want me any longer,"

"Hush up, hush up, don't talk so. How do you know but you are the very one I've been a thinkin' on: and now I'm goin' to tell you, Charlie, what my mind is. You've been a good fellow all the time you've been here. You mind what I say, you don't spend nothin', only for your folks to home, you work early and late, and you have done more to make things look bright and smart. than any one ever did here afore, and then I may as well say it first as last, I've taken a notion to you. You seem just as if you was my own flesh and blood. And I feel just as sure that you would n't do nothin' to harm me, than my own son would."

"Oh, thank you, sir."

"But hear what I was goin' to say, and hush up, or you'll set me a chokin', and then we shall have to leave things in *statter quo;* hush up, and now I tell you, after this, *you are to be my partner.*"

"Oh, Mr. Thompson!"

"Drat it, don't make sich a to-do—you see Charlie—you see."

But Mr. Thompson had become so excited by his sympathy with Charlie, whom he perceived to be almost beside himself with wonder and joy, that he began to see things double, and to make motions with his lips that did not amount to any thing.

"Oh, Mr. Thompson, what can I ever do to repay you? Oh, sir, I will work night and day, and do exactly as you say. Oh, what will they say at home."

Mr. Thompson after a short period of unavoidable silence on his part, went on again from where he had left off.

"You see, this comes of bringing up, for you won't lie, come what will, and you're civil to folks, and that brings the custom to the store; but you see I ain't a goin' to have a word said about this to a living soul but just your own folks. It ain't nobody's business but our own, we don't owe any one, and don't mean to, and now that's the end on it. No it ain't, neither—now, Charlie, what do you think I've got for you?"

"I don't know, sir, I am sure."

"Where's them books you made such a fuss about? the 'count books?"

"There, sir; I found that case at home, and I have painted it, and put it in behind the desk there, and the books are in it."

"Well, just come here," and Mr. Thompson moved along toward the desk behind the counter.

"Just git me the books."

"All of them, sir?"

"I want the one with the names in."

And Charlie handed out the ledger.

"Now just turn to your name—you've got it there, ain't you?"

"There, now that's it—Charles Leslie. Well, now, jist put down on the credit side, under your name, one thousand dollars. Put, put, put it down, don't you hear?"

Charley did as requested, but the big tears kept dropping on the ledger.

"Now, don't you think that I gi'n you that, for it ain't no sich thing; I am glad of it, and gladder than if it had been gi'n to me. It's come from a good friend o' yours, and it's to be your share of the capital to begin with; but hush up now. It's time to shut up shop, and you want to go home, and see your good sister; I most think she's an angel from heaven, and that all your good things is a comin' to you for her sake. She'll tell you all about the news, for I'm so husky and out o' breath I can't talk no more, and you need n't look so, as if you wanted to know all about this thing, for I sha'n't tell you nothin' more. So jist shut up shop and go home like a good boy."

It will hardly be worth while to tell how Charlie felt as he was barring the windows and closing things fast, for the night, nor how bright the stars shone to him, nor how beautiful the water looked, as it lay like a molten mirror reflecting the spangled heaven.

There was a heaven of joy in his young heart, for dear ones were to be told the news, and he was to feel their tears of happiness upon his cheek, and to know that he was that very hour to be the spring of hope and consolation to those whose sadness and sorrow he had long felt, and done his best to relieve. No, we need not tell all this. The heart that can not follow that bright boy as he bounds along the old beaten path that leads to his home, and read the meaning of his animated look, and enter without being told into the happy scene that awaits him, could not be much wiser for our description—and those who can will need no pen to make the vision clearer.

Blessed be God! our life is not all a waste. Sin has not taken away all its beauty. There are some tints from heaven yet streaming in the midst of the ruin. Hours of bliss, when the heart riots in untold ecstacy, amid the rich outpourings of social love. Hours that well repay months and years of firm endurance and patient toil. But they can only be known in their fullness by those who fear God and keep his commandments.

Mr. Leslie had indeed settled with Folger, but he had lost his home. It was to him a sad moment when he signed the deed which conveyed from him and his forever, the estate which had so long been the inheritance of his ancestors. But a stern necessity demanded it; he well knew there was no alternative between that and a slavish bondage.

The amount of surplus, after canceling all obligations to Folger, was small: only a few hundred dollars. And with this he was to begin the world at an age when its turmoils and care ought, in general, to be on the wane. He had realized the depth of the descent down which for years he had been sliding. There was indeed a slight hope that the young man who had taken such an interest in his affairs might recover the property out of which he had been wronged, but the hope was too faint to yield much encouragement to his heart.

His only refuge—and it would have been all-sufficient had he relied in full confidence upon it—was, in trusting to the care and guidance of that hand by which he had hitherto been sustained. Experience had done something toward confirming his confidence, but he knew not what further trials might be needed for the correction of his delinquencies. He tried to trust, but could not drive away his fears.

The morning after he had parted from his dear Carrie found him busily engaged at his usual labors, and the more so as he was making preparations to leave the city for a few days, in order to procure a place of residence for his family. The cloud which had encompassed him so long was lifting up; he did not know it, nor how soon a bright sky would be over him. He heard footsteps approaching his room, and in a few moments he had the pleasure of beholding the cheerful countenance of his friend Douglass. Mr. Douglass was a man of business and wasted few words in the small talk of life. He had therefore scarcely been seated when he began to make known the purpose of his visit.

"I have been thinking, Mr. Leslie, about your affairs, and as you have frankly answered my inquiries as to your true condition, you will excuse me for my interference. I have learned by a long course of experience that the best way to help a friend is to put him in a way to help himself. If I judge rightly, your desire is to engage in some employment that will enable you to provide for your family?"

"You have judged rightly, sir; and no labor that I can perform will be deemed too hard, if such an end can be accomplished."

"Exactly so, sir; your health, Mr. Leslie, I am convinced, is failing under your present circumstances. There are but few situations that I can think of, adapted to you, or rather—pardon my freedom, sir—for which, from the fact that you have not been trained to business, you are qualified."

"That is my greatest trial, Mr. Douglass."

"I have no doubt of that, sir, and you would not wish a situation as a mere sinecure."

"By no means, sir; I wish to earn my living in a way that would be honorable."

"I understand your feelings I believe, sir; and I will be short in my communication. I am about sending a vessel to Madeira; I need a person whom I can trust, to take charge of an outward cargo, principally of staves and flour, and one competent to select a return cargo of wine. In fact, the office is that of supercargo. I believe you are fully competent for the purpose. The voyage will be just what you need for the recovery of your health, and the perquisites will be handsome. Now, sir, if you think well of my offer, the situation is at your option."

"My dear sir, you have, by your preface to the offer you have made, forbidden me to think that this is a mere act of kindness on your part, and yet I can not but look upon it as such. If you really think my services can avail you, I most heartily accept your offer—and—"

"Nothing more need be said, sir; I have thought the matter well over, and have nothing further to say. A few weeks will be necessary before the vessel will be ready for sea, and you will probably need that time in making preparations to leave your family. You had better at once, sir, resign your present position, as you will need all your time, some for yourself, and some part of it will be required in confidential communication with me in reference to the business to be intrusted to your care. And further, sir, I would say, both Mrs. Douglass and myself will esteem it a peculiar favor if, after this, while you are in the city, you make our house your home. It will be more convenient, you know, under present circumstances for both of us. You will accede to this?" and Mr. Douglass arose and gave him his hand in parting.

"I can not say nay, sir. And yet your kindness is so unexpected, and my claim upon you so slight!"

"Not a word, sir; we have long wanted to know you for your daughter's sake. She has taken all our hearts by storm. So good morning, sir. But stop; one thing I had like to have forgotten. You may need some advances on account of your commissions, for extra expenses in making an outfit—that you shall have, sir; but we can arrange these matters at our fireside. Good-day, sir, and be sure to be with us at dinner time."

Mr. Leslie could only press the hand of his kind friend as he walked with him to the door.

And now his little room is light about him. Hope sparkles from the walls, and from the table, and from the slate roof before his window, and from the little patch of sky beyond. *He is now a man.* He is to know the bliss of being able, by his own energies, to provide for those his heart cherished so fondly. And from the fullness of his heart went up to heaven the incense of gratitude. A new life opened before him. It should be a life by the grace of God faithful to his obligations.

But a stranger scene awaited him! Another messenger with good tidings was approaching. It was a short time only after Mr. Douglass had left the room, when Mr. Leslie was summoned to the door by a gentle knock.

"Mr. Ralston! good morning, sir! I had not expected a visit from you so soon."

"It is quite unexpected to me too, I assure you sir."

The demeanor of young Ralston toward Mr. Leslie was marked with deference and respect. He bowed low to him as the latter gentleman cordially grasped his hand. And as he took the seat which was offered him, Mr. Leslie could not but notice that a deep flush had suffused his countenance.

"I am happy to be able to say to you, Mr. Leslie, that your difficulties with Mr. Folger have been brought to a favorable issue." And taking from his pocket-book a paper he handed it to that gentleman.

Mr. Leslie read it carefully, and then, turning to the young man,

"What does this mean, Mr. Ralston?"

"It means, sir, that Mr. Folger has given you a quit claim deed for that property; you are again in possession, or will be, so soon as I have ejected the persons who are busily engaged in despoiling it."

"How has this been obtained? for what consideration?"

"The consideration was probably of more consequence to Mr. Folger than perhaps you or I know of—at least than you probably have been made aware of. It was, however, without the receipt of money, and given freely. But, sir, that you may understand the matter, permit me to tell you what has taken place."

Clarence then related as well as he could the scenes of the last evening, with which the reader is now familiar. Mr. Douglass had said nothing to Mr. Leslie on the subject, as it had been agreed between them that Clarence should be the bearer of the tidings. It was impossible for Mr. Leslie, however, to remain seated during the recital. He was wrought up to the highest pitch of feeling, and he walked the room in a state of great excitement.

"What unmitigated villainy! my poor Carrie! where is she? I must fly to her!"

'Be composed, sir! all is well now; I parted from her this

morning, quite happy in the company of her good friends Mr. Thompson and Mrs. Crampton, and she is now no doubt well on her way home."

"But may not the villain make another attempt? I shall not feel safe to leave her a moment without my protection."

"Fear nothing on that account, sir. Mr. Folger is safely lodged in the hands of the high sheriff of this city to answer for a crime committed years ago. The evidence necessary having but just been gathered, he will now reap the wages of his iniquity."

"And if I understand aright," said Mr. Leslie, grasping the hand of the young man, "you have been the deliverer of my dear child! Oh, sir, I can not tell you what my heart feels; I can only thank you! yes I can pray God to bless you! Oh, you can not tell! God only can know, what my feelings would have been had your efforts failed!"

"I know, Mr. Leslie, that I can not realize what your sufferings might have been, but I must now in all candor say to you, that they could scarcely have exceeded mine."

Mr. Leslie looked at young Ralston with marked astonishment. "I hope, sir," continued Clarence, "that I shall not forfeit your regard by speaking thus plainly; I ask you to hear me patiently for one moment." But as Mi. Ralston's communication can not be of much interest to the reader, it being on subjects of a private nature, we must pass over it, merely remarking, that in the course of the conversation that ensued, Mr. Leslie was for the first time made acquainted with the fact that the young gentleman who had taken such an active part for his interest, was a son of Randolph Ralston of Clanmore. Neither need we give the result of the conversation further than to state that an agreement was entered into by the gentlemen to start on the morrow for Princesport.

Mr. Leslie was spending his last evening in company with the kind-hearted Mrs. Barstow, who had done what she could to make his sojourn with them agreeable. She heartily rejoiced in the change which his affairs had taken, and contrary to her usual habit, referred to circumstances in the past history of herself and husband.

"I've never told you about these things afore, Mr. Leslie, because me and my husband never like to talk about them.

But things are coming out now, and I s'pose they'll all be public in a few days. We've been dreadfully treated! But as it is all come out of our own family like, we did n't like to say any thing about it. Although Mr. Folger ain't no blood kin."

"Folger! What! Do you know Mr. Folger?"

"Folger! Oh, la me! But then I suppose there's a good many of that name! But, I'm a thinking there can't be many so bad. To *me* there ain't but *one Folger*. His first name is Tobias. He's a rich man, or he has passed for a rich man. But we're afraid it has n't been well come by. One thing we are sure of, some of it ain't.

"This man married our daughter, an only child—oh, she was a lovely creature as ever you laid your eyes on! and so mild and gentle, just like a dove!

"Well, Lucy—her name was Lucy—took a great fancy to him. He was a spruce young man as ever you see, and made a great show out in the country, and all said he was rich, and we living in a plain way, you know, it took with a young creature like Lucy. She was only seventeen. Her pa did n't fancy it much; the man, he said, was too smooth. He did n't like, he said, to see a man talk as if butter would n't melt in his mouth. But he could n't bear to baulk Lucy, so he let it go on. Well, they got married and came here to New York, and it all went very well for a while. They lived in a fine house, and all that; but it did n't last long. Something was the matter with Lucy, but we could'nt know what it was. She grew thin and pale, and wasted away, and at last she wrote to us, that she couldn't be happy any more, unless we came to live here too. She wanted her mother where she could see her once in a while. She felt as if she could n't live long if we did n't come. Well, what could we do? We had a snug property where we was, and lived comfortably. But we must sell it if we moved to the city. So at last we let it go, and took the money, and thought maybe with the income of it, and what little my husband might do, why, we could get along on it here. And so we might; but somehow Folger persuaded Barstow to put his money into some concern or other, I don't know now what it was, and that was the last of it. Folger somehow contrived to save himself, but ours was all lost. Well, there we was, out of house and home, and all our living was what my husband got from his place in Folger's office. But that had like to have been the worst of all. For some things happened, and Folger got a bad name, and it had like to have stuck to my husband too; for when Folger broke up his business it was the hardest thing for to find a place; people was afraid of him, and if it had n't been for a man that knew Barstow, and that he never could do a dishonest thing, we must have been in a dreadful condition. But we have made out to live."

"Did your daughter leave any children?"

"One child, only one! a little girl; and oh, that's the worst of the whole! You see I have n't told you yet that my father left quite a nice little property to my daughter. He might better have left it to us her parents, and we could have taken care of it for her. But he passed us clean over, and gave the whole of it to Lucy. It was a nice house and lot in the city. Well, what has become of that, we don't know. For my husband has such a mortal dislike of Folger that he never could bear to go near him to say any thing about it; and what is worse, we don't know whether the child is living or not! The moment the mother was dead, you see, he just took the child, and put it off among strangers, and we've never heard a word about it, and it's now seven years since our daughter died."

"Had she signed away the property before she died?"

"We don't know nothing about it! But we think by his putting the child away off so, among strangers, to keep it out of the way like, that maybe he has managed to dispose of it. But we don't know, and that's what Barstow has gone about this evening. He's heard that Folger has been took, and he's got a lawyer with him, and they are gone together to look after things. But if I could only know that the dear little thing was living, I should n't care. But it is hard to have it all just so."

"I believe, Mrs. Barstow, strange as it may appear, that your little grand-daughter is yet living, and is at my house, under the care of my wife and daughter!"

"Oh, dear, how you do talk!"

"I am sure of it, madam, if the Mr. Folger you mean should happen to be the one with whom I am acquainted. Where did he remove to from New York?"

"That we don't know, neither. He went off unbeknown to us. The case is, that when our Lucy died, we was most heart-broke. Oh, it was a dreadful thought how she'd been treated! You see he did n't beat her, nor starve her, nor turn her out of doors. He didn't do that. But to my notion he did worse! Oh, I can't tell you! But the poor thing, you see, had loved him, and her whole heart, I suppose, was just placed upon him as though he was all the time a loving her. But when she found he began to grow cold, and keep silent, and never speak a word to her, and maybe stay away whole days, and whole nights too, and when he'd come home never take no more notice of her than if she had only been a housekeeper, you see, she just drooped right down, wilted away, like a tender plant that you pull out of the ground and let the sun shine on its roots. And at last she heard things! But it ain't no matter. He killed her! He was her murderer! Though maybe he never laid a finger on her. And we felt it so then! and Barstow could n't never bear to go near him, nor to speak to him, about any thing. But now he feels, since things has turned up so, that it is his duty to look after matters a little. But, oh, dear! if it should be that you have got that dear blessed child! I shall be so happy!"

"It can be easily ascertained, Mrs. Barstow, when your husband returns. He will know whether we are speaking of the same individual. But I am glad to hear there is some hope that the child has property he can not deprive her of. He will most probably be stripped of every thing that he owns."

Mr. Leslie, however, was obliged to leave before the return of Mr. Barstow, but he gave such directions, that, should their anticipations prove correct, there would be no difficulty in having access to the child, which would be necessary, should a guardian be appointed over her.

It was a happy moment with Mr. Leslie, when he found himself seated by the side of his young friend Clarence Ralston, in the early-stage coach, and about to start from Hoboken, on their way to Princesport. A severe ordeal he had passed through. Brighter prospects now lay before him. Energy, and resolution, and patience would yet be needed. But hope was now present to stimulate and support.

The sun had just risen, and his rays were streaming across the summit of the great city, and every spire sparkled in the glorious light. And when he caught the first glimpse of his old dear home, the sun had circled the heavens, and was near to his setting.

Some sad thoughts were mingled with the thrill of pleasure, which the sight of home afforded. It was *his* no longer. Those trees planted by the hands of his ancestors, would no more yield their fruits to him! He and his could never more enjoy their shades, nor walk over those rich fields, with a sense of ownership!

True, he had suffered much in his efforts to retain the place, and had long been familiar with the probability that strangers must, ere long, possess it. But he could not know the peculiar trial of parting with a home sacred to the memory, until it had passed from his keeping.

At length they have stopped before the well-known gate, and a buzz is heard in the dwelling, and dear ones are hastening to meet, half-way, the husband and father. Nor are those who serve, far behind, for old Bob is hobbling round, from the kitchen-yard, and Aunt Luckie stands in the door with her clean apron already raised to wipe away the tears. Good heart, how she rejoiced to see the fond father embraceing in silence those from whom he had so long been separated. But why is that? and who that fair young man on whose arm lovely Carrie leans! and how proud and happy he appears! What does it mean? And little Willie comes tearing in from the garden, and almost upsets the good woman in his haste to get through the door, and into his father's arms. Willie has missed that father much, and his tears are flowing because he sees how pale his face is now, and he does not like the change. And Luckie cries out too,—she can not help it.

"Ah, Luckie, you are sorry to see me, ha!" and away she runs to hide somewhere and have her cry out.

"Father," said Carrie "wait, wait for Daddy. He is trying to get to you."

And her father turns, and both hands of master and servant are tightly clasped together.

"Oh, master, 'Ratio! master 'Ratio! Tank God, me see you once more!"

But the tear on the old man's face tells more than his words can, and the master dares not trust himself to speak; nor does the old man need ought else beside that silent grasp of the hand, to assure him that his master's heart is true as ever.

And now they are all gathered in the old parlor, and Clarence seems quite at home, and Carrie has a glow upon her cheek more bright than has been seen since her days of childhood. And the curls which dangle about her fair neck seem to have been arranged with unusual care. And as she walks the room, or sits and holds converse with her dear father, with every feature sparkling with beauty and life, the eye of that young man rests upon her, and seems to be drinking in sweet draughts of happiness.

And now quick steps come through the hall, and a tall bright boy, almost a man in height, is in the door and in his father's arms.

"Charlie! my dear, good boy! How glad I am to see you!"

And well that father may press him to his breast, and then, holding him off, look with admiration on his manly son. For that boy has proved a fond and faithful keeper of his father's trust. By day and night has he been ever ready to supply his place, and every dollar he has earned has been sacredly devoted to filial duty, and his heart is now aching to unfold the joyful tidings of his new condition, and to relieve his father's heart from anxiety about the future.

And now parents, and children, and servants, are all bowing down together. It is an hour that calls for special thanksgiving, and the father has learned from the trials of the past that there is no place where support can be so surely obtained, as at the throne of grace. And amid the sunshine of joy, with his flock about him, how can he refrain from leading them to praise with him, the kind hand that had so graciously led them!

Blest hour of sorrow! if it bows the heart
In sweet submission to the chastening rod;
Blest hour of gladness! if its joys impart
The love that pours its incense up to God.
The purest bliss that thrills the bosom here
Is but a ray of light from heaven's brighter sphere.

CHAPTER XXIX.

Clanmore had been to Clarence the scene of so many calamities! He had witnessed there so little that his memory wished to recall! Death, too, had done his work there under circumstances so appalling that, beautiful as was its situation, he had resolved to dispose of it, and commence for himself a new home, where the objects around him would not be constantly bringing to mind the scenes of the past. He was now about to visit it for the last time in order to make arrangements for its sale.

It was a lovely day, and as he rode through the highly cultivated fields of that fine valley, and beheld the marks of that care which had been his father's life-work, he could not but heave a sigh at the thought how soon a stranger's hand would be directing its improvement, and perhaps changing the whole aspect of the place.

As he drew near the old mansion, and its noble proportions attracted his notice, he could not but admire the skill manifested in its construction, and the care which had preserved it for nearly a century in a condition as fresh and firm as though just finished. It had, too, a more cheerful aspect than he ever had remarked before. The heavy shutters of the windows were all opened, and rooms which had seldom been permitted to receive the light were now visible through the openings of the rich drapery. And there was an air of life about the premises which he had no expectation of beholding.

"Massa Clarence! massa Clarence! you welcome home!" It was Juba, who had approached unnoticed, and thus saluted his young master. Clarence at once gave the old servant his hand.

"Ah, Juba! I am glad to see you, I can hardly feel that I

an coming home. It is a sad place to me! and I think it must be to you. I hope I shall soon get you all into a new home! Is there company here, Juba?"

"No, no, Massa Clarence! no company but just the kitchen folks and Maggie. But I don't know what get into that woman. She been and opened all the windows of the best rooms. Old missus neber allow them to be open only maybe for the quality folks. But that woman will do her own way."

Clarence knew that Juba had some jealous feelings in reference to Maggie, now the sole mistress in the house department. He felt therefore no alarm as to her doings. And seeing her honest face smiling upon him as he was about to ascend the stoop, he left Juba to his ruminations, and receiving her hearty welcome, followed into the house.

"You looked so airy here, Maggie, I almost expected to find company!"

"Ah, no, Mr. Clarence, there's no company to bless us now-a-days. But, seeing I expected you along about these days, I thought it might be better just to make the house put on a gleesome air to you. It's no gude way, as it seems to me, to be livin' in the dark when a body can have the clear sun a shining in, and the air of heaven a blowing through. And I wad have you just gang with me and look at the beautiful rooms. Ye have not been in them for a lang while, if ever, as I'm a thinking, for the mistress was jealous of opening them, except at a gathering of the great folks. And of late years, ye ken yourself, there was no much company."

Clarence willingly accompanied her, for in truth some of the rooms he never remembered having seen, except in the dim light afforded by an open door. There was the blue room, as Maggie called it, from the fact that the drapery of the windows, and the bottoms of the chairs, and the covering of the sofa, were all of that color. It was the first they entered. The door into it opened from the wide hall. It was indeed richly furnished. A heavy Wilton carpet covered the whole floor; massive high-back chairs; highly polished card-tables; a tall book-case; and a long marble table, all of black walnut, stood in different positions around the room, shining as though they had just received a new coat of varnish. Varnish, however, would no more have been allowed in those days, on valuable furniture, than upon their powdered wigs. The polishing had all been accomplished by the hand, with the aid of wax and brush.

The curtains of the windows, as well as the bottoms of the chairs, and the covering of the sofa, were of silk damask. All the wood-work of the furniture was curiously carved, and seemed designed to be as costly in its execution, and as difficult to keep free from dust, as the ingenuity of man could devise.

As a whole, however, the impression of elegance and stability could not be mistaken.

Clarence stood a moment looking at the various articles of furniture, and then at the wainscotted walls of the room, with its heavy cornice around the ceiling, tipped at intervals with gilt, and giving a fine lively appearance to what would otherwise have had a heavy look.

"It all looks, Maggie, as though you had bestowed much care upon it. Every thing is as fresh and free from dust and stain as though newly made."

"Thank you for saying it. I thought you wad be pleased to see the sun once a shining through the big windows. And sich a sight as is to be seen from them, there ain't in many a mile."

Clarence stepped to the window. It was the first time he had ever looked from them. A rich lawn spread immediately before him, on which nothing could be seen but the thick velvet grass closely shaven. A few large shade trees were scattered about it; but none of them obstructed the view beyond. The valley with its winding stream, its fields and forests, lay in panoramic distinctness, and even the blue tops of the eastern mountains, some forty miles distant, could be clearly seen.

"It is a charming prospect, Maggie!"

"You may well say that! The like is not to be seen gae where you will—not this side of the big water. Ye may see the like in Scotland, but I doubt an ye find anither like this ane, short of that. And now will ye jist look at this ither apartment?" And from the bunch of keys she selected one that fitted a large door, so formed as to be taken, by a slight view, as part of the wainscotting.

"I call this one the sunny room, for I ken not what else to name it. For it has a grand chance to the sun-light on a times of the day, gin it has fair play, and no kept out by the shutters. There now, there is no one hour of the day, winter nor summer, that if there is any sunshine without, that ye canna have it here. And the curtains, and the seats, and the sofa, and all, is of the same color. It makes a body's heart dance. Sae light an airy and pleasant to the view."

Clarence walked around in silent admiration of its neatness, and at the same time with sad thoughts at the reflection how little joy had really been imparted to their owner by all the expense lavished in the fitting up!—and Maggie continued,

"I never remember seein' these rooms used but once, and then it was during the hard winter, when the great gineral lay at the Forge. Him and his lady, and a smart retinue of ginerals, and servants, and what not, came to a visit, and your mother had both the rooms opened to onst, and a grand sight it was, for the table was loaded with silver, which had been stowed away from common; and the chandelier that hangs there was full of burning wax candles. And the officers was glistening with their regimentals. But the greatest sight to me, was the gineral himself. Ah, me! I'm a thinkin' he must have had Scotch blood in him. I could think of naething but Wallace, or Douglass, or the Bruce. But he had nae a bit of the Scotch tongue. It was nae much he said, but it was as precise and staid-like as auld Knox himself. I'm a thinkin' ane wad nae want to be told twice to do his bidding, for to my mind he wad expect it to be done and no questions asked But that's the only time I remember these rooms both to be opened. Ye see yoursel they are designed for one and the same purpose. And ye approve of my opening them, Mr Clarence? But, if you say the word, it will be but a short work to bar the shutters."

"Oh, certainly Maggie, certainly I think you have done right! It has given me a new view of the place. I almost wish it was so that I could feel satisfied to live here."

"And waes me! and what for no! and have nae I been a brushin' up, and making a' things look like new, and for your ain sake! And where wad you live? Ye wad nae be forsaking the auld homested that has been sae many generations the home of your fathers? waes me! and what can the bairn mean?"

"Why, Maggie, you know how sad to me must be every thing connected with this place. I need not repeat to you the many trying scenes I witnessed. What contentions about property! What hard feelings between parents and children! What hard words, sometimes! and the last of all, what sad events conspired to close the lives of my parents and brother! I fear there can be no blessing to its inheritor."

"And what for no? Do you think the Lord wad visit upon the innocent the doings of them that—waes me that I must say it!—the doings of them that feared him not? Gin ye had mingled in the fray, and had sought to get your share, and more than your share, by fair means or foul, ye might then weel misdoubt fornent the blessing. But your hands are clear of them doings, that I weel know. Ye stood for the right, and peace of your parents. Ye had nae longings for the place, and wad willingly have seen them have it that hankered sae for it. But the Lord wad nae have it sae. It was decreed to you. And yours it is, fair and square. And are ye goin' to despise the good land that has been put into your hands? Just as if the blessing could nae come to you here as anywhere else—gin you seek in the right way?"

This was a view of the matter Clarence had not taken; and so intent was he upon its consideration, that for some time there was not a word spoken by either—at length Maggie resumed,

"And what wad you do with the place, Mr. Clarence? Surely it wad grieve your heart to see strangers a walking over your father's lands! and altering things to suit their mind! and a' the old tenants driven off, and maybe this grand house, fit for a prince to live in, turned into a nasty inn! and clowns a drinking their punch in the very room where ye now stand!"

"Maggie, Maggie! say no more. Perhaps I have judged wrong! I believe I have! I must come here and try to set up a new state of things. But perhaps you may not fancy the lady I should get for my wife. You might feel obliged to leave!"

"I was nae thinking of myself, Mr. Clarence. I've been here, to be sure, many years, and hae seen many things I did nae fancy, and hae had to put up with many things that flesh and bluid was nae sae weel pleased to bear. But I ay mended the matter by thinkin' that, be where I might, sin and sorrow wad be biding near neighbors, and ready to be visiting me, whether or no, and I have nae great fears that the leddy wha wad be pleasing to ye could be a very hard ane for others to please. But is it sae? and hae ye found one to your mind?"

"I believe I have, Maggie."

"And the Lord be praised for that! and now, do ye nae remember how I told ye it wad be sae? When ye were sae sair and heart-broken because your mither forbad ye to have aught to do with that beautiful lass that ye was sae taken with, did nae I tell ye just to go on and mind your parents and do your duty like a gude bairn, and things wad turn to the right for ye in the end?"

"Yes, you did, Maggie, and I had the pleasure of hearing my mother thank me on her dying bed for having yielded to her so patiently, and requesting me not to be influenced in my choice of a wife by the motives she had formerly urged."

"I heered her say it while ye was standing by her bed-side, and the tears bedewing your eyes. Oh, there was a great change in her thoughts when once the hand of death began to touch her! and she went out of the world a very different person from what she was when a livin' in it. We maun hope for the best. Some canna have the vail taken away until death comes and gives it a rent. But are ye in truth goin' to bring us a leddy? and where do ye get her? and when are ye coming?"

"In a few days I expect to be married, Maggie, and if this is to be my home, I see not but that you have every thing in readiness; and I know not, if she were a princess, that she could expect a much handsomer home to come to. But what would you say, Maggie, if I should tell you that the lady I expect to marry was once that same pretty girl I loved so much?"

"The Lord be praised! can it be so?"

"It is so, Maggie! only she is much more beautiful and lovely now. She has been through scenes of trial, and will know how to feel for the poor and those who are dependent upon the will of others; and as I shall see to it that she has plenty of means at her own disposal, I know she will suffer no one, far or near, to want what money will procure for their comfort."

"The Lord be praised! and may all your rich hopes come truly to pass! But, Mr. Clarence, I hae ane thing to say to ye, and then I have done. Ye maun begin right as ye mean to end right. Ye are no' accountable for the past. That is gone and sealed up to the great day. But ye are the master now. And as the doin's here from this day forrard will be laid to your door, gin ye allow them within your gates to break the Sabbath-day, and spend it in strolling through the woods, and idle talking, and jesting, and turning their backs upon the house of God, because it is not very convenient to go there, ye will have to answer for it—ye yourself!"

"I know it, Maggie, and I have resolved what to do. I shall at once build a small neat church close at hand, and convenient for all the tenants. And I intend that I and my household shall go to the house of God in company. And I shall also build a comfortable house for my good foster-parent, Mr. Rice, and he and his good wife shall live near us, and we will have him for our minister."

"Oh, that will be like heaven upon earth!"

"And I design, Maggie, to have family worship, night and morning, and all the servants and hired men living in our house shall be present. I know, Maggie, there is no blessing to the household that does not call upon God."

"Oh, that I should live to see this day! and will you wife be to the same mind with you, do ye think, in this matter?"

"Yes, most cordially! She could scarcely love me, Maggie, if she thought I had no heart to serve the Lord!"

"Only to think of the wonders of the Lord's hand! 'The night cometh and also the day!' There is a blessing for Clanmore yet! Ah, Mr. Clarence, you may think it nae much that a puir body like me has been long a prayin' for you, and for a blessing upon them that has gone, and upon the place, and the people. But it is even sae—and if to no one else, there is a clear streak in the sky to my een. The finger of God is in it."

Clarence having fully determined to make Clanmore his future home immediately ordered some improvements which he thought would please the taste of his Carrie, and then repaired to Hazleton that he might put a stop to the labors of those who had been despoiling that fine property. The powers with which he had been invested were sufficient to accomplish that, and also to make a disposition of the timber already cut for the benefit of the true owners.

A few days were required for this, and for what arrangements he thought necessary, in preparation for bringing home the dear one to whom his heart had so faithfully clung.

And then the sumptuous coach, the old "state carriage"

which his mother had kept for special occasions, with the four noble blood-horses trained for her own use, were ordered. And with a joyful heart he departed for the purpose of consummating his long cherished-wish.

It had been concluded, before he left Princesport, that no steps should be taken for the removal of Mr. Leslie's family, until Clarence should return. But as the time was passing away, in which Mr. Leslie would be able to remain at home, and as he might be called away sooner than he anticipated, he made a partial bargain for a dwelling-house. It was of small dimensions, and greatly in contrast with their old house. Yet not a murmur was heard. Parents and children had together been in the deep waters. The rod had been upon them—it had proved the chastening rod of a father. They had turned with loving hearts to Him who smote them, and as they rebelled not, when suffering under the severest stroke, so as their trials began to lessen they were happily prepared to take with gratitude every alleviating circumstance.

The day when Carrie was to give her hand to the man her heart had chosen, was to be determined also at his return. It was therefore with mingled feelings that she heard the announcement "that Mr. Ralston had arrived." And when she saw the splendid establishment which had drawn up at the gate, and beheld the bright smile of her lover as he hastened to meet her, a strange fluttering affected her maiden heart. The beginning of the final scene was indeed at hand!

We will pass over particulars which the reader can as well fill up from his or her own imagination. And also the substance of a long interview which young Ralston and his lovely Carrie enjoyed, on the afternoon of his arrival. It must have been a happy one, if we may judge from the appearance of Carrie as she entered the apartment where her father and mother were seated, leaning on the arm of Clarence, and holding in her hand a paper, which, with a smile of joy, almost belied by the tear that fell upon her fair cheek, she with a kiss placed in her father's hand, and asked him to read.

It was a short document, and easily comprehended, although its effect upon Mr. Leslie was almost too much for his manliness.

"What am I to understand by this?" And he looked with intense interest, first at his daughter and then at young Ralston, whose countenance also manifested deep excitement.

Carrie at once threw her arms about the neck of her father.

"It means, dear father, that he to whom you have given your Carrie, has put you in full possession of your home once more. It is yours now, I hope for life. O may you long, long, live to enjoy it!"

"Believe me, Mr. Leslie," said Clarence, "your struggles with the stern realities you have had to encounter would long ago have ceased, could I, consistently with peculiar circumstances have interposed as my heart dictated. This estate, sir, has been virtually yours from the hour you sold it and released yourself from the claims of that bad man."

"You was then the real purchaser!"

"I was, sir; I concealed my interest in the affair by employing an agent, lest my act might be construed into an attempt *to purchase* the hand I wished to win *by love alone*. Yet, had I failed in my pursuit, and your daughter, whom I have loved for years, been unable to return my affection, it would have made no difference in the disposition of this property. But my dear sir, I can now rejoice that all my purposes have been accomplished. I have won the prize I so intensely longed for, and you are again the master of your own homestead."

"And you are the unknown friend, too who has interposed for my son, and purchased an interest for him in the store of Mr. Thompson?"

Clarence slightly smiled.

"I may acknowledge it now, sir. But I did that for Charley's sake alone. I saw how ambitious he was to get ahead, and I wished to encourage the noble spirit he manifested in endeavoring to aid his family."

"And you too have used an influence even in a foreign land for the benefit of my dear Henry? I have a letter which has just reached me, giving information of a singular interference of a gentleman at Canton in his favor, supplying him with means, and procuring for him a situation which will probably be to him a future fortune!"

Carrie was looking earnestly at the blushing countenance of the noble youth whose hand she held, to know whether this charge was also true, when another smile of acknowledgment caused her to throw herself upon his bosom.

"My own dear, noble Clarence!"

"I am richly repaid, had I done a thousand times as much. I have loved you for yourself, and all connected with you for your sake, and shall ever hold them as my own dearest kindred."

"And although we can never repay you," said Mrs. Leslie, rising and placing her hand upon his arm, "for the light and happiness you have shed upon us, yet all that parents can do while we live, to comfort and bless you, I promise for myself and my dear husband."

"I accept the offer, Mrs. Leslie, and ask a mother's kiss."

"My dear, dear son!"

"All I can say, Mr. Ralston," said Mr. Leslie, as he held the hand of his future son, "would indeed feebly express what I feel! May this dear child prove to you what she has to me, and carry to your heart and your house the blessing which has never failed to enrich all whom she has ever loved."

"And now, dear father," said Carrie, "you will not feel a necessity for going abroad. You will now have a competence, and can spend the remainder of your days in the bosom of your family."

"My dear child, much as I love you all, and pleasant as my home would now be to me, no consideration would induce me to step aside from the path into which providence has led me. The bitterest ingredient in the cup which I have had to drink was the thought that I was disabled by my past training from taking some station in the ranks of useful labor for your support. Now a way is open for me to do something, to learn something, and I wish to live long enough to prove to you all that your father has the resolution to undertake, and the ability to accomplish, his duty as a man. I owe it to my dear boys. I owe it to you all. As you love me, all of you, throw no hinderance in my way."

Tidings fly fast through a household, and while the happy parents and children were yet reveling in the joy which these communications had imparted, the door was gently opened, and two individuals appeared, each endeavoring to urge the other in first.

"Oh, come in, Mr. Thompson, come in!" and Carrie hastened toward him, all the party following, to bid the old man welcome.

"Come in too, Aunt Luckie!" but Luckie, seeing the old

gentleman safe in, betook herself speedily away. Luckie was too happy to stay long in any one place.

Mr. Thompson seemed much overcome not only by walking, but by his kind reception; and without making any reply to the expressions of joy at his presence among them, he quietly took a seat, and kept his handkerchief moving about his face either to hide his confusion or something else.

"Mr. Thompson," said Mrs. Leslie, "you must never knock again at any door of this house, nor wait for any one to usher you in. We consider you a friend entitled at all times to a free entrance. The very sight of you warms our hearts."

"And my house, too," said Carrie, as she stood by him with her hand on his shoulder "wherever it may be," and she looked up smilingly at Clarence, "will be happier to me, no matter how happy it may otherwise be, when I shall see your kind face beaming upon me within its walls."

"And I, too, Mr. Thompson," Clarence chimed in, almost interrupting the lovely speaker. "My home, my heart, and my hand, will ever be at your service; such friendship as yours I value beyond all price."

The old man had to keep his handkerchief moving.

"You have all said enough! I don't want to hear nothin' more; hush up, hush up." This he said by way of smothering his own feelings. "I ain't maybe long to live, for I know I've been a jogging along for a good many years, and there can't be a great many on 'em left. But in all I've seen, there ain't been nothin' that has given me half the pleasure that that woman has gin me by what she has just telled me. But I've always been a thinkin' that a man as had such a daughter as Miss Car'line, must sooner or later have good luck a coming to him."

"Oh, Mr. Thompson!"

"You may say Oh, but it don't alter the case, and I can tell this young gentleman—who I don't feel no ill-will to—that if so be it is that he has had the good luck to get her to say Yes, I hope he'll be thankful for the mercy, and make much on her. But what I've come for now, ain't just to tell you all how happy I am to hear of all the good that has come to this dear family. I was a comin' in, when that woman came and took hold of me. She is a good friend to you all, as I take it, for I never see a creetur so clean out of her head for joy. But you see Captain Thomas, of the sloop *Fanny*, has just got in, and he came into my store a bit ago, and says he, 'Thompson, I've got a passenger in my boat as I don't know what to do with. She's been the sickest creature all the way that you ever see. We've had a rough time on it, to be sure, and been pretty well knocked about all the way, but I thought when we got to the dock she'd be better, but she ain't able to stir. And she says she's come to see Mr. Leslie, and that he lived in her family.' 'Hush up,' says I, 'gin that's the case I know her too, and I'll go right aboard;' and so I did. It's the woman. But I see she wanted women's help, and so I went home and sent my galls right aboard to see what they could do for her. She's dreadfully pestered for breath, and has other ailin's besides."

"Can it be that Mrs. Barstow has come, father?"

"It is even so, Miss Car'line, I've seen her with my own eyes."

Carrie determined at once to go down, and was waiting for her father to accompany her, when the announcement was made "that a carriage had just come to the gate" and immediately a very fleshy woman, was seen waddling up toward the stoop. Carrie and Mr. Leslie hastened to her, and each taking an arm helped her into the house.

"You will feel better soon, Mrs. Barstow: the motion of the boat, and the air of the cabin have not agreed with you."

"It almost suffocates me to think of that little confined bit of a place. I almost felt like going down into a tomb when I got to the bottom of the cabin stairs. But I dare n't say a word, for I was in such a stew to get here! And then such a time as we've had! The wind a blowin', and the waves a tossin' us about, and all the cabin things a flying, first one side and then the other! I just set right down on the floor and held fast to any thing that was n't a movin'. And then sich a sick critter as I've been! and no air! not a breath to get, and the doors all shut. I clean give up, and thought it would be the last of *me*. But, oh, dear! I'm so happy to see your face again!" turning to Carrie, "and you look a great deal better, Mr. Leslie! and, do tell! is that lear child with you?"

"What, Lucy? Oh, yes, you shall see her in a few moments."

And Carrie hastened from the room to prepare the child to see her hitherto unknown relative.

"And you feel assured, Mrs. Barstow, that Mr. Folger of this place was the man who married your daughter?"

"Oh, it's all come out now, wonderful. He has been took, you see, and when he found it was all up with him, he was so cut down that he was just as humble as a kitten. And Mr. Barstow has been appointed guardian, and the property is all safe, and a pretty property it is too! But somehow he did n't get his deserts, for he contrived to throw them off their guard, and has slipped off to sea somewhere or another. But, oh, dear! Is that my baby!" And Mrs. Barstow raised her hands in amazement. Carrie had prepared little Lucy for a pleasant interview, and the child seemed anxious to behold one to whom she could look as a mother.

"And is this my darling Lucy?" And close to the breast of her who had once folded the parent in a like embrace, did the fond grand-parent draw her offspring, and they wept together.

"The very image of her mother!" And holding her off she wiped away the tears and gazed upon the child.

"And you will love me yet! won't you dear?"

"I love you now, dear grandmother."

"Oh, you darling!" and again the child hung upon her breast, and then tears flowed freely.

"That I should ever live to see this day! But you need n't fear that you shall ever be taken far away from this dear young lady! We shall live near to her, wherever she lives."

"You mean to leave the city, Mrs. Barstow."

"You see, Mr. Leslie, Barstow can't stand it there! what with standin' at the desk, and what with other things, he grows worse, and he's sick of the city."

"I don't wonder at it," said Mr. Thompson, who had been looking on with no little interest. "I'm sick of it too."

"And do you live there?"

"I've seen enough on it, without living there. It ain't a place fit to live or to die in."

"Oh, well, they have to die there, whether or no. The air is bad, and not much of it any how. And my husband is glad of a chance to get out of it; and so he says we'll go somewhere or another, and I've made up my mind that where-ever that dear young lady lives, we will get a little place near at hand, and then Lucy can see her old friend, and I know Barstow will get his flesh again, or some on it, at the least, when he ain't all the time a breathin' pizen into his stomach, and has something green and fresh to look at."

Splendid weddings are now such common events, that a discription of one could scarcely prove interesting; we must therefore leave to the imagination of our readers the beautiful bride and her happy lord in all their tasteful decorations, and the joy that thrilled their bosoms when the solemn rite was ended, and the minister of God pronounced them man and wife.

The morning which followed the wedding was one of nature's most perfect specimens, where sky, and earth, and water, presented their fine contrasts blending in harmonious beauty.

The sun had just risen over the vast extent of water, and his slanting rays rested on the distant headlands, and the white sails, and far over upon the summits of the western hills, waking all nature into life and song.

Before the gate of Carrie's much-loved home stood the beautiful establishment which was destined to convey her, from that which had been the delight of her childhood, to the mansion where, hereafter, her pleasant words, and kind care, and cheerful smile, were to shed their light, and create within her influence a home that all might praise.

The whole family have followed the departing couple to the gate, and the liveried servant stands holding the open carriage-door ready for their entrance.

"One more kiss my dear dear child." Her arms are around her father's neck—a moment she rests in his silent embrace, and then with him whom she has chosen for her life's partner, takes her seat within the carriage.

"Miss Carrie, my young missus!" and the rough hand of old Bob is raised toward her. She saw the tears on his old honest face, and her heart, already excited to the utmost by the parting scene, would not allow that she should speak his name or say good-by, but she pressed the hand he had held out, and he saw her eye dropping the silent tear.

"God bless, you, Miss Carrie!"

The scene has closed, and all are returning to the house but Aunt Luckie and old Bob.

"I knew it, and I always knew it; she was worthy to have

a prince, and if he ain't a prince he's as good as one, and as rich as one; was n't it beautiful, Daddy?"

The old man was straining his eyes to keep as long as possible a view of the receding carriage; he did not remove his gaze as Luckie spoke, but merely replied,

"Pretty nuff."

"And only to think, Daddy, how it has turned out! Did n't I tell you he had taken them into the wilderness to give them vineyards and oliveyards from thence, and now he's done it."

"Me know nuttin' 'tall about dat, Miss Luckie! me no see dem tings you talk about! and den you say toder day, how changed Massa 'Ratio!"

"And don't you think, Daddy, there is a great change in him? He is so good!"

"Miss Luckie, you don't know nuttin tall about dat man! Massa 'Ratio no change, neber! Ain't I 'tended dat man when he baby! ain't I lived wid him all my life! Massa 'Ratio good baby, good boy, good man; you know maybe about dese tings you talk so much dem vines! and de olives! me no see dem tings 'bout here, nowhere! But Massa 'Ratio *always* good man! and me tank de Lord he got his old place once more! dere ain't no such in dis breathin world! me want to live and die here, and den dey must carry me to dat churchyard where old massa lay."

Aunt Luckie saw that her efforts were vain to make the old man understand what to her seemed so beautiful and true. She therefore shut the gate and walked thoughtfully toward the house; while Bob hobbled round into the kitchen-yard, to his favorite seat on the chopping block.

Dear reader, we must again part. And as there will be always some last words unsaid, when friends are separating, which they wish had been thought of before it was too late, so probably it may be with us. But if the interview has been pleasant, let that thought atone for omissions.

THE END.

1864.

A NEW CATALOGUE OF

BOOKS

ISSUED BY

CARLETON  PUBLISHER,

413 Broadway,

NEW YORK.

Mrs. Mary J. Holmes' Works.

DARKNESS AND DAYLIGHT.—*Just published.* 12mo. cl. $1.50
LENA RIVERS.— . . A Novel. do. $1.50
TEMPEST AND SUNSHINE.— . do. do. $1.50
MARIAN GREY.— . . . do. do. $1.50
MEADOW BROOK.— . . . do. do. $1.50
ENGLISH ORPHANS.— . . do. do. $1.50
DORA DEANE.— . . . do. do. $1.50
COUSIN MAUDE.— . . . do. do. $1.50
HOMESTEAD ON THE HILLSIDE.— do. do. $1.50

Artemus Ward.

HIS BOOK.—An irresistibly funny volume of writings by the immortal American humorist and showman; with plenty of comic illustrations. . . 12mo. cloth, $1.25

Miss Muloch.

JOHN HALIFAX, Gentleman. A novel. 12mo cloth, $1.50
A LIFE FOR A LIFE.— do. do. $1.50

Charlotte Bronte (Currer Bell).

JANE EYRE.—A novel. . . . 12mo. cloth, $1.50
SHIRLEY.— do. . . . . . do. $1.50
VILLETTE.— do. . . . . . do. $1.50

Edmund Kirke.

AMONG THE PINES.—A thrilling work. 12mo. cloth,
MY SOUTHERN FRIENDS.— do.
DOWN IN TENNESSEE.—*Just published.* do.

Cuthbert Bede.

VERDANT GREEN.—A rollicking, humorous novel of student life in an English University; with more than 200 comic illustrations. . . . . 12mo. cloth, $1.50

Richard B. Kimball.

WAS HE SUCCESSFUL?— A novel. 12mo. cloth, $1.50
UNDERCURRENTS.— do. do. $1.50
SAINT LEGER.— do. do. $1.50
ROMANCE OF STUDENT LIFE.— do. do. $1.50
IN THE TROPICS.—Edited by R. B. Kimball. do. $1.50

Epes Sargent.

PECULIAR.—One of the most remarkable and successful novels published in this country. . . 12mo. cloth, $1.50

Miss Augusta J. Evans.

BEULAH.—A novel of great power. 12mo. cloth, $1.50

A. S. Roe's Works.

A LONG LOOK AHEAD.— A novel. 12mo. cloth, $1.50
TO LOVE AND TO BE LOVED.— do. . . do. $1.50
TIME AND TIDE.— do. . . do. $1.50
I'VE BEEN THINKING.— do. . . do. $1.50
THE STAR AND THE CLOUD.— do. . . do. $1.50
TRUE TO THE LAST.— do. . . do. $1.50
HOW COULD HE HELP IT.— do. . . do. $1.50
LIKE AND UNLIKE.— do. . . do. $1.50
A NEW NOVEL.—*In Press.* do. $1.50

Walter Barrett, Clerk.

OLD MERCHANTS OF NEW YORK.—Being personal incidents, interesting sketches, bits of biography, and gossipy events in the life of nearly every leading merchant in New York City. Two series. . . 12mo. cloth, each, $1.50

T. S. Arthur's New Works.

LIGHT ON SHADOWED PATHS.—A novel. 12mo. cloth, $1.50
OUT IN THE WORLD.—*In press.* do. . do. $1.50
NOTHING BUT GOLD.— do. do. . do. $1.50

The Orpheus C. Kerr Papers.

A COLLECTION of exquisitely satirical and humorous military criticisms. Two series. . 12mo. cloth, each, $1.25

M. Michelet's Works.

LOVE (L'AMOUR).—From the French. 12mo. cloth, $1.25
WOMAN (LA FEMME.)— do. . . do. $1.25
WOMAN MADE FREE.—French of D'Hericourt, do. $1.50

Novels by Ruffini.

DR. ANTONIO.—A love story of Italy. 12mo. cloth, $1.50
LAVINIA; OR, THE ITALIAN ARTIST.— do. $1.50
VINCENZO; OR, SUNKEN ROCKS.— 8vo. cloth, $1.50

Rev John Cumming, D.D., of London.

THE GREAT TRIBULATION.—Two series. 12mo. cloth, $1.25
THE GREAT PREPARATION.— do. . do. $1.25
THE GREAT CONSUMMATION.— do. . do. $1.25
TEACH US TO PRAY.— do. $1.25

Ernest Renan.

THE LIFE OF JESUS.—Translated by C. E. Wilbour from the celebrated French work. . . 12mo. cloth, $1.50
RELIGIOUS HISTORY AND CRITICISM.— 8vo. cloth, $2.50

Charles Reade.

THE CLOISTER AND THE HEARTH.—A magnificent new novel, by the author of "Hard Cash," etc. . 8vo. cloth, $1.50

The Opera.

TALES FROM THE OPERAS.—A collection of clever stories, based upon the plots of all the famous operas. 12mo. cl., $1.25

J. C. Jeaffreson.

A BOOK ABOUT DOCTORS.—An exceedingly humorous and entertaining volume of sketches, stories, and facts, about famous physicians and surgeons. 12mo. cloth, $1.50

Fred. S. Cozzens.

THE SPARROWGRASS PAPERS.—A capital humorous work, with illustrations by Darley. . . 12mo. cloth, $1.25

F. D. Guerrazzi.

BEATRICE CENCI.—A great historical novel. Translated from the Italian; with a portrait of the Cenci, from Guido's famous picture in Rome. . . 12mo. cloth, $1.50

Private Miles O'Reilly.

HIS BOOK.—Rich with his songs, services, and speeches, and comically illustrated. . . . 12mo. cloth, $1.25

The New York Central Park.

A SUPERB GIFT BOOK.—The Central Park pleasantly described, and magnificently embellished with more than 50 exquisite photographs of the principal views and objects of interest. A large quarto volume, sumptuously bound in Turkey morocco, ... $25.00

Joseph Rodman Drake.

THE CULPRIT FAY.—The most charming faery poem in the English language. Beautifully printed. 12mo. cloth, 75 cts.

Mother Goose for Grown Folks.

HUMOROUS RHYMES for grown people; based upon the famous "Mother Goose Melodies." . . 12mo. cloth, $1.00

Stephen Massett.

DRIFTING ABOUT.—A comic illustrated book of the life and travels of "Jeems Pipes." . .. 12mo. cloth, $1.25

A New Sporting Work.

THE GAME FISH OF THE NORTH.—One of the best books on fish and fishing ever published. Entertaining as well as instructive, and full of illustrations. . 12mo. cloth, $1.50

Balzac's Novels.

CESAR BIROTTEAU.—From the French. 12mo. cloth, $1.25
THE ALCHEMIST.— do. do. $1.25
EUGENIE GRANDET.— do. do. $1.25
PETTY ANNOYANCES OF MARRIED LIFE.— do. $1.25

Thomas Bailey Aldrich.

BABIE BELL, AND OTHER POEMS.—Blue and gold binding, $1.00
OUT OF HIS HEAD.—A new romance. 12mo. cloth, $1.00

Richard H. Stoddard.

THE KING'S BELL.—A new poem. . 12mo. cloth, 75 cts.
THE MORGESONS.—A novel. By Mrs. R. H. Stoddard. $1.00

Edmund C. Stedman.

ALICE OF MONMOUTH.—A new poem. 12mo. cloth, $1.00
LYRICS AND IDYLS.— . . . . do. 75 cts.

M. T. Walworth.

LULU.—A new novel. . . . 12mo. cloth, $1.50
HOTSPUR.— do. *in press.* . . do.

Author of "Olie."

NEPENTHE.—A new novel. . . 12mo. cloth, $1.50
TOGETHER.— do. *in press.* . do.

Quest.

A NEW ROMANCE.—*In press.* . . 12mo. cloth,

Victoire.

A NEW NOVEL.—*In Press.* . . 12mo. cloth, $1.50

Red-Tape

AND PIGEON-HOLE GENERALS, as seen by a citizen-soldier in the Army of the Potomac. . . 12mo. cloth, $1.25

Author "Green Mountain Boys."

CENTEOLA.—A new work, *in press.* 12mo. cloth, $1.50

C. French Richards.

JOHN GUILDERSTRING'S SIN.—A novel. 12mo. cloth,

J. R. Beckwith.

THE WINTHROPS.—A novel, *in press.* 12mo. cloth, $1.50

Jas. H. Hackett.

NOTES AND COMMENTS ON SHAKSPEARE.— 12mo. cloth, $1.50

Miscellaneous Works.

ALEXANDER VON HUMBOLDT.—Life and travels.	12mo. cl.	$1.50
LIFE OF HUGH MILLER, the Geologist. . .	do.	$1.50
ADAM GUROWSKI.—Diary for 1863. . .	do.	$1.25
DOESTICKS.—The Elephant Club, illustrated. .	do.	$1.50
HUSBAND AND WIFE, or human development.	do.	$1.25
ROCKFORD.—A novel by Mrs. L. D. Umsted.	do.	$1.00
THE PRISONER OF STATE.—By D. A. Mahony.	do.	$1.25
THE PARTISAN LEADER.—By Beverly Tucker. .	do.	$1.25
SPREES AND SPLASHES.—By Henry Morford. .	do.	$1.00
AROUND THE PYRAMIDS.—By Gen. Aaron Ward.	do.	$1.50
CHINA AND THE CHINESE.—By W. L. G. Smith.	do.	$1.00
WANDERINGS OF A BEAUTY.—Mrs. Edwin James.	do.	$1.00
THE U. S. TAX LAW.—"Government Edition."	do.	75 cts.
TREATISE ON DEAFNESS.—By Dr. E. B. Lighthill.	do.	$1.00
LYRICS OF A DAY—or newspaper poetry. .	do.	$1.00
GARRET VAN HORN.—A novel by J. S. Sauzade.	do.	$1.25
THE NATIONAL SCHOOL FOR THE SOLDIER.—	do.	50 cts.
FORT LAFAYETTE.—A novel by Benjamin Wood.	do.	$1.00
THE YACHTMAN'S PRIMER.—By T. R. Warren.	do.	50 cts.
GEN. NATHANIEL LYON.—Life and Writings. .	do.	$1.00
PHILIP THAXTER.—A novel.	do.	$1.00
LITERARY ESSAYS.—By George Brimley. . .	do.	$1.50
HAYING TIME TO HOPPING.—A novel. . .	do.	$1.25
THE VAGABOND.—Essays by Adam Badeau. .	do.	$1.00
EDGAR POE AND HIS CRITICS.—By Mrs. Whitman.	do.	75 cts.
TACTICS; or, Cupid in Shoulder-Straps. .	do.	$1.00
JOHN DOE AND RICHARD ROE.—A novel. .	do.	$1.25
LOLA MONTEZ.—Her life and lectures. . .	do.	$1.50
DEBT AND GRACE.—By Rev. C. F. Hudson. .	do.	$1.50
HUSBAND *vs.* WIFE.—A comic illustrated poem.	do.	50 cts.
TRANSITION.—Edited by Rev. H. S. Carpenter.	do.	$1.00
ROUMANIA.—By Dr. Jas. O. Noyes, illustrated.	do.	$1.50
VERNON GROVE.—A novel.	do.	$1.25
ANSWER TO HUGH MILLER.—By T. A. Davies.	do.	$1.25
COSMOGONY.—By Thomas A. Davies. .	8vo. cl.,	$1.50
NATIONAL HYMNS.—By Richard Grant White.	do.	$1.50
TWENTY YEARS Around the World. J. Guy Vassar.	do.	$3.50
SPIRIT OF HEBREW POETRY.—By Isaac Taylor.	do.	$2.50

Lightning Source UK Ltd.
Milton Keynes UK
UKHW02n0945120218
317657UK00002B/22/P

9 780483 683723